I0628731

HART OF DARKNESS 2

KING OF HART

HART OF DARKNESS 2

KING OF HART

VIOLETA M. BAGIA

PRESS

Copyright © Violeta M. Bagia 2025

The moral rights of the author have been asserted.

All rights reserved. No part of this publication may be reproduced, stored in or introduced into a retrieval system or transmitted in any form or by any means, electronic, mechanical, photocopying, recording or otherwise without prior written permission from the publisher.

This novel is entirely a work of fiction. Names, characters, places and incidents are either the product of the author's imagination or are used fictitiously, and any resemblance to any person or persons, living or dead, is entirely coincidental. No affiliation is implied or intended to any organization or recognizable body mentioned within.

First edition published by Solstice Publishing in 2017

Published by Vulpine Press in the United Kingdom in 2025

ISBN: 978-1-83919-628-7

www.vulpine-press.com

To those who shipped Sydney and Vaughn – this one is for you!

PROLOGUE

ILLARION

THEN

Tears burned the inside of my eyelids. Ace couldn't be gone. Not like this. We needed more time. Bozhe, there wasn't enough time.

A never ending, all-consuming rage took hold and the Darkness I held at bay, began to burn.

"I wish I told you in person too."

Her mind grew quiet, and I couldn't hang on to her flickering thoughts anymore. Her soft hands were limp in mine.

"I love you, Ace, I love you. Please, please don't leave me. *Moya zvezda.*"

Tears slipped from my eyes as I lowered my forehead to hers.

"Please, stay with me. Stay with me."

My words and cries blended into one, painful, deafening kaleidoscope of agony. My heart refused to accept what my mind was telling me.

But I knew it through to my core. She was gone. I barely felt Aurel's arms around me pulling me away as the paramedics rushed to her side.

Whatever he was saying got lost in the chaos, blood rushed through my head, and I couldn't make out the words he was telling me, or the sirens signaling the arrival of more of our men and more medics.

Troy bucked and yelled, knocking an agent to the ground.

1

"This is your fault!" he screamed in my direction.

Someone pulled him away.

More medics rushed in.

It was my fault. Troy was right.

Aurel pulled me against his chest and I clutched at the fabric around his arms.

The medics worked tirelessly but it was over. She wasn't going to come back from this, I'd already felt her heart giving out.

"They're taking her to the Agency Hospital," Aurel's voice broke through the pain. "Come on."

My heart fell through the floor. How in the hell could I accept that this was going to be the rest of my life?

I'm so sorry, Westen, I failed. You trusted me and I failed.

A sob rippled through my body before I could stop it.

Someone pulled me up into the back of the ambulance then I collapsed against the door ignoring everything else. Sometime between hearing my name lost in all the noise and reaching the hospital, I found myself seated in a small plastic chair beside Aurel, trying to figure out what the next few steps would look like. I'd go home. Eat. Sleep. Then what?

Aurel paced the corridor.

And when Donna finally came out, I knew for certain. She shook her head and Aurel dropped into the chair beside me releasing a chain of expletives in Romanian I'd heard only once before.

Donna crouched down in front of me, taking my hands in hers. "We're ready for you."

"She's gone," I said.

"You should say goodbye, they would have wanted that."

My eyes shot up, and Aurel shifted in his seat beside me, I shot him a sideways glance before looking back at Donna, getting to my feet.

Her eyes widened as she stood, one hand on her hip the other covering her mouth like she wanted to stop the next words on her lips. "Oh Illarion, I'm so sorry…you didn't, you didn't know?"

Aurel was beside me in a heartbeat.

My eyes swung back to Donna.

Her lips were set in a hard line. "Illarion, I'm so sorry. She was pregnant."

***

NOW

Holding onto whatever semblance of strength I could muster, I walked ahead.

As I neared the apartment building, I stopped, pausing briefly trying to gather whatever courage I could. Once I was certain I could do this, I moved again. I gripped the edge of the railing as I took each step up to his apartment. I swallowed hard, and took a deep breath, as I knocked on his door.

Ace had been taken away to our hospital and Troy was kept in the dark. It was classified. Her death was kept under wraps for a week now, a week during which he called me over and over asking about her, and I had to lie.

Inside, the TV was silenced, then rushed footsteps neared the front.

I came face to face with Troy Johnson. Her best friend, her solace, the one person I'd promised above all else, that I'd keep her safe.

"I'm sorry," I said quietly. "I failed her, and I failed you."

I had no time to register the right hook that cracked across my face. I staggered backward slightly but stood firm.

"This is your fucking fault!"

He hit me again. I let him. The burn jolted me. It was the first time I felt anything since becoming numb.

"You let her die!" he screamed again.

And when he threw another punch, I blocked the hit and wrapped my arms around him.

"You fucking asshole!" his voice cracked. "You were meant to protect her!"

He tried to shove me back. He was strong but not strong enough. As he thrashed and cried, I felt his resolve dying.

"You were meant to keep her safe!" he broke down. "This is your fault."

"It is my fault."

Troy pulled back and thrust his hands through his hair.

I slipped my hand into my pocket finding the black card I'd held onto knowing that once I handed it to him, it was over. It was really done. Definitive.

"The Agency is holding a private funeral."

Troy took the card and kept his eyes down.

"I'm so sorry," I whispered again before leaving.

CHAPTER ONE

ACE

A grin swept his cold features setting his face into a cruel demeanor. "You're incredibly perceptive."

My breath caught in a pathetic attempt to calm myself.

"Where am I?" I repeated, painfully aware of the wavering in my voice and the fact that my body was frozen in place, just like the time he'd ambushed me and Illarion.

"The Giver and the Taker—together again." He laughed, mocking what I'd said to Damon.

How could we have read this so wrong?

My heart sank—where was Illarion now? Did he know I was alive? Would he even be looking? Was Troy alive? Too many thoughts consumed me, I didn't even know how much time had passed. I didn't know anything.

But I knew that the fear climbing through my heart like icy water, was real.

I tried to move my hands, to call on the Darkness but nothing came through. It was there though, deep within where I couldn't reach it.

He stood beside my bed, his hip resting lazily against the edge. "You're questioning why you aren't able to feel your powers inside you."

My mind shot off in all directions. He wasn't just talking about the warehouse, no...no there was something more.

"You fought through some of my strongest compulsion—made me rethink everything."

I couldn't speak.

"You do remember, don't you?"

Words refused to form.

He laughed and gently brushed my hair forward letting his fingers graze across my cheek.

Jerking my head back from him, I hissed as the pain from all my broken bones made me rethink doing that again.

Undeterred, he swept his fingers along my cheek again and then roughly squeezed my face and forced my eyes to his.

"When I saw how strong you were, I had to take precautions, after seeing what you were capable of, I thought it best to keep you sedated, at least until you were ready to be awoken."

His eyes travelled across the bed to the small metal tray, a bright blue liquid stared me right in the face.

"Now I know you're familiar with this on a very intimate level, if I'm not mistaken?"

My eyes remained transfixed to the syringe.

Oh, I was acutely aware of the Serum, of what it could do to us of what it had done to me at Sergeant Luke Grimes's hand.

"A very powerful, young Sensitive discovered a way to modify it for us a few years ago, he's been fine-tuning it, testing it for us once Grimes handed over all of his research."

"Why are you doing this to me?"

He smiled, turning to me, syringe in hand.

I couldn't take my eyes off the blue liquid as my heart faltered in my chest.

"The effects will take hold in approximately ten seconds. And then." He grinned. "You and I are going to do some incredible things."

"What do you want from me?"

Before my mind could begin to process the level of shit I was in, he pressed the needle into my neck.

My heart raced as I looked up at him.

"You already know your half-brother was an idiot, he didn't know that the transfer wouldn't have worked, but I do."

His eyes narrowed as he pulled the needle away from my neck, quickly I looked up at him and that was the last thing I remembered. My eyes closed, and the Serum took hold.

***

When I opened my eyes, I was happy to see that I was in a lovely, bright room. The sun shone through the half-closed blind to my left, and to my right, a heart monitor beeped, slowly, loudly.

"How do you feel Ms. Hart?"

I turned, meeting his crystal gaze. "I feel fine."

"Are you ready to begin your work?"

"Yes."

"Excellent, help her up." He spoke quickly to two nurses who hurried in and obediently helped me up and out of bed.

They lowered me into a wheelchair then he sent them away.

"Now I'd like to set some ground rules."

"Of course."

We continued through the grand house, and I noted that the vastness was exceptional. It was the most beautiful home I'd ever seen.

The staircases were lined with Persian runners; the walls were painted in a rich burgundy adorned with exquisite gold-framed paintings from the sixteenth century. The ceilings were so high you could fit a fifteen-foot tree in here.

"You're staying in my home as my guest, I expect you to obey the rules. You shall address me as Master, do you understand?"

"Yes, Master."

"Good. First, you will not wander the home or grounds unaccompanied. Second, you will not be late to dinner, and lastly, you will not, under any circumstances question me or my orders."

My eyes flicked up, why would I question him?

"Do you understand these three rules, Ms. Hart?"

"Yes, I do, Master."

"Good. Now I'm going to show you to your room. I will lock it at night and unlock it at sunrise, unless I need you for something, understand?"

"Yes, Master."

We stopped at the foot of the stairs, and he helped me up to my feet. Ignoring the pain in my side, I carefully took the steps one at a time. We stopped when we reached a large door which he unlocked with a key that he slipped back into his waistcoat pocket.

"New clothes, shoes, and toiletries are all ready for you. Come down for dinner at six and do not be late."

"Thank you, Master." I nodded, painfully shifting my weight to my other foot as soon as the door was closed.

I moved to the large bed and sat on the edge, letting my fingers sink into the soft, velvet blanket that sat atop the sheets. It was all so beautiful.

The whole room was themed in red and gold. Like the rest of my Master's house.

My room had mahogany floorboards and a thick, red square rug in the centre of the room which made it feel incredibly cozy. The large, wooden, four poster bed sat centered on top of it. The sheets were white with red and gold patterns intricately weaving in and out of the fabric.

The writing desk was also dark in color as were the wooden shelves surrounding it. They were stacked with classic literature and books I'd never even seen before. I walked over to the shelves and a quick inspection confirmed that they were all first editions. Most people never had access to things like that.

I tore my attention from the books and slowly made my way over to the walk-in. It was brimming with dresses.

I pulled a lacy, black one out and pressed it to my body smiling lazily at my reflection in the floor-length mirror.

Deciding that this was my favorite, I took it to the bed and laid it out. I needed to shower first, then I would get to wear it.

There were dozens of perfumed shampoos stacked neatly in the niche, citrus, musk, floral and vanilla. I chose a vanilla one and indulged in the fragrance, and as the water washed it out of my hair, I felt it; a deep, almost sorrowful hum, in the depths of my heart.

I threw my hand out in front of me, stopping myself from falling through the screen.

"What the hell?"

Just as it came, it was gone, and I felt normal again.

I turned the water off and dried myself. When I turned, catching my reflection, I stopped abruptly. My hands hovered over my stomach. I knew the scars were there from the fight I had with Damon, and the new ones across my ribs were from the warehouse, but a different kind of pain had my attention. An emotional pain. But where my hands lay flat over my skin, there was nothing visible.

I shook my head, tearing my gaze from the reflective surface and got dressed.

The black lace hung perfectly over my curves. I loved it. I pulled my damp hair into a low, tight bun and left my room heading downstairs for dinner. I couldn't be late.

As I made my way down, I felt the pressure inside my head building, but I couldn't place it, I swallowed hard and tried to force myself to calm down. I gripped onto the railing as the long train of my dress trailed down each step.

"Ah, here she is." My Master got to his feet with his arms outstretched.

"You look lovely, I'm glad you found something you like."

"They're all lovely, thank you so much."

"You're very welcome. Sit?" He guided me to the chair nearest to his.

I obliged, waiting patiently for permission to speak.

"My son will be joining us for dinner, I hope you like veal."

I looked up as another occupant joined us.

His son must have been in his mid-twenties, but far too mature for his years. He looked haunted; it was deep in his gaze like he'd seen things that had shaken the foundations of his belief system.

Bright, blue eyes scanned my face making me flinch at the intense stare.

"Daniel, this is Acacia. Ms. Hart will be joining us for a while."

Daniel looked away, sitting on the other side of his father.

"Will she be staying longer than the others?" his voice had a rough edge to it which his father seemed to ignore.

"Yes. Ms. Hart will be staying much longer. Indefinitely I hope."

Something inside me shifted. Again, it was a feeling I couldn't quite place. But it was familiar. There was an aching, a longing, for what? I had no idea.

"Ah, the food is ready."

I followed my Master's gaze to the four staff who walked in carrying plates of food, drinks and bread.

One of them caught my eye.

It was an open, silver dish with a white cloth and a syringe with pretty, blue liquid.

Daniel's gaze drifted over to me. It was only a quick glance, but I saw it before he turned away.

My Master nodded at him. "Go on."

He took the syringe off the platter and walked around to my side of the table.

When he knelt beside me, I held out my arm, pulling the sleeve up. Daniel's eyes caught mine. A small, niggling feeling of dread washed over me, but very faint, almost undetectable. I drew my arm back.

"Acacia," My Master's voice boomed across the dining table making me recoil. "Do not make that mistake again."

I immediately put my arm back.

"I'm sorry. I'm sorry, Master."

I dropped my gaze to my arm; Daniel swabbed the inside of my elbow before he pressed the needle into my skin. A tiny hiss left my lips, but I quickly stifled it before he could get angry at me.

"I'm sorry," I heard Daniel whisper quickly before he was up and gone.

I couldn't have imagined that. *What was he sorry about?*

Slowly, everything in my mind faded except the dinner.

We ate, they spoke, I drank and then my Master helped me to bed. I fell asleep, but somewhere in my consciousness, threads of memories pieced themselves together.

I remembered closing my eyes and feeling the fabric of the dress leave my body. I remembered rough, calloused hands touching me, coasting across my hips, slipping through my hair but they didn't feel right. Something was off. They weren't his, they weren't *Illarion's*.

I shot up. Illarion. My breath caught as a shaky sob wracked my body. Weeks of emotions hit me like a storm battering a fragile shore.

Weeks, weeks had passed and my baby, *our baby* was dead. I'd been beaten and tortured. Illarion's face haunted me as he held my body. I

11

was brought here by *him*, my *Master* was the Taker, he was Ugly Shoes. Oh God. How had I missed this?

I wrapped my arms around my middle. Everything was so damn hazy. *Why couldn't I link one coherent thought to another?*

The Serum. Of course. Fuck. *Why was I even able to work that out?* Maybe something was wrong with the Serum, maybe they weren't using a strong enough dose. But that wasn't it.

I scratched the inner part of my elbow while my gaze darted across the room. It was a fortress, a prison cell trimmed in gold and lace.

I thrust my fingers through my hair, what the hell was I going to do?

The windows were barred, the door was locked, and the vents of course, were too small in these massive mansions.

Think, Ace, think.

My phone. I rushed over to the wardrobe. I vaguely remembered seeing my old clothes there, surely there had to be something I could use.

I dropped to my knees and rummaged around in the dark, there were endless rows of shoes, ridiculous heels no one should walk in, but not my old clothes, he must have taken them. I slapped my palm to my face. Of course, they wouldn't be there. He wasn't an idiot.

And what the hell was I doing wearing this shit? The dresses above me loomed like some twisted fantasy. I was going to be sick. I stopped abruptly when I recognized two of them from Damon's house. He must have purchased them all for this asshat. Holy hell.

I got to my feet and ran to the bathroom, dropping to my knees. I clung to the toilet bowl and threw up. My hands reached up around my neck, but my fingers came up empty. My usual gesture of comfort was gone. Troy's necklace was gone.

Tears stung the back of my eyes then the last few months started flooding back.

Being with Illarion, training with Aurel, laughing with them… and Troy… another bout of nausea hit me. All the thoughts my mind had locked away somehow came crashing into me. I threw up until there was nothing left.

My heart was shattered. And I was so screwed.

Certain that no more surprise bouts would hit me, I pulled away and flushed the remains. I dragged myself to my feet and walked back to the bed.

I stopped short. I couldn't sit on it, not when he touched me like that. Oh god. What else did he…I refused to finish that thought. Surely, he wouldn't have…no one could be that messed up.

An insidious little voice inside my mind told me I was being naïve.

I drew in a long breath and swept my hands over my hair. I needed to think. I needed a way out. If only I could reach Illarion. I focused on him, trying to find that pull, that familiar hum, but it was gone. Of course it was gone. I was blocked off from everything and everyone. I was dead for all intents and purposes and this Serum only made it more believable.

My heart twisted as my mind grew clearer. He said he'd kept me sedated while I recovered which meant that yesterday's dinner was just the first…

Helplessness tightened my chest. Illarion didn't even know I was alive and, if he didn't know I was alive, he wouldn't be looking for me. I was on my own to survive this hell of unimaginable terror.

I walked over to the wall and sat, bringing my knees to my chest. Crying wouldn't help me right now. I forced myself to even out my breathing and get it together.

What was I going to do and how was I going to get out of this? That's all I needed to do at this stage, one step at a time. Solve one problem and then another.

My ears perked, as I picked up on a hurried set of footsteps coming toward my room. I got up and backed myself against the window. Quickly glancing around, I searched for something I could use. There was nothing aside from the big ass books. Shit. I pulled one out of the shelf, ran back to the bed and ripped the pillowcase off a giant pillow and shoved the book inside, clutching it tightly.

I still hadn't regained all my strength, but if I needed to, I'm sure I could still fight, and the makeshift weapon would be enough to stun the intruder.

The key turned and I braced myself but instead of Ugly Shoes, I saw Daniel. He quickly stepped inside, closed the door and looked around the room.

"Ms. Hart?"

Standing completely still, I stayed hidden in the shadows gripping the pillowcase.

"I'm not here to hurt you. I need to talk to you, please, there isn't much time before my father comes back."

Silently, I stepped out from the corner, and he quickly turned in my direction. Damn, the kid had some good hearing.

"My father doesn't know I'm up here," he started, motioning for me to follow him to the writing desk.

Hesitantly, I followed him and eyed the small parcel he was holding out. It was complete with newspapers and magazines tied neatly with twine. When I didn't take the package he gave the pillowcase in my hand a quick look, his brows shooting up for a moment before he gestured to the desk.

I set my weapon down beside me, close enough to use but not within his reach and he set the bundle down on the surface.

Keeping a safe distance, I wrapped my arms around my middle. "Who the hell are you?"

"I'm Daniel."

"Yeah, I got that when your father introduced us."

"You remember?"

"I remember. So, I'm asking you again, who the hell are you and who is your father?"

He winced. "I'm sure your file notes at the Agency have mentioned my father by name, a few times."

Glaring at him, I waited for a proper answer.

"Simon Dalca."

I released a long breath. "Well shit."

"Take it you've heard of him, then."

The Agency didn't have a complete profile on him, but they did know that he was a Romanian national who was responsible for a lot of black-market dealings, selling and buying information pertaining to government uses of Sensitives, where they were inserted, who was undercover and what they did.

He also dug around a lot searching for some clandestine group we'd only ever heard rumors about – they were called the Legion. The Legion was said to belong to some seriously cashed up ghost. Word on the Agency books was that the Legion were made up of genetically modified ex-soldiers who were deployed to do jobs no other agency wanted to be attached to.

"Yeah, I've heard of him."

"Then you know how dangerous he is," Daniel muttered.

"It hasn't eluded me."

On the surface, he was a well-respected man, his money and power made him so. People feared him, people protected him and so, the Agency never got any closer than the information we'd already had, which was minimal.

Then again, maybe Damon Cale had something to do with that.

My evil half-brother who all but trafficked me to this asshole, evidently had many people under his control and it made a lot of sense now. He pulled strings no one even knew were there.

Daniel sighed fiddling with the parcel on the desk.

"I can imagine you've got a lot of questions," he said drawing my eyes to him.

"Damn straight I've got questions. I don't even know where to start."

For a moment we looked at each other while he stood transfixed by the writing desk. Curiosity piqued but skepticism still held me back, there was no way I was about to trust this kid. Who knew what other messed up tricks Dalca had up his sleeve?

"Why are you here?" I demanded.

"I can't stop the frequency of the doses my father orders me to administer, but I can start to alter the potency."

"And you expect me to trust anything you say."

"No, I don't. But right now, I'm the only chance you have."

"You and your father are criminals. Don't think for a second that I don't know what the fuck you're doing to me."

He ground his jaw, looking away for a moment before he met my gaze again. "And I'm trying to make this better."

"Why?" I shot back. "Why the hell do you care? Do you come into my room at night as well?"

"Jesus Christ, no," he spat, shaking his head. "No. I'm here to help and right now I'm all you have."

"Why the hell would I believe you?"

"Because I'm not like him!"

I closed my mouth, taken aback by his response and the obvious disgust at my insinuation.

"I could never. Fuck. You have to believe me."

"Not likely, kid. You know what they say, apple doesn't fall too far and all that shit."

"I am not like my father."

We stared each other down for a moment before Daniel took a small step forward and I instinctively shot back. His demeanor shifted. He backed away and stuffed his hands into his pockets. His body language told me he wasn't a threat but my experience thus far in this house of horrors told me to keep my guard up.

"Let's say I believe you, what's the catch?"

"I have to do it over a period of time."

My previous reluctance to trust him went out the window when desperation to survive kicked in. "How much time?"

"Four months."

"Four months?" my heart sunk.

He nodded, holding my gaze.

"Why?"

"Number of reasons, first being it's risky enough as it is and, if I'm not careful with how much we alter it, he'll figure it out and he'll kill us both."

"Second reason?"

"If I don't alter it slowly enough, the withdrawal will kill you."

"It's better than nothing," I heard myself say.

"It's not going to be easy."

"I can handle it."

He scrubbed the back of his neck. "Tomorrow, he'll start to draw from you…even on the Serum, even with all the pain blockers, you'll feel it."

"Why are you helping me?"

"Because I've seen so many before you suffer and die because they weren't strong enough."

"Strong enough for what? How many have there been?"

"Too many. I lost count."

"What?" Terror coated my insides.

"I tried to lower the dose, but they couldn't hold out long enough."

My eyes filled with tears for the lost women who never got to go home, never got to see their loved ones. Were they married? Were they moms? A tear slipped down my cheek, and I quickly swatted it away. I would honor them by living and killing this asshole.

The pain in his eyes was sincere, he hated what was going on. And, suddenly, my outlook wasn't so bleak. I couldn't get a read on him, but the sincerity I heard in his voice was real. And maybe, with him, I stood a chance.

He straightened up, towering over me, he was almost as tall as Illarion, and much taller than his father and for the first time, I really took notice of how he looked. His hair was short and tousled, just like Troy wore it. He was lean and very athletic.

"Tomorrow will be hard." He let out a long breath and scratched the back of his neck. "But I'll start to bring the dose down. Just keep that in the back of your mind. It will help ground you, okay?"

When I didn't reply, he turned his body to face me.

"You with me?"

Snapping my mind back to him, I nodded.

"Keep it in your mind. It's important, no matter what happens, keep that hope there."

"Wait, what are we talking about here? One percent a day decrease?"

"Point eight, to be precise…I can't bring you to zero percent without proper medical attention. It'll be like going cold turkey on a cocktail of all the worst drugs combined. It could kill you."

"Got it."

He gave me a pointed look like he didn't believe I was capable of surviving this. "Try to get some rest."

18

"Thank you for these." I nodded at the parcel.

"Hope it helps," he said, then left and locked the door behind him.

With a sigh, I collected the bundle and made my way over to the bed and sat on the ground beside it.

I flicked through the magazines and the newspapers. The dates spanned more than two months, from December through to the end of January. I'd been out for more than a month. And I missed Christmas. Damn it.

My previous assessment was correct. Weeks had gone by. And now, I would have to be here for at least four more months until the Serum was out of my system.

I couldn't settle the pain in my heart. The dull ache was still present even if nothing else was.

Finally, I brought my attention back to the pile of random reading material and when I started flicking through it, a smaller, handwritten set of notes fell out.

As soon as I saw the handwriting, my heart stopped. I would have recognized it anywhere. The elegant strokes on the paper were as elegant as the man himself.

Illarion had written to me. There was no address, just my name. But here they were. Daniel had brought them to me. *How did he get these?*

I refused to say goodbye, I can't accept that you're gone. I write these, taking them to your post box, hoping that if I say all the things I should have said, I'd feel better. I don't.

I can't feel you anymore, I felt your life slip away as I held you in my arms. I felt the fire die inside you. How am I meant to live with that? To have felt that?

I can't let you go.

I love you.

Tears welled up and my heart sank. I pressed my hand to my mouth, stifling a sob. I wiped my eyes and carefully placed the note beside the pile of newspapers.

Aurel came back to the Agency, you'd have loved that. You probably would have punched him for being a hypocrite, but he said he needs the distraction. Being at his house reminds him too much of you. He loved you.

He cared for you probably a lot more than I would have liked.

You would have laughed at my jealousy. I just want to hear you laugh again.

But I don't blame him. You're easy to fall for, Ace. I did. Before I even met you. You're infectious, everything about you draws people in. I wish I had told you all of this when you were here.

I want to resign. I can't work there anymore. But I won't. I need to stay and find closure for you.

We found out that Damon had been shielded by the Taker. He managed to hold the veil over him for more than a decade, so no one would have ever known or sensed anything was off. But you did. I remember the first time you met him. I should have acted then. Whomever the Taker is, he was behind your attack, Damon coming for you, all of it.

I found out at the school, I never got to tell you that. I never got to tell you a lot of things.

For that, I'm sorry, I'll never forgive myself. This is my fault.

My stomach twisted in knots. God. There was no way I could even tell him that it was Simon Dalca, if I could have somehow reached out, he would know where to look, he would know how find me.

Tears coursed freely down my cheeks.

I looked down at the pile, dozens of them were spilled across my lap. I couldn't do this. I couldn't look at them; I couldn't feel that pain.

I dropped the rest of them into the pile, then I bundled them together, stashing them safely under my mattress.

Four months. Four months was what Daniel needed to get us the hell out of here. I could do it. I had to do it.

I pulled the covers off the bed and draped them over myself on the floor using the red rug to cushion myself.

Finally, I let sleep take me, hoping I'd get some rest because tomorrow would suck, but it was going to be the beginning of my countdown.

CHAPTER TWO

ACE

I did not sleep well. Images of Illarion kept playing on my mind. My heart was aching for him.

His face always came to me first, the way he looked when I forced him out of the warehouse, the way I *felt* him running, knowing that he would be too late.

But throughout it all, I would never forget the pain I felt when we lost our unborn child as an eternal reminder of a life I would never have.

Sighing, I pulled myself up off the floor and moved to the wardrobe. Another horrendous dress to wear, another day to be a slave. I pulled out a dark blue, silky gown. I didn't bother with a shower. I wouldn't be lucid enough to care about that.

Dalca was waiting, a smile wide on his lips. I put my game face on. I smiled from ear to ear and sauntered gracefully toward him. This was just like being undercover. *I can do this.* I cringed inwardly as he took my hand and twirled me around. I felt his eyes on my body.

"Beautiful." He sighed. "Come now, we have some work to do."

I followed him, obediently.

He led us through a large set of stained-glass doors, through to a room deeper within the mansion. I made a mental note of all the doors we'd walked through, the amount of time it took to clear each room, and how much staff he had in each part of the house.

Astonishment rendered me speechless. This was insane. How did something like this exist in New York? My heart sank unless we weren't in New York anymore.

"This is my private office. This is where we will greet our business guests." He motioned for me to enter. I heard the lock click into place before he joined me inside.

"Please, sit."

Obliging, I moved toward the chair and sat.

"Now, before we greet our first guest, my son has prepared another dose for you, and a quick bite to eat for breakfast."

My heart hammered in my chest. I could feel the fear creeping up on me. Everything was counting on me being able to hold my façade.

"Yes, Master." I nodded with a smile.

He leaned back in the heavyset, leather chair steepling his fingertips as he studied my face.

Hold it together, Ace.

I was a trained spy. A damn good one at that and I knew how to do this. I turned my attention to the detailing around the room, the walls, the paintings and the other assortment of décor filling the space.

I studied the fireplace and paid extra attention to the flickering flames inside it. If I was going to sell this drugged-up thing, I was going to sell it well. I smiled to myself and kept my eyes on everything long enough to seem preoccupied, but quick enough to show that my attention wasn't that of a lucid person.

Finally, he turned his gaze away, and the tension inside me settled.

"Do you like it here?"

"Oh yes, it's the most beautiful home I've ever seen." I let my gaze drift away from him.

"Good. I want you to stay with us. You and I will be working together for a long time, and I know a beautiful woman like yourself shouldn't be alone."

Oh God. I threw up a little.

This was a bad situation. I forced my eyes to remain ahead. On the one hand, I needed to play this part, not only my life was on the line. On the other, how could I pretend that I wanted this animal touching me? I was on the verge of a full-blown, hysterical breakdown.

He got up, letting Daniel in.

Hold yourself together, Ace.

I took a deep breath. I could do this.

"Nice and quick now, Daniel, we have some work to do before our guests arrive."

***

I looked up at my Master and waited for him to speak.

"Our first guest has arrived."

I got up and followed him through the double doors and into another adjoining room.

There was a man tied to a chair, his face was blank, and unresponsive.

"Acacia, sit down, right there." He pointed to the chair in front of the man.

As soon as I sat, my Master took my hands and placed them atop the man's then he knelt beside me and pressed one hand over mine and the other, on my cheek.

A sharp, piercing bolt of pain shot through my hand and into the man's. He jumped. His eyes widened, meeting mine. A flitting realization crossed my mind. He was afraid. Of me.

My Master pulled his hand free.

"Well done, Acacia. Now we know how powerful you are, let's get to work."

He stood up and walked around behind me.

"Concentrate on the man before you, I want you to focus on everything inside him, you're going to transfer it to me. Understand?"

Nodding, I did as he said, I forced my eyes to the man's, ignoring the terrified expression on his face. His brows were furrowed and the lines in his forehead deepened with each jolt.

As soon as our eyes were locked, that same, sharp pain exploded inside me piercing my heart and my brain all at once.

It was different from the way the Darkness felt when it coursed through my veins. Where the Darkness felt consuming it still felt as though it belonged to me, this though, this was foreign and violent.

My grip on the man's hands was tightening. I dug my nails into his skin and grit my teeth. Everything inside me was screaming. I had to do this for my Master. I had to prove my worth.

Searching inside him, I felt the essence I was looking for. In Sensitives, our evolved Sense looked like different colored threads of silk, some were course, some were smooth, and some were woven through other colors. But his was simple. A white, thin string moved through his body, I grabbed onto it and pulled.

His energy shifted, and I felt it pouring into me.

It felt like hours, though it was probably only minutes, until everything inside him was gone. My Master released his hold on me. I sank into the chair, my head falling forward.

Heavy tears clung to my lashes.

I wiped them with the back of my hand and focused on keeping my breathing even.

"Enough for today," he spoke, softly in my ear, pulling my braid back. He pulled the elastic out running his fingers through the length of my hair and lowered his lips to my ear. "Keep your hair out. I like it better like this."

"Thank you, Master."

I'd killed the guy. His eyes were blank when I left. Something about that disturbed me.

I stood in the bathroom naked for a while before I turned the water on and stepped in. It hadn't even warmed up yet but something about the icy, cold stream was welcoming. Everything else felt numb, this didn't. The disconnect between my body and emotions was alien.

My body struggled with each sharp gasp, but my mind wasn't keeping up. *Why couldn't I feel anything?*

I turned the water off, dried myself then picked another dress. Green and black lace, with a low back. I stepped back holding it out...something...something I couldn't quite place niggled at me.

It was pretty, a long train adorned the back, and the lace sleeves were beautiful, but something about *this* dress was odd. Like I'd seen it before?

No. That was ridiculous, my Master didn't share, I knew that already.

Ignoring my own paranoia, I held it up against my body and smiled. I knew the perfect heels for this one.

Ducking into the rows of shoes, I found them. Black, insanely high and the tiniest strap around the ankle and toes. My Master would love this. As instructed, I also left my hair out, making sure the loose waves fell neatly over my shoulders and went down for dinner.

Just on time.

"Ah, beautiful, Acacia, come." He stood and held his hand out.

I took it and followed him around the large dining table and sat.

"I'm especially fond of this dress on you."

My eyes travelled up to his. "Oh?"

"An old friend helped me pick them for you. This one was his favorite too."

"An old friend?

"Someone no longer with us, I'm afraid."

A few moments of silence passed, as he watched me. He then gestured for the staff to bring in the food.

"Are you hungry?"

Hungry was an understatement, I was starving, but my stomach was churning.

"I don't think I can eat, I'm sorry."

"Are you feeling unwell?"

"A little," I admitted. "I'm sorry."

"No need for that."

"I will have my staff prepare a dish for you to take back to your room."

"Thank you."

"Now tell me, how did you sleep?"

"Well, thank you."

"I hope I didn't overstay my welcome last night?"

Something inside me shifted, I felt the wrongness of it, but I couldn't seem to grasp what was making me feel like that.

"Of course not."

For a moment he held my gaze sending a sensation of caution rushing inside me, before he looked away, I returned my attention to the food in my plate.

"May I be excused?"

He nodded, gesturing for the staff to pack my food.

"Get some rest. Tomorrow we will return to work. We have a lot to do."

It was hot, I was barely walking but somehow, I was making progress. The desert sun was high on the horizon and my heart was heavy, I was alone, I was hurt, Alex…Alex was gone…he'd died, he died for me…but I got out. I survived…I stopped abruptly. Was I hallucinating? There was someone walking toward me, they were a silhouette against the bright orange sun.

My eyes flew open and everything from the day before came crashing into me, yet it was Alex who made my heart break in two.

I closed my hand over my mouth stifling a sob.

It'd been so long, so much time had passed—why was he on my mind now? I, I couldn't pin it…it was like Dalca had unlocked memories, things in my past that haunted me and hurt me when I was wide awake.

The breath I'd been holding, came out slowly. Alex had known all about me. What would he think about me now? Would he be disgusted with the monster I was becoming?

Gripping the blanket tightly, I drew it over my head and closed my eyes. It had to get better. It had to.

CHAPTER THREE

ILLARION

I took another swig of the scotch I'd poured minutes ago, the seventh glass from the third bottle. The vodka had run out. I laughed and Aurel stopped talking.

A Russian who ran out of vodka—it sounded like the start of a bad joke.

"Brother." He sat on the edge of my desk.

I'd moved into the office. I spent more time in here than anywhere else in this vast, empty house. It was perpetually like a tomb in here now.

No amount of heating could chase away the cold and no number of bright days could cast away the grey. Elsa tried to pry me out but, after the first three weeks, she slowly stopped trying until she didn't anymore.

Now she came without letting me know, to collect the food I barely ate and cleaned the glasses I left scattered around the place.

"Illarion," Aurel said. "You with me, man?"

"What?"

"This isn't healthy."

"Why are you still here?"

"Because someone needs to make sure you're eating and sleeping."

"Elsa's here."

"Elsa called me."

My eyes snapped up to his. Dark shadows circled his eyes, he must have been exhausted. Yet he was here. Day in. Day out. Constantly by my side, even when I kicked and screamed, in moments of terror when I woke from nightmares.

It had been two months since Ace died.

He bowed his head and scratched the back of his neck.

"You don't have to do this." I reached for the bottle.

Before I could refill my glass, Aurel took it from my hand and placed it on the table just out of reach.

"You need to stop. I'm not going to sit here and watch you kill yourself."

"I'm...*coping*."

"You're not coping." He shook his head, shifting back against the edge of my desk. "You're drinking yourself into oblivion and you're on the fast track to the grave."

I sighed, pinching the bridge of my nose. "I miss her."

"I know."

***

ACE

Four long and agonizing weeks had gone past. Day after day, I struggled with the addictive properties of the Serum, while the coming down and withdrawals grew stronger.

Daniel tried to spend as much time with me as he could, but it wasn't always possible. His father was around a lot more than he was in the beginning. It seemed as though he didn't really trust his son.

Sucking in a deep breath, I peeled myself away from the toilet and washed my face. I was getting a little too used to wrapping my arms around the cool, ceramic bowl night after night.

A tap on the door drew my attention to it.

I tossed the small towel aside and walked into the main room. My stomach grumbled as soon as I spotted the bag of McDonald's he held up.

"How are you holding up?"

I took the bag from him and sat on the floor against the leg of the table. He sat in front of me.

"I feel like I'm dying, slowly, painfully, one night at a time. How about you?"

Daniel sighed, clearly unamused. "He's out for the day."

"Where'd he go?"

"Didn't say anything to me, but I did see something on his desk about Long Island."

My eyes shot up.

"Is that important?" he asked.

"Illarion lives in Long Island."

"Surely it's a coincidence."

"I know you don't believe that."

He paused for a moment. "Maybe he's running surveillance."

"I bet he is."

Discarding the wrapper, I dug into the Big Mac, stuffing a few fries into my mouth every few mouthfuls or so.

Illarion could take care of himself, I had to believe that. I forced myself to refocus. I had to look after me right now.

"We need to hurry this dose thing up," I spoke around the fries.

"We can't, I told you before—"

"It's dangerous, I know."

"Then you know I can't speed it up."

I stuffed a few more fries in my mouth before washing them down with some soda.

"I can't do this for that long," I said evenly.

He frowned.

"The others didn't go through what I am with him...did they?"

He looked away for a moment before returning his attention to me. "No."

A breath caught in my chest, but I nodded.

"Ace, I'm sorry."

"Yeah," I looked away, I didn't want him to see me cry. "I know it's dangerous, but I won't let him hurt you, if I'm lucid enough to fight, I will fight."

"You know it's not me I'm worried about."

Daniel tossed his half-eaten burger in the bag and wiped his hands on the small napkins.

"If we don't do something sooner, I..."

Air caught in my throat. I couldn't finish the sentence. I couldn't afford to let my mind wander to those nights I was completely under the Serum and had no recollection of what I'd done...or what was done to me.

"I know there are things that I don't want to ever remember, I know what he does to me when I'm not in my own head. It doesn't take a genius to work it out...and Daniel, I can't do it."

He scrubbed his eyes, his blond hair falling over his face.

"I'm not asking you to cut me off completely, just speed it up. That's all."

"It's not that simple."

"Yes, it is!"

"Ace. Listen to me."

"Don't," I shot. "Don't try to rationalize my life in this hell, with math and science."

"I'm trying to rationalize this by not killing you!"

I closed my mouth. He let out a long breath.

"I'm sorry," he said sternly.

"I don't remember everything, but I remember enough. I can piece it together. I cannot stay here and let him," I sucked in a sharp breath and wiped my eyes. "I can't let him keep doing it to me."

"I have to do some calculations."

"Thank you." I nodded, dropping my gaze to the brown, paper bag.

"Yeah."

"Has he told you why he's doing this?"

"Practice."

"For what?"

"He doesn't tell me anything, but I did hear him mention that there was a plan to take the Agency. Apparently, there's a weapon."

"A weapon?"

He shrugged. "I know he was searching for you, trying this whole conduit thing on the others to make sure he didn't kill you when he finally got you. I assume part you being here is working out how to find the weapon."

I mused for a moment. There were still so many missing pieces, things I needed to know.

"Okay…can you get something for me?"

"What do you need?"

"You can't make contact with anyone from the Agency, or anyone connected to it, your father has people everywhere," I ripped a sheet from the notepad and scribbled down an address. "So, you need to reach this person. She was my contact when I was in the military. She is the most secure, untraceable person I know."

"Why can't we get her to contact Illarion? She's super covert and all that, surely, she could get the message across."

A lump formed in my throat. I had thought of that, I went through a dozen scenarios and each one brought me to the same shitty conclusion.

"Because Dalca will kill him. If he's in Long Island, it means he has eyes on him. I can't chance it."

"What do you need?"

"Information about the running of the Agency and how Sensitives came to power… the information is at St Augustine's. That's where she'll need to go."

"The school?"

"Yes. Illarion didn't tell me everything, but he wouldn't have left me behind unless he knew something that changed the game. I also have a feeling that whatever he's searching for is related to something called the Legion, maybe this weapon has something to do with them. If so, that's where the info will be."

Speaking his name aloud brought a fresh pain to my heart but I couldn't afford to let emotions get in the way, not now.

"Okay. I'll contact her later today."

"Wait," I said quickly. "I need you to get my hospital records too."

"From when?"

"My admission before your father took me."

"What are you looking for in there?" he asked, folding his arms across his chest.

I wet my lip drawing in a breath through my nose.

"I was pregnant. I need to know what…I need to know if I'm okay otherwise."

Daniel's face paled.

"The information will probably be redacted or hidden. Can you still get it?"

"Might take me a bit but I'll see what I can do. My father will be back at six. After dinner he has another Sensitive he needs."

Another Sensitive he needs me to kill. I cringed.

"We're down to eighty-nine percent today."

The sudden tightening in my chest warned of the breakdown I knew was coming. I couldn't do this; I didn't have it in me. God knew I wanted to survive and to fight, but this... this was too much. I wrapped my arms around my chest and took a deep breath pushing back the lump in my throat.

"Ace, I—"

"I know. You're doing what you can. Thank you."

I turned my attention to the bed, and the letters hidden under the mattress. It had been two weeks since I'd read Illarion's letters. My heart tripped over itself.

"How'd you get the letters?"

He leaned against the door. "I overheard my father mention that you were in the Army and everyone who travels as much as recruits do, has a postal box. Or at least had. In your case it was still active."

"Right."

When I was alone, I pulled out the stash of letters and sat down, curling up against the foot of the bed.

I keep dreaming about you.

Every night I see your face, you're always the way you looked that last night in the cabin. You're peaceful and happy.

You tell me about our baby, and we make plans. Me and you. Can you believe that?

I should have been there, I never should have left you, it's the biggest damn regret of my life. I think about all the mistakes I'd made and if I could go back, there are so many things I would have done differently.

The point is moot though, isn't it? It's too late and I sit here writing these letters hoping that if I explain myself, it will make the pain ease, but it doesn't. The guilt is raw, I feel it getting heavier every day. But I deserve nothing less.

Aurel came to the house today. He asked me to come back to the Agency. I don't know if I told you already, I left. It was too hard. But now Elena and Michael need help. They have a great team of agents there, but he says I'm still the best agent they have.

Truth is, I don't think I have it in me anymore. Everything I'd ever done in this job was for a cause greater than me, and now that you're gone, what else can I do there?

Christ, I miss you, Ace. I miss you so damn much. How do I do this? How do I move on? I don't know that I can.

Illarion

I swallowed the giant lump in my throat. His pain was so raw it cut me. I couldn't imagine what he was going through out there. He wouldn't move on. He would let this pain rile him up until it finally killed him.

I pulled free the next letter and opened it, swatting away a stray tear with my free hand.

I saw my mother today. I don't know why I went. I told her everything. And when I did, I felt it, there was an understanding, like she wasn't surprised.

She knew. Didn't she? When you went to see her, she knew about the baby, about the prophecy.

No matter what we did, it would have ended the same.

I can't get my head around it. I don't even know her, how could some-one let another person walk into a trap like that?

I feel your energy everywhere in my house. I'm afraid to be lucid enough to feel it all. But then I'm terrified that soon, your energy will disappear, and you'll be gone. I can't let you go.

I don't think I'll ever be able to let you go.

Illarion

Well, that made sense, I thought Sonya knew more than she let on.

I wrapped my arm around my stomach and leaned back against the mattress.

Tears spilled over my cheeks. Illarion would have been a perfect father. He would have taken such good care of the three of us, our own little family. He would have loved our child as much as he loved me.

Swallowing back the nausea, I folded the letter and reached for the next one. Each word, each stroke of pen on paper made me feel as though I was with him, breathing in his scent, feeling his skin on mine, hearing his voice as he spoke these words.

God, I missed him. I didn't think it was possible to love someone as wholly as I loved him.

I reached for the next letter and held it open.

I went back to the Agency; I'm trying to live whatever life is possible to live without you.

Elena has been wonderful. She was as distraught as we were.

You never knew this, and she kept it from you for a reason, so did your parents. Elena is your aunt. Your mother's sister. You already know they wanted you away from this world.

Like the rest of us, she regrets the way she handled it all. She blames herself, too.

She hates that she was blind to Damon and that she brought you to the Agency in the first place.

I don't know who I am anymore…I drink so much I pass out most nights and then, I dream about you. Always those same dreams…it's the only time I'm happy. If that's what you can call it.

I hit Aurel today and nearly broke his jaw. He and Michael came to check on me and he took away my scotch. I nearly killed him, Ace. Sometimes I forget how addictive the Darkness can be. I welcomed it. I enjoyed it. They had to take him to the hospital.

Michael knocked me on my ass. If it wasn't for him, I don't know what I would have done to Aurel. They took away all the alcohol in the house and they've been coming back every night.

I don't know if I can sleep without it.
Illarion

My mouth dried up. Illarion hit Aurel. *Drinking? Passing out? Elena?*

God, he was unraveling. Just like me. My world and his, was falling apart. *What was happening to him?*

I read over the letter again. He was losing himself. He was breaking.

Panic shot through me, no. No. He couldn't. He couldn't break like that. He was my lifeline. Without him, I would have given up. I fought because *he* kept me fighting.

As much as I tried to steady my breathing, the damage was already done. I was losing it. I couldn't think, I couldn't breathe.

My mind spiraled. *Elena, Elena was my aunt? God. How did I miss that? How did I not recognize those same, warm eyes my mother had?*

Where was my mind? Where did I keep losing myself? I shook my head and folded all the letters back together and pushed them under the mattress. Shit. I'd lost track of time, and I was late for dinner.

I pulled on the first dress that came free from the hanger and pulled my hair out of the elastic. I ran down the stairs nearly bowling over one of Dalca's staff and stopped, breathless, just outside the dining hall.

"You're late, Acacia."

My heart raced as his eyes locked onto mine. Shit. I stopped a few feet away from him, averting my eyes. Daniel's stricken expression shook me as his gaze darted between me and his father.

"I'm so sorry, Master."

Dalca got up, stalked over to me and in one, swift move he slapped me across the face so hard that the impact sent me backward into the door, slamming it shut.

I lost my footing and fell. The rage grew tenfold, and I forced myself to hold off. Memories of that day at the warehouse flashed before my eyes.

He stood above me, and his ugly shoes connected with my stomach. I grit my teeth. *Hold it together, hold off, stay calm.* I forced myself to breathe. My throat constricted, and I suppressed a scream, forcing my eyes shut as another kick threw me flat against the door.

"I'm sorry, I'm sorry, please." I whispered holding my hands up in surrender.

I hated myself for cowering the way I did. Even if I wanted to fight back, to break cover I couldn't. Pure terror seized my insides, wrapping around my heart locking my muscles in place.

Daniel made a move to get up but was stopped before he even took a step.

"Sit down!"

"She said she was sorry!"

"There are three simple rules I've implemented here." He crouched down, hovering above me, he roughly pulled my face up to his and I cracked my eyes open. "Now, is that too much to ask?"

My entire body was shaking.

"It won't happen again, please Master, I deserved that."

"Get to the table, clean your face up."

Obeying him, I stumbled over and dropped heavily into the chair ignoring Daniel's horrified expression and the pounding in my jaw.

I took the napkin and pressed it to my face. I just couldn't catch a break.

"Daniel." He nodded to his son. "You know what to do."

***

"Follow me Acacia," my Master said, after we had finished our quail and truffled mash.

He led us through an opulent set of doors opening into a white room. The staircase went up from either end, meeting in the middle on the first floor, a large painting of a battle scene I didn't recognize, hung above it.

"You remember your colleagues from the Agency?"

"I remember Damon Cale."

"Yes, Damon was just one of the men working for me. I have many other agents in place."

"Spies?"

"I prefer the term, loyal followers." He looked at me, with a smile. "With you, Acacia, I'll get exactly what I need."

He stopped me when we reached the door. When he turned me to face him, I held my breath. He traced his fingers across my cheek and when I winced, he cupped his hand over it gently.

"I'm sorry about that, I truly am. I only expect you to follow my rules."

"Of course, Master. I understand."

"Does it hurt?"

I shook my head.

He lowered his face to mine and pressed his lips to the stinging skin, then he said, "Come. The man you'll meet today has been working at the Agency for twelve years. He's a powerful Sensitive evolved in Sight."

I walked in after him and sat down. The man was tied up with his palms facing up.

"Do you recognize him, Acacia?"

When his eyes locked onto mine, I tried to think back to where I remembered him.

I searched his eyes looking back through not only my memories but his too.

Once I had what I needed, I looked back up at my Master.

"He was at the Agency's base in New York when I first went there. He was in a meeting room, listening to Agent Lazarev speak."

My heart felt funny. *Why was I feeling like this?*

"When I walked past the meeting room, I was taken to another where I spoke with three board members."

"Good, now what I need you to do, is go back to that meeting room. Get into his head, I need what he saw on the board. He has eidetic memory, and he has the information we need. Understand?"

"What am I looking for?"

"I need to know who has the lockdown protocols."

Something about that sentence made a pang of warning shoot through me.

"Understand?"

"Yes, Master." I shook away the uneasy feeling and reached forward, pressing one hand to his chest and the other to his cheek, ignoring the pleading look on his face.

"Please, Ace, please don't do this to me..."

Jerking back, I forced an even breath out, but my Master only placed my hands back into position.

"Please Ace, Illarion and I are friends, *you* and I are friends! You know this!"

My breath stalled, but I didn't know why.

Ignoring the way he trembled under my touch, I forced his eyes to mine and a white, blinding flash stunned me as I was sucked into his memories, racing through months and months of information until,

41

finally, I was in the meeting room looking up at the board and the information on it.

"There are three men in that room with the information I need."

That same warning echoed inside me. *I shouldn't give him this information.*

Agent Lazarev was pointing to a graph. Around him there were pictures and files on the locations of safe houses and weapons depots. On the meeting table scattered in messy piles there were files I couldn't make out. I looked up and took note of all the information my Master needed. My eyes found Agent Lazarev's. He wasn't really looking at me, I knew that, but the feeling was there again, making my heart chase itself.

Then his eyes left mine, and I felt a sudden sadness envelope me. I watched as his attention was stolen from the room by someone outside. My heart stopped when I saw that it was me. His attention was completely taken as I stopped and looked at him, I was rushing to get to the meeting with Elena. I remembered this part...a split second turned into eternity, and I felt him...

Before I could look at him again, I was back. My Master was looking down on me while he stood with his hands tucked neatly in the pockets of his brown suit pants.

"Get yourself cleaned up; I'll be there later to talk to you."

Was he displeased? Did I do something wrong?

"Now."

Closing my mouth. I got up and made my way back to my room. I traded the gown for my night dress, taking a few minutes to clean up, I brushed my hair and teeth and padded back over to the bed.

Why was I so tired?

Looking over at the clock, I noticed that more than four hours had passed since dinner and quiet footsteps stopped outside my room.

"Acacia." He pushed the door open, standing by the mouth of my room for a moment, watching me, eyes sharp and focused in the dark.

When I made a move to get up. He closed the door, locking it behind him.

"Sit down."

I did. I pressed my palms flat against the soft, white sheets and watched as he walked over to me. His eyes were dark and serious.

"What did you see in that Agent's head?" he asked.

When I didn't reply immediately, he took two, quick strides toward me and slapped me.

A shocked gasp left my lips, and my hand instinctively reached for the stinging skin.

"I won't ask again."

"Nothing…nothing I shouldn't have…you saw everything, Master."

He slapped me again this time the force threw me backward onto the mattress. In the second it took for me to draw in a breath, he was on top of me.

My lungs struggled to take in air as his grip around my throat tightened.

"Do not lie to me."

I tried to tell him that I wasn't. That I only saw what he wanted me to see. But I couldn't do anything. I couldn't speak.

Finally, he released me, and I turned to my side sucking in as much air as I could.

"You saw Lazarev," he said, firmly.

I nodded curling in on myself.

"What else did you see?" He grabbed both my hands and pinned them across my stomach, making sucking in breaths almost impossible. No matter how much I tried to move, I couldn't.

He leaned down so his face was inches from mine and I felt his hand pull the hem of my nightdress up, he pressed his palm to my leg sweeping it up higher and higher.

My breath caught and suddenly, I was terrified. Fear gripped its hand around my heart like a vice and then my mind snapped. The haze that kept me floating in and out of lucidity, was gone. No. No. *No.*

"What else did you see?" he repeated, running his hand along the hem of my underwear.

I forced my eyes to stay open. I couldn't falter now. *Hold it together, Ace.*

"I saw his face," I whispered.

"But you felt something too. Didn't you?"

His hand was too close. I could feel the Darkness building inside me. I was freaking out. Slowly, he pushed my legs apart and ran his fingers along the skin on the inside of my thigh.

"What did you feel?"

"It's familiar, the feeling, like…like I'm connected to him."

"Did you recognize him?"

Terrified that he'd do something if I didn't answer I nodded.

"Yes, I, we were together. We worked together."

My tongue was heavy. If he didn't leave soon, I would throw up. God, I couldn't do this.

Trying to hold my façade and keep myself together, was becoming impossible. I was crumbling and he saw it.

"You used to sleep with him," he said, so matter-of-factly like it was a dirty thing we had done. "You remember that?"

"Yes," I stammered.

He lingered, his hands too close to my core, sickening heat radiated from his skin as he let out a long, hot breath. He squeezed my face with his free hand, forcing my eyes up to his while his other remained on my thigh.

"That will never happen again, you're mine. Do you understand me?"

I nodded.

"No one, but me will touch this body again unless I say. Is that clear?"

"Yes, Master."

My breath faltered, freezing in my throat as he swept his hand up higher.

"Can I trust you, Acacia?"

When he moved his hand closer, my breath hitched, a scream was on the verge of escaping.

"Hmm?" he asked again, running his fingers along my trembling skin.

"Yes," I breathed. "Yes, you can trust me."

"If I think you're lying to me, Agent Lazarev won't be safe anywhere he goes. Not in that big mansion of his, not within the walls of the Agency, not even in the protection of the most fortified place on this planet."

Tears stung the back of my eyes making my throat constrict.

"And I know somewhere deep down where you still know who you are, you know how much you love him."

Tears slipped onto my cheeks.

"So, don't give me a reason to cut his life short. Do not make the mistake of thinking you can outsmart me."

"You can trust me." I hissed, choking on a sob.

"I know you're in there, Acacia, I know you're lucid when the Serum wears off, so if you're in there now, make no mistake, I will find him, and I will kill him if you give me reason to."

"I'm not lying. You can trust me."

I held my breath until he was off the bed and the lingering touch from his hand was gone.

"Get some rest."

Then he was gone.

"Oh my, God." I sobbed out loud, pulling my knees to my chest. I couldn't do this. I couldn't let him do this to me. I couldn't pretend. I couldn't anymore.

***

ILLARION

I woke with a jolt again. My body was covered in a fine sheen of sweat and I knew that I'd been thrashing in bed again.

I looked across at the mess of pillows on the floor beside the bed. I swung my legs over the edge and dropped my head into my hands.

Tears came again like they did every morning. This wasn't normal. Grief came in all forms. I knew how this worked. But not like this. These dreams, this pain, it wasn't normal.

Dragging myself from the bed, I groaned as last night's drinking reminded me of my own mortality. My vision hazed out in front of me, and a slight sway told me to sit back down.

For a few seconds I did, allowing the world to realign. Aurel would be disappointed. I'd retrieved the fine whiskeys I'd been saving for a special occasion, the stash he and Michael didn't find during their purge. My head was pounding, and my mouth was dry. No matter how much water I drank it never seemed to quench it.

A sound outside drew my attention as I pulled my arms through a sweater ignoring last night's T-shirt still clinging to my body. I probably should have taken time to shower, but I couldn't find it in me to care.

Pulling the door open, I stopped when Aurel gave me a pointed look, glancing over my choice of attire.

I pushed past him.

"You look like hell."

"Thanks." I muttered, heading straight for the kitchen.

I rummaged around two shelves coming up empty, and when Aurel's incessant tapping drew my attention, I let out a breath of relief as he tossed a box of Advil over.

"Did you get any sleep?" he muttered.

"Maybe an hour or two."

He shook his head and sat at the bench. "Want to talk?"

"No."

"Illarion."

"I know," I exhaled, pressing both palms flat to the cool surface. "I can't. Not yet."

"You've bottled everything up, brother, you need to let someone in."

That same pain that I'd learned came whenever I thought about her, began to thrum inside me, pulsing steadily with the beat of my own heart. It was like her presence was still here. Only in some way, she was suffering, just like me. But another feeling, a nagging instinct inside me told me this was something I couldn't ignore.

"I see her in my dreams," I said, quietly.

Aurel didn't respond, but he was listening.

"She's not like before," I ran a palm over my jaw, jarred by the alien feeling. "She's tired and in pain. I don't know why I'm seeing her like that."

"You're hurting, you're going to see all sorts of painful things."

"Not like this. She changes like time is still going somewhere."

"Your mind is torturing you."

"I deserve it."

"Illarion, no. This isn't on you, it never was."

"Why am I seeing her like this?"

"What are you seeing?"

"Someone's with her. I don't know who he is. But I see everything through her eyes. Like she's pulling me into her consciousness."

His eyes darkened.

"He hurts her every night, and she cries. She begs him to leave but he never stops," I paused. "But you know the worst part? She's calling for me to help her. She reaches out. She's not lucid, not completely but she still calls for me. She still has faith that I can save her."

I laughed harshly. Aurel hung his head, reaching over and squeezing my hand.

It was undeniably my own personal hell, signed, sealed and delivered by the devil himself.

A brief second of intolerable silence filled the still air. I was painfully aware of every hot tear searing its way down my cheeks.

"I've dreamt about her before, Aurel but these dreams are new," I looked up at him. "She tries to fight this man but he's always stronger than her. Something is stopping her."

"They're just dreams," Aurel whispered.

"Why does it feel so real?" I shook my head. "The pain in her eyes is real."

"You need to get more sleep, I mean it, Illarion. Proper sleep, not passing out because you're wasted."

I didn't know what I could say to that. My heart was beyond repair and my soul vacant. Aurel held my gaze. He must have seen something in my eyes that shook him because I felt the apprehension rushing through him.

He released a long breath before pushing away from the counter, "I'll get some food organized for the fridge. Make sure you eat."

"Where are you going?"

"I need to meet with Michael. I'll see you tomorrow."

CHAPTER FOUR

ILLARION

I bolted upright, barley keeping myself seated on the lounge. I'd fallen asleep. Damn it.

Another horrific dream shook me to lucidity. This time it was different. I didn't see her the way I usually did. This time, I saw through her eyes. It was dark and she couldn't see further than an inch from her face. When she looked up, all I could see were papers and books—a desk. Her face was pressed down on a desk.

I didn't need to see the rest to know what was happening to her. Every few seconds or so, I'd feel a jolt of fear rush through her and into me and then she'd squeeze her eyes shut and cry, pleading for me to save her.

I rushed off the couch dropping to my knees at my desk, then I threw everything up into the wastebasket filled to the brim with empty bottles.

The image was still burned into my retinas as the last remnants of sleep broke away, but it was the voices taunting her that made me throw up.

I wiped my mouth and dragged myself to my feet, then I took another bottle of whiskey from the bar behind my desk. I didn't bother with a glass this time.

Glancing at the clock, I recoiled, it was just before seven in the morning.

"Illarion," Aurel's voice boomed from down the hall.

I looked up.

"You have to stop this."

"Leave."

"I'm not going anywhere."

"Drink?"

"You didn't touch any of the food I made you yesterday." He reached for the bottle. This time, I didn't stop him.

"Fell asleep."

"I'm glad to hear it, but you need to eat something."

"Not hungry."

"I know," he said, leading me toward the kitchen, anyway. "Anna's coming to see you."

My eyes shot up to his.

"She said she was meaning to visit for a while, but you kept missing her calls."

"I wasn't missing them."

"Yeah, I got that," he said sternly. "She cares about you, we all do."

"I don't want to see anyone."

"Donna's coming over with her. It's done."

I sighed and sat when Aurel motioned to the chair.

"When are they getting here?"

"Six," Aurel said, over his shoulder while he cut up some vegetables and dropped them into a pot of water.

"Thank you."

He stopped and turned briefly. "For?"

"For all of this."

"You don't have to thank me for this, man. I'm here, goes without saying."

"I haven't made it easy," I whispered.

"There's nothing easy about this, I wouldn't expect any different."

When I stayed quiet, he turned back to the food and continued chopping. A few minutes later he added some pasta to another pot and turned back to me. He handed me a bottle of water and took one for himself.

"Not much of a breakfast food. But you need something a little more substantial."

"Don't know how well *substantial* will go down."

He leaned his hip against the bench and watched me for a few moments. He didn't say a word, and he didn't have to. He knew. He saw it when he stayed over.

I cleared my throat. "I'm not sure that I can come back from this."

"You will."

Tightness in my chest made my breath turn stale.

"You'll come back from this. You'll go back to work. You'll find your way."

"I'm not sure I want to."

His jaw squared and he set down his bottle, "I've never known you to quit a damned thing in your life, Illarion. Not when your father was killed, not when your mother was hurt and not now. That isn't you. Understand?"

"I'm not so sure anymore."

"I am," he bit. "And you will get through this."

"Christ, Aurel. How do I do this without her?"

"One day at a time. I'm here."

***

After surviving five long hours sitting in the sun in total silence with Aurel, I'd managed to break away long enough to retreat to my room where I stayed until it was time to greet our guests.

I got up and got ready for dinner.

Pulling my hair up, I smoothed down my grey t-shirt along with black jeans and dark boots.

This was a mistake. I shouldn't be going down there. I should be staying here, in this room with the bottle that was calling my name.

Anticipating my apprehension and the probability to cancel on him, I felt Aurel approach before he knocked loudly on the door.

I pulled it open, resting my elbow on the wall.

"You weren't thinking of bailing, were you?" he lifted his brows.

"Wouldn't dream of it."

"Get your ass down there," he said, sternly and jerked his head motioning toward the stairs.

"I'm going."

He grabbed my forearm and stopped me.

"No one is expecting you to host a party. Just be there with us. That's all I'm asking."

"I'll be there."

We walked down the remainder of the staircase in silence.

Aurel stepped ahead of me and squeezed my shoulder gently before pushing the door to my lounge open.

The ashy smell of crackling fire drifted through the room once again making my chest tighten.

Donna and Anna were seated on the couch, talking quietly and when we approached, they stood. Both women looked across at us, sadness and apprehension coursed through them filling the air causing it to dip into a pit of angst.

When I forced a smile, Anna let out a nervous breath and moved toward me. She tentatively wrapped her arms around my waist and when I tensed, she promptly retreated.

"I'm so happy to see you," she whispered.

Happy. I flinched inwardly. Happy isn't the adjective I'd have used in this scenario. But I smiled and hugged her back then Donna when she stepped into my space.

Aurel shifted beside me, his whole body buzzing with emotions. He was anxious, but he was happy that I came down, he was *happy* that I was trying and me? I was coping—floating through this experience like I was viewing it as an outsider, counting down the minutes until they left, and I could go back to my room.

"Drink?" I said, *happy* with my suggestion.

Aurel shot me a warning look. When Anna eagerly agreed, he dropped whatever he was about to say.

Her nerves were flashing all over the place making my insides tighten.

I needed a strong drink, or two.

When her hand grazed mine, I sucked in a sharp breath and rushed out of the room, finding myself gasping for breath in the bar while I steadied my breathing. When I was sure I'd be able to form more than a single word, I returned, a couple of bottles in hand.

"I have wine and scotch," I said, dryly.

Aurel took the scotch from me and placed it away from us. Smart move.

Leaving me with the wine, I set down four glasses and poured us each a drink.

Aurel and Donna began talking, catching up on what he'd missed since he left the Agency while Anna and I moved to the far end of the room, looking out over the garden.

Anna stayed quiet while I drank silently. Then she left and returned with the scotch.

"Donna has to work in the morning, she wanted me to pass on her apologies."

I nodded and turned back to the sky.

Anna poured two glasses and handed me one. When her fingertips brushed across my hand, I flinched, jerking back.

"I'm sorry." She laughed nervously. "I must be all static."

I looked down at my hand.

"I didn't get a chance to speak to you at the funeral."

"It was a long day," I muttered.

"She was an incredible woman, Illarion."

"She was." I blinked back the haze coating my eyes and looked down at the glass.

A gentle hand on my shoulder drew my attention.

"You doing okay?" Aurel knelt.

"Yeah." I held up my glass. "I'm alright."

"Good." He smiled and hugged Anna. "I'm off to bed, make sure he gets some sleep."

"Will do." She smiled and turned back to me.

When Aurel left, I took the bottle of scotch and poured some more, much more than one would normally pour. Anna frowned and reached over for the bottle. When her hand cupped over mine, I froze.

"You've had a few," she whispered, swaying.

"So have you."

"Come on." She tugged until I let go.

As she leaned over me to put the bottle down, I caught the scent of citrus and coconut. I breathed in deeply and stopped when she moved back and grazed my arm with hers.

"Aurel said you weren't looking after yourself."

"I'm doing fine."

"You don't seem fine," she whispered.

She sat too close. Her arm was touching mine and the fire in the background made the room double in temperature. Anna took off the light sweater she was wearing, and my eyes quickly darted away.

Her full breasts filled out the silk shirt and every sharp breath she took made her chest rise and fall, causing every nerve inside me to fire.

It was the alcohol flowing through my veins, I knew it was because no woman would ever make my heart race like Ace did.

Sucking in a sharp breath I shot to my feet then rushed outside onto the balcony. Cold stinging rain rapidly drenched me. It was a welcome relief from the heat.

Anna called to me over the howling wind, but I ignored her. I gripped the edge of the rail and looked up at the sky, closing my eyes hoping to God and Beings that somehow, they would give me strength to be the man Ace thought I was.

But I was breaking and there was no coming back from it. When lightning cracked, splitting the sky in two, Anna rushed outside and wrapped her arm around me, urging me to come inside.

I followed her and when I finally inhaled, after holding my breath for so long, I broke. My wet hair clung to my face, hiding the burning tears.

She gripped my face in her hands, but I didn't hear a single word she was saying. It was so loud in my head, there was so much noise. When she leaned in to wrap a towel around my shoulders, I brought my hands to her cheeks, and I kissed her.

For a moment, she was frozen. Pain and acceptance and hope flared through her and then her hands were in my hair and her lips were over mine. I moved quickly after that, pulling off her wet shirt and she moved even quicker pulling off mine. I picked her up and in one fluid motion laid her down on the soft rug beside the fireplace. I reached into a wooden box beside the giant plant and retrieved a condom. A pang of guilt shot through me remembering the times Ace and I spent here.

Ace was gone an angry voice inside me hissed.

I ground my jaw and pushed it out of my mind. I watched Anna through hooded eyes as I worked the wrapper. She bit down on her lip when I moved toward her and lowered myself over her.

The fire roared as her breathless gasp was lost in the raging thoughts flashing through my mind when I brought our bodies together.

I gripped her hips as I moved, faster and harder, letting every emotion disappear, letting every thought grow silent as all I focused on was the way she cried out when I moved with her, the way she dug her nails into my back when I dipped my lips to her pulse.

As a tremor started between us, I pressed my cheek against hers and closed my eyes. I didn't want to feel anything other than this release; I didn't want to hear her breathless voice as my name became a plea on her lips. I didn't want to hear the insidious voice inside my head telling me that I was betraying *her*.

Crying out, she gripped my arms as spasms rocked her body and I held her. My fingers brushed across her cheek and before another word could pass, I held my breath letting the shudder bring me to a quiet crescendo.

I quietly got up and collected her clothes and handed them to her. I couldn't, bozhe, I couldn't be here. Not like this. Not after what I'd just done. I ignored the way she pleaded with me to stay, and I walked, I walked without a single shred of dignity left. I was broken.

Chapter Five

ACE

As much as I could fall asleep every night and zone out for the most part, it didn't bring me any peace. Whatever took place during the day came flooding back when I closed my eyes. Whatever he'd done, somehow starting to creep back up on me when it was still and silent. And then there was the night I'd completely blocked out, the night he brought his friends over. I had no idea what else took place after they'd watched me drain another Sensitive, and the logical part of me which seemed to drive most of my higher reasoning these days, told me I was grateful for it.

It wasn't hard to piece together the missing information though. What else would they have been there for? It didn't take a genius to realize two and two made four.

Two weeks had passed since Daniel brought me new letters from Illarion, two weeks since I killed another one of this idiot's victims and two weeks since I stopped crying when he came to me in the night. I sat on the edge of the proverbial fence, weighing up whether I should just try to make a run for it, or whether I listened to Daniel.

There was nothing miraculous he could do to speed up the process. Simply put, I was too reliant on the drug, and I was still too dependent on daily doses to be able to safely go without which was all obviously by design.

It was day twenty. We'd be hitting eighty-four percent, and the last few weeks had been hard to say the least.

Master Jackass had me suck information out of more than fifteen former and current employees of the Agency. I lost track of what information I handed over. It was the same thing, day in and day out.

I knew what happened every night he came to my bed. Marks on my body told me infinitely more than my hazy, clouded mind did.

But the survival mechanism inside me blocked everything out. Every painful moment, every terrifying touch, every agonizing hour.

But the hours when I was lucid between doses, were the moments I feared the most. I remembered those moments and those moments would stay with me forever.

Those were the days I'd look outside the window and push myself inside the broken and shattered shell that had become my body, as he breathed heavily into my ear while his hands roamed across my skin. Those were the days I squeezed my eyes shut while I waited on my knees, in the dark, for the heart-stopping sound of the lock turning.

I kicked off the covers and sat on the edge of my bed, ignoring the newly formed bruises on my wrists. My own body was betraying me in a sick twist of irony. I'd probably be dead before we made it to Daniel's deadline.

Burying my head in my hands I took a deep breath and sat, breathing, letting it all sink in. I was still here though. I was still alive.

I could do this. I looked down at my arms and jerked when I realized how violently I'd been scratching the inner part of my elbows.

The itching was getting worse, and I looked like hell. I ran my hands up and down my arms. I'd lost so much weight I barely recognized my own body.

Kneeling beside the bed, I reached for the letters, hopeful that at least they would chase away the ever-present pain on the forefront of my mind.

I keep dreaming about you. But these dreams are different now. They terrify me, Ace.

Every night I see your face, you're always in pain, you're suffering. You cry but no one comes to you. You call for me, but I'm not there. Your hand hovers, reaching like you see me, but it's not possible.

Your mind betrays you; you see things that aren't there, you feel things but when you wake you don't remember. You're alive, but your heart wants to die. You plead and plead, and it goes on and on. I never see past that.

The suffering is too much, Ace, it kills me. It's killing me every night. Why am I seeing you like this? I tried to speak to Aurel about it, but he doesn't know how to help, no one does.

I keep thinking one day I'll wake up and it would all be gone, just a bad dream. You'd be here, in my t-shirt, watching me work...you'd be reading a book.

I don't know. I don't know anymore.

I've been spending time with a woman. She's been around a lot since you left. I don't know what I'm doing, Ace. I feel like I'm making a mess of everything.

She works at the Agency. She's kind, she's a good friend, a distraction. God knows I need one right now. She listens, and I talk. Always about you. That's all I can do, that's all I have. I have to keep talking, thinking about you.

Illarion

What the hell?

It couldn't be. Jealousy began to form an angry knot in my stomach. I should have been happy that he was talking, speaking to someone. But I couldn't help it. I couldn't help the pain that settled and burned inside.

I was alive. Right here. Suffering and alone and he was spending time with a woman.

Tears pricked my eyes, and my breath stopped short. *My hand instinctively went to my heart—did he care about her? Did he hold her the way he held me?* I was alive, I was right here! Going through a hell I wasn't sure I'd survive. Stopping my faltering breath, I tried to breathe in deeply and blink through the haze.

I swallowed the dryness in my throat and read over the letter again and each time I read it, the words cut me a little more. How could it be? How could he be seeing my dreams?

It wasn't possible as much as I hoped to God that it was, I knew I couldn't use any of my abilities in this house. Dalca must have had some serious shields up. *But I'd broken through, somehow, right?* Through the dreams. It's why I felt our connection spark to life when I saw his face through that agent's eyes. Maybe that connection, through that time in space connected us again here. It's also why Dalca freaked, he saw it and panicked. He could ward the crap out of this house and drug me until I drooled into the carpet, but if I was as *divine* as they'd kept telling me, then he'd need more than just wards and Serum to keep my power suppressed.

I quickly folded the letter up and reached for the next one.

The pain is worse now, Ace. You're in so much pain. I can't sleep anymore. I haven't slept properly in days. I feel your pain whenever I close my eyes.

It's as though you're breaking through some kind of shield and you're pushing and pushing, trying to break down those barriers but you can't. You're always reaching for me, begging me to help.

Even Anna can't help now, she tries. She wanted to come to your grave with me, to help me grieve. I can't. I feel like you're not really gone. And if that's true, it means you're out there somewhere, suffering and I'm failing you all over again.

Where are you, Ace? Are you suffering somewhere?

Please, tell me, find a way to tell me.

Is this my punishment? Because I failed you?

O Bozhe, if it is, please find a way to tell me. I'd take it for a thousand lifetimes if I knew you were okay.

Please find a way to tell me.

Please.

Illarion.

My eyes filled with hot tears. Anna was trying to get through to him, to comfort him and be there because I couldn't. It should've been me there. It should've been me holding him. Not Anna.

A quick flurry of footsteps drew my attention. They weren't king jerk off's footsteps; I knew the difference, so my body relaxed when Daniel stepped inside.

"I have the information for you."

My eyes shot up.

"What's wrong?" his face dropped.

"Nothing, what have you got?"

He gave me a pointed look. When I shook my head, he frowned then handed me two folders.

"It was hard work getting those hospital records, Ace. You were right when you said they might be redacted. They were sealed and hidden so deeply I had a hard time finding them. So, I don't know what's actually left."

"Did you read them?"

"No, of course not. That's your business."

"I appreciate that." I sighed, hating how my heart slammed against my ribs in anticipation to what I was about to read.

"There's something else."

"What?" I looked up at him.

He stood with his arms folded tightly across his chest, his face slightly downturned. "Your contact said there was heavy surveillance on Illarion's house."

"He wasn't bluffing."

"No." Daniel sighed.

"No one followed you?"

"I checked. I did all the things you told me."

"Tell me again."

"I didn't use turn signals, I took extra turns, stopped at the store, and waited an hour. Even ordered breakfast for good measure."

Relaxing, I took the folders to the writing desk and sat down. Daniel stood beside me, looking over my shoulder at the file from St Augustine's.

"What are you looking for in there?" he asked.

"Honestly? I'm not sure."

"But you'll know when you see it?"

"I hope so."

"Anything in particular?"

Casting my eyes over the papers, I drew my fingers over the sheets.

"There was a prophecy, something about the Divine Sensitive and the Celestial Beings—I think it may have something to do with what Dalca's planning, something to do with both Divines."

"You don't think it has anything to do with the Agency, do you?"

"No." I said firmly. "I think whatever he's trying to do with the Agency is a means to an end. He's planning something much bigger than that."

"You really think you'll find that in there?"

"I don't doubt it, but the information will be hidden, maybe encrypted."

I closed the folder and tucked it under the magazines, then I pressed both palms on the desk and inhaled sharply, ignoring the hospital file staring up at me.

"Ace…"

The tension was rolling off him, you'd think he was about to take the Bar Exam.

"I'm alright." I sat down and looked up at him.

"You're not."

Leaning back in the chair I chewed the side of my lip and scrubbed my face. "You're right. I'm not."

"I try to stop him."

"I know that."

My foot tapped restlessly on the rug beneath me. I tried my best to ignore him, he was suffocating me, all this emotion was going to kill me.

"The addiction is taking hold," he said, pressing a hand to mine, stopping me from scratching myself.

"It's fine."

"It's not fine. Lowering the dose only helps take the veil off, the addiction will still stand. It's serious shit."

"Yeah, I can see that," I muttered. "Sodium pentothal, Rohypnol and a little something else."

"Something else being heroin," he bit.

"Yep."

A pregnant pause settled between us. He looked away momentarily before he focused his attention on me again.

"You need to get me something else."

"What?"

"Anything, just, make me forget. I need something else to complement the Serum, get me something to make it stay in my system."

"You want me to get you something to keep the Serum in your system?"

"I need you to trust me," I managed through shaky breaths. "My body doesn't hold onto drugs, not for long anyway."

"Then why do you want something more?"

"I'm lucid when he comes to me now, I know everything he's doing. I can't...I can't do that anymore."

There were things I was afraid of and then there were the things I knew would kill me if I stopped fighting. I found his eyes and a second later I lost it, tears began rushing out of me and I was afraid I'd never be able to stop them.

"Did you know that he brought friends one night?"

Every word was getting stuck in my throat and every word sliced me with a fresh pain.

"I know," he ground out. "I know because after he left you, I was there to pick you up. I know what he does."

"And you're refusing to help me!"

"I cannot do what you're asking!"

When my resolve died, and I broke into breathless sobs, he moved to take my hand, but I pulled away. I pushed out of the chair and rushed back, tripping over my own feet which sent me careering into the ground.

Daniel reached out for me then I completely lost it.

The air was punched out of my lungs. I wrapped my arms around my stomach trying my best to stop myself from throwing up.

"Get me something to make me forget, I don't care what it is!"

He didn't protest. He didn't try to talk me out of it. "I'll have something for you tomorrow."

Nodding, I dropped my head into my hands, hoping that he would just leave. A few minutes later, he did. When I was alone, I let everything out, all the pain and suffering, all the agony, all the torture I was putting myself through, all the thoughts of Illarion and how much I missed him and the fear that even if I got out of here, Ila wasn't mine anymore.

As much as that all hurt, right now, I had work to do. I geared myself up then walked over to the desk with the files Daniel had brought back.

He was right. My hospital records were heavily redacted. There were more blacked out blocks across the text than words. I skimmed across the laundry list of reported injuries then stopped when my eyes coasted across the part I needed.

Gestational age of foetus estimated at eight weeks. hCG levels normal. Miscarriage caused by severe abdominal trauma. Foetus could not be saved, mother at risk of death without immediate intervention. Full hysterectomy was performed. Mother died in theatre. T.o.D: 23:16. Doctor D. Davis.

I must have read the simple paragraph more than six times before splashes landed on the paper making it impossible to see. I realized then I'd been crying.

I wiped my face before I closed the file, tucked it away somewhere Dalca would never find and I slid down against the wall, resting my chin in my knees.

So, that was it. He'd taken everything from me. Not just what was, and what is but what could have been.

CHAPTER SIX

ACE

The next time Daniel came, the mood was heavy. There was no banter, no smiles, no small talk.

He pushed past me after he locked the door and sat on the edge of my bed.

"I did some research." He held out a small parcel. "Sadly, it's exactly what I thought. Heroin."

Holy fuck. The bottom of the bottom.

"It'll match the effects of the Serum, but it'll block your memory receptors. Same composition. You won't remember anything. At least until your body starts to flush it out which as we know, won't be too long."

Heroin. That was a new, all-time low.

"That means repeat doses, right?" I managed.

"Sadly, yes."

He prepped the syringe without saying anything else. After a few moments he looked over at me. I didn't hear what he was thinking but I didn't have to. The look in his downturned expression was enough to make me feel as disgusting as I should have.

I cleared my throat. "How did you get it?"

"Perks of being his son. I get to know some pretty fucked up people. Bored rich kid wanting a buzz. No one asks questions."

Sadness overwhelmed me. I loathed what I was asking of him, this was the only thing that would keep me alive and the only thing that would buy me the time we needed to get the hell out of this house.

He gently pulled my arm into his lap, and he fixed the rubber tourniquet around my elbow.

"Are you sure you want to go through with this?" he asked quietly.

"Yes."

"Because we can look into something else."

"There is nothing else. You said so yourself."

He sighed. A few agonizing seconds later he pressed the needle into my skin.

I leaned back on the bed, gently letting my body fall into the softness beneath me.

"Thank you," I managed to whisper, letting my hand fall free.

"Christ, Ace." He looked away from me. "Don't ever thank me for this."

"Then thank you for helping me forget."

A muscle in his jaw worked. "We're down to sixty-eight percent tonight."

I nodded against the pillow.

For a moment he didn't say anything, then he looked down at me. "Did you read your file?"

"I did."

"Do you want to talk about it?" he asked gently.

My eyes coasted up to him just as the warmth started to spread through me, making my fingers tingle.

"I was right about the baby. Two months."

"Shit, Ace. I'm sorry."

I swallowed hard and swatted away a stray tear. "The report said repair wasn't possible. They took everything out."

Daniel's eyes drifted shut for a moment before he let out a chain of expletives in Romanian. I didn't know the language, but I knew enough.

"What can I do?"

"Nothing, it's done now," I whispered, forcing a tight smile. "Before you go, please give me the letters."

When the letters were safely in my hand, Daniel left, and I was alone with Illarion.

I cannot handle the dreams anymore, Ace. They're so real. You're clearer in my head now. I see you, all of you.

You don't look like you did when I saw you last. Something about you is so haunted. Your expression...it breaks me.

What's happening to you?

Who is he? The man I keep seeing? His face is always veiled by something, but he hurts you. I can see that. I can see the blank expression on your face when he touches you, but your eyes...I can see the pain in them.

I don't know how many more of these dreams I can handle.

I'll never forgive myself.

Illarion

My eyes wandered from letter to letter, dozens of them, all telling me how much he was suffering because he was seeing everything through my eyes. How could I ever face him? How could I look into his eyes if I ever got out of here?

Aurel came by again, this time he drank with me. He says that when he looks at me, he sees the pain in my eyes and it's almost as bad as seeing you die.

The dreams have been happening every night now hitting me harder and with more pain than before. He must believe there's more to it now. But what else could it be?

I'm so tired, I don't sleep. I don't try to stop crying now. Anna sees it, she refused to leave, so she stayed the night.

I don't think there's any strength left in me, not enough to get through the night and face the day. The dreams are terrifying but my life without you is a living nightmare.

I don't know which is worse. I feel your strength depleting, you're giving up.

Aurel is worried about me. He doesn't leave my house anymore. He stays with me until I'm asleep and when the nightmares wake me hours later he's by my side again. He knows Anna's here, he doesn't say anything, but he knows my mind is a mess.

Last night I saw you begging, pleading to end it. Your eyes are as dull as the day I watched you die in my arms.

He's hurting you so much and it never ends...I wish I could make it end. Why is this happening?

Illarion.

Silent tears wet my cheeks as they fell. I wasn't giving up. I just wasn't letting myself feel anything anymore. Maybe that was giving up? Maybe taking heroin was as cowardly and as weak as it got. But it was the only thing I could do now.

***

Pretending that I was under the Serum's effects wasn't hard anymore, my body was slowly shutting down. The drugs were taking a toll, and when Dalca sat down joining me and Daniel I looked past his face, to a spot on the wall.

This was the second or third week taking both drugs now, I couldn't remember for sure. But they were doing the job.

"Daniel, the Serum."

I groggily lifted my head and held out my arm. As my head rolled to the side, I caught a glimpse of the skin inside my elbow. It was horrible. The skin there was black and blue, dozens of puncture marks stared back at me.

"This is two months, Father, this is the dose that killed the others."

He hesitated for a moment before his father spoke up.

"She's not like the others. Do it."

Fifty-two percent. I could do this.

Daniel knelt beside me and pressed the needle into my skin.

"I'm sorry," he whispered, pulling back.

***

My Master stood beside me with a glass of scotch, twirling it in his hand.

He didn't ask me to work tonight, instead, we sat in his library by the fire, talking.

"Do you remember your last operation in Iraq?"

"Yes, Master."

"Tell me, Acacia, do you regret leaving?"

"No." I answered, keeping my eyes on the flames. "It was the right choice."

"How so?"

He reached over and swept my hair behind my ears.

"I was done with all the death."

"Death is a part of war, no?"

"Not when it was substantiated by bad orders and people in power who didn't care about the lives they were condemning."

He mused, returning his attention to the fire.

We remained quiet for a moment, immersed in the raw power of nature seemingly harnessed and contained in such a simple manner.

"Do you know why I'm doing what I am?"

I shook my head slowly.

"I'm doing it because I think that we've lived like rats hiding in sewers for far too long. There was once a time when Solaris and Aaryon ruled over our kind and the non-Sensitives. Somewhere along the line, we lost that, maybe they stopped caring or maybe we became complacent."

"Do you think that it will make a difference?"

He thought for a moment and then turned to me, cupping his hand over my cheek.

"I think if we work together we have a better chance. We will make them listen."

Letting that thought imbed itself into my mind, we settled into a comfortable night.

***

I raised my arms and inspected the damage; I'd been scratching again. My skin had scabbed up where I'd been ripping the flesh apart. Bruises had formed everywhere else.

Pulling the covers off my body, I walked over to the shower and climbed in before the water was even warm.

If I died right now, it wouldn't be so bad. I wasn't as depressed as I had been. Daniel was nice, the drugs were helping. Illarion's letters kept me company.

With shaking hands, I reached for the shampoo on the edge of the shower but when a wave of vertigo shot through me, I lost my balance. I stumbled forward and hit the edge of the niche.

I dropped like a stone clutching my head. The clear water quickly turned red and then panic set in.

No matter how much I tried, I couldn't get up. I couldn't reach. I was too weak and whatever I grabbed onto slipped under my soapy hand.

I reached up as far as my arm could and pulled a towel in with me. At least if someone found me, I wouldn't be completely buck-naked.

When the water started rising, I burst out laughing.

I laughed when it lapped over my ears, and I laughed when it covered my mouth. I blew tiny bubbles until the water covered my nose. That's when I stopped laughing.

My body was covering the drain, and I was too high to get up.

The towel grew heavy around me until my eyes went under and all I could see was red water.

I closed my eyes.

Guess this wasn't so bad, there were worse ways to go. I would finally be at peace. No more Dalca. No more nightly visits. No more pain. No more drugs. I'd see Illarion someday in the next life and he'd stop feeling my suffering.

Just as I'd made peace with my less-than-graceful death, I felt two, strong arms around my shoulders, pulling me out of the shower and across the floor. I cracked my eyes open as soon as I could and sucked in a deep, greedy breath.

Daniel. I looked up at him and grinned.

"Your hair looks good wet," I said.

His eyes darkened as he moved my wet hair from my face, "You could have died."

"You're actually really hot, you know that?"

He ignored me and helped me sit up, propping me against the wall. His eyes coasted across my body finally stopping on my head.

"Christ that's a serious cut. Wait here," he said before getting to his feet and rummaging around in an overhead cabinet. When he came back, he tilted my chin up and taped a gauze to my head.

"How do you know how to do all this?"

"I read a lot."

I grinned, closing my eyes. "Smart and sexy."

I heard him scoff.

"You know, if you were here at night instead of your dad, I'd be pretty happy with that."

"Ace," he said, trying to dry my hair with a towel, "you need to stop talking."

"Do I make you uncomfortable?" I cracked my eyes open.

He thought I was attractive; I'd seen it in the way his eyes would drink me in completely, and here we were, naked and wet, well I was at least.

When he didn't reciprocate, I reached for his hand.

"Don't you think I'm beautiful?" I bit down on my bottom lip and looked up at him.

"You need to stop, Ace. Please."

A frown tugged on my lips. "I mean, I, I know these bruises…And my head."

"It's not the bruises," he whispered, catching my hand and stopping it from trembling. "It's not you, your head or anything."

Inching closer, I reached forward, grabbing a hold of his collar. His wet hair dripped over my skin, and I noticed in this proximity how luscious and full his lips were, his icy blue eyes were filled with kindness and something else; fire fueled by passion and want.

As I moved closer to him, he wrapped his hand around my wrist.

"Please, stop."

"You don't think I'm beautiful," I whispered, slumping back. "God, this is so embarrassing."

"You know I do." His hand shot out, catching mine when I pressed it over the scar on my cheek. He shook his head, trailing his fingers across the mark. "But this isn't right, none of this is."

"It can be," I whispered.

"Ace…" his voice broke with pleading as he closed his eyes, his hair falling over his face, shielding the creases in his brow.

I knew it then; he'd let his walls down and his resolve was gone. I trailed my fingers across his cheek drawing his face and eyes up to me.

When he opened his mouth to protest, I made my move. My hands found the nape of his neck and my lips crashed into his, stifling any attempt of pushing back.

His lips were cold from the water he'd just saved me from but the heat from his body warmed me.

Without warning, he pushed me back and shook his head. "We can't, Ace. This is wrong."

Everything was gone from me, everything was breaking, everything was falling apart. I got up, desperate to put as much space between us as possible—

My thoughts were interrupted as he moved, lightning fast. His body was flush against mine, pinning me to the bathroom door before I could take my next breath. As his hand roamed across my body through the towel, the other cupped my cheek.

There was no hesitation on his part anymore. The low sound from the back of his throat was caught on my lips when I let him walk us backward, pressing me flat to the tiles.

My heart thundered in my chest as his hands worked quickly, wrapping around my hair, pulling me closer.

It didn't take me long to pull his wet T-shirt off and I didn't know why I was so shocked when I saw the taut lines of his abdomen. He was well-defined, perfectly tanned. He was tall and broad. My eyes took all of him in, his golden hair fell around his eyes, while the shorter parts stuck up in a cute, messy fashion.

As our lips collided, he broke free and pulled back, abruptly drawing a sharp gasp.

"I'm sorry," he breathed, smoothing his hands through his hair, "I don't know what I was thinking, I'm so sorry."

"What are you talking about?"

"That was completely inappropriate, I can't believe I let that happen, after everything here..."

"I wanted it to happen."

"It doesn't matter. It's wrong, *I* was wrong. I was out of line, you nearly died in there."

I couldn't do anything but shake my head. My heart was in my stomach, my cheeks burned with each word.

"You need to be careful; we need to lay off the heroin," he said, finally after a long silence.

"No, no you can't do that to me."

"And you can't keep acting like you want to die." He stepped closer to me and that previous energy firing through us returned.

"I don't want to die."

When his gaze dropped, my resolve did too.

"I don't want to die," I repeated.

Before another moment passed, his lips were back on mine only this time there was nothing rushed in the action. It was slow, sensual like it was the most difficult, yet simplest thing to do.

I released my hold on the towel, letting it fall to my feet and drew him closer to me, pulling his hand to my body, letting it coast across my skin.

As he moved us back toward the door, he picked me up and wrapped his arms around me, where he held me against him never breaking the kiss.

He quickly undid his jeans with his free hand and stepped out of them before returning his hand to my hip.

My hands found their way to the curve of his back where I pulled him closer until our bodies were flush against each other. I arched up against him, feeling a wild rush of emotions spark and ignite within me.

A gentle hand ghosted across my stomach. He pressed his palm flat to my rib cage and up higher until he swept over my breast, drawing a sigh from me.

His lips were full, his hot breath was intoxicating and the way his arms tensed when he pulled me closer, floored me. A deep ache filled my belly rising with each sweep of his tongue across mine.

I desperately held on, throwing everything into this moment. He brought his hand between us and his gaze met mine. He stopped, his eyes searching my face for permission. This was the moment I should have told him to stop and go to bed, that he was right about this being wrong. But I did neither of those things. Instead, I twisted my fingers through his wet hair and kissed him.

Understanding passed between us then he eased our bodies together stifling my gasp with his lips.

I dug my nails into his shoulder and cried out when he let his hand fall to my lower back and pull me closer.

My heart raced, everything inside me was unraveling, pent up pain and fear, complete ecstasy and joy—all rolled into one dangerous burst that consumed everything. When his eyes found mine and I saw that same expression haunting him, I broke.

A breathless gasp was lost on my lips as we both reached the point that would change everything.

His hand splayed out on the door next to my head and his eyes closed, blonde lashes fanning across his cheeks as a breathless gasp parted his lips.

He brought his mouth to mine stopping the fierce cry that was filled with so much emotion I feared it would break me down completely.

And when the first wave exploded inside me, I gripped his shoulder crying out. He held on tighter, every breath, every move filled with more frantic energy, and as another wave broke me down, I shattered.

Breathless gasp after breathless gasp brought fresh tears to my eyes. I held onto him and squeezed my eyes shut, so desperately hoping he wouldn't hear me cry.

Regret filled the space between us as his hands smoothed my hair down my back, telling me that somehow it would all be okay.

***

I woke up with a smile, for the first time in forever, a real smile. Illarion was in my dream. His soothing voice, his beautiful eyes, those experienced hands.

And then my smile was chased away by a deep regret and even worse than that, anger.

Daniel deserved better, he cared about me, and I'd practically used him. I was so fucked up it wasn't even funny. Whatever I tried to tell myself to justify it, fell short—nothing made this okay. Nothing about my actions was excusable.

Forcing myself out of the bed, I threw on whatever I found in the wardrobe and sat back down with a sigh. We were getting closer. Day eighty at thirty-six percent Serum, one hundred percent heroin.

When I was clean, I could slowly feel the hum inside me again… it was barely there, but I knew soon, it would be back full force.

If only I was brave enough to tell Daniel to stop the heroin.

Frustration at my own cowardice consumed me. When did I decide to stop fighting?

When I managed to get up and stop pitying myself, I pulled out the letters and looked at them. Daniel had brought another small pile of them last week.

Elena came to the house and dragged me outside personally. I know it hurts her a lot.

I don't even know what I'm doing most days. I wake up, I drink, I pass out. Aurel stays…Elena goes…sometimes, even Michael visits.

It's impossible to sleep but it's harder to stay awake. Wherever I turn I see your face haunted by pain and agony. When I close my eyes, I feel you breaking. I don't know what to do.

I can't even see straight anymore. I don't remember the last time I ate, or really slept for that matter. All I keep tabs on is the amount of whiskey I've had and the number of times I watch you scream for them to end it.

The last dream I had of you, two nights ago, was quick. You let go.

After that, I told Anna to leave. I couldn't look at her without feeling like I was betraying you and hurting her. It's all messy, Lyubov. I've made a mess of it all.

You don't struggle now. You don't yell, or fight. You close your eyes, and I see the torment wash over your still features.

Christ. I don't know that I can live like this.

Illarion

My spine straightened.

Illarion was never one to give up. Never.

He was slowly falling apart and everything he said, was true. I looked over the letter again. I had let go. I was letting Dalca win without even fighting.

I threw the letter aside and rushed to the bathroom.

"Ace?"

Cringing, I leaned back enough so I could answer.

"I'm in the bathroom."

"It's five in the afternoon…did you just wake up?"

Wow. *That late?* Time was slipping from me.

I struggled to my knees and got up with Daniel's help.

"You really need to shower, seriously."

"I know, I'm sorry."

Tears pricked my eyes as I caught a glimpse of my reflection. I was a fucking mess.

The physical stuff was bad, but inside me, where I used to be a good person, that's where the real ugliness lay.

Daniel stopped behind me, keeping a few feet between us and his eyes downcast.

"Ace—"

"Don't say it." I shook my head. "And please don't look at me like that."

Soft footsteps came toward me.

Tears rapidly formed and I couldn't stop them this time. I threw my hands up to my face and tried to contain it as much as possible.

Daniel pulled me away from the mirror and into the bedroom. When I felt him leave, I turned to face him. He disappeared into the bathroom before returning with a wet towel and a small bowl of water.

"This will pass," he spoke, softly, brushing my hair behind my ears. "You're going to survive this."

His words burned a hole in my chest and the goodness of his soul crushed me into the mattress.

Without another word he cleaned my arms, and my face then moved to the matted, crusted ropes of hair hanging limply over my shoulders. He paid careful attention to the angry, open wounds inside my elbows. My nails had broken and chipped away long ago, but it still didn't stop me scratching at my skin and tearing it to shreds.

I had no dignity left.

I kept my eyes averted. I was too ashamed to look at him and see the judgment in his sapphire eyes.

Once he was done, he took the bowl and towel away and came back with a brush. I let out a laugh when he began to brush my hair.

"What you've gone through and how you've survived is… it's nothing short of amazing, Ace. Don't ever doubt your strength or your worth."

"I'm an addict." I cringed at the confession.

"Not by choice."

"Doesn't make me feel better."

"I know, I don't think much will at this point. But you've got to know how strong you are, how proud I am of you."

My gaze found his. He gave me a little smile then returned his attention to my hair.

"And last night," I rubbed my eyes shaking my head. "Daniel…God, I'm…it was—"

"I know. I get it. You don't have to say anything."

If I wasn't feeling like a real bitch before, I was now.

"When we get out of here, I'm going to stay until it's all out of your system and until you're no longer drawn into it. Deal?"

I smiled, closing my eyes.

CHAPTER SEVEN

ACE

I *closed my eyes, letting all my walls down, I was safe now...I could always be bare with him. I could always show him the darkest corners of my soul and he'd still see the light in me.*

I could show him all the demons hiding in the depths of my mind and he'd offer to show me his.

He traced his fingers across my skin, sending shivers across my body. He always had that effect on me...his hands always undid me, and his kisses always unraveled my soul...

I closed my eyes as we drifted to sleep together breathing in the familiar scent, the familiar safety his presence brought me. I never thought I'd feel this again.

Tears slipped through my closed eyes and his hands found mine, holding them against his chest so I wouldn't be afraid, so I knew there was nothing to be afraid of again.

Beside us, a small girl slept soundly with her tiny hand gripping Illarion's finger. It was our precious daughter, the one I knew I'd never meet but in here, I could hold her forever.

I woke up, jolting in my bed.

A sad, painful reminder that I was still here, shocked me to lucidity. I was still at Master Asshole's house, and I was still weeks away from making it out.

And my child, whom I would never meet, started making more regular appearances. I cried most mornings but not today. Today I was just tired.

Rubbing the sleep from my eyes, I sighed before rolling out of the bed, literally crawling to the bathroom.

It was easy to see now why all the others died months ago. I was a supercharged freak, and I still felt every aftershock of every pull of power.

It also begged the question—why did he need me? He was the Taker, he was a Divine, just like I was. Whatever he was doing here, it was about me.

Groaning, I pushed myself to my feet doing my best to ignore that little revelation and stepped into the shower, slowly and carefully. I only let a small trickle of water escape the showerhead, figuring that if I passed out, it would take a lot longer to fill to the brim before it could kill me. I'd come too far to die by shower, now.

I washed last night's blood and bile from my hair, and scrubbed at the itchy, raw skin on my thighs and forearms, deliberately pressing harder than necessary.

The pain shot through me as blood pooled around the flesh wounds before disappearing under the stream of hot water, but it felt so good. I lowered myself to the tiles. I could do this. Only twenty more days.

I walked into the room as steadily as my feet would allow. Daniel was waiting for me. I sat beside him.

"How do you feel today?" he asked, turning to look at me.

"I dreamt about him last night."

"Yeah?"

He was supportive, but I didn't miss the pang of hurt that flashed across his eyes.

We'd made a nice, little team lately. He would ask how I was, and I would talk. Sometimes I'd just lie quietly, sometimes I'd have more energy. He would inject me and let me forget everything. But he always listened, and he always remembered what I told him.

It felt good to speak about Illarion, to feel like he wasn't just a memory that I was afraid to lose.

Silent tears fell. I couldn't stop them, maybe I didn't want to. Emotions rolled through me, overwhelming my senses. I could feel a lot more now, but I still couldn't control it because the shields and wards Dalca had in this house, were still stronger.

Pure, relentless rage filled Daniel's veins as his trembling hands smoothed my wet hair down my back. I didn't need power or abilities to know that. We both had a lot to be angry about.

"Tell me more about him."

"He told me that he loves me." I smiled, tasting the tears as they fell. "In one of his letters."

"How could he not?"

That was a loaded question. Would he still feel the same way? Knowing about all the things that happened in this house?

"He always thought I was beautiful," I said quietly, like it was a definitive, past-tense statement.

"Because you are."

"I'm not anymore." I closed my eyes. "He writes about a woman who cares for him, he tells me that he feels like he's betraying me."

"Who is she?"

"A woman named, Anna. Someone from the Agency."

He tightened his hold around me. "I know it doesn't feel like it now, but when he sees you again, everything will be back to normal and everything you had between one another will come back."

"He'll never love me like this."

"I know how much he loves you, Ace. Nothing will change that, ever."

"You're sweet, Daniel. But I'm not naïve, I know how this goes, I know what Anna is to him."

"You need to believe in yourself more, and in him."

"Yeah," I murmured, sighing.

I pulled myself together and got up. I had to sort myself out. I had to make it through the next three weeks by any means necessary.

"My father is out for the day. Do you want to go for a walk?"

"You'll get in trouble. I don't want you to get hurt because of me."

"He won't be home until dinner and the staff won't say anything. Come on," he said holding his hand out to me.

"I don't know, Daniel."

"Come on, you need it. Trust me."

"He'll hurt you."

"He won't know. I've got some good friends here, people who won't say anything to him."

"Are you lying to me?"

"No," he said gently.

I released a long breath before taking his hand.

***

He linked his arm through mine and together we made our way through the grounds. We had to stop every few minutes since I wasn't exactly in the best health of my life, but it was nice.

It felt good to be outside.

"How did you and Illarion meet?" he asked gently.

"We were assigned to work together. At the Agency."

The first day I met him, came to my mind.

"He must be one hell of an agent."

I nodded leaning into him for support. "He is. He told me in one of his letters that he quit because he couldn't be there anymore, but they asked him to come back."

"Did he?"

"Yes. His friend was worried about him."

"What else does he say in his letters?"

We rounded another winding path and walked up paved steps alongside a grand fountain.

"That he misses me, that life is hard for him now. Anna helps a lot, but he sees me suffering."

He stopped walking, holding me up. "How?"

"I'm not sure."

"Does he know you're alive?"

"He hopes that I am. But he doesn't know. There's no way he could. Whatever he's seeing must be my mind doing it subconsciously."

"Through dreams?"

"Maybe. Times of high stress. I don't know."

He rubbed his chin. "That's heavy."

"I know. I hate that he's hurting so much."

"What has he seen?"

My eyes flicked up to his. "According to his letters, everything."

"What do you mean?"

"He feels all of it. I must push it into him through our connection."

"But he can't differentiate between that and a dream?"

"No, the Serum is keeping me blocked. I can't feel him, and he can't feel me. So, he probably sees them only as dreams. Mind junk and all that, rather than an actual attempt of communication."

"But some Sensitives can walk dreams, right?"

"Some can, yes. I don't know whether I can."

"I'd say by what you've just told me, you can, and you are."

I looked across at him, contemplating what he'd just told me.

"You're calling to him for help because you know what's happening to you, even with the heroin. I did this to you for nothing."

"That's not true. It helps. Believe me it does. When I sleep, I see Ila, I don't see Dalca or what he's doing to me. I don't feel the pain. I'm not scared."

"They're only blocked memories, Ace. You know they'll come back as soon as you stop taking it."

"I know. And when they do, I won't be here. I'll be out there where it's safe. I'll be able to deal with it and process it all properly."

He sat down on the step and dropped his head into his hand. I followed suit, enjoying the sound of the tranquil water cascading down beside us.

He took a deep breath. "I'll kill him myself."

"You won't have to."

Letting that thought settle, we quietly walked back to the house. Daniel locked the door to my room when he left, and I sat on the floor with my pile of letters.

I dreamt about you again, I've been trying to stay awake. I can't sleep knowing what I'm going to see. But I know it's the only way I still feel you, it's like some sick and twisted way that fate has let me keep you.

Next week will be five months since you died. Five months. I don't even know how I can quantify the days. They're just numbers. Just numbers on a clock. Time goes on, but not for me. For me, time stopped when your heart did.

Everything now is just existing.

I watched you cry again, you're so weak, you're barely holding on now. I don't know what's happening to you. I don't know if it's real, or if it's a punishment. Whatever it is, it's getting worse.

You're getting worse. You call to me, every night.

Every night I fight the Darkness inside me, if I let it take hold, I wouldn't feel this anymore. I wouldn't feel your pain.

I know you wouldn't want that. You're the only reason I get out of bed every morning. Knowing what you did, for me.

I'll never forgive you.

I love you.

Illarion

In my heart, I'd always known that the decision was going to make him hate me, I think I knew it as soon as I pushed him out of the warehouse.

Gripping the letter, I took a moment to compose myself. I peeled my eyes away and put the letter back with the others then I got ready.

I put my game face on, and a glamorous dress and made my way down to dinner.

***

"We're serving a lovely Salmon on sweet potato puree, tonight."

I forced a smile as the asshole spoke.

I laughed when he told the lamest jokes possible, and I feigned interest when he told the most boring stories.

Daniel watched my act in silence. I didn't need to look at him anymore to know what was going on inside him. I was down to only twenty percent Serum.

I still couldn't control the hum connecting me to Illarion, but I could feel the pull of the familiar light inside me, constantly battling against my Darkness. My strength was coming back. It was a slow simmer at best, but it was there. Only a few more weeks.

As was the usual practice, I rolled up my sleeve for Daniel and let him administer the dose.

It didn't take hold like it usually did, I was still me, though hazy. I could still keep tabs on my own thoughts and feelings, but his orders still had their effect…I followed him reluctantly through the house, into the back office where he did his business and sat down waiting for the next guest I'd be killing.

Just like every other night, it was a man who had done nothing to deserve his fate at the hands of this maniac.

He explained how he was controlling the Agency and how he's been able to do it for years. I tried my hardest not to knock him out there and then.

But I had to keep this up, for mine and Daniel's sake.

"I need you to get into his head and retrieve the last known information about the undercover Sensitives."

My brain was still hazy, compliant to his wants and desires but now I could hold some of my own ground.

There was no way I would give him all the Sensitives. That would be enough for him to destroy all of us and then he'd have access to all the Agencies around the world.

No. He wouldn't be getting that from me. I swallowed the fear and took the man's hand in mine.

I focused my eyes on his and without much effort at all I was in his head.

He oversaw all mission guidelines. He was the one who briefed us, told us what each mission would entail. He would explain what we would need, timings and everything important. He had all this information in a file saved under each agent's name. I remembered him. He was at the Agency when I first started, he and Josh prepared all our case notes for the Ritz infiltration.

Quickly, through all the rapidly changing memories I saw it, the file with every single known, undercover mission and agent. I focused on some of the names, mostly on the ones I knew were already out of the field and capable of protecting themselves and pushed that information into Dalca's head.

Satisfied that I had fulfilled my job, he released me and sent me back to my room.

I dropped into my bed, pressing my face into the soft, white pillow.

A groan left my lips, and I did my best to ignore the blood pouring from my nose. The wetness warmed my face reminding me of my mortality and the very real possibility that I wasn't going to make it out of here alive.

As I closed my eyes and willed sleep to find me, I heard the latch release on my door and heavy, purpose-driven footsteps come to me. I clenched my fists at my sides and squeezed my eyes shut.

As a rough and heavy hand landed on my back and drifted under my nightdress, I let the tears fall until there was nothing else until sleep finally took over.

CHAPTER EIGHT

ACE

The last fifteen days had been torture. I was less focused than before the dose was reduced and I racked my brain trying to work out why. Then I realized, as though it was the only valid reason all along; I was dying.

A short-lived laugh escaped my lips as I sat on the edge of my bed.

I couldn't die now. That would just be cruel.

There was so little life left in me, so little strength, I wasn't naïve. I knew what this meant. I knew how much these months had cost me and slowly, reluctantly, my mind wandered to Illarion's mother. *I wasn't far off, was I?*

I bowed my head feeling the relentless pressure on my mind. The Serum was pulling me apart and the heroin was barely holding the shattered pieces together. Only five more days and I'd be free. One way or another.

Daniel stepped through the door like he had every other day, the familiar pouch he carried with him made my heart swell in anticipation.

When my eyes swept up to his face, they fell on the fresh cuts and bruises marring his face.

"What happened?" I shot up.

He walked over to me and pushed me back down.

"Daniel. What happened?"

He turned away avoiding my gaze.

"Daniel."

"It's nothing." He finally looked at me keeping his hands folded in his lap. His eyes trailed up and down the flesh wounds dotting my arms.

"Did he do this to you?" I demanded.

When he didn't reply, I raised my brows.

"Daniel?" I encouraged. "Did he do this to your face?"

He nodded.

"Fuck. Why?"

A few moments of silence passed between us before he cleared his throat and spoke.

"He was in your room last night. I couldn't just stand by…"

"I will live through this. He needs me. But he'll kill you. You know that."

Shaking his head, he looked at me, his eyes brimmed with tears. "All these months, I've tried to stop him, I did, I really tried, Ace. You have to believe me."

"Hey," I took his hand and squeezed it, "I know you did."

"It's not good enough."

"Please, don't do this." I smiled. "Don't argue with me. I'm a big girl. I got this."

He didn't believe a word I said.

I gently punched him in the shoulder.

"I will be okay as soon as we're out."

His eyes were dull and full of exhaustion, but he nodded.

"I promise. I'll be alright, just don't get yourself killed because of me."

"Fine." He shook his head, hating every word I was saying. Thankfully, he changed the topic. "How are you doing today?"

I shrugged. *How was I doing?* Fine considering that the memories kept coming back in waves, hitting me every morning, like I was watching some sick, twisted family movie and I was the star.

Master Jackass didn't even bother with pleasantries anymore. He hit me and beat me every other night when I resisted and then he'd break down and get on his knees begging me to forgive him. But I was still here. I was surviving somehow.

I let the rage consume me and used it as fuel. He thought he was destroying me and taking everything away when in reality, he was arming me with everything I needed to beat him when the time came.

I smiled, as honestly as I could, and turned to him, pulling up my sleeve.

"I'm fine."

He took my arm and tied the tourniquet above my elbow.

"Don't stop at the half dose."

His eyes found mine. "Ace…"

"Do it."

He wet his lips then nodded and prepped the needle.

He squeezed my hand before gently placing it in my lap. "It's late, we should head down for dinner."

***

Together we sat, waiting for his father. When he finally showed, the usual proceedings took place. He ordered Daniel to inject me and then he watched while I ate, while my nose bled, while I struggled to keep anything down, then finally, he led me to his office.

"I'll be with you shortly," he muttered, leaving me alone.

I dropped heavily into the chair.

My mind wandered all over the place, fragmented memories pieced themselves together and then drifted apart like my own mind couldn't muster the strength it took to hold on to them.

A quick look at the clock told me more than an hour had passed since he'd left me.

Footsteps outside alerted me to his presence. I stiffened as the door opened and then swallowed hard. He was alone. That was a bad sign. He shut the door and locked it.

"You don't look too well, Acacia," he said, stalking over to me and lifting my chin up with his bony finger. "Feeling a little under the weather?"

His eyes found mine and a breathless second later, before I could even register what was happening, he'd yanked my head back by my hair and stabbed a syringe into my neck.

My heart skyrocketed and no matter how much I struggled and fought my arms kept hitting nothing but air.

A breath caught in my throat as my eyes followed his hand. It was another dose, another *full* dose of the Serum. No. No this could not be happening.

I scrambled away from him, backing into the wall by the fireplace.

"Now." He smiled, kneeling next to me when my legs gave way and I fell. "Tell me what my son has been doing, aside from fucking you."

A scream was building in my lungs. No, no, *no*.

"Hmm?"

The words were on the tip of my tongue, burning, begging to be released. I bit down until I drew blood. Squeezing my eyes shut, I fought the Serum. *I had to fight.* Whatever happened next, I couldn't give in.

He wrapped his hand around my throat and dragged me up to my feet and pushed me backwards until he slammed me into the wall making the obnoxious framed artwork rattle beside my head.

"Answer the question."

"Fuck you," I hissed, opening my eyes.

He grinned, but not the kind of grin he'd usually have given me. No. this was new, this was a whole lot of bad, and a whole lot of unknown.

"I suspect you only have a few more minutes of lucidity left. Make them count."

His hand slipped under my dress, and I tried pushing against him, praying that I had some strength left. When he tried to pull at the hem of my underwear, I managed to lift my knee between us and shove him back.

"Fuck you."

"Only a whore would have such an eloquent response."

"You're a fucking pig." I spat, hitting him right in the face.

His body tensed as he wiped the spit with his free hand, and then that grin widened. "I will keep dosing you until you answer me, and believe me, Acacia, you will beg for death."

I grit my teeth swallowing the blood in my mouth.

He smiled, showing all his teeth.

A quick, brutal punch landed on my stomach and when I doubled over, his hand shot out, wrapping around my wrist. His other fist slammed into my ribs, and I heard the crack before the pain registered. I let out a muffled cry and tried with whatever was left inside me, to fight him off.

He grabbed me by my hair and flipped me around before he slammed me onto his desk and yanked my arms behind my back locking them in place. My face was pressed against paperwork and pens, digging painfully into my bruised cheek.

He stepped between my legs and pushed my feet apart. I heard his belt buckle clank as he undid it with his free hand.

"What has he been doing? How are you able to fight the Serum?"

This time, I grinned. "Because I'm the Divine fucking Sensitive. You should know. You made me."

A sharp, furious breath came in response. I knew he would hurt me for this. I had no way out now and I wasn't going to make it easy. He roughly pulled the flimsy fabric of my underwear aside and I braced myself in anticipation.

"You're going to beg me to kill you, Acacia."

"I'm going to fucking kill you before that ever happens."

He roughly shoved my dress up my back exposing my entire lower half.

Before he could do anything, the door to the office swung open, breaking off its hinges, and in a heartbeat, Daniel was on him. He threw his arms around his father's neck and pulled him backward, off me. I slid off the desk and dropped to my knees.

Damn it, the Serum was taking hold. I could barely see straight. I tried to grab hold of the table, but I couldn't make my hand work.

Through blurry eyes, I looked up at the scene unfolding before me. This was it. This is how I die. The thought kept repeating, over and over, until I was curled up on the floor, trying desperately to stay awake. I pulled my dress down as much as I could to save what dignity I had left.

Daniel wasn't giving up; he fought hard against his father. His upper hand was his height and his strength, but his father's, was the skill I knew he had in hand-to-hand combat. He kicked my ass at the warehouse, and I was damn good.

He threw Daniel into the wall, smashing the framed artwork, sending the shards of glass all over me. Daniel recovered and reached for his father's legs, kicking out at his knees until a loud pop signaled the shattering of a kneecap.

Grabbing my head, I desperately tried to stop the pain. The dose was too high, too much in a short time. This was going to kill me. Panic set in and my vision dimmed.

"Daniel." I managed a whimper, folding in on myself as convulsions began to rock my body.

From the corner of my eye, Daniel looked at me, horror flashed across his wide eyes. We were in trouble.

A single, ballsy move was all it took. He launched his foot into his father's face. He was already injured so the impact served its intended purpose. He dropped but he wouldn't be out for long.

Daniel moved toward me, and without a second to spare, he pulled me up into his arms and ran. At some point, before I blacked out, I saw him steal a set of keys and then we were gone.

***

Darkness followed me as I stepped outside into the world. Dazed and confused I felt him, I felt the familiar hum draw me to him. He was so close; I could feel him now.

Tears sprung to my eyes as I let the feeling consume me. So long, I had waited so long.

I stood in the warm evening wind. I looked up to the sky, the day turned cold and blackness followed.

Storm clouds crossed the sky opening up, releasing a downpour.

The raindrops fell in quick succession wetting me, drenching my hair but I didn't care. The rain was beautiful, it was all beautiful, I hadn't seen it for months. Suddenly, all the months of pain, of terror, of fear faded into the back of my mind.

A relieved sigh left my lips as I saw him. He stood a foot away, scared to move.

Slowly, his gaze found mine and time slowed down as he knelt.

***

I stretched my achy body out and pressed my hand to my face. I needed him. I needed Illarion so badly. I wiped the few tears that wet my eyes and turned my attention to the heat burning through my hand.

Damn it. I was burning up and nausea welled inside while I did my best to ignore the rapidly, building headache behind my eyes. A moment of panic set in until I realized I wasn't in Dalca's house.

Relaxing slightly, I looked around taking in the room. I'd spent more than enough nights in hotels and motels to be able to recognize which category my current room belonged to.

This was the latter.

I didn't need to look further than the small mini bar holding the ancient TV up or the less-than-perfect blinds blocking out the morning rays.

I pulled myself up and out of the bed, swinging my legs over the edge. I expelled a long breath, pinching the bridge of my nose. Sweet baby Jesus. Everything was pounding, even my blood sounded like the bass at a rock concert.

My ears perked up as soon as a set of footsteps came closer and stepped just outside the door. Fear gripped my heart and I moved backward. I looked around for something to use as a weapon and then shot the idea down. I wasn't strong enough to stand, let alone fight.

The pounding in my head intensified as I focused, I tried whatever I could to break through the barrier still holding me back.

"It's me," Daniel called, and I relaxed.

He walked in carrying two large paper bags.

"I have food and supplies."

"Where are we?"

He put everything on the table and walked over to me, helping me to the kitchen.

"Southport Motel," he said, taking everything out, laying the items on the table in front of us.

There were gauzes, bandages, antiseptic lotion, and even a sewing kit. But my eyes fell on a bag of jelly snakes and a box of doughnuts.

"Are you hungry?"

"I'm starving."

He handed me a plate with a doughnut.

"You need to get your sugar levels up, try to eat as much as you can."

"What's with the sewing stuff?"

He smirked. "Oh, you know, in case I get bored and feel like fixing your clothes."

I gave him a mock scowl and laughed.

Returning my attention to the doughnut, I took a few careful bites, eager to feel the taste on my lips.

He watched closely; no doubt ready to throw a bucket at me.

"How do you feel?"

Carefully taking another bite, I shrugged. The mood drastically changed. As much as we forced the light-heartedness, the underlying issues were still there, poking and prodding, reminding us whenever we dared to think of anything else.

"How badly are we screwed?" I asked.

He scratched the back of his neck before folding his arms across his chest. "I don't have any doses of the Serum with me and, to safely bring you off it, we needed to do it slowly. It's going to be dangerous, but we'll manage it." He sighed. "That last dose he gave you really screwed things for us."

"What are the odds that I'll actually survive the detox?"

"I don't know."

"Daniel, you're one of the smartest people I know, I mean I'm pretty high up there but you're a genius when it comes to this stuff."

"Knowing sucks."

"You're not wrong. Tell me."

He sat and turned his chair to face me.

"At four percent, you would have needed to continue with at least a week's worth of doses, slowly bringing the percentage down while alternating between that and an opioid antagonist, only then would it be safe to take you off it completely."

He paused making sure I was following, I nodded my understanding.

"Now you'd need at least three weeks' worth of doses to bring you off and I don't have any."

"So, what do we do? Can't we use an opioid antagonist like you said? Methadone, right? That should be easy enough to source."

"Yes and no." He shook his head looking up at me. "Methadone can only take you so far, the Serum can't be replicated."

"Heroin is a root of the Serum, part of the composition, right? I'm sure a seedy place like this wouldn't have a shortage of suppliers. We could use that."

"Not the right part, it won't work. Now we're weaning you off the Serum and heroin. This is going to be a lot harder than I would have liked."

"What about Rohypnol or sodium pentothal?"

"No. I don't know the exact composition, and even then, I don't know how to do that."

"So, what do we do?"

"We're going cold turkey whether we want to or not. It won't be easy."

"I didn't come this far to die now, whatever comes, I'll do it. I can do it."

"You need to be prepared for the shitshow you're about to endure, Ace."

"I am."

"Right now, you're still under the effects of both. You were dosed twice yesterday so you still feel relatively fine. When it wears off, this will be bad, I'm not going to lie."

"I get it. Where do we start?"

He took a breath and got up disappearing for a moment before returning with a can of soda. He sat back down handing me a small cup with three white pills in it.

"The two round ones are methadone, that'll take the edge off the heroin, the other is Kaopectate. It should help with nausea."

"What about the Serum?"

"We're going to work on taking the edge off the heroin first. That's far more potent at this stage."

I looked at the pills for a few moments and then popped them in my mouth, washing them down with the soda.

As the weight of everything I was about to go through, settled in my veins, I realized how terrified I really was. I wanted to have Illarion by my side through this.

But I couldn't do it. I couldn't reach him. Not when I knew Dalca had eyes on him. He was probably waiting for me to make a move.

But there was one way I knew we could try, but it wasn't an option, not when I was so weak.

Closing my eyes, I brought my feet up to the chair, hugging my knees.

"You need to rest as much as you can, you're safe here."

"I feel too wired to sleep."

"You'll crash soon. I'll be here when that happens."

"Appreciate it," I nodded down at the comfy trackpants and hoodie I was now dressed in. "This you?"

"Yeah, I had a go bag ready for when we had to leave the house. Kept it stocked with clothes and shoes for you, not much else, sadly."

"You're amazing."

"I wouldn't go that far." He gave me a weak smile and eventually got to his feet. "Get some sleep."

I nodded and watched him leave. I moved to the bedroom and collapsed into the sheets. Minutes turned into hours as I tossed and turned in the small bed. Eventually my body gave in, and I felt sleep come over me.

CHAPTER NINE

ACE

My eyes shot open as violent dreams rocked me to lucidity. My hand jack-knifed into the air desperate to fight off the terrors haunting me, but it hit nothing.

Pressing my hand across my heart, I took several deep breaths until I managed to realign my breathing with my heart. I turned my head and my eyes fell on Daniel.

I'd made it back to the couch at some point in the night and he sat with his back to me, sleeping in an awkward position.

For a moment I allowed myself to sit with what took place over the last six months. My soul had been brutally tortured. I was broken; completely shattered and torn wide open. Fragments of what used to be me, curled up deep inside, locked away where none of the pain could reach me.

With whatever strength I managed, I made my way across the floor and buried my head in the black bucket. I heaved and threw up all the contents of my stomach. Reactive tears sprung to the back of my eyes.

A soft, gentle hand rubbed my back and pulled my hair away from my face. I heard the tired sigh leave his lips.

He was mumbling what should have been soothing words, but they weren't doing much to make me feel better. Detoxing was one of the worst things a person could go through, especially after months and months of subjection to the same, potent drugs.

I was addicted, but not only by my own will and not just your usual run-of-the-mill drug. No, this was much worse than anything the non-Sensitives created out of boredom and self-destructive tendencies.

When the Serum began to spread through your veins, it was like injecting liquid ice into your body. It spread through the blood, blocking your heart, and freezing it in place. Not a single thought or action belonged to you anymore.

Unfortunately, I was special. I felt almost everything. I felt pain and the loss of control as though I was merely a bystander watching my life become a train wreck but unlike Sensitives, something in my DNA forced the drug out of my system at record speed which meant that I was basically detoxing all the time, hence the need for repeat doses.

My eyes snapped shut when the next, painful wave rolled through me, splitting my skull in two. This time I felt my muscles tense and then spasm.

"Breathe through it," he said.

Another bout of nausea hit me, and I doubled over. There was nothing left to throw up.

I reached out and grabbed his arm, clutching onto him, praying that the contact would somehow ground me and keep me alive.

He wrapped his arms around my shoulders, holding me tight, rubbing my back as I cried into the bucket.

My body was struggling; it couldn't cope with the sudden lack of drugs running through my veins anymore. I felt the fever creeping up, inching toward the fatal degree and I knew I didn't have long.

"It'll get easier, just breathe through it."

Tears slipped out of the corners of my eyes. I let out a frustrated cry, collapsing against the cool, rough carpet.

I curled in on myself and the convulsions began, again.

"It'll be over soon. Just focus on my voice."

"And then what?" I ground out.

"And then you'll deal with what comes after."

"I-I don't know that I can."

"You can and you will."

Another painful convulsion rocked me and the tension in my body snapped, I tightened my arms around my knees. A small, pathetic whimper came out.

Deep in the back of my mind, where my Senses remained hidden, I felt the slightest shift allowing me to open up to him. He was upset; he didn't know how to help. He was scared that I would die.

He pulled me up, circling me with his arms so that my back was firmly supported against his chest while I instinctively brought my knees up.

He reached behind us pulling forward a small bowl filled with water.

"It's going to be okay." He pressed a small, wet towel to my forehead wiping away the sweat that had begun to bead on my slick skin.

"I can't, I can't do this—" I was cut off by another violent tremor.

His hand was cold against my cheek but his arm remained tight around me.

"You can, Ace."

Forcing my breathing to even out, I pressed my head back against his chest. "This...this really sucks."

"I know."

When he tried to turn me to him, I snatched my arm back and buried my face in my knees. I couldn't face the pain. I didn't want to. I curled up and pleaded to whoever would hear me that it would be over soon. I couldn't...I couldn't do this anymore.

"We have to call him."

"We can't." I squeezed my eyes shut. God knew I wanted to, I wanted to see Ila so badly. "Too dangerous."

"We have to…I can't help you Ace. I…I don't know what I'm doing."

"Yes, you do."

"No. I don't. I thought I did but I'm so out of my depth here. He can take this pain from you, you know he can. You're going to die like this."

I tried to open my mouth to argue but his hand squeezed my shoulder. He gave me a knowing look.

"Please. You're not going to make it through the night. I can't help you. That's the truth."

His skin had paled several shades. He was right. We needed help, we needed someone who could help to ease the symptoms, someone powerful enough to do it.

"Okay…we'll do it, we'll call him." I fought back the stupid thoughts running through my head.

The probability of me making it through the connection, *if* I could even manage to hold on long enough to reach him, was minimal.

Daniel cupped my elbows pulling me up to sit against the couch.

"You look like hell, Ace."

I laughed under my breath. "Yeah."

I'd lost so much weight over the last four months. Whatever he encouraged me to eat came back up minutes later. My stomach was twisting itself into painful knots. I was going to die of starvation before the drugs killed me. Great.

He handed me a cup. The peppermint permeated the air around us making my stomach lurch again.

I held the cup firmly.

A few minutes of silence passed between us before I looked up from the liquid swishing around in the cup. He folded his hand over mine, helping me to keep it steady.

"We can't pick up the phone and call him. Dalca has eyes and ears everywhere. We need to get into his head through our connection," I started.

"How do we do that?"

Turning my gaze away, I paused for a moment, contemplating how I was meant to explain that he had to do exactly what his father had been doing to me for more than four months.

"You have to go through me the same way your father did."

"No. I can't do that. I'll kill you."

"You won't, it'll be fine."

"There's got to be another way. I won't do that to you."

"There isn't. Contacting him any other way will alert your father. I'm not willing to risk that."

My head was splitting and the nausea deep in the pit of my stomach was starting to reappear. I only had a few minutes' reprieve between each bout, but I couldn't handle much more of it.

"What you're asking me to do is going to hurt you, Ace. It's going to put you at risk and make this worse."

"You said so yourself, we need him." I paused, breathing through the stabbing pain behind my eyes. "I can handle it and if it makes it worse, well, Ila will be here to fix it."

His lips formed a tight line, the crease in his brow deepened. "This is a bad idea."

"It's the only idea."

He thrust his hands through his hair. "I'm not even a Sensitive, can I do this?"

Glancing up at him, I sighed. Son of a bitch lied to his kid all along. He didn't even know.

"You are," I managed.

His face was set in a hard line.

"Your evolved Sense is Hearing. I suspected it the first night I met you when you brought me the letters. But I wasn't sure."

His eyes shot up, meeting mine.

"Didn't you ever wonder why you always seemed to know what I was thinking?"

"Why would he keep this from me?"

"Same reason he's able to do what he does. Anonymity. It was safer if no one knew, not even you."

"How then?"

"He's a Divine. He would have been able to hold whatever he wanted back from you and everyone else. It's how he had so many people at the Agency working for him including our director."

Daniel looked down, digesting everything I'd told him.

"You have to be quick; it needs to be quick."

A moment of silence passed between us. He caught my attention, shaking his head.

"I'm not okay with this."

"You won't hurt me. I promise."

I rested my face on my knee and placed the cup down carefully making sure I didn't spill it all over myself.

"I don't know how long we've got till I pass out again. I'm not feeling so good."

"What do I do?"

"I'll get you in, the connection between us will alert him straight away but you won't have much time. You need to be concise. Please just make sure you reach him."

"I'll reach him."

My heart swelled. I was going to see Illarion again.

"Are you ready?" I asked.

When he nodded, I placed my hands on his; like I'd done to all of Dalca's victims. A pang of guilt shot through me. I was a murderer, there was no way to spin that.

Pushing that thought aside, I concentrated on the present, because as soon as the connection was made, it could be my last attempt.

He got comfortable, leaning against the coffee table.

"When you feel me connect us it'll be like a welcoming hum. You'll be drawn to it. Just follow it, that's all you have to do. Don't fight it, don't pull back, let my power pull you in."

"Got it."

I closed my eyes and began to focus. I ignored the faint trembling in my hands and the throbbing inside my skull.

Sucking in a determined breath, I pressed my palms flush against his, grounding myself. Then I began the search for Illarion. I looked for the connection, any sign of the warm, gentle buzz that used to bring me so much comfort all those months ago.

At first, I couldn't sense Illarion at all. I was seriously out of practice. But before long, I felt the familiar warm, sliver of gold light that connected us. Just like riding a bike.

Readying myself, I pressed one hand over Daniel's heart and tightened my hold on his hand.

"When I open my eyes, you'll connect with me and he'll find you," I spoke softly, calmly. "Be quick, I don't know how long I'll be able to hold us together."

His hand stilled in mine.

"It'll be okay," I added for both Daniel and me.

As soon as I opened my eyes, that same, blinding torture would begin again. I would be ripped apart from the inside and a part of me wanted to ditch this entire thing and take my chances with Daniel. But I shut that part down immediately. Illarion was worth it. He was worth everything I did and would do. I smirked to myself. After everything, he'd be so pissed that I still thought that way. Then, when the humor left me, I suddenly felt so afraid.

What if when I reached him, he didn't want to see me? What if he didn't want to help? What if he…?

"Ace?"

I pushed that thought away. Only one way to find out. "Ready?"

He stirred in front of me, and the slight shift in energy told me he was.

Before he could say anything, I opened my eyes and locked onto his. A painful, sharp breath was ripped from my lungs. My scream was stifled by the force at which my head was thrown back. Pain pierced my skull and then a white, blinding flash burst across my vision and then it was silent.

***

ILLARION

I closed the book, tossed it across the small table and watched as it knocked over an empty cup sending it tumbling over the edge.

Anna left it there the last time she was here. A white coffee cup with her pink lipstick mark boldly staring at me like an eternal reminder of what I'd done.

Massaging my temple, I pressed my elbow to my knee and dropped my head into my hand ignoring the ever-growing pile of Agency paperwork.

Michael had assigned me to a research job, tasked with finding out everything I could about a clandestine group called the Legion. There wasn't much known about them other than the fact that they employed skilled individuals who performed unnamed operations no one took credit for.

There were rumors filtering through underground channels that they were genetically amplified ex-marines. It was rumored that they were people who were either MIA or KIA. It was a dangerous problem to have but it was so insignificant. It had nothing to do with Ace or who the Taker was or why she was killed.

We had no justice for her, no closure. Just an unmarked star I walked past every morning at the Agency.

There was no proper goodbye, closed casket thanks to the strong spiritual beliefs all Sensitives abided by thanks to our Gods, Aaryon and Solaris. It sickened me. They weren't worthy of our worship.

Was there any point doing any of this anymore?

Part of me knew Michael had given this task to me to keep me occupied and keep me living. Another part wanted to throw in the towel and…and what? Move somewhere? Start a new life? No. That kind of thing wasn't in my repertoire.

So, I did as Michael asked, I worked on the files, worked on whatever he sent me and tried to live the way Ace would have wanted me to.

I scratched the back of my neck and recoiled when I felt the rough callouses on the heels of my palms. I don't know why it shocked me so much. Maybe because it was the first thing I'd really felt since going sober. It had been almost two weeks now. Two weeks and not a single drop of alcohol touched my lips.

I exhaled sharply and looked across at the files on the table. I wasn't coping regardless of what I'd spun to Aurel.

My mind kept me locked inside a hellish prison that seemed to torture me by replaying every decision of my life.

Had I done all I could have for her? Was I right in keeping my distance? Should I have approached her outside of the Agency when I found her in Iraq? Should I have told her how I felt before everything went wrong?

111

Should I have gone to Iraq sooner and made sure Westen survived? Would she still be here if he was?

I got up and thrust my hands through my hair.

Every thought came back to her. Ace, Ace was lost.

I scoffed. She wasn't *lost*. She was dead. She was dead because of me and Troy was right. It was my fault. I was meant to protect her. I was meant to keep her safe, not get her killed.

And then there was Anna. God, I'd screwed that up on an astronomic level.

She'd been a good friend, and I couldn't believe she stuck around even after I'd turned to ice when I told her to leave. But she came back, she always came back, and that made it worse.

Giving in to the rising tide of self-pity, I reached for the bottle and contemplated breaking my newfound sobriety. But the way Ace would look at me now, made me re-think.

I got up, grateful for the quiet, uneventful night. It was the first night she didn't come to me in my sleep. Bozhe. How I hated myself for being glad that I didn't dream of her.

I stretched my shoulders out and paced the room. I'd made some progress on the task Michael had assigned but the rest would have to wait.

Aurel and I were meeting later to go over the latest information we gathered from the infiltration of the Alabama house.

He'd spent the better part of the morning gathering all the relevant weapons we'd need for the next infiltration. The previous assault on the house was a failure.

A woman had been there. We found gowns, shoes and make-up. But I couldn't tell who they belonged to or when they left. By Aurel's assessment and the information Josh was able to uncover, we estimated that whoever was there had been gone at least a week.

The house had Celestial markings all over it, even if Ace had been there, I never would have felt her. I didn't know how long the wards were set for, maybe now they'd faded, maybe now when I went back...

No, I shook my head and brought my mind back to the same conclusion. Maybe I was just crazy, maybe I'd finally broken. I didn't bother talking to Aurel about it, he'd looked at me like I was crazy before.

Coming to think of it now, I wasn't too far off. I barely recognized my own thoughts anymore.

Sighing, I brought my hand to my eyes and rubbed them. I couldn't do this without her, without seeing that smile again, or hearing her laugh. I couldn't do this without the hum in my heart...

Straightening my back, I shot up. The hum. The hum was there. It wasn't possible unless she was...

"Ace?"

No. No there was no way. It couldn't be. But I felt it, I felt *her*. And I was clean, nothing was impairing my Senses.

Concentrating on it, I closed my eyes. It was weak. Barely there. But I felt it. Like I felt it before she was gone.

Slowly, it was coming into focus, like a fine master tuning the strings of a piano, it was out of key, but it was still there. I squeezed my eyes and focused.

"Come on, Ace. Come on, lyubov. I feel you, talk to me. Come on," I whispered to the empty room.

"Illarion?"

I jumped. I hadn't heard anyone talk to me like this since...since she died. It was a distant, familiar feeling that felt strange and normal all at once.

"Are you there?"

I heard it again. But it wasn't her. It was a man.

"Please, if you can hear me, my name is Daniel. We need help. Ace needs help, she doesn't have much time."

My heart hammered in my chest, and I balled my fists at my side.

"Where is she?"

"We're at the Southport Motel, please hurry, Illarion."

The connection faltered.

"You have eyes on you. Stay safe," he said.

Then he was gone.

My body tensed. I knew it, I had hoped but now I knew.

Ace was alive.

CHAPTER TEN

ILLARION

Tears found their way to the surface and Darkness consumed every thought in my mind. I'd clutched at the last, fading memory of her, her smile forever imprinted in my mind, letting my own mind torture me repeatedly because that's all I deserved. But now I had something more to live for.

I stuffed a tablet, first aid supplies, medicine, pain killers, and clothing, everything I thought she might need and my cell into a duffle bag and rushed outside into the warm, summer day. I threw the duffle into the passenger side and slid in, keying in the coordinates for the Southport Motel.

My mind raced as I drove. Endless possibilities rushed through my head. *How was she alive all these months? Who contacted me? Why wasn't she able to do it herself?*

As each question rolled around inside me, I grew more and more furious. My heart fell into the dark void I'd kept all my shame locked up in.

Those dreams…they were all a reflection of what was happening to her and for months I was here, unable to help her, too caught up in my own misery to read the god damn signs.

I hit the steering wheel with my palm. When I should have been holding onto her in my dreams and figuring out her attempts to contact me, I was letting Anna in.

Every time I saw Ace, she was different. Not drastically, but enough to see that she was changing. Her hair was a bit longer, her skin a little paler, her body had changed too. She was sick, she was losing weight.

I sped down the highway. Christ, if only I had been smarter, if I pulled my head out of the bottle, I would have figured it all out.

The GPS instructed me to take another right turn and continue until I arrived in approximately twelve hours. I reached into the glove box and retrieved the Smith and Wesson I'd purchased off Agency records. Checking that it was loaded, I stuffed it into the side of my duffle.

Something was keeping Ace shielded from me and I'd be damned if I went in without backup.

Twelve hours and I would see her. I held in a shaky sigh and increased my speed. *Just hold on Ace, I'm coming.*

***

ACE

I jolted awake.

Icy tendrils of fear crept over my skin sending a flush of goosebumps over me. I cracked my eyes open searching the room. My eyes stung like I'd been caught in a desert storm while my mouth felt like I'd eaten a bag of cotton. And the killer migraine from before, well that was intensifying.

When I tried to clear my throat I stopped, my insides felt like sandpaper and the more I tried to suck in deep breaths, the more they wouldn't go in.

Close beside me Daniel shifted, drawing my attention. He sat with his legs crossed, reading a magazine. His head tipped in my direction.

"Hey, you good?" he asked quietly.

The familiar feeling of the metallic taste building in the back of my throat sent a fresh coating of saliva to fill my mouth.

"Sick…"

He gently placed the bucket in my hand and moved my hair back. It took a second flat for the contents of my stomach to come rushing out.

"Did it work?"

"Yes." His voice was rough. "He's on his way. Just hold on a little longer."

I wanted to answer him, to tell him that I was trying but God, I couldn't even form a sentence.

"You're doing great," he murmured, gently pulling my hair back. "He'll be here in no time."

"New York is kinda far," I whispered.

"Well, with the type of cars I know he drives, he'll cut that trip in half."

I laughed while I held onto the bucket.

Confident that no more vomit would come, I drew back and let him help me up to the couch again.

"Do you want to go outside? Get some fresh air?"

I managed a half-nod.

Before he helped me up, he handed me the three pills again, just like yesterday and the day before, and the day before that. I took them with a glass of soda and let him pull me up to my feet.

"Are you good to walk?" he asked, as we inched our way toward the front door.

"I think so," I whispered, closing my eyes against the blinding pain in my head. I winced and even that small movement felt like an icepick hitting my brain.

"Okay, nice and easy," he instructed, looping his hand around my waist. "We won't go too far."

As we stepped into the warm, gentle summer breeze, a flood of emotion rendered me speechless. I never thought I'd be free.

As we rounded the corner, an elderly lady came up to us with a wide smile.

She nodded to Daniel and then turned her attention to me.

"Lovely day isn't it, dear?"

Forcing what I hoped looked like a smile, I managed a nod.

"Are you both enjoying your stay here?"

"We are, thank you." Daniel smiled tightening his hold on me.

"If either of you needs anything, my husband and I own this little place so we can get things from out of town if you need."

"Thank you." I smiled.

Daniel led me to a park bench and gently eased me down. "I'll be back in a minute. I just want to see if they can get some things for us."

"Where did you get the other stuff?" I croaked, cringing as the sound met my ears. All the throwing up had lacerated my esophagus.

"A rest stop a few hours away," he said, and then frowned. "I had to stop to get you water. You don't remember?"

I shook my head.

"It's okay, you were out of it," he said, as he squeezed my shoulder bringing my attention back to him.

It wasn't okay. It was the heroin.

"I'll be back in a minute," he repeated and then left.

I let my mind wander to Illarion. What would he be thinking? Would he be beating himself up? Would he be wondering what to tell Anna? The name made me flinch. No. I couldn't do that to myself.

Up over the horizon, I noticed a thick cover of trees and shrubs, and down below I heard the intoxicating sound of waves crashing into a shore. It immediately brought a smile to my face, there was a beach.

"Do you have a pharmacy nearby?" I heard Daniel ask the lady.

"Sadly, no. The nearest town is two hours away."

"Do you have any medicinal supplies here?" Daniel asked, keeping his voice low.

"What kind of medication does your friend need, dear?"

"We need aprepitant or dolasetron for starters," Daniel said softly. "I have a list of other things."

There was silence for a moment and then the woman spoke again. "As far as anti-nausea medication goes, I have some left over from my chemo treatment, would that work?"

"Whatever you can spare will help, thank you so much."

"You're welcome."

They both went quiet and when I looked over my shoulder I saw Daniel coming back.

"How'd you know she would have the stuff?"

"I hoped."

"You heard."

"When we first got here." He nodded. "She's a cancer survivor. Six months and counting."

My stomach knotted.

Twisting back to lean against the bench, I nodded to the horizon. "It's so beautiful."

Birds dotted the cloudless sky while the trees swayed gently above us and children's laughter filled the air.

My heart sunk. I couldn't pull my mind away from the sorrow inside and the choices that were ripped from me.

"There's a beach," he said, drawing my attention to him.

"Yeah," I whispered.

"We can check it out if you want?"

"Maybe later."

"Yeah, of course." He looked out over the sky. "I'll make you something to eat."

"I'm just tired."

"I know," he breathed out and stood, pulling me to my feet, "but you need to eat something. It's all part of getting better."

Daniel held onto me as he led me back through the door and helped me down onto the couch again. I pulled off the sunglasses and tossed them aside.

When he came back, he handed me a plate with a sandwich cut into two neat halves and a bottle of red Gatorade.

"Try to eat as much as you can." He sat beside me. "When she comes back with the dolasetron, it will help even more."

I slowly ate, washing it down with the Gatorade.

"You're doing really well."

"I'm a mess, look at me."

"You're doing well," he repeated.

"I've never felt so useless in my life, I'm completely dependent on you and these drugs." I put the plate on the couch beside me and leaned back, resting my head on the cushion.

"There's nothing wrong with asking people for help."

There wasn't. When someone could be helped.

"Hey." He stopped me mid-thought.

"I'm beyond help, Daniel, look at me."

He leaned against the windowsill and folded his arms across his chest. "I'm looking, and I don't see it."

"You're blind then."

"You're being ridiculous."

"Ridiculous?" I shot back. "You're an ass."

"God, that's not what I meant, I'm sorry."

I stood up and pushed past him. I picked up the plastic pill bottles.

"Is it going to fix everything your father did to me?" I unscrewed the lid. "You think this will save me?" I spilled them into my hand. "You think that maybe I'll forget how he raped me every night?"

"Ace. Don't."

"Nothing can save me, Daniel. Not a damned thing. Not these pills. Not you. I'm too far gone for that."

"Ace, stop."

"You stop!" I screamed and threw the pills at him, watching them scatter all over the floor. "Stop trying to save me, there's nothing to save! He made sure of that!"

"You're going to hurt yourself." He darted toward me, but I threw the bottles at him.

He dodged them and reached me grabbing my arms. An ugly sensation of panic set in as he held them, pinned to my side. Feeling his strength overpowering me, I stopped struggling and dropped to my knees. And then came the tears.

"Get off me!"

"Stop fighting. You're hurting yourself."

Another torrential downpour.

"This isn't you, try to relax, just listen to my voice."

"Get, get off me...please."

"It's me, Ace, you're safe. Just listen to my voice."

When my body and mind finally got on the same page, I relaxed, letting out a low whimper.

"Okay," he said pulling me into a seated position. "We knew this wasn't going to be a walk in the park, but we've got this, you're okay."

"I'm sorry."

He smoothed my hair down my back. "You don't have anything to be sorry for. Just stay with me, okay? Keep breathing, keep fighting. Don't give up."

"Thank you," I sobbed.

"Come on." He helped me to my feet and onto the couch and covered me with a blanket. "Try to get some sleep." He scrubbed his chin, fluffing the pillow for me. "He'll be here soon."

My heart stuttered, Illarion...

"Then you'll feel even safer," Daniel added, and I caught the double meaning in his words.

Every time I'd managed to fall asleep, Daniel's father came back to me in my dreams, chasing me, tormenting me. I could never run fast enough. I could never hide. He always found me. But the more my power returned and the hold of the Serum dissipated, I became more confident in my ability to hide my location and my surroundings even in my dreams. Dalca searched through my mind trying to find any clues as to where we were. But he never would and knowing that I'd protected the conversation between Illarion and Daniel through my mind, he wouldn't be able to find out that way either.

That gave me enough comfort to sleep, at least for a few hours here and there but I couldn't function like that for long. I needed proper rest. I was running off sheer will at this point.

Maybe Daniel was right, maybe having Illarion here would help me feel safer.

***

It was sometime in the afternoon when I awoke with a start once again reaching for the bucket and throwing up. I gripped the edges of the plastic and exhaled. This was getting worse.

Daniel's eyes found mine as I pulled myself free from the bucket. I wiped my mouth with the back of my hand.

I couldn't quite make out what he was thinking, but the concerned look was more than enough to worry me.

Taking the bucket away, he left me kneeling on the ground.

It had been days since I could get up and shower or do anything for myself that didn't involve the toilet. It was humiliating, to say the least. I was helpless and that was the worst thing I could imagine.

"I'm sorry," I said, softly. The energy shifted in the room, and I knew he had heard me. "I know you hate this as much as I do."

He came in and stood leaning against the door frame.

"It's not fair to you, I'm sorry."

"Please stop apologizing," he said, pinching the bridge of his nose. "I promised you that I would help."

"You're not obligated to stay with me."

"I know that." He replaced the bucket with a clean one and sat beside me. "And before you say I'm doing this out of guilt, I'm not. I'm doing this because I care about you."

"Yeah. I got that."

"I'm sorry, I shouldn't have said that."

"It's fine. I'm the asshole here, not you."

"You're not an asshole."

"We had sex," I said flatly. "And we bonded over collective trauma."

"I'm not expecting anything from you, Ace. That's not why I'm hanging around."

"Why then?" I looked across at him.

"Because despite all this bullshit, I consider you a friend. God knows I don't have an abundance of those."

I flinched and our eyes met briefly. "I'm sorry."

"Please stop apologizing."

I sighed. "Can you help me to the shower?"

"Yeah, of course."

He took my hand and led me to the small bathroom. I stood back while he set the water, letting a small trickle flow only. When the water was hot enough, he stepped back.

"Need me to, uh, help?"

Chuckling, I shook my head. "I think I've got it."

He flushed but nodded.

"Thank you."

"You got it." He disappeared faster than I could blink.

The smile stayed glued to my face as I stripped and stepped into the stream. I tipped my head back, letting the water do its thing. I slathered on a stupid amount of soap and even more shampoo, once it was all rinsed out and I dried off, I smiled. Finally, I felt more human.

When I got out, I noticed a folded pair of track pants and a tank top. I inspected the clothing and grinned to myself. They were taken in, made smaller and more fitted to my current form.

I dressed and checked them out in the reflection. I pulled the door open, surprised to see Daniel waiting by the door.

He straightened when I walked out. "They fit."

"You are full of surprises."

He grinned. "Picked up a few life skills from my father's staff."

"Thank you, Daniel."

"You're welcome." He chuckled. "Anyway, I was waiting to tell you that I have to go see our hosts and ask them to pick some stuff up for us from the store."

"More supplies?"

"Figured since Illarion will be joining us soon, we'll need more food. You're okay if I leave you for a bit?"

"Yeah. I'm good, go."

He left and I dropped into the sofa, stretching out my achy body. The moments of silence were the ones that I feared, I didn't know how strong my will was, nor did I know if I could fight him if he came to me again. He made it abundantly clear that as soon as I closed my eyes, he'd be there, somehow shredding those barriers I'd loosely built up.

And now, with the link weakening, and my strength slowly coming back, it took every bit of control I had to keep myself grounded.

Before I could fight off another bout of nausea that clawed at me I dived off the couch and buried my head in the bucket again.

The contractions forced a broken sob to come free.

Stammering back, I gingerly drew my hand to my face, wiping my mouth. I flinched as my clammy palm burned under the touch of my hot cheek. God, I was burning up again. I pushed to my feet and made a line for the door.

It should have cooled down enough by now and I needed fresh air. A quick glance at the clock told me that Daniel had been gone a little under an hour and the sun had since set. I pulled the door open and the Darkness inside me followed as I stepped outside into the world.

Dazed and confused, I shook my head, gripping the door as a wave of something I couldn't place, washed through me. It couldn't be, but...it felt so real, I felt him, I felt the familiar hum spark to life.

It was just like before, so real, so safe. He was so close; I could almost feel him now. Tears sprung to my eyes as I searched the dark around me. God, it had been so long. I stood in the warm evening wind looking up to the sky.

Storm clouds crossed the horizon opening up, releasing a summer downpour.

The rain drops fell in quick succession drenching me in a matter of seconds. My heart stuttered as I felt it. Suddenly, all the months of pain, of terror, of fear, faded into the back of my mind. And a relieved sigh left my lips as I lowered my gaze and there in the middle of the small path leading to the motel room, I saw him.

He stopped a few feet away, his dark eyes searching mine, he was scared to move. He was watching me, his eyes were wide, his lips parted.

Slowly, I took a step down, and he took one forward and then time slowed like my heart. The surrounding trees stilled, and the wind grew silent, the only movement came from us. He dropped his duffle bag beside him before he fell to his knees, crashing into the wet surface of the gravel path. My heart fell in on itself.

His eyes filled with tears and his emotions rushed into me like we'd spent no time apart at all. But it wasn't joy that coursed through him this time. These were dark and painful feelings, oscillating between despair and guilt.

He remained silent for the longest time. The pain in his eyes tore down my walls as he looked up at me.

My name left his lips in a reverent sigh.

This was really over. He was really here.

Before I could say a single word, he was on his feet, moving toward me, through the rain, through the dark. The moment he reached me and his skin touched mine, everything around us roared to life. Above us lightning cracked across the blackened sky, shooting bolts of light through the air.

In that brief second of light, I saw the agony marring his features. Those hauntingly, beautiful dark eyes found mine and then his arms were around me, holding me, feeling everything coursing through me. I broke down. My legs gave way, and he tightened his hold on me.

"You're here," I whispered, against him, "oh my God, Ila, you're really here."

"Moya zvezda, o bozhe." He pulled back, cupping my face in his hands. "Ace, my Ace."

CHAPTER ELEVEN

ACE

Illarion turned and the two men keeping me alive for the last six months, finally met.

Daniel's smile didn't reach his eyes when he looked to me and then to Illarion.

"You two should get out of the rain," he said softly, pushing the door open and holding it for us to pass through.

He took the bags into the kitchen and set them on the table. Beside them, he placed two new bottles of pills. Illarion didn't miss a beat. His eyes narrowed and quickly found mine.

"Not now," I ground out.

Illarion pulled his wet coat off and slung it over the chair. I realized that I was drenched too. Daniel walked around me and grabbed a small towel I'd noticed belonged to a pile of fresh ones he kept beside the couch.

"Here."

I took it from him and draped it around my shoulders. The three of us stood silently.

"Well, this is a hell of a meeting," I said, trying to lighten the mood.

Before either of them could say anything, another bout of nausea ripped through me. Deciding that I absolutely was not about to throw up on the floor in front of Illarion, I quickly turned and made a run for the bathroom, reaching it just in time.

Illarion came after me and before he could follow me inside, I slammed the door shut and locked it.

This is not how I wanted him to see me. I dropped to the floor, my knees barely catching me. Ignoring the tears rushing down my cheeks, I buried my head in the bowl and brought everything up, food, water, blood.

"Ace?" his voice was laced with a roughness I'd never heard. "Please let me help."

"Give me a minute." I closed my eyes.

God. I couldn't even face him. I didn't want him to see me like this. Now that he was here, I was terrified. I was ashamed and I barely recognized myself.

Fresh tears spilled breaking me down.

When it finally stopped, I flushed the toilet and curled up against the door, my skin soaked up the coldness of the wooden barricade. I had to face him. I just couldn't right now. I closed my eyes and pressed my hand above my head to the door, willing him to feel me, to know how sorry I was.

***

ILLARION

A shift of energy behind the door drew my hand instinctively to the wood separating us. I pressed my forehead to the cool surface and reminded myself that she needed space, she needed to feel ready to talk to me.

She was afraid. She was blocking me out on purpose. I choked back a sob when I realized that a part of her didn't want me in there. But the other part called out to me.

"Give her some time," Daniel said behind me.

The air surrounding him was dense. He was tired and mentally exhausted.

Grinding my teeth, I balled my fists at my side and stood. Daniel took a small step back.

"What did he do to her?" I demanded.

When I turned and found his gaze, he looked away, but I didn't miss the hesitation in his eyes. They were haunted, like he'd been through far too much, seen too much. He was young, but his eyes were that of a wise man, a broken man.

He shifted his weight onto his other foot. "Too much, Agent Lazarev."

"Daniel? Right?"

He nodded.

I folded my arms across my chest. "Tell me what happened."

His thoughts raced, forming then fragmenting as his own power chased them away. He didn't want to tell me. He didn't want me to know what she went through and when I caught glimpses he fought hard to shut them down, condemning them to the back of his mind where I couldn't reach without prying.

He wasn't an experienced Sensitive which made me think either he didn't know until recently or, he wasn't given guidance on how to explore his gift.

"It won't change anything," he said.

"I know that."

"She doesn't want you to know."

"The dreams were real."

He nodded slowly. "She told me she thought she was reaching out to you."

"Who was he? The man she kept showing me?"

A few moments of silence passed between us before he spoke, "My father."

My heart fell. God damn it. The puzzle was finally complete. The bastard was the Taker. The man we were sent to apprehend and search for at the Alabama mansion. The lead was good, coming from an old Russian informant but by the time we got there, they'd already cleared out.

"Simon Dalca."

"Yep." Daniel scrubbed his jaw, leaning against the door frame. "Had your Agency fooled, used Cale as a scapegoat."

"And kept everyone in the dark."

"Including you."

The jab hurt but he wasn't wrong. I ground my jaw momentarily looking away from the dark glint in his eyes.

I was the fool who basically handed Ace to them. The Agency had leads on Simon Dalca for months, but they refused to infiltrate because they didn't have enough information. We knew he was a Romanian national who had migrated to the United States after his wife died under suspicious circumstances. His son, Daniel Dalca was raised here and kept hidden by the hush money Simon threw at anyone who looked in their direction.

Simon had billions upon billions of dollars to his name through both legitimate and black-market business deals. In the public eye, he was as clean as the president. Off the books, there weren't enough papers to write down the crimes he'd committed.

I bit back the anger bursting inside me. We'd let him slip through our fingers. *I'd* let him slip through my fingers.

"He did that to her every night?" I heard my voice break.

"He used her. He knew the transfer wouldn't work, not like it does with other Sensitives."

"What did he do?"

"He forced her to Collect their gifts, he kept her sedated on the Serum. She didn't know what she was doing."

I wet my lips, composing myself.

"She was afraid of what you'd think." Daniel stopped, looking down at his feet. "But she didn't know what she was doing, the Serum blocked everything."

"How did she start breaking through it?"

"I lowered the dose, every day, but even before that, she was coming off it."

"That's when she began remembering the kills and the nights," I muttered, finally understanding. That's when I started dreaming of her. She'd broken through a part of his wards.

"I tried to stop him."

Tears filled my eyes and the helplessness inside me grew, quickly overtaking the anger. My shoulders sagged. I was supposed to protect her. I was supposed to be the one to keep her safe.

I was going to be sick. I closed my hand over my mouth steadying my breathing.

"She begged me to find a way to make her forget. Agent Lazarev," he whispered.

"Bozhe," I muttered to myself. "What did you do?"

"I gave her heroin. It was the only thing I could do. In the beginning it worked well, she didn't remember anything, she didn't feel much but then she started talking about you and a woman. I don't know."

"A woman?"

"Yes. She read the letters you sent her. After that, she changed."

"You found my letters?"

He nodded, wetting his lips.

My stomach tightened in coils. The helplessness and confusion she felt in the dreams, the sudden change in how I felt her. She was trying to forget the torture she went through and then she learned what I'd done.

A shaky sigh left my lips.

"Please give her some time, she needs you…she just, she's ashamed, she hates what she's become."

"I'll wait as long as I have to."

***

ACE

I pulled myself up off the floor, finally managing to stand on my own two feet. I washed my face in the small basin making sure I was presentable.

A quick look in the mirror drew my attention to the insides of my elbows. Without looking again, I pulled down the sleeves of my sweater ensuring they covered every inch of my skin and let my hair fall over my shoulders. It was long enough that it covered most of my gaunt features.

This wasn't okay. I wasn't an idiot. I wasn't beautiful anymore; I could never expect him to feel the same way about me. The mess I'd become wasn't just going to get better with some makeup and new clothes. No, this ugliness went soul-deep. I was rotten inside.

After everything that happened, I wasn't the strong woman he fell in love with. I wasn't the confident Divine Sensitive destined to make peace for us. I was the coward who begged for death, who gave in to the drugs because I couldn't handle the pain.

Somewhere between losing myself and who I was, I'd lost Illarion too. First when I hosted my own pity party and then when I slept with Daniel.

Another gentle tap at the door caught my attention.

"Please, let me in, Ace."

Illarion's voice was thick. And the pain in his words grew heavy around us.

132

Without even realizing that I had walked over to the door, I opened it. His dark eyes found mine and the weakest hint of a smile crossed his lips.

Slowly, he brought his hand to my cheek, but he let it hover, uncertain, then he stepped back.

I wanted nothing more than to fall into his arms, to hold him, and to let him hold me. But so much more than what I *wanted* mattered right now. I needed to get better. I needed to heal so that when Dalca came, and I knew he would sooner rather than later, I'd be strong enough to stand my ground and fight.

He'd caught me unaware and unprepared. I would not make that same mistake again.

Illarion followed me to the small bedroom and closed the door behind him.

I stood with my back to him, arms wrapped around my stomach.

"I'll wait as long as you need me to wait, Ace."

I blinked back the tears.

"I know *I'm sorry* doesn't even come close, but I am so sorry. I'm so sorry I didn't find you in time. I'm so sorry for failing you, for failing to be your protector. I'm so sorry…"

I turned and finally found his eyes. The way his lips parted, like a plea was on the verge of escaping, completely undid me. "You couldn't have known, Illarion."

Everything that had been holding me together, shattered. An endless stream of tears began and the apprehension holding Illarion back, disappeared. Before I could take another breath, he was in front of me, his arms tightly wrapped around my body.

Without warning, I broke down and began sobbing into his chest, clutching at his shirt pulling him closer. I held onto him for dear life.

My body shook as one of his hands cupped my cheek while the other combed his fingers through my hair.

"Lyubov," he whispered in my ear, "God, I've missed you."

I cried harder.

"I should have figured it out. I saw you, the dreams…"

He knotted his fingers through my hair and pulled me tighter against him.

My body recognized the familiar hum inside as soon as he was with me, my body knew as did my heart, he was the only reason I had survived. But I didn't miss the fact that the hum felt different like it was faltering.

My knees grew weak, and that same feeling of helplessness tore up my insides. Everything I'd been holding in was pouring out of me and all the strength I was holding onto, was fading.

"Talk to me, I'm here."

Shaking my head, I clung to him, I couldn't, what was I meant to say? He brought us both down to our knees when my legs gave way. He rubbed my back, knotting his fingers through my hair.

"I'm here, Ace. I'm here."

Months of pent-up fear, agony, and pain cascaded down my cheeks.

The hum inside us was broken, but he was fighting. Shattered pieces of his soul were desperately trying to hold on. Inside him where I usually felt joy and passion when he was with me was now filled with guilt and intolerable pain.

"I love you," he whispered, lowering his forehead to mine, he ran his thumb across the marks on my cheek, "moya zvezda. I love you so much."

My breath slowed, and another choked sob came in response as fresh tears spilled from my eyes. I pulled back and looked up at him.

When his dark lashes lowered, tears slipped down his cheeks. He gently took my hands in his and squeezed them tightly.

"Forgive me," he whispered. "Please forgive me."

This time I reached up, cupping his cheek in my hand, feeling his skin under my fingertips.

"You kept me alive, Ila, your letters kept me fighting."

He frowned, lowering his forehead to mine. "I failed you."

"You forced me to survive."

His dark hair was pulled back like he always wore it, but his face was unshaven and unkempt, far from the immaculate way he usually looked. It was all indicative of how rough the last six months were on him.

My living nightmares had become his too.

A silent moment passed between us until he gave me a small smile and led me to the bed. When I looked at it longingly, he chuckled and pulled the covers back.

"I'll take the chair."

"You don't have to." I tugged him toward me.

He released a long breath then sat. He looked at me desperately until I sat down beside him.

Together, he brought us both down into the soft mattress and drew the covers over us.

I rested my head on his chest and folded my arm across his stomach. He closed his hand over mine.

My heart stammered. This was going to be the hardest conversation of my life. I had no doubt that he would have questions. And I knew he would wait as long as it took, but the truth was, I would never be ready to talk about it. Talking about it would mean admitting that it hurt, that every night there chipped away a part of my soul. It was devastating to admit. I was broken wide open and I didn't know if I'd ever really be okay.

"What did he do to you?" his voice was barely a whisper as he drew gentle lines across my bruised wrists.

He swept my hair from my face.

"I don't even know where to start." I drew in a long breath, letting him pull me closer.

"Anywhere, Lyubov."

When I struggled to answer him, and instead tightened my hold around him, he responded by wrapping his arms around me, enveloping me in a safe cocoon.

And when that moment of silence passed between us, I cleared my throat. My fever was spiking again.

"Help me take this off."

He got up and helped me peel off my sweater before fitting me beside him again.

"I'm sorry." I swallowed hard. "I didn't want you to see me like this."

I felt his gaze coast across my body.

The curves I usually had were gone, I was so thin I barely looked like the same person he would have remembered. The hideous open wounds on my arms from scratching were angry and red contrasting starkly against the pale of my skin beneath them.

"Christ." He kissed the side of my head.

"I never wanted you to see this."

"You never have to hide anything from me, you know that."

"I know."

He pulled my arm up and over so that we were lying face to face, his eyes never left me.

"You're exhausted, Lyubov," he whispered.

"It's the dreams, I can't…"

"I'll watch over you. You're safe with me. Your mind is safe with me, I swear to you."

Like my body knew it could relax, I finally felt sleep come for me and I closed my eyes. Letting the warmth of the darkness cocoon me, I let go and drifted off into silence.

CHAPTER TWELVE

ACE

*Y*ou're going to keep running and I'm always going to find you, Acacia."

My eyes darted around in the dark. Where was he?

My heart sped up as my breath danced around in front of me.

The blackness was growing, building faster and faster, the air was getting sucked out as though I was inside a containment chamber. There was no escape. There was nowhere to go.

The cold was suffocating, I couldn't find my breath, I couldn't contain the nausea.

"When I find you, you will wish that you stayed, because every night you endured there will be nothing compared to what I will do to you when I find you. And remember my little threat to Agent Lazarev?"

Tears stung my eyes and when I tried to hold them back, they only came faster.

"You think just because you're with Lazarev, you're safe? You're not safe anywhere. I will find you and I will make you repent."

Fear rippled through me like an endless wave of emotion.

"The only reason he isn't dead yet is because I've got far more I need you both for."

Attempts to break free were shut down. He shot forward out of nowhere wrapping his hand around my throat, forcing my eyes up. I fought his grip on me but he was inside my head pushing me under. I screamed against the pain exploding behind my eyes.

"I will find you, Acacia!"

***

I bolted upright. Illarion was beside me pulling my hair free from my face as I leaped off the bed straight for the bucket.

"Easy, lyubov," he whispered, running his hands up and down my arm. "Nice and easy, I'm right here."

"Did he get through?"

"No."

"You're certain?"

"I'm certain. I shielded your mind."

Trying my best to nod, I managed to jerk my head.

My palms were pressed into the carpet like they would somehow ground me. If I could laugh, I probably would have. This was beyond a joke.

"Is it always this bad?" He moved closer to me.

I jerked my head again.

"Is he always trying to get past your shields?"

"Yeah," I whispered, feeling the burn of tears. "He's trying to find me."

"He won't get anywhere near you." He was doing a good job keeping his emotions at bay but the long breath he expelled, let him down. "I'll get you some water."

"Thank you," I murmured, keeping my head safely inside the bucket.

A few moments later he was back at my side and Daniel stood at the door with his arms crossed. He wanted to help but he didn't move.

Illarion helped me to my feet and into the bathroom, stopping us beside the basin.

Cringing, I looked down at the clothes I was in. I was pretty sure there were chunks of toast from two days ago stuck to the fibers. Didn't I clean it all up yesterday? Or was that the day before…?

"Here, drink this."

Taking the water from him, I gulped half of it down in one go.

"God." I hung my shoulders. "I'm disgusting."

"You're not," he said, pressing both hands to either of my cheeks. "You're perfect, like always. Maybe in need of a shower, but still perfect."

I stepped back, shaking my head as my stomach dropped through the floor. "I'm so sorry."

"It was a joke, Ace," he whispered and then, I think the real heaviness hit him.

I didn't laugh, or even crack a smile. Had this been six months ago…well things would have been different. Now, I wanted to curl up into a ball and die.

Humiliation made my cheeks smolder as though I was burning up from the inside. All I could do without breaking down was step back and wrap my arms around my chest.

"I'm so sorry. Christ, I wasn't thinking."

"I should shower," I insisted, pulling back when he tried to reach for me again. "It's pretty bad. You're right. There's toast and soup, maybe even blood and I'm kind of smelly."

"Hey." He cut me off and pressed a gentle hand to my cheek. "You do not smell."

"I do."

He let out a long breath and his hand went to the back of his neck. As I stood in front of him, tears stinging my eyes, I found myself wondering whether we could ever just be normal again.

"Do you want me to help?"

"No."

"I want to help you."

"I'm fine."

"Ace…" He wet his lips and then stepped closer. "Please. Please let me."

Considering his offer, I wordlessly nodded. He turned from me, giving me privacy to undress though it wasn't necessary. He'd seen me naked before, but not like this.

When I heard his clothes come off, my heart thundered.

He cautiously turned to look at me. When I gave him the go-ahead, he moved toward the shower. His eyes remained focused on mine but he never let his gaze wander and I was grateful. He stayed in his underwear and I did too.

When the water warmed up, he took my wrist and tugged me to him.

He stepped into the warm stream first and then let me come inside. The shower was much larger than a standard one but not quite as big as his. It would serve its purpose. He dropped a towel on the tiled floor making sure it covered enough surface for us to sit. He turned me in his arms and guided us both down.

The water cascaded over us and with each minute that passed, more and more pain was lifting. Illarion's chest was pressed firmly against my back making the rapid racing of his heart reverberate through my body. I closed my eyes against the torturous distance between our souls and bowed my head.

His arms wrapped tighter around me while he whispered soothing words into my ear in Russian.

Between the suffocating barrier pushing us apart both on the account of my Dalca induced issues and the woman occupying Illarion's mind, my composure went to shit.

A sob crept up on me before I could stop it. It bubbled over and tumbled out of me in a mess of unintelligible words. Illarion pulled me into his lap letting me curl into him. When the tears passed he reached for the shampoo and gently washed my hair.

He took his time, letting his fingers gracefully massage my scalp and then my neck, before carefully rinsing all the shampoo out. When he was done, I took a deep breath and let him wrap his arms around me again. He pushed my hair over my shoulders turning his attention to my body.

He took his time washing around the bruises and the welts, avoiding the cuts, and delicately treating each wound with the care he gave everything. Tears welled again.

"Thank you," I whispered, turning in his arms when he helped me to my feet.

He brushed my hair behind my ears and smiled. A warmth spread inside my heart where it had been cold for so long. His warm honey eyes closed for a moment, and I reached up and grazed his cheek, smoothing his hair behind his ears.

"We should dry off," he said quietly and reached behind me to turn the water off.

Keeping him where he stood, I reached up on my toes, and carefully pressed a soft kiss to his lips. He froze for a moment, then when I twisted my fingers through his hair, he lowered his face, slowly dropping his hand to my hip, kissing me back.

The kiss was tender, slow, and careful, he held me close and at the same time, he gave me space and with each second that passed, a little of the weight started lifting.

"We should dry off," he repeated, letting his lips linger close to mine.

I smiled against his mouth.

"It's getting cold," he said, unmoving.

As goosebumps broke out across my skin, I shivered in response and agreed.

When we were changed into fresh clothes, he led me back to the bedroom. Daniel was setting out fresh blankets and sheets. I kept my eyes averted when he looked over at us. I didn't know what Illarion was feeling from him, but I could feel his emotions flaring all over the place. When he was done making the bed, he stopped by the door. Had Illarion asked him here?

"Do you want to lie down?" Illarion asked me, breaking the silence.

"I don't think I can sleep."

"That's okay."

I pressed the heels of my palms to my eyes and took several deep breaths. Illarion shifted beside me, he was an emotional wreck. The emotions that ran through him rapidly changed from concern to sympathy to rage.

"I'm going to help you." He stepped closer, holding his hands out. "If you'll let me."

"It's too much to ask you to do this."

"You'll never have to ask me, come."

I chewed my bottom lip but nodded, taking his hands. I followed him to the bed and sat.

"Advil and water, right?" Daniel asked. "Anything else?"

"No, thank you," Illarion replied.

Daniel disappeared for a moment leaving me and Illarion alone.

"I don't know how I'm meant to get through this," I said, finally acknowledging the truth of the situation.

"When your mind feels clearer, you will have direction and I'll be here to help however you need me to."

"The worst part is that I can't even distinguish between the emotional pain and the physical. Everything is just hard."

"I know, Lyubov. This will help."

When Daniel came back, he stopped by the door clutching the water bottle.

Illarion and I sat face to face. This kind of healing could knock someone about badly and I wasn't certain I'd be able to help Illarion if I was so weak already. So, I knew that's why he'd asked Daniel to stand by. He was here to help in case Illarion passed out.

"Give me your hands, Lyubov."

I did.

Before long, a calming feeling began to spread through me and the pain that was constantly present was starting to fade just a little. I winced when I saw the flare of pain in his eyes. A few minutes later, he dropped my hands and swayed on the bed.

Daniel made a move but then stopped when Illarion steadied himself.

A transfer of feelings like that was difficult at the best of times, but when it was *taking* pain, the way he'd just done, was intolerable.

"I'm so sorry, Ila," I murmured, brushing my fingers across his cheek. "I'm so sorry you have to go through this."

"Don't ever apologize for that…" his voice trailed off before he looked at Daniel and then back at me.

There was agony in his eyes, but he didn't move any closer and he didn't touch me again.

I laid down and Illarion got up. Daniel left the bottle and the Advil by the door before leaving us alone.

"Try to get some sleep, Ace."

Illarion drew the covers over me and moved toward the small armchair by the window. When he sat, he blocked himself off from me.

There were two types of hell. The kind that waited for those who'd committed sin and then there was the hell you made for yourself. I curled up and buried my face in the pillow, letting silent tears fall, wetting the fabric beneath me. This was my hell, eternally emotional, forever dragged back to the nightmares.

Finally, like a switch was flipped, I worked out why I was constantly feeling this way—I was broken.

***

ILLARION

Darkness filled the room and only the small flicker of light, from the streetlamp outside, filtered through the dark blinds. Even in the still blackness I saw her tremble under the covers.

It took everything inside me not to get up and go to her but I couldn't. The pain inside me now was at its worst, my head was splitting and the shallow breaths I'd somehow managed to produce were spliced with pain.

I took the water and pills Daniel left and took a couple before finishing off the whole bottle.

If this is how I felt, and I'd only taken a fragment of it from her, I couldn't fathom how much she was suffering. I gripped the edges of the armrests biting down.

I couldn't do a damned thing to help her. It was like seeing her in my dreams all over again only this was worse. Then, I'd drunk myself to a stupor so I didn't have to deal with the guilt and the possibility that she was out there somewhere. Now, I couldn't escape the truth when it was right here in front of me. I'd left her there.

I dug around the duffle I'd shoved under the small table and retrieved my gun setting it on the table in front of me.

Looking down at the steel of the Smith and Wesson, I drew a shaky hand over it and sighed.

Finally, after what seemed like hours, she fell asleep and the breath I'd been holding escaped. I took the few moments of silence to check my phone. Aurel had called at least a dozen times as had Michael and Elena.

More than a hundred emails filled my inbox and a few dozen texts.

An email from my Russian informant caught my eye. I straightened in my seat and opened it.

Information about the Legion is buried deeper than even I can reach, Comrade. You might need to change your approach. I believe there is something much more important about this unit than even your agency understands. Watch your six. Stay safe.

I let out a long breath filing that information away. I would give it all my attention when I could.

I quickly sent Aurel a text telling him I was fine and that I'd check in when I could, and then I switched the phone back off and placed it on the shelf closest to me.

There I leaned back, closing my eyes for a few minutes.

***

ACE

I awoke to the light creeping in through the small cracks where the blinds didn't quite reach the edges of the windows. A quiet murmur beside me drew my attention.

My heart caught as soon as I saw Illarion sleeping on his knees beside me.

His dark lashes fanned across his cheeks while the dark strands of hair that escaped from the elastic fell across his eyes. His fingers gripped the comforter as he murmured in his sleep.

I didn't think it was possible for my heart to love him anymore than I already did. Everything about him captured my heart, it gripped and held on like last night's conversation would just be an after-thought.

And I knew he would wait. God, he would wait for the rest of his life if that's what I asked. But I couldn't, I didn't want to do that to him. *But could I let him in? After everything?* My eyes were wet again.

He stirred, a moment of realization flashed across his eyes, and he shot to his feet.

"I'm sorry, you were having a bad dream...I shouldn't have—"

"It's okay."

"No, it isn't." He shot me a quick look, his eyes skimming the welts across my torso. "You need space, and I shouldn't have..."

He shook his head, and before I could say another word, before I could apologize for startling him, he was gone.

He slipped out of the room, closing the door behind him. I got up to follow but stopped myself.

Sitting back down, I pressed my hands to my face.

A tap on the door caught my attention.

"I have your pills for the day," Daniel announced. "Can I come in?"

"Yeah."

He pushed the door open, and the God-awful creak of the ancient wood made me flinch.

"How do you feel?" he asked, handing me the pills.

"Like I've made a mess of everything."

"What are you talking about?"

He sat down beside me.

I swallowed the pills and put the glass down on the floor beside my foot.

"With you. With Illarion. He wants to be there for me, but I can't..."

"You need space. And don't worry about me."

"I can't even be near him…God, Daniel, I want things to be how they were." I groaned and got up, pressing my hands to my hips.

Dalca had taken everything from me; my confidence, my strength, my smile and that was just the beginning of a list I couldn't even fathom going through just yet.

Daniel got to his feet and crossed the room coming to stand in front of me.

"You need some time. He gets that."

"I love him…" I whispered, barely recognizing my own voice. "I don't want him to give up on me."

"He knows that and he won't."

"What if I push him away? What if he…"

"He won't leave," he said, softly. "He'd be crazy to." He tacked on at the end.

Suddenly, I felt like a real jerk. Daniel wasn't an idiot, and I wasn't ignorant.

"Do you feel like going for a walk?" he asked quickly.

"Sure."

He gave me some time to pull together a semi-decent outfit and once I was outside, he led me into the bright summer day. There were dozens of kids and their parents just like there had been yesterday and the little old lady walking on her own spotted us again.

I looked a little more presentable today though.

The nausea hadn't eased up much but that would take longer and, instead of feeling better that Illarion was here, I felt worse. Guilt gnawed at my insides and shame ate at me from every damn angle.

I questioned myself at every turn. I second-guessed my decisions the moment the thoughts formed. There was nothing of me left. Dalca had seen to it that I'd never be the same person Illarion had known. The bitter taste of anger burned through me. He'd broken me down, torn me apart into tiny pieces and sat back, watching the shit show unfold. *He'd taken everything.*

"Yesterday, when you were resting, I found a way down to the beach. Want to see it?" he asked, ignoring every thought I'm sure he heard.

"That sounds nice."

I followed him down the gravel path running my fingers across the overgrown ferns.

"When I was a kid, my mom used to take me to the beach. When she died, I stopped going. It was too hard."

"How did she die?" I asked, keeping my eyes on the water approaching ahead.

"My father killed her."

My eyes shot back to his. "Oh God, Daniel, I, I'm…I don't even know what to say."

A small smile tugged on his lips. "She deserved better. He was horrible to her, made it look like an accident."

"What did he do?"

"Drowned her in our pool, waited until nightfall to call the cops who were all of course on his payroll. Wasn't hard to do in one of the most corrupt governments on the planet."

"That was back in Romania, right?"

He nodded before his eyes returned to the horizon ahead of us.

"We don't have to go…" I said quickly, catching his hand, stopping him.

"You said once that you loved the beach, that it made you happy."

"Daniel, it does, but—"

"Let me do this for you."

I considered him for a moment before relenting. "Okay."

He pulled his wrist free and stuffed his hands into his pockets and continued without giving me the option to argue further.

I followed silently.

We crossed a small, wooden bridge which led us down to the shore. Just ahead, the beach and the ocean came into view.

A lump formed in my throat. The beach did make me happy. Especially at night, when the night chased away the day and the ocean reflected a million tiny stars. You couldn't tell where the sea ended and the sky began.

The sun shone brightly above us, warming my skin.

Daniel walked up to the water pulling his sneakers off. He tossed them to the sand and rolled up his jeans.

A smile broke across my face. The beach clearly had a calming effect on him too.

Copying him, I sat in the sand and pulled my sneakers off, rolling up the cuff of my jeans.

There was no one in sight, it shouldn't have surprised me as we were pretty far from any major cities and, from what I'd gathered when we walked down here, most wouldn't have even known there was a path leading down to the shore either. I braved the sun and slowly pulled off my jacket.

The welts on my arms had started to heal and, thanks to my healing genes along with what Illarion had done, I didn't look like a punching bag. But what was the deal with the cuts I'd sustained at the hands of Damon?

A thought popped into my mind, it was improbable but not impossible. I'd heard of poison-tipped arrows and darts, what if the blades and bullets were laced with Serum too? It would make sense.

Letting a deep breath settle in my lungs, I shook my head. It didn't really matter; the damage was done, and it wasn't just on the surface.

Parts of me were erased, parts that not only took away what made me a woman, but also a future I had no chance of having.

I sighed, turning my attention down to the shore. I watched as Daniel walked up and down in the shallow water, stepping over the small waves crashing at his feet. When a rogue wave slammed into his legs, wetting his jeans, I laughed louder than I'd intended earning a mischievous grin.

Before I could react, he was coming right at me. He ran across the beach. I jumped up and shrieked, trying to dodge his attempts to drag me to the water. I laughed, trying to catch my breath. When he caught my wrist, he yanked me toward him.

"Now you're going to get your ass handed to you." He laughed dragging me in.

"Not cool!" I laughed continuing my fruitless attempt to pull free.

Sadly, my coordination hadn't come back and I tripped over my own feet going face first into the water.

Not only did I forget to close my eyes, but I also didn't close my mouth quickly enough. I swallowed a mouthful of salty seawater.

When my fingertips brushed across sand, I dug my fingers into it and pushed myself up. Daniel reached down for my arms to pull me up, but before he could, I swiped my leg out, tripping him over, throwing a handful of the wet slush at his chest at the same time.

A laugh was cut short as he went down.

Together we sat, in knee-deep water, covered in sand, completely clothed laughing like two idiots. It was amazing.

My wet hair clung to my exposed skin while the longer bits in the water fanned out around me. Ironically, it was the first time in a long time that I felt normal.

"You're smiling," he said, softly, tucking a strand of hair behind my ear.

"Thank you, Daniel," I said, dropping my gaze. "You've done so much for—"

My words were cut short when Daniel looked up, and I followed his gaze stopping on Illarion.

He was standing on the shore, his hands tucked neatly into his pockets.

Daniel got up, helping me to my feet. "Talk to him."

"I will."

He gave me another look, a smile playing on his lips before he left me standing in the cool water. I watched curiously as he walked past Illarion, the two men shared a quick exchange I couldn't make out.

Illarion's gaze returned to me. He pulled off his boots, tossing them aside and joined me in the sea.

He stopped a foot away. For a moment, neither of us spoke. Finally, he stepped a little closer and cupped my elbows gently.

"I don't want to lose you, Ace."

I tried blinking back tears, but it was pointless, they came anyway.

"I know you need space, and I've been racking my brain, trying to work out what to say, what to do, and I'm lost. All I know is that I cannot lose you, I'm not asking anything of you, but please, don't push me away."

When I opened my mouth to protest, he stopped me by stepping closer and sliding his hands up to my shoulders. I stiffened for a moment before his hold loosened.

"I know you don't need me, I get that, but I need you. I need to know you're here. I need to see that you're alive."

My heart thundered in my chest. "You're wrong."

"About what?"

"I do need you," I whispered, "more than ever. I want you here, I want you with me."

A silent understanding passed through him.

Our connection relayed everything that I had gone through, he heard every thought inside me, he felt every bit of pain and in return,

I saw it in his eyes. This was something we'd both lived through in different ways and I couldn't discount the pain he'd experienced.

I pressed my hands to his forearms when he cupped my elbows. He lowered his forehead to mine and I reminded myself to breathe.

"I don't know how to do this, Ila. That's the truth."

"Then we'll learn together."

I looked up at him. "There's a lot to learn."

"I don't doubt that and I understand there are things you don't want to talk to me about…" He trailed off bringing his hand to my cheek wiping a stray tear with his thumb. "But we will get through it together."

Illarion threaded his fingers through mine and pressed a kiss to my forehead. We would be alright. I knew we would.

CHAPTER THIRTEEN

ACE

When the sky opened up and summer rain began to pour, we walked back to the motel. Daniel had gone to sleep and left us both some soup on the stove.

When I managed to hold my food down, I was going to request at least ten Big Macs, a sickening amount of fries, and endless soda.

We ate silently until both our bowls were empty, then he took them away and sat back down, keeping his eyes averted.

He didn't look up at me, but I could feel the tension building around us.

"I'm going to try to get some sleep," I said.

"That's a good idea."

For a moment, we stood in the crowded kitchen, needing to say something, but saying nothing. Eventually, I gave him a quick nod before making my way to my room. He didn't follow.

From the corner of my eye, as I turned, I saw him by the table.

"You can stay in here, Illarion." I rubbed my arms dropping my gaze. "If you want."

Without another word, he crossed the distance and met me at the door.

He leaned against the frame, his arm was so close to mine that we were almost touching, but he kept his distance.

"Are you sure, Ace?"

"I'm sure," I murmured, without looking up at him.

"Okay."

He took his place in the small armchair by the window as I climbed into the bed and pulled the covers over myself.

I heard him remove his jacket and pull the blanket out from the shelf.

A few minutes later he went quiet, and I heard his breathing even out. He'd been living off coffee and fumes. He hadn't been getting any sleep and it was finally catching up with him.

I pulled off the covers and lowered myself onto the bed looking up at the ceiling, his quiet breaths were the only sound resonating through the darkness.

The hum inside me was quiet and low but it was content, having him close by.

A quiet murmur drew my attention, Illarion was having a bad dream. Nightmares of death and past battles tormented him. I'd seen them before when I slipped into his mind accidentally. But those dreams weren't the only ones that found a deep, dark spot in his mind. Now he had mine too, all the times I'd pushed my fear and pain into him, all the times I had subconsciously reached out to him.

The Darkness inside me wasn't mine alone, it raged through him in the same way. It was threatening to burst to the surface. I figured that the only reason it hadn't so far, was because he was keeping himself intoxicated. Alcohol had a numbing effect on any abilities we possessed, and much like more serious drugs, such as heroin, for example, it dulled whatever burned inside us.

Soft sounds of distress began to fill the silent night. I padded over and knelt. I brushed my fingertips across his cheek, grazing the stubble on his face, tracing over the faint scar on his cheek—a mark left from the last night I'd seen him in the warehouse.

He stirred under my touch, his dark lashes lifted revealing the beautiful, whiskey eyes I took so much comfort in.

The last remnants of sleep left him as he reached down for me, gently running his fingers through my hair.

"Everything okay?" he asked quietly.

"You were having a bad dream."

His brows furrowed. "I'm okay, Ace."

"They were because of me."

"Don't do that," he said gently. "Don't put that blame on yourself."

I sunk back to the ground wrapping my arms around my chest.

He reached down, pulling me up to him.

Words failed me, but my tears did not.

Clutching at the soft fabric of his shirt, I inhaled deeply and buried my face in his chest.

"Talk to me."

I tightened my hold around him, which did little to appease him. I was sure that the pounding of my heart against my ribcage was telling of the imminent breakdown I was about to have.

His body tightened before he pressed a firm kiss to the top of my head.

"I'm sorry," my voice broke as I tried to hold it all in. "I'm so sorry, Ila."

"There is nothing to forgive, Ace."

He tried to stop me but the words wouldn't stop now.

"There is. God, Illarion, there's so much." My arms folded over my head as I shook it over and over. "The things I did…"

Holding me at arm's length he tilted my chin and his dark, stormy eyes found mine.

A muscle in his jaw moved and the storm in his eyes grew darker. "Ace—"

155

"I can never undo the things I did, Ila. I'm a horrible person. I don't deserve you."

"Don't say that." He captured my hands and drew them to his chest pressing them over his heart.

"I hate myself Ila."

"Don't say that, please don't." His voice cracked.

Whatever had broken and chipped away inside me, was breaking inside him, too. There were things that time could fix and then there were the things it could not.

"I do, I do, Ila, I hate myself. I hate what he did to me. I hate what I did to the men he brought to me. I hate what I did to us," I couldn't stop, I couldn't breathe, the words kept coming, and the tears kept raging. "I hate who I am…"

"Lyubov, stop." His hand slipped to the nape of my neck and tried to ease my face up to his. "Look at me."

"I hate him, I hate him so much, Ila…please forgive me."

Stars began to form around the dark edges of my vision and vertigo overwhelmed me. My head grew hazy and when I swayed on my knees, he pulled me against his body, he helped me to the bed where he eased us both down and wrapped his arms around me.

"There's nothing to forgive, you're safe now, you're safe with me."

My body shook against him as uncontrollable tears surged through me my body.

"I hate what he did to me!" I pulled back covering my face with my hands.

"I won't let him hurt you again…" he took my hands and slowly pulled them free from my face. "Look at me, Ace. I swear to you."

I squeezed my eyes shut and tried to turn from him.

"Ace, look at me."

Reluctantly, I turned my face up.

"I'm here with you, no matter what."

"You can't love me, not like this, Ila, not the person I am now. Not after the things I've done. I killed so many people, so many of our friends, people we worked with."

He closed his eyes, taking in a deep breath and when he opened them, I noticed that tears clung to his dark lashes.

"I've never loved anyone as much as I love you, Ace. The way you were. The way you *are*. What you did was because you had no choice."

Nothing he could say would make me forget, nothing could make those feelings go away.

"Every night he came to my bed." I closed my eyes, digging my nails into his arms. "Every night he made me cry…"

Illarion stilled. His fingers stopped drawing gentle lines on my skin and his breath stalled.

"And the nights he didn't, he made up for when he came back, and I let him. I let him do whatever he wanted because I just wanted it over. I wanted to die."

As the admission left my lips, a Darkness I didn't recognize began to rise. I thrust my fingers into my hair and pulled. I pulled until I could barely hold the scream in. Illarion wrapped his hands around my wrists until I let go.

"At the warehouse, the things he did to me, he killed our baby, Ila. He never worried about getting me pregnant, he didn't have to because he destroyed me. He took everything away from me."

Illarion pulled me against him, whatever strength he had, was fading. There was no masking the agony in his staggered, labored breaths now.

"When I couldn't take it anymore, I made Daniel bring me drugs. Ila, drugs! I took heroin, I took it so much I stopped caring, it didn't matter anymore. I didn't care about the men I'd killed when I collected their Senses. I did whatever he asked. I stopped begging to die…"

Illarion's tears fell onto my cheeks, mixing in with my own. He ran his fingers through my hair pulling me closer against him. With each broken sob, his heart thundered in his chest beating as rapidly as mine.

"I saw you one night, through another Sensitive's eyes. I was so high I barely recognized you, Ila. What kind of person am I? How can you love me? How can you stand to touch me? How can you be here when he did that to me every night?"

Rage filled my veins, and I pushed against his chest shoving him to the ground. A scream built inside me, and I hit him again and again until he was on his feet, his arms out, backing away.

"How can you love me?" I screamed.

"Lyubov," he said, firmly as he backed up. "You need to breathe, look at me and breathe."

"How can you say you want to be here when you know what I did?"

The fury was building, and a blinding, white rage intensified inside me. The Darkness was slipping through the cracks. My vision turned black as his trembling hands reached for me.

"How can you think this body is beautiful?" I shouted, pulling the sweater off.

He averted his gaze, looking down at the floor.

"Look at me!" I screamed, feeling nothing but the burning under my skin, pulsing through my super-heated veins.

"Look what he did to me!"

At some point, Daniel had busted through the door and his wide eyes met mine. Illarion held his hand out, warning Daniel to stay back.

"Look at me Illarion! Do you still love me? Do you still want to touch me?"

Daniel stood frozen by the door, Illarion placed his body between us as a shield.

"Yes!" he yelled back. "Yes, because I love you, Ace!"

"You don't even know who I am anymore!" I laughed harshly letting the Darkness spread through me. It reached around my heart like a cold, angry vice.

"I know who you are."

"No, you don't, Illarion."

His nostrils flared as he watched me. I took a step toward him.

"I let him do whenever he wanted to me, every single night! Do you still want me, Ila? Do you still want to fuck me?"

"Stop this!" he shouted pushing Daniel back when he tried to run in.

Illarion stepped toward me but I locked onto his mind and stopped him. Pain flashed behind his eyes as my grip on his mind took hold. I forced him down and he stumbled to his knees.

The floor beneath my feet started to rumble and Daniel stammered backwards, throwing his hands out against the wall to break his fall.

"Look at me, Ila! Does this body turn you on? Do you still want to fuck me? Do you still want to fuck me like you fuck Anna?"

His eyes watered.

I stepped forward lowering my gaze and my voice, "Am I really who you want? Or is she?"

"You are everything to me, Ace."

"Is that why you're here?"

"Of course it is!"

I laughed and ignored the fierce tears streaming down my face.

"Sure it's not guilt?"

"Ace, stop."

Numbness settled deep in my heart, and I did the only thing I knew would bring forth some sort of feeling. I reached down for my arm and scratched as hard as I could. I ripped and tore at the already fragile flesh letting the blood free from my veins.

The more I tore my skin open, the fiercer the vibrations in the floor became. Daniel was yelling something that I couldn't hear.

Illarion moved forward and I forced him back.

"Stop!" he shouted, finally finding his voice. "This isn't you!"

He tried to move; he was fighting me. A shrill, hollow laugh escaped from my lips. A laugh that was too cold to belong to me.

He was no match, he couldn't beat me, he wasn't as strong as me, no one was as strong as me.

The Darkness spread through my veins reaching my fingertips.

I stepped over the discarded clothes at my feet and gently ran my fingertips across his face sending a jolt of electricity into him.

"Ace!" Daniel yelled when Illarion bucked under my touch.

I crouched beside him and ran my hand over his heart, he jolted, trying to jerk back as his shouting turned into staggered breaths.

"You're killing him!" Daniel shouted again.

But he was at my mercy too, he wouldn't be able to move, he wouldn't be able to break through my hold. And if I just pushed a little more, this whole building would come down around us and there'd be no more noise, no more pain. It would all be quiet...

Daniel jerked beside us, his eyes darting to the cracks breaking out across the walls.

"Stop it!" Daniel shouted.

Before I reached down for Illarion, he reached up for me, he wrapped his hand around my wrist and forced my eyes to his.

"Look at me," he stammered, through gritted teeth.

"Let go." I hissed, trying to pull free. But his hold on me was strong. Too strong.

The trembling in the floors grew. The cracks across the flaking walls exploded sending weblike fractures all over the surface.

"Look at me, Ace, let it go, let the Darkness go."

Desperately trying to pull my hand back, and break free from his gaze, I froze when I realized that the Darkness was dying... it was dissipating...what the hell...?

Just like that, the rapid fracturing of the walls and shaking in the floor, stopped.

"Let it go, Ace, let it go...you can do it...let it go. You don't want to do this, remember how you felt last time, think of how it consumed you. Let it go."

His voice broke on the last word and so did my hold. I stammered backward falling hard into the carpeted ground.

Illarion was in front of me, holding my face in his hands. "Lyubov?"

A shaky, breathless sob left my lips as I looked across at him and at Daniel's wide eyes, and then down at my body.

Illarion pulled me up into his arms. "Get me something to cover her."

Daniel reached for the robe hanging by the door. When it was folded neatly over me, he left.

Illarion tipped my face up.

"I nearly killed you..."

"You weren't in control," he said quietly, rubbing my knee.

"I would have killed you if you didn't fight back." I finally found his eyes. "I could have killed you both."

"You're okay now, that's all that matters. Just focus on right now."

"I nearly took the building down."

"Your powers are strong. But you're not in control."

"I'll hurt you."

"You won't."

Before I could say another word, he lowered his lips to mine, and that familiar feeling I could never forget no matter how lost it got in my memories, brought me right back to the man I loved. The man who believed in me. The man who would never let me lose myself.

When I pulled back to search his eyes, he drew his hand across my cheek tilting my face up. "I will always bring you back, Ace. That's why we're connected, that's why we were destined to be together. I've got you, Lyubov. Always."

"What if you can't help me anymore?"

"I promised you once, that I'd never let you lose yourself. I won't break that promise."

Chapter Fourteen

Ace

Convulsions broke the last shred of sleep from me as I stumbled off the bed and rushed across the room to the bathroom. Before Illarion could follow me in, I slammed the door shut and locked it.

The cracks in the walls had reached the bathroom too and Illarion had done a good job patching up the door jamb which had dislodged from the frame. I ground my jaw and tore my gaze away.

"Let me help you."

I ignored him and gripped the toilet bowl throwing up the soup from last night, or earlier today? I had no idea.

The days were all bleeding into one.

Rubbing my sweaty face, I closed my eyes and ignored the tears that came whenever the strain overpowered me.

"Please, Ace." His voice was muffled by the door, but his emotions were coming through a lot clearer now.

The longer I was off the Serum, the clearer I felt everything else. Including the elusive presence in his heart.

Anna kept making an appearance. It was turbulent in his heart. He felt guilty for hurting me and terrible for hurting her. I ground my molars and reached up, flushing the toilet.

I had to keep my emotions in check. Last night was dangerous and if Illarion hadn't stood his ground to talk me down, I wasn't sure I would have been able to stop myself.

I sucked in a long breath and pushed Anna out of my head. Call it selfish or childish but I couldn't give a shit. I was the one who suffered and Illarion's emotions were drowning me.

"Ace?" he called gently.

Composing myself was a lot harder than I thought. But I managed to clean myself up.

I unlocked the door, walked back to the toilet, closed the lid and sat.

Illarion came in and for a moment he looked at me, assessing whether I wanted him there or not before he finally walked over and knelt in front of me.

He cupped my cheek, tilting my face up to his.

His emotions were flashing through the room like a fireworks display. I shoved my snide remarks down and forced myself to simmer down. I looked down at my hands folded neatly in my lap.

"We need to talk about Anna," Illarion said gently.

My eyes snapped to his. He gave me a knowing look. Right. He would have caught all that.

"Not right now." I shook my head.

"I understand. But we need to stay on top of your power."

"You mean my emotions."

"That's part of it, yes."

"Won't happen again."

"You power is unrestrained right now."

"I won't lose control again," I clipped.

He wet his lips like he was about to say more then, instead held his hand out to me, "Come on, it's more comfortable in there."

"What time is it?" I asked, following him to the bed.

"Just after seven. You slept through most of the night."

"First time in a while."

He sat beside me keeping a few feet between us. Apprehension stopped him from moving closer.

Turning my head, I found his eyes.

"Is Daniel okay? He saw a lot last night."

He brushed his thumb across my knuckles, "I spoke to him. He's fine."

"He doesn't know much about the Darkness…or me and what I am, not really."

"He knows about Divines, I take it."

"He knows what Dalca is like. We're different."

He leaned back, resting his head against the wall. "That animal has no right being what he is. He doesn't deserve that power."

Groaning in frustration, I shook my head and ran both hands through my hair.

Illarion was still, but his eyes were roaming across my body. A line in his jaw feathered as he looked over me before glancing across the weblike fractures around us on the walls.

I looked away ignoring how vulnerable I felt for the first time ever with him. He was questioning my ability to control the power running through me and he wasn't wrong to be.

"I could have killed you, Illarion, this isn't safe for you. I'm dangerous." I got up, putting some space between us.

His lip quirked into a half smile and before I could decipher the gesture, he was standing and slowly walking over to me. "I know you're dangerous."

"And it doesn't scare you?"

"No."

Something about the look in his eyes made my breath catch. I bit down on my lip and forced myself to drag my eyes away from him.

I might have been through hell, and I might have been a shadow of my former self, but my heart and my body remembered exactly who I was before. I remembered how I felt around Illarion, I remembered how my heart raced when his eyes found mine. I reached for him, instinctively grazing my fingertips across his cheek.

My hands found their way to his forearms, and he stiffened as I trailed my fingers across his taut skin feeling every muscle as he tensed. He was unsure, eager but cautious.

"I don't trust myself, Ila. You shouldn't either."

"I trust you."

His voice was thick, laced with unspoken questions.

Stepping closer, I looked up into his dark, hooded eyes and drew my hand over his cheek.

Touching his skin and being able to feel him beneath my fingertips was so overwhelming that I barely managed to draw in a breath. When his hand slipped to the nape of my neck, he lowered his forehead to mine and my defenses came tumbling down.

Every thought that ran through his mind was conflicting. He wanted me and he wanted this moment, but he was afraid that I couldn't handle it.

A cautious breath left his lips as he drew me closer to his chest. "Ace, we shouldn't. This is too soon."

"I know what you're thinking..." I closed my eyes feeling his heartbeat against my cheek. "But you're still wrong."

Illarion tipped his head back, sighing loudly. "We can't do this right now."

Choosing to ignore what he just said, I traced my fingers along the hem of his shirt, dancing closely to the edge of his belt. A few inches up and I'd feel the defined ripples along his taut stomach, a few inches down...

He closed his hand over mine, pressing it flat against his stomach.

166

"Don't."

"I *need* this." I fisted a handful of fabric from his shirt and pressed my forehead to his chest.

For a slow moment, he didn't say or do anything and then in a quick, precise movement he wrapped his arm around my waist and turned us around, swapping positions.

He bowed his head bringing our foreheads together again. "God knows I need it too. But we can't, you know we can't, Ace. You need time."

"Are you worried about me losing control?"

"No, Lyubov. I'm worried that this will push you too far."

"I keep seeing his face." The truth of those words burned through me. "I want to forget, I want to feel *you*, I want to see your face."

"Lyubov."

"Make me forget," I whispered, cupping his cheek, forcing his eyes to meet mine.

At long last, his lips found mine. He kissed me deeply, carefully and with such passion that every single touch and every single kiss sparked a flame within me.

His pain coursed through me morphing with mine, but deep down the pain was slowly getting chased away by something else: hope.

He cupped my cheek and deepened the kiss. My body responded as it always had. It remembered every touch and every pulse of electricity that shot through us. Regardless of the pain and fear normally consuming my waking thoughts. In this moment, nothing but Illarion was on my mind.

He pressed one hand above my head, against the wall while his other slid behind my back lowering slowly until it was resting on my hip.

"Are you sure?" his voice was so soft, so quiet I had to strain to hear him. And God how I'd missed hearing it.

His hot breath danced on my lips as his hips pressed into mine.

"Yes," I managed a breathless response. "I am so sure. I need you, Ila. Please."

He didn't waste another moment before he picked me up and carried me over to the bed, a silent moment of apprehension coursed through him before he gently lowered me onto the sheets.

Before he could say another word, I tugged at the button on his jeans and, in no time, I had him where I wanted him.

My legs tangled with his, quickly, rapidly drawing our bodies together and closer. His breaths were ragged against my cheek as he pulled my track pants down and tossed them aside. I arched up, letting his hands roam my body, feeling every inch of me.

Fragments of memories that had been frayed started to piece back together but deep inside me, where the broken pieces lay, something else started creeping through the darkness. With each hot breath against my cheek, I felt the impossible weight of Dalca's body on mine.

No. This was not happening. I wouldn't let it.

I dug my nails into Illarion's shoulder hoping to God that it would ground me. The heat of his skin beneath my fingertips did little to vanquish the terrifying fragments slithering through my mind.

I squeezed my eyes shut to push Dalca out. But it was no use.

No. Fuck no.

He wasn't going to keep ruling over my life like this.

I kissed Illarion, forcing my mind to remain present. But as Illarion's hand coasted across my breast, I felt panic rise when my mind brought me right back to the nights in Dalca's house of horror.

Illarion reached down for my hand and when his fingers circled my wrist, a part of me shattered.

He wasn't going to win. Not here. Not now.

Illarion's hands continued roaming across my body and the moment his fingers slipped to the band of my underwear, my entire body froze. In an instant I was transported back to my bed in Dalca's house, trapped beneath his body, held in place by invisible forces that controlled me just like he was controlling me now.

Tears burned my eyes but the scent of Illarion's cologne dragged me back to the present.

No. Dalca wasn't going to win.

I reached down for the band on Illarion's Calvin's and when I tried to tug them down, he pressed his hot cheek against mine, drawing in a ragged breath before stopping my hands.

Before I could reach up for him, he pulled back and remained hovering above me, his elbow depressing the pillow beside my head.

"What's wrong?" my raspy voice broke the silence, stilled only by the dark, stormy look in his eyes.

"Ace, I can't."

"Why?"

"Tell me you're here with me."

"I'm here."

He searched my eyes. "You're lying."

I felt a frown tug at my lips.

"You're lying. Your heart is racing, your mind is everywhere. I can't hold onto any fragments for longer than a moment."

"I'm here." I tried to reach for his face, but he moved quickly.

He removed himself from the bed and turned his back to me. He ran his hands through his hair as he stood, his body tense.

"Ila, look at me," I said, sitting on the edge of the mattress.

I wanted to be firm, I wanted to keep my voice level, but I couldn't. Every word was heavy on my tongue and every breath seemed to break my barrier. He was going to leave this room and if he did, it meant that he was leaving me, that it was all over.

Fear whipped through me.

"Ila. Is it because of him? Because of what he did to me?" my words were barely a whisper.

He shook his head and crossed the space between us kneeling in front of me. He brought his hands to my cheeks.

"Nothing he did could make me stop loving you. Or stop wanting you. But this, it's too soon. You're afraid."

When I tried to shake my head in protest, his hands held me in place.

"I can see it, every time you look at me, Lyubov." He closed his eyes for a moment, and for a moment I stayed silent feeling him course through my mind and my soul. "Whenever I touch you…" His voice broke when his eyes met mind again. "I feel your heart, I can sense the fear. Your body freezes as though you're afraid of me. I feel your pain, you're remembering."

"Ila I'm not scared of you."

"No, but your body isn't distinguishing between who is here now and who hurt you." He traced his thumb along my cheek. "I *know* you're afraid, I don't blame you, I never should have done this."

"Please, please don't go."

He looked at me through wet eyes but remained silent.

"I need this, Ila."

He brought his hands down to my biceps.

"I need this too, God, you have no idea. To feel your skin on mine, to feel *you*, to kiss you…but when I look into your eyes, there is so much fear, Ace."

"I'm not afraid of you."

"I know it's not me you're afraid of, or maybe you are, I don't know."

"That's ridiculous. I'm not scared of you, Illarion. I could never be afraid of you."

"Things are different, you're holding parts of yourself at bay, and I know it's to protect yourself. But I see it, I can feel it, Ace. I can't look into your eyes and see that fear when you look at me when I'm touching you."

"Ila. Please."

He captured my hands in his and brought them to his lips. He kissed my knuckles and then he drew back.

As he moved away from me, a sudden, heart wrenching thought floored me. What if he'd expected something different when he saw me and now, it was too much? That thought broke me in two.

"I need some air," he said, quietly, taking a step back.

I moved toward him, but he was quicker.

In a matter of moments, he had his jeans and T-shirt back on and seconds after that, he was gone, leaving me on my own.

Seconds, it had only been seconds, but that's all it took.

Chapter Fifteen

Ace

The look on Illarion's face burned through my mind every time I closed my eyes. It had been more than two weeks since I'd watched him leave my room that night.

Dalca had ensured that I would never be touched by another man ever again.

I didn't know how or when it happened but somewhere between Illarion leaving me and my own mind tormenting me, Dalca made an appearance in my mind as though a door was suddenly opened in my defenses.

"What did I say, Acacia?" he taunted me. *"Didn't I say that no man will ever touch this body again?"*

"Get out of my head."

"I'll be seeing you."

I managed to push him out, but the damage was done. He knew how to get inside, and he showed no signs of backing down.

He pushed himself into my head whenever he pleased and taunted me with the things I feared most: Illarion had left me, and it was all because of what was left of me.

The more he said it, the more I started to believe it.

And round and round it went. Day after day, everything following became a jumbled mess.

Illarion became more and more concerned, his constant attempts to draw me out, failed continuously and, eventually, even Daniel stopped trying to pry me from my room. All throughout their attempts, Dalca kept cooing in my head.

And so, it went on. Days turned into nights and eventually, two weeks had gone by and here we were. Only basic, necessary words were exchanged and I mostly stayed silent, in my own head and in my own bubble of safety.

Illarion tried to talk to me, Daniel told him to give me space, they'd argue, and I'd sit like a robot, staring into nothingness.

"We have to leave," Illarion said, kneeling in front of me taking my hands into his.

Attempting to blink through the haze, I nodded, keeping my eyes straight ahead.

"Look at me." His voice was soft on my ears, but it echoed loudly. "I don't know what's going on in your head, Ace, but we don't have time to sit and wait here anymore. Do you understand what I'm saying?"

When I didn't respond, he gently tilted my head up with his fingers. "Please. It's not safe here."

When even that failed to get my attention, he let out a long breath and squeezed my hand.

"I know you don't want to go anywhere with me right now, but we must leave. There's been chatter about Dalca's movement." A desperate edge in his voice caught me off guard and the name shot my nerves into overdrive.

He bowed his head. "Please, Ace, we have to go. We've stayed as long as we can, I didn't want to move you until you were feeling better, but we can't stay here any longer."

"Daniel..." I managed to whisper.

Nodding, he drew my attention back to him.

"Daniel is coming with us."

"Where are we going?"

"Home."

***

About an hour in to our drive back to Long Island, Illarion handed me his phone. "Aurel would love to hear your voice."

"You haven't told him?"

"No. I thought it'd be best coming from you."

My heart stammered, I looked down at the phone, his number was already up and all I had to do was press call.

After a few moments deliberating what I would say to him, I swallowed back the nerves and pressed the phone to my ear.

A few, quick rings later, which honestly felt like an eternity, I heard the familiar voice.

"Finally. Do you have any idea how many times I've called. You better have a really creative excuse for ignoring me, for the last four weeks. I've been worried out of my fucking mind!"

"Is seeing me, a good enough excuse?"

The silence on the other end was piercing.

"Ace? Is that you?"

Closing my eyes, I exhaled. "Yeah."

"How? What?"

"It's a long story...but I'll tell you when I see you."

"Are you coming home?"

"Yes," I whispered. "I'm coming home."

He laughed and the full sound warmed my heart.

"This is..."

"I know. I'll see you soon."

A moment of silent understanding passed between us before I handed the phone back to Illarion. He brought it to his ear. "Have Elsa prepare the guest rooms."

After a few quick exchanges with Aurel, he hung up, replacing the phone in his pocket.

"He's missed you, a lot," he said, turning his face to me.

"I've missed you all too."

Illarion's jaw squared. Something had changed between us. Not just because of the hell I'd been through and not just because he couldn't stop seeing the fear in my eyes. But *I* had changed. And it scared the hell out of me.

Daniel shifted in the back. *How could I have forgotten that this was obviously hard for him, too?*

He was uprooted and pulled out of his own home. I rubbed my face and turned back to look at him.

"Is there someone you want to call?"

He smiled but shook his head. "No family here, thanks though."

"You always have a place with us, you know that right?"

His lips quirked into a smile. "Thanks, guys."

Illarion caught his eye in the rear-view mirror and gave him a quick nod before bringing his attention back to the road for yet another long stretch of silence.

As the drive reached the ten-hour mark, and the sky grew dark, I heard Daniel's breathing deepen and even out. I leaned back in the leather seats and turned my face to Illarion.

"I know what you're thinking," I whispered.

I heard him shift and turn his head slightly.

"You think I don't love you, at least not the same way. Because of everything that happened."

"Do you?" he asked.

"I could never stop loving you."

"But something has changed."

"I've changed, Ila. But inside, who I was, how I loved you…that hasn't."

The sigh that left his mouth was a painful one. I was numb. I could admit that. I surpassed the torrent of emotions that raged through me and now, well now there was nothing.

I turned my head back and leaned against the headrest again.

"Then why won't you let me in?" he asked.

"I have my reasons."

"I can see that. Is it because of what I wrote to you about?"

"In part."

He turned to the road, wetting his lips for a moment.

"You don't have to say anything else," I added. "Maybe that's for the best right now."

"But we do need to talk."

"And we will."

Somewhere between Washington and Baltimore he reached over and took my hand. "I never meant to make you question my feelings for you, I'm sorry for what I did."

"Yeah, me too."

"I deserve that."

"It wasn't a jab." I glanced across at him. "We've both been there, we've both done things we questioned."

"Talk to me." His voice was firm, but I felt it, for the first time. He was afraid of what was left for us.

The lump in my throat doubled.

He squeezed my hand, and I didn't have to look at him to feel the apprehension coursing through him. He didn't know who I was anymore. He didn't know who he was.

I pulled my hand free and folded it across my other hand in my lap. I ignored the pang of pain as it shot through him, but he kept his hands to himself.

"We'll talk, but not now."

"Okay, Ace."

He gripped the wheel tightly, his knuckles blanching under the pressure.

I felt the truth of Dalca's meaning echo through my mind. No one would want me the way I was. He'd made sure of it.

"You've lost faith in me," Illarion said after a while.

"I've lost faith," I corrected.

He looked at me quickly, searching my eyes before his eyes went back to the road.

The torture inside him started again. I hated that I'd made him feel as though he was at fault. None of it was true, of course. He didn't fail me. He never could. I didn't blame him. He was the reason I survived and pulled through, the reason I didn't give up. He was the reason I stopped begging to die.

But a part of me buried deep in the pit of my own angst, was angry. I was left alone to suffer, and I didn't know how I would ever get past it.

After several miles of dark highway passed, he pulled over onto the side of the road and got out of the car. Quietly, he closed the door, careful not to disturb Daniel.

He stalked across the road where he stood up straight running his hands through his hair.

His body shook and from here, I couldn't tell if he was crying or shaking from rage.

I quietly opened my door and I walked over to Illarion. His body tensed as I approached.

"I'm sorry," he said, quietly, keeping his back to me. "I just needed to stretch my legs."

"I can drive. You're tired."

He looked across at me and shook his head. He took a step toward me and brought his hands to my elbows.

"Are you punishing me? I don't understand."

"I'm not punishing you."

He stepped back thrusting his fingers through his hair.

"I'm not punishing you," I repeated, shaking my head. "I just, I have nothing, inside, at all." My voice cracked before I could stop it.

"What are you talking about?"

He furrowed his brows, looking right into my eyes.

"I don't feel anything, in here." I took his hand and pressed it over my heart.

His dark eyes searched mine. He stepped closer, one hand fell to the curve of my jaw.

"There's nothing, anymore, I thought there was. But then the pain dulled, and the numbness came. Then everything else was gone. He said this would happen and he was right."

"What are you talking about? Who said what?"

"Dalca. He told me this is how it would go. He told me I was ruined that no one would ever want me again. And it's true, isn't it?" I whispered. "You see what I am now."

"No, Ace, I—"

"It's okay. I get it. It's better this way."

He brought our foreheads together. "Dalca is a vile, despicable bastard. He isn't right about anything, and I know you're scared, and you must be feeling so many things but none of what he taunted you with is true."

"You're wrong, Ila. I don't feel anything about Dalca anymore. I remember it all, I just, I don't know, I don't care. I don't feel it. I don't feel *anything*."

He guided my face gently up to his and brought his lips to mine. What once would have warmed my heart, now did nothing at all. I pulled back and wet my lips, before I dropped my gaze from his.

"We should get back on the road, we shouldn't be out in the—"

Like my breath was suddenly stolen from me, I stopped, almost doubling over when the wave hit me.

"What's going on?" he shot.

"Someone's coming."

His eyes scanned the horizon and returned to me. "Which direction?"

"I don't know."

Panic set in as I turned from him, letting my eyes sweep the surrounding woods. I couldn't see anything. But I knew what I felt.

"Ace? What are we dealing with?"

"I don't know. But they're getting closer. We have to go. Now!"

Illarion didn't wait for me to elaborate, we both ran back to the car. The second we were seated; he shifted the Hummer into gear and we were moving.

Before Daniel could speak, headlights appeared in the tree line. My heart raced as I looked across at Illarion. He floored it down the highway, whoever was coming, was coming in hot.

They navigated the rough terrain of the forest, keeping up with us in their ATVs.

"What the hell is happening?" Daniel shot.

I chanced a look back and swore. There were another three sets of headlights coming from the forest.

As the trees thinned out, they swerved onto the road and began gaining on us.

"Ace? What's going on?"

I looked back at Daniel and grit my teeth. "They're coming for us."

"My father?"

"Yes. He's been taunting me for weeks." I shook my head.

"Hold on," Illarion said firmly, shooting me a look. "This is about to get rough."

He didn't have to tell me twice. I gripped the roof handles and held on tight. He veered off the road and up the embankment into the thin cover of trees.

"They've got ATVs!" I yelled.

"I've got a Hummer," he shot back. "Hold on."

Holding my breath, I braced myself as we sped toward an incline. Illarion accelerated and hit the dune hard, sending the Hummer up and over. When it hit the ground on the other side, I held in a surprised shriek and turned back to check.

"They're still coming."

"I can see that."

"Go that way," Daniel said quickly, leaning between us.

Illarion followed his directions and sped toward the small opening.

"I know these woods. There's a river coming up," Daniel added.

"ATVs can cross rivers," I snapped.

Daniel shook his head. "Not with these currents."

Illarion gripped the wheel tighter and gave me a quick look before hitting the gas and aiming right for the clearing.

Daniel sat back down and strapped himself in.

"How deep is the water?" Illarion asked.

"We'll be fine," Daniel answered.

"Not what I was asking." Illarion ground his jaw, checking the mirror again.

"Jesus." I checked my seatbelt and gripped the roof handles tighter.

A glance back confirmed that they were still there. I counted five ATVs quickly gaining on us. Illarion hit the riverbank and my breath caught as soon as I saw the rapidly rushing water.

"Can we make this?" I looked over at Illarion.

"This car weighs more than six-thousand pounds," Illarion said quickly.

"Those currents are moving pretty damn fast," I said breathlessly.

"We can make it," Daniel said from the back.

We both turned to look. The ATVs were still coming, but as the Hummer hit the water and the current quickly pushed us sideways, the ATVs stopped, skidding in the riverbank.

Illarion's eyes were fiercely focused. His knuckles were blanching as he struggled to hold onto the wheel as the rapids pushed us further and further down the river.

I gripped the edge of my seat and looked around. There was a good fifty feet between us and the other side.

Illarion grit his teeth, breathing deeply as the rage of water continued to rip the wheel from his grasp, sending the Hummer out of his control.

A rapid rush of panic entombed me when I looked down and saw the water rushing inside.

"Oh my God, Ila."

"It's okay," he said firmly. "The car can take it."

He shifted the gears; I heard them grinding under the pressure. There was no grip. The tires had nothing to hold onto.

And then, finally, I heard the sweet sound of the engine roar as the tires made contact with a sandbar.

Illarion wasted no time getting into gear. He floored the Hummer, holding the wheel tightly and after what seemed like the longest time, the water inside the cabin started receding and we were nearing the riverbank.

As soon as we were on solid ground, I let out a long breath and leaned back in my seat, throwing my hands over my face.

Illarion stopped and engaged the handbrake.

"You both alright?"

"Yeah," I breathed.

"Daniel?"

"Yeah, I'm good."

"Okay." Illarion nodded, removing his hands from the wheel.

They trembled as he dropped his head with a shaky breath.

I squeezed his arm gently. "Are you okay?"

He nodded silently, clenching and unclenching his fists. He let out an even breath and looked back at me.

That was too close. We both knew how determined Dalca was and if I hadn't have felt what I did, we would have been captured. He'd seen firsthand how desperate Dalca was when he tried to get into my head through my dreams.

Neither of us would take his threats lightly.

Illarion swallowed hard and after a few moments, he tore his gaze from me, shifting the Hummer back into drive.

***

Illarion's beautiful, cobblestone mansion came into view.

It was bittersweet and God, the bitterness burned strong. *She* would be here, but Aurel would be too, and I needed a sense of normalcy.

The path leading up to the house was surrounded by tall pine trees and it looked just like I saw it last.

Six months had passed since I'd been here. In a way, it felt like I was here just yesterday while at the same time, it was as though a lifetime had gone by.

His home was beautifully illuminated showing off every tower and chimney stack as far as the eye could see. Just up ahead, Aurel stood with his arms folded across his chest.

Illarion took the Hummer around to the left and parked just in front of the door.

Aurel's eyes widened as his gaze took in the sight of the vehicle. I was sure there were dings and scratches and water pouring out from all crevices.

But as soon as his eyes landed on me, whatever he was preoccupied with before, was forgotten. Before I could reach for the handle, he'd already pulled my door open.

"How are you here?"

I hugged him tightly.

When he pulled back, he held me at arm's length. His gaze swept over my face and arms and I didn't miss the look that flashed across his eyes.

I reached up and cupped his cheeks. "You look like shit, Aurel."

He laughed and hugged me again. "You know grieving does that to a person."

"Oh, is that the excuse you're going with?"

"Still a punk, I see."

"Still a shitty liar, I see."

He chuckled, pulling back to look at me again. "I can't believe I'm looking at you."

There was the briefest hint of sadness in his eyes before he forced a smile.

A subconscious reaction within him drew my attention to the grand entrance of Illarion's home. A woman stood silently with her hands folded neatly in front of her lap. Her eyes darted between me and Illarion. Even though his mind was all over the place his eyes never left me.

Illarion remained fixed in his spot and just like the first time I'd seen him since all this began, the storm battering down on our connection came in and out of focus.

Swallowing my pride, I looked back at Aurel and forced a smile.

"Let her get some rest," Illarion said, speaking for the first time since we got here. He clapped Daniel on the back before walking past. "This is Daniel; he's staying with us."

Aurel nodded without breaking eye contact with me.

"I'm fine, I could use the air," I said, noticing the redhead watching the exchange.

"Walk?"

"Please," I agreed.

Before Illarion could say another word, I turned and began the familiar walk down the path which led to the garden.

Aurel followed me, although he was silent, I could hear the questions burning on his mind.

When we made it to the garden that was surrounded by thousands of tiny fairy lights above, I stopped by the wall of flowers taking in the scent of the roses.

Aurel turned me, his hand found the curve of my cheek.

Emotions filled him and I saw it in his eyes before I felt it. He was overwhelmed and confused. I should have removed myself from this equation immediately, but I didn't. I stayed. I enjoyed it. I watched his eyes drink me in, I watched in fascination as he grew more and more conflicted about what he was feeling and why. So did I. I didn't think this way about Aurel, I cared about him as a good friend but right now...

"I can't believe I'm looking at you."

"I heard you missed me."

A small laugh broke free from him. "Yeah, you can say that."

He led me to the small, stone bench.

I sat down and tipped my head back, looking up at the lights above us.

"You're different."

The words themselves were simple, but what cut me was his tone.

He was digging deep, pulling apart the walls I'd put up trying to focus on what I didn't want him to see. The truth that pulsed under the surface. The truth I'd become insanely good at hiding.

But he saw more than I wanted him to. He was a powerful Sensitive and, from all the ones I'd seen over the six months, he was probably the most powerful Sight one around.

He saw Dalca and fragments of images I couldn't hold back.

I focused on a small spot in the garden directly across from us.

"Ace." He got up and crouched in front of me.

His hand guided my face up while he searched my eyes like he was reading a picture book about my life.

"I can see some of the pain, what did that son of a bitch do to you?" His eyes searched mine, digging deep through the memories I was trying to hide.

"There's too much to tell. Please don't make me."

"You don't have to do anything you don't want to."

I closed my eyes for a moment and when I opened them, I was met with so much compassion that it tore all my defenses down.

"Illarion said he thought you were alive. We should have listened…I should have listened."

"You can't blame yourself, neither of you can."

He bowed his head, gripping my hands in his.

"I can see the pain, somewhere inside you…but something is blocking it."

My gaze flicked back to his. I frowned. Something was blocking off everything inside me, I'd felt it for days now, but I thought it was just me going into shock or something.

"What do you mean?"

"I don't know." He shook his head a little before his frown deepened, concentrating on me again. "Something is blocking you from me. I can't see past it."

"My walls."

"No, no that's not it." He shook his head.

I cleared my throat and got up, pushing past him. "We should get back. I'd like to shower, find some clothes that fit."

"I'm sure there's plenty in there for you to choose from." He chuckled and then added, "Welcome home, Ace."

***

Some time had passed since we'd arrived. I managed to shower, help Daniel settle in, give him a full tour of the expansive grounds and I managed to avoid Illarion, Aurel and Anna. I even managed to close my eyes for a few hours and get some rest, waking just before noon feeling somewhat refreshed.

I leaned against the rail on my bedroom balcony taking in the fresh air. I'd say that it had been a successful day.

We survived a forest car chase, a rapid river, and I hadn't even cried. I hadn't shouted or tried to kill anyone with my Darkness or crack any walls.

A quiet tap at my bedroom door, drew my attention—Illarion pushed the door open and gave me a weak smile.

"Can we talk?" he asked, as he came and stood beside me keeping a foot between us.

"Sure." I shrugged, turning away.

"Did you manage to get some rest?"

"I did. Few hours."

"I'm glad."

The conversation died. He shifted beside me searching my eyes. He was torturing himself again. We had something in common.

I'd seen my lowest point when I barely recognized myself and what I was doing. I'd made the decision to sleep with Daniel just like Illarion made his choice. He denied that she meant more to him but she made him happy when it counted.

She was there for him because I couldn't be, and I was still miserable.

There was something so poetic about it. I couldn't be angry about that; I couldn't hate her for it and I couldn't hate him.

Instead, I directed the tension and anger at myself for feeling what I was. How could I be such a hypocrite?

"I don't think talking is going to help." The moment the words left my lips I didn't believe them and neither did he.

He bowed his head, leaning heavily against the railing beside me. "Please don't shut me out."

"I don't know what you want me to say, Illarion." I glanced across at him; he kept his eyes down and away from me. "Honestly, tell me what you want to hear, because I have no idea. I don't know anything right now and the one thing I was sure about..."

"I can never apologize enough for that and for what I made you feel."

"You've nothing to apologize for. I was dead as far as you knew. I don't blame you for that, for finding comfort in her. That's not what this is about."

"Isn't it?"

"Not completely, no."

I looked away again and he remained quiet for a moment before he turned and stuffed his hands into his pockets. A haunted expression met me.

"It was two months ago, when I first began dreaming about you and what you were going through. I was drinking, a lot. Most nights I didn't make it to bed and the nights I did, well I didn't sleep much anyway. One night, Aurel invited Donna and Anna here for dinner.

"I got so drunk I could barely stand. Donna went home, she had patients in the morning, so she had an early night. Anna stayed with me. At some point, it all became too much, I couldn't breathe, Ace, I was drowning so fast I thought I'd never come up for air. I rushed outside, I remember the cold and the rain and then she was there…"

"You don't need to explain anything to me."

"I do," he shot back, folding his hand over his heart. "I do."

Christ.

"God, I was so broken. Ace, I couldn't think without you, I couldn't…" He stopped for a moment and looked up at me, before he could notice the tears staining my cheeks, I swatted them away. "Anna was there, she listened, it was different talking to her, Aurel had his own grief…but she was there, for *me*."

"Ila—"

"It was a mistake. I knew it was, and I was selfish."

It took everything inside me to remain quiet and let him gather his words.

"She put the pieces back together, even if it was just when she was there. I'm so sorry."

He dropped his gaze.

My stomach churned as my heart tightened into angry coils. I couldn't lie and deny that it didn't hurt. It absolutely shredded me but what I was about to tell him, would probably hurt more.

"I hurt you," he whispered, his voice barely audible. "I can understand your reluctance to let me in now."

"I slept with Daniel."

Whatever was on the tip of his tongue, was silenced. He rested his hip against the rail as he expressed a long breath, his eyes lifted meeting mine.

"I knew about you and Anna." I wet my lips, dragging in a long breath. "You thought I was dead, that was your reason. What was mine?"

He ran his hand across his jaw.

"I was in a bad place, a lot was wrong, a lot that didn't make sense to me and Daniel was there. That's the truth. I wanted to feel wanted; I needed to feel wanted. There was nothing else there. I used him."

Illarion let out a long breath.

"I know that's not an excuse and I'm sorry for what I've done, for who I am now."

He opened his mouth to protest, but I stopped him.

"There's nothing more to say, Ila, we were both in a bad place, we both did what we had to, to survive."

Illarion scratched the back of his head. Bet he didn't think that's where this conversation would go.

Without anything more, I forced a smile. "I really wanted to get some training in if you don't mind."

He nodded, understanding right away. He gave me a small nod and then he was gone.

I let out the breath I was holding and bowed my head. So much for not crying today.

***

A full two hours passed before I gathered enough courage to face the day. I pulled on a pair of sweats and a tank top threading my hair through a baseball cap. I pulled on a pair of sneakers and grabbed my boxing gloves and then made a beeline for the back of the house.

Elsa had kept everything as I'd left it and I knew Illarion had everything to do with that. Fresh pain seared through me.

As I neared the door, I stopped abruptly. Anna sat with her back to me reading on the porch. Her cropped red hair was fastened neatly behind her ears with a thick, green ribbon matching her long cardigan.

I contemplated leaving when I saw her, but the briefest moment of confidence found me, so I decided against it and moved toward the door. I needed to leave the house, and I needed to get to the gym.

Adjusting my baseball cap, I tightened my hold on my gloves and walked with my head held high.

As I neared the door, I sucked in a breath and pulled the sliding glass door open. A moment of panic set in when she turned around and looked up at me.

She shot up, quicker than I was expecting and stood deathly still. Her eyes were a fierce shade of green surrounded by red circles. She'd been crying.

Now up close, I recognized her. She was the woman I saw talking with Donna, the first time I'd visited Josh. I forced a neutral expression.

She clutched her book, her knuckles blanching under the pressure as she looked at me.

Not giving her the opportunity to say anything I made a move to leave and much to my dismay, she spoke.

"Agent Hart."

I stopped, shifting my weight from one leg to the other, anything to alleviate the tension.

"I really have to go."

"It won't take long," she said, quietly, and I heard her move.

Oh boy.

I turned to face her and pulled my gloves to my chest.

"I've had this conversation in my head a million times before I even knew you'd be here and every time I did, it was worse than before. The truth is, I don't know how to say what needs to be said."

"Nothing needs to be said."

"I respect you so much, you've no idea. I've read all about the work you've done, your time in Iraq, Special Forces. You're a legend on the field and off."

"Thanks for the accolades, but it's really not necessary—"

"I've been losing my mind knowing that you're here and that, that I overstepped my boundary with Illarion."

My heart constricted hearing her say his name. I let out a long breath and centered myself. "Anna."

"Please, let me finish, I need to say this."

Figuring that arguing wouldn't do anything, I stayed quiet and gave her a curt nod.

"I care about Illarion, I always have, for years—from when I first handed him his identification badge to now. But I know that his heart belongs to you. I'm not trying to break anything up, you weren't here, and he was shattered. Losing you destroyed him. I reached out as a friend. You have to believe that I never intended for things to go where they did. I'm not that person."

Casting my eyes to the trees on the horizon, I held in a long breath and wet my lips before I looked back at her. "Whatever happened when I was gone, it's between the two of you," I said, as evenly as I could. "It's not my place, Anna, not anymore and I would appreciate it if we refrained from discussing this again."

I still couldn't shake the image of his hands on her body, imagining him loving her the way he would me. I turned from her and left.

Throwing all my strength into a sidekick, I watched with satisfaction as the bag swung back, nearly coming off the hook.

Before it came back down, I switched positions and aimed, ready for the next strike. Again, and again until the skin on my bare feet turned red.

Then I turned to punching. I slammed one fist into the bag and then the other, over and over until I couldn't feel my arms anymore and then I pulled my gloves off, continuing without them.

The pain in my body wouldn't slow me down. I was beyond that, mind over matter was a hell of a thing, especially being trained in hand-to-hand combat, especially coming from a POW situation. I punched harder and harder with each blow until the skin around my knuckles tore.

Strong body meant a strong mind and I'd conditioned myself to a point I was able to almost shut all my emotions down.

When I started bleeding all over the mat, I stopped.

"Ace."

My shoulders reactively dropped, and I let out a sigh as Illarion's voice boomed through the gym.

Could I really not get any time alone today?

As he neared, I turned toward him, aware that his eyes fell to the blood at my feet.

"Jesus, Ace."

"What are you doing here?" I asked, heading toward the basin and away from him.

"Ace, stop."

"Please, just leave." I yanked my shoulder back when he pressed his hand to it.

"Look at me," he murmured, his hand fell to my wrist, and when I didn't pull back, he slowly turned my hand in his.

I heard a sharp inhale as he looked at the skin on the other hand. Hating the way his touch always undid me, I pulled myself away.

"It'll heal, you know that."

"You're being destructive," he said, softly, taking my hands in his.

"I think you know a little about that?"

"A little."

He turned the water on and placed my hands in the stream without breaking eye contact.

Damn it, the proximity was suffocating.

"Why are you here?" I asked sternly.

The concern and angst in his eyes undid me. I felt my resolve weaken as he turned the water off and wrapped my hands in a towel.

"Let me take a look at your hands," he spoke quietly, keeping his eyes locked with mine.

He was holding his power over me; I could have fought it. I was strong enough to but I didn't. Maybe this illusion was what I needed. Maybe it made this feel real.

"Fine."

He led me to the bench and sat me down, returning a moment later with a fresh towel, some water, and ointment.

"How can you even want to be here?" I asked.

He didn't answer me, not straight away at least. He remained quiet for a few moments like he was gathering his thoughts, and then he looked up at me.

"I won't deny that I'm hurt." He swallowed hard and returned his attention to my hands. "And I can't begin to imagine what went on in that house. But I can understand needing to feel human, in any way possible with whomever possible."

The more he spoke, the more I felt humiliated.

He stopped what he was doing and looked up at me.

"Do you care about him?" he asked.

My heart fell through the floor, and I looked down at my hands in his.

"Because I can…I understand—"

"No." I shook my head. "Not like that."

"Okay."

He returned his gaze to the bandage he was applying and continued working in silence.

"Do you love her?" I asked.

"No, Ace."

For a moment we looked at each other.

"You didn't come here to fix my hands."

"No, I came to talk to you about something."

He squeezed some cold cream onto my hand and gently massaged it onto my skin before tentatively bandaging it. As he moved onto my other hand, he looked up at me.

"Anna told me she spoke with you."

So that's what this was about.

I was getting ready to argue, when he stopped me with a gentle squeeze of my thigh.

"She knows you're hurting and God knows this isn't how I wanted you to meet. I'm sorry."

"Yeah, ambush wasn't on my bingo card for today."

A ghost of a smile crept across his lips.

He was calm, his eyes conveyed that too in the way they searched me completely, focusing on my face and my reactions.

"Why won't you talk to me?" he asked.

"What am I meant to say, Illarion?" I asked, struck by the way my voice shook. "In all honesty, what do you want me to say?"

He bowed his head for a moment as he finished bandaging my other hand. "The truth, Ace. Please. Tell me why you're shutting me out and don't say it's because you've changed. I don't believe that."

For a moment, we sat in silence, my hands in my lap and his eyes seeing right into my soul until I couldn't take it anymore. I got up, pushing past him, and walked toward the door.

"Please don't." His voice caught me off guard. "Don't walk away from me, don't run."

I stopped.

That moment cost me. Before I could move, he was behind me, his proximity stealing my breath and what should have set my nerves on edge, instead made my heart race.

I turned.

His hands gently circled my wrists and then his eyes found mine. He was seeking permission to be close, to touch me, to be near me.

When he looked at me like that, I couldn't think straight. I closed my eyes, composing myself.

He knew that I wasn't afraid of him, of being close but he still wanted to be sure I was comfortable and that was exactly why we could never get back what we lost. When he looked at me, he would always see that fear in my eyes. He was right back at the Southport Motel even if I didn't know it then.

"Tell me to leave, Ace, tell me to stop chasing you but don't stop talking to me. Tell me what to do."

When I opened my eyes, his were filled with apprehension and fear.

"I don't know where to start." I laughed nervously.

"I hurt you," he began, dropping my hands from his. "For that, I can never apologize enough. Tell me what you're feeling."

"We hurt each other," I corrected. "When I read about Anna, God. It broke me."

Illarion's eyes darkened, and he rubbed his hand across his mouth.

"I know I have no right to say that, after what I did with Daniel but I can't pretend it didn't hurt a lot, Ila."

He nodded, letting out a long breath.

"I held onto hope." I wet my lips. "It's all that got me through the nights when the Serum wore off but after that night...after I read that..."

"You started to let go."

The words burned between us like acid. He knew it, I knew it. It was a sick, shameful secret I harbored, one I never wanted to admit.

"You were my salvation, Illarion, I saw your eyes when I closed mine. I felt your touch when I was screaming to stop feeling his and when it was over, I imagined that you were holding me, not Daniel.

"I wished it was you who was there to pick up the pieces when I couldn't stand anymore. But after some time, I wanted it to be Daniel. I wanted to know that someone was taking care of me, that someone still wanted me even after Dalca...after he was done with me."

Tears slipped from his eyes, falling over his cheeks as he opened and then closed his mouth. Pain flowed through him. I shouldn't have said any of the things I did. I shouldn't have let him feel the pain but something inside me felt like he needed to feel it. When his heart cracked with hurt, I was shocked at the relief I felt. What was wrong with me?

My hands shook with each shallow breath I drew in, it was soul crushing like a sickening, twisting pain coiling in the pit of my belly. It was like a shitty breakup, only this was worse, it was a choice made for us when we'd both been stripped of the ability to make our own.

"Is that what you needed to hear?" I asked. "I don't hate you or Anna, or what happened but I can't say that I'm okay with it because, in all honesty, Illarion, I don't know how to move past this. I don't know that we can. We both screwed up."

He started to say something, but nothing came out. I reached up and cupped his cheek.

"I forgive you, Illarion, and I hope that someday, you can forgive me. But we can't do this. What we had, what we *were*—that's in the past."

"Ace—"

"I'm not the same girl, Ila. I don't even know who I am, but she needs to learn how to live again. She needs to learn how to smile and laugh, and right now, that's all I can do. That's all I have strength for."

His eyes left mine and the pain pulsing beneath the surface rolling between us doubled. Illarion was breaking.

"Please understand. Please give me space."

"Is that what you need from me?"

"Yes. Right now, I need you to leave me alone."

He nodded. He was shattered but he didn't fight me.

Ending the conversation on my terms, I turned from him and pulled the door open. I stopped for a second and turned back.

"I know this isn't how things were meant to be and I wish to God we had more time before..." I wet my lips. "I'm sorry I broke your heart Illarion."

His lips slowly parted but nothing came out. As if it took great effort, as if it was the hardest thing to do, he looked down, letting me walk away.

CHAPTER SIXTEEN

ACE

I looked down at my hands as I washed the blood from my knuckles. Illarion's bandages did their job, but I'd bled through anyway.

Just as I was getting ready to take a shower, a tap on the door drew my attention.

"Punk, it's me." Aurel's voice carried through the door. "Can I come in?"

"Sure." I got up with a grin, pulling the door open.

"Want to go for a walk?"

"Now?"

"Why the hell not?" He shrugged. "The gardens are lit up like a circus."

I smirked, glancing across at the window. The sun was low on the horizon but there was still some light. "Let's take a walk then."

The warm night was alive with the sound of insects nesting in the floral oasis and birds soaring high above. Aurel led me toward the garden, keeping the conversation light.

"I heard you met Anna," he said.

"You heard right."

"Damn. How did that go?"

"As good as it could have."

When we reached the benches, he sat down while I made my way to the wall of roses, plucking one free.

"Didn't see her at the house." I said, sitting down beside him. "Where is she?"

"Illarion asked her to consider spending less time here."

"How'd she take that?"

"She gets it."

I wet my lips and nodded. Bet she did. I chastised myself and reined it in. At least he didn't know the other part of the story.

"When she started coming here, I didn't want to see it. I knew where it was going. He was drinking so much," Aurel said, quietly, keeping his eyes ahead.

My throat constricted.

"Ace, he loves you."

"I know he does."

"But you don't want that anymore?"

"Want isn't the word I'd use."

"Then what?"

"I don't know."

Silence descended in the garden and for a moment he didn't speak until he looked across at me.

"When he told me who'd taken you, I knew it was bad. Knew we'd all been played, and you ended up paying the price for it."

"You can't even imagine, Aurel."

His jaw squared and he shook his head.

As he continued trying to pry through my shield, I got up and walked toward the flowers and focused on keeping my heart rate in check.

All I had to do was concentrate on here and now, breathing and making sure he didn't see anything I didn't want him to.

A shift inside me that felt all too familiar and terrifying made my breath catch.

Then Dalca's voice came into focus like a taunt inside my head.

He'd been pushing at my barrier the second I learned how to hold it up.

He still had no idea where I was at any given time but he did manage to break through my walls for a few seconds at a time when I wasn't concentrating. I snapped my eyes down to my feet so he couldn't see anything identifiable and work out where I was.

"You're damaged, Acacia. The sooner you understand that the sooner you'll stop damaging those around you."

"Get out of my head!" I hissed.

Aurel shifted behind me. "What?"

"Nothing," I said quickly, smoothing my hand over my hair.

I was two steps away from looking like a lunatic.

Dalca was gone. I'd forced him out of my brain. How the hell was he still able to get into my head? I ground my jaw, focusing on Aurel once I was sure it was safe. I exhaled through my nose.

Aurel's brows were knotted.

"You okay?" he asked.

"Fine."

"You sure because I'm pretty sure I heard you say something."

"Just talking to myself."

"Right. That's totally normal."

"Totally." I smirked, keeping the mood light.

He dropped it.

I turned my attention on the flowers surrounding me, trying to ground myself. God, that was too close. He was getting too ballsy.

No more than a few seconds passed before Aurel was behind me, I could feel the heaviness in his step as he gently turned me so that we were face to face.

"You sure you're okay?" he asked again.

"I told you I'm fine."

He stepped in, closing the space between us. A small, non-existent distance separated us. That same, intoxicating feeling shot through me. What in God's name was happening?

"Something is definitely blocking you from me."

"What is it?" Panic surged through me. Could he see Dalca picking through my brain?

He frowned, searching deeper. "Can't tell but it's strong. I'm worried."

"Don't be, I'm all good. I promise."

He exhaled, the crease in his brow told me he didn't believe me.

He dropped it though, then stepped closer making my breath catch and a warm fuzzy feeling to spread through me. I was confused, suffering from PTSD, that was it.

I wasn't suddenly developing romantic feelings for Aurel. But as his eyes found mine and the raging storm in the ocean blue orbs intensified, I wondered whether it was always there but hidden away because I was so taken by Illarion.

No, that was ridiculous, I told myself. But the more I allowed myself to see him, the more my mind wandered to his eyes, his lazily messy but gorgeous hair...He looked just like when I'd seen him last, he still wore his dark blonde hair half up half down, those dimples in his cheeks when he smiled were gorgeous, but that glint in his eye was missing. He was torn and tired, these last six months had re-shaped him.

Not only was his mind all over the place with worry for me, but the red head also made an appearance as well.

He stopped my racing thoughts when he reached up and gently traced his thumb along my lower lip. I didn't react and for a moment he didn't either. We were both frozen and stunned. Then, in a heartbeat, his hands were on my hips, pulling me toward him and then his lips were on mine and my mind snapped from pure euphoria as I kissed him back into pure panic mode.

It took a second flat for me to absolutely lose it.

He pushed me back against the wall, trying to slip his hand under my shirt and when I finally found my voice, a choked cry escaped.

Regaining some higher reasoning took more effort than I cared to admit. I pressed my hands flat to his chest and I pushed him back until he stumbled. His expression changed when he, too, realized what he had just done.

Holy hell.

I covered my mouth with my hand, sucking in long, greedy breaths trying to calm myself down.

A series of shallow gasps came out before I could stop them and all I could do was clutch at my chest, trying to steady my breathing. And then the tears came.

What the hell was wrong with me and what had just happened here?

"Ace, I, I'm so sorry." A quick flash of remorse shot through him. He moved toward me, and I stammered backwards. "Ace. I don't know why I did that, Ace, you have to believe me."

"Don't, please just don't."

I pressed my hands to my face and sucked in a deep breath.

There had to be an explanation. Something that made sense on some level because right now, the only thing I knew was that I was terrified of my best friend, horrified of being in the same space as him.

When he stepped toward me, I shot him a look before turning on my heels.

The back of my eyes burned as I walked through the garden back to the mansion where I saw Illarion, seated on the steps. Anna was right there beside him. So much for asking her to spend less time here. For the love of God.

Illarion got up as I approached and, as soon as I found his eyes, he knew something had shaken me. His gaze darted up and behind me locking onto Aurel.

Before I could take a second to register what he was doing, he was already halfway across the courtyard, speeding past me and rushing Aurel.

Oh no. This was going to be bad.

"Stop!" I finally found my voice as I ran back toward the entrance to the garden. "Don't!"

Illarion had knocked him to the ground, but Aurel was quick and in one, precise move he pushed Illarion off and threw a punch, hitting Illarion square in the jaw.

Both men grunted as each went for a hit the other might not anticipate.

"What the hell were you thinking?" Illarion yelled, as he tried breathlessly to regain his composure.

"I didn't mean it!"

"Didn't mean it?" Illarion clipped. "You're out of your mind."

Aurel's eyes flared with anger, but neither were about to stop.

I screamed when Aurel rushed Illarion and when another fist met Illarion's jaw, throwing him backwards, I screamed for them both to stop.

Illarion ran at him, throwing his weight around Aurel's midsection and they both went into the ground, hard, sending pebbles flying in different directions.

"How the hell could you do that?" Illarion shouted, pressing his forearm against Aurel's throat.

When Aurel shoved him off he scrambled to his feet. "Let me explain!"

"Explain how you came onto her?" Illarion shot back and rushed him again.

When Illarion moved again, I ran at Aurel who was closest to me and reached for his arm. He jerked backwards so quickly that his shoulder slammed into mine, tripping me. If I wasn't standing on uneven surface, I would have been able to steady myself, I would have been able to recover but thanks to my already unstable state of being, I felt myself falling.

Time slowed, much like it did at the warehouse—I saw the edge of brick path as clearly as I would have seen it if I was casually walking by.

Illarion's eyes met mine for the briefest moment as he reached out to catch me. His fingertips brushed mine, slipping through my fingers

He knew what was coming. I knew what was coming and neither of us could stop it.

I hit the ground. Hard.

A blinding pain shot through me, silencing the scream about to erupt from my lips.

Broken, shattered cries came out instead as Illarion hovered over me, his trembling hands afraid to touch me.

"Don't move, Ace, don't move."

I tried to nod, but nothing happened, nothing at all. Oh God.

"Call the medics now!" he shouted to Aurel who was already halfway to the house.

Daniel dropped to his knees beside us. Anna stood, shaking behind him, tears brimming in her eyes. When did they get here? Had they seen the whole thing?

Sweat broke out across my face, and I felt it mixing in with my tears.

Unable to move a single muscle, I lay sprawled out across the path while Illarion's hands gently brushed my cheeks.

"They're on the way, just hold on."

I was completely stunned. His panicked eyes found mine as his hands brushed my hair free from my face.

"Everything's going to be okay. Just keep your eyes on me, Lyubov."

The pain inside me twisted into angry, tight coils. I wanted to tell him that I was sorry and that I was scared but when I opened my mouth, all that came out, were whimpers.

"Don't try to speak, just look at me, that's it, keep your eyes on me," Illarion said gently, trying to force a smile.

As the approaching sirens got louder I felt my vision darken pulling me under.

And then I heard it. The quietest, faintest whisper of words. Words from a voice I recognized from long ago, from the warehouse right before I died. My brain struggled to focus, but the same melodic tone beckoned and called to me.

"You need to let go and trust us."

CHAPTER SEVENTEEN

ILLARION

I stood back as the medics rushed in, getting to work.

If I didn't rush Aurel, she wouldn't have been trying to stop us. This was just as much my fault as it was his.

I couldn't swallow the lump in my throat and, whenever I tried to speak, my voice broke.

One of the medics walked over to me, guiding me to speak in private.

"We've stabilized her spine but, from what I can gauge as a preliminary assessment, it's not looking good, Agent Lazarev."

I bit down on my lip, forcing my eyes to remain focused. "Will she be okay?"

"We can't make any assessments until we've completed all the scans. For now, I think it's best to keep her sedated until we know more."

As each word passed between us, my heart grew heavier and heavier.

He placed a gentle hand on my shoulder and led me to the ambulance. When I was cleared to do so, I climbed in after them and sat down as close to her as I could.

A short breath came free when I saw the brace around her neck, holding her firmly against the stretcher. Her eyes were closed but they moved rapidly under her lids.

The medic who met me inside looked up before taping an IV to the inside of Ace's elbow. "We'll run a full workup when we reach the hospital."

I nodded wordlessly.

She gave me a sympathetic smile. "These other injuries, Agent Lazarev?"

"POW situation. She returned home a few weeks ago."

"Understood. Has she had a medical assessment?"

"Not yet."

"I'll make sure we check her over. Some of these wounds look like they could use some attention."

I nodded my understanding.

We had been riding in the ambulance for just over ten minutes when we finally slowed down and pulled into the hospital.

In a matter of seconds, the medics had the stretcher down and rushing off toward the larger, emergency doors.

"You'll have to wait by the ER."

I nodded and fell back, watching as Ace disappeared behind the glass.

Aurel's footsteps drew my attention, before he said a word, I turned on my heel and faced him. He was only a foot away, but whatever he saw in my eyes made him stop whatever he was about to say.

"What in the hell were you thinking?" I hissed.

"Illarion, listen to me. I don't know what came over me."

"You expect me to believe that?"

"Believe that I would never hurt her!" his voice rose. "You know me."

I stepped toward him, closing the distance until only a foot remained. "I don't want you here now. Go home."

"Brother, please."

"No," I hissed, lowering my voice when I noticed we'd drawn attention. "You know what she's been through. Why would you do that?"

"I honestly have no idea, Illarion. You have to believe me. My mind went blank, I don't know what I was doing."

"That's for damn sure."

His gaze was wide and disbelieving. When I searched his eyes and his mind, for any sign of what happened I was shocked to find nothing at all. He was completely blank, just like he'd said. It was strange, as though his mind was warped and wiped. I'd never felt that before. I exhaled sharply through my nose and shook my head at him.

"I can't do this right now. Go home."

When he finally accepted that there was nothing he could say to justify what he'd done, he let out a breath and backed down. He nodded, glancing at the viewing window, then back at me.

"Brother, I'm so sorry."

"Go home."

After what seemed like an eternity, he finally turned and left.

The breath I had been holding in finally broke free and I found myself walking back to the window as though it were my only tie to her.

My eyes caught movement down the corridor and a relieved sigh found my lips. Elena and Michael pushed through the double doors.

Elena wrapped her arms around my shoulders, giving me a quick look.

"Illarion, where is she?" Michael asked gently.

Nodding to the surgery, I kept my eyes averted.

"Have you heard anything?" Michael asked.

Shaking my head, I pulled back from Elena.

He nodded, squeezing my shoulder. "I'll find a doctor."

Not more than ten minutes had passed since Michael left when I saw him coming down the hall with a surgeon who unfortunately wasn't Donna. She was on leave, and she wouldn't be back for a few days.

Focusing on them, I tried to get a read on their thoughts, but they were both silent. Damn the Agency and their hospitals. Everyone was secretive here, using wards to protect their thoughts.

"Agents." The surgeon nodded to us before gesturing for me to follow him to an office at the end of the hall.

My heart thundered in my chest as each step grew harder. I didn't need to read his thoughts to know.

He closed the door behind us as we each took a seat in the provided chairs.

He looked to me first and proceeded with the usual apology, then he told us the news and then I didn't take in a single, other word as my mind assaulted me with a million different scenarios where I saved her, where I managed to catch her, where I was quick enough and close enough.

She would never walk again. She would never use her arms again. She would be considered lucky to live at all.

I leaned back in the chair and felt my body go cold.

Elena's hand found mine and squeezed. The gesture was alien. Her fingers trembled, and I didn't dare look at her. She was crying.

"Her healing," I said promptly. "She'll heal, won't she? Like always, our DNA—hers is stronger."

The surgeon gave me a pointed look and Michael gently squeezed my shoulder, bringing my attention to him.

"Sensitive's DNA doesn't work as it should when it's suppressed."

Elena sighed. "She still has traces of Serum in her veins, Illarion."

Of course. I knew that. The tangy taste of fear coated my insides. She was still detoxing from Dalca's hell house. Her abilities weren't just suppressed by Serum though, there was heroin too. I saw firsthand how much that had taken a toll on her mind and considering how long she was exposed to the potent doses; it was no wonder there were still traces in her system.

"There's something we can try," Michael said, rising from his seat.

My eyes shot up, catching his, I watched as he and Elena exchanged knowing glances ignoring the surgeon who shook his head.

"Yes. It can work," Elena said.

"What? What can work? What are you talking about?"

The surgeon interrupted me. "It's nothing short of expecting a miracle."

Michael slammed his palm on the table, rattling the kinetic sticks into motion. "It can't make her any worse!"

My eyes darted between the two men until Elena finally stood up. A woman like her had a certain poise that commanded silence and attention. Both men went quiet.

"I'll speak to her, I'll ask her," she said.

"She's unconscious," the surgeon said firmly, sitting back down.

"She's my niece, I can communicate with her. I'll explain it."

"Explain what? What are you talking about?" I shot.

When neither of them answered, I looked back to the surgeon who averted his gaze from me and found a keen interest in the kinetic sticks twirling in front of him.

Michael pressed a hand to my back and forced my attention to him. "The Celestial Beings."

Elena looked at me with hope in her eyes.

I found myself shaking my head before I even answered. "Absolutely not, we can't rely on them."

"Anything is worth a shot," Elena's voice was weak.

"They have done nothing for us." Anger and frustration coupled with how damn exhausted I was, took over. "Look at what they've allowed her to live through!"

"We don't know how they work," Elena said.

"That's a damn understatement. They can't be trusted," I snapped.

The surgeon looked at me apologetically and I rubbed my eyes dropping back into the chair.

"I can't condone these pseudo medicines, but she is your niece, Elena, do what you must. Just don't drag this young man down this path and give him false hope."

She nodded her thanks and before I could form another thought, she pulled me to my feet and dragged me outside.

"This will work," she whispered to me. "I know it will."

CHAPTER EIGHTEEN

ACE

First the sound came back, and then the heat and, finally, the light as I cracked my eyes open.

I forced my gaze around the familiar, dreamlike state I knew all too well, it surrounded me as it came in like a thick, dense fog.

As panic shot through me, a monitor somewhere near me, out of view, came to life. I tried to look for it, but I couldn't move. I tried to get up, but nothing worked. That's when the proverbial shit hit the fan. I lost it. My insides churned, and I barely managed to suck in oxygen and then came the full-blown panic attack.

My heart sped up until the machine beside me seemed to cease beeping and, instead, it became one long, continuous wail. I wanted to scream or kick and shout but nothing, *nothing* happened. I was sure my heart was going to explode.

I sucked in a deep breath and closed my eyes and when I opened them, a soft, gentle voice sounded beside me.

"Try to stay calm."

My eyes flicked up and found a pair of stunning, green eyes, much like my own and much like my mom's.

"Elena."

She smiled, pulling up a chair beside me and swept her hand across my cheek, just like mom always did.

I blinked back the wetness in my eyes.

"You look so much like your mother, Sweetheart."

My heart swelled as dark brown hair tumbled over her shoulders framing her beautiful face. She was tall and elegant just like my mom had been. Somehow, I'd missed the height in the gene mix.

"You've been so brave."

"I'm so scared," I whimpered.

"Oh, Ace, I know you are, Sweetheart."

Closing my eyes, I felt the tears break through my lashes, wetting my cheeks as they fell.

"It's really bad, isn't it? This isn't just a dream."

Before I even asked, I knew what the answer would be. Elena shifted beside me and pressed her hand to my cheek, wiping the tears that had fallen.

Her eyes were warm, they drew me in and within the deep, green pools I saw hope and determination.

I looked away and squeezed my eyes shut, forcing the tears to stay put.

"Please, don't let Ila see me like this. I don't want him to see me."

Her hand stilled against my cheek.

When I opened my eyes again and found hers, she smiled and this time the smile wasn't filled with sadness.

"I promise. I won't let him see you."

I nodded against the pillow and then a question formed on my mind. *How did I not think of this before?* "How are you here? In my head?"

She moved across to the other side of my bed and sat by my side.

"Only people with the same bloodline are able to enter your mind when it's sedated the way you are. There are of course artificial ways we can induce these visits but not in this case."

"Why are you here?" I asked, my voice hoarse.

A little of my world shattered when she pressed her hand to my cheek again. "There's something we can try. I can't promise that it will work."

"Anything is better than this…do it…whatever it is."

"Okay." Her voice was quiet as she leaned in and pressed a kiss to my forehead. "Close your eyes, Sweetheart. Don't open them until you're asked to."

Taking a deep breath, I did as she said. My eyes drifted shut and, as soon as they did, the atmosphere shifted, and the surrounding energy moved. Elena had moved away and another person… no, it wasn't a person it was something else entirely, joined us. I'd never felt anything like it. It was powerful, both heat and cold radiated from it as it moved around the room.

When it stopped, I felt the air around us thicken, it went completely silent save for the quiet breaths coming from whatever was beside me.

I really wanted to open my eyes, I wanted to see what *it* was.

Without warning, I felt it touch me.

A cold, smooth hand fell to my forehead, and another lifted my head and came to a stop at the nape of my neck.

Slowly, the cool touch warmed and an intense heat radiated through me. Through both points where it was touching me, pressure built, and before I could prepare for what happened next, I was sucked back in time.

I was watching myself in Iraq, kissing a man I'd loved. I was ambushed and tortured and then I was at the Agency, meeting Illarion and, eventually we were at his home and Aurel's and then the warehouse. I watched myself dying and waking up at the Taker's house.

Tears slipped through my closed eyes as memories assaulted me, hammering the pain right back when I thought it was lost and finally, the time traveling me, was facing Illarion. It was only yesterday, when

I told him I was numb, that I didn't feel anything anymore. As though a plug was ripped from the bottom of the ocean, the emotions came flooding back, roaring and crashing into me in a flurry of motion.

Everything I'd blocked from the Taker's house came flooding back, all the rage and fear, the helplessness and weakness. All the times I thought death would be better than a life there, and the shame. I wanted to scream; a scream so complete from the depths of my soul but I couldn't. Whatever was in the room with me was so strong it stopped everything and blocked it from rising to the surface.

Then I was standing face to face with Dalca, but it wasn't a memory, it was real, it was right here and right now. My heart raced so fast I thought I was going to die.

"You play a dangerous game, Divine," a disembodied melodic voice said.

Dalca grinned and before he could reply, a thunderous, powerful jolt reverberated all around me like an earthquake and one, quick flash exploded, then Dalca was gone.

I was back in my body, lying in the bed, with its hands on me.

"Open your eyes." The voice was far away, but it echoed clearly in my head and the familiarity struck me. It was *the* voice. The one I heard at the warehouse and again just before I blacked out.

When I did, I was startled by the bright, silver eyes staring back at me.

"It was Dalca…" I heard myself whisper.

"The Divine had planted himself in your mind. He's gone now."

Planted himself in my brain? I felt sick all over again.

"Was that real?"

"Yes, in a different plane. Where he can find you. You're free of him now."

The Being moved over me, the angelic, translucent face looked masculine with a strong, sharp jaw and aquiline nose as though it was chiseled of stone.

From the corner of my eye, I saw Elena clutching my hand in hers. I still couldn't feel it, but I could feel the heat spreading inside me. Whatever *he*, if they went by our binary rules did, was bringing back all the other feelings and emotions I seemed to have lost.

The face broke out into a smile. "Yes, Solaris and I go by your binary rules. I am a male and she; my half is female."

I closed my mouth.

He lowered his face close to mine and stopped an inch from me, his silver eyes deepened to a gunmetal grey as he narrowed his gaze. I suppressed a gasp as he rapidly moved closer still, I could see right through him.

His lips were moving in rapid succession murmuring something so low I couldn't make out a single word.

Beside us, Elena moved. "Can you help her, Aaryon your Divinity?"

The Being moved his head slightly, yet his eyes never left mine. "She's been through a great deal."

My breath caught, his voice was comforting and terrifying all at once.

"I can see the Darkness coursing through her. Because of it she is dangerous."

I didn't dare look away from him, my eyes widened as he drew his hands away from me and pressed them on either side of my face.

"The pain is feeding the Darkness."

His words rang true, somehow. The Darkness was growing inside me, I'd felt it for months, slowly building and simmering, threatening to take over at any point.

Aaryan's eyes narrowed burning through me, I could feel him inside me, poking and prodding through all the deepest, darkest corners of my soul where Dalca had been. All the things I hated about myself were dredged up, brought to the surface, like all the years I worked on keeping them hidden were nothing at all. He found them, pulled them out and tossed them aside without any effort at all.

My eyes brimmed with tears.

"She's powerful," he said, again only this time he pulled back and broke his hold on me.

As soon as he did, I felt the compulsion break. God, he was strong. I'd never felt anything like it.

It was like the Serum only this was via thought, and not even in person, he was in my head.

My mind reeled until it stopped, and Elena's words came to the front of my mind.

Only people with the same bloodline are able to enter your mind when it's sedated the way you are.

And then, as though it was the only thing which made sense, I realized what he was. The Celestial Being I descended from.

Elena came to my side once again drawing me out of my thoughts.

"Will you help her?"

He looked down at me and nodded. "We will help the Divine Sensitive."

"Thank you, so much, Aaryon, your Divinity."

He cast her a quick look before returning his gaze to me.

The breath I was holding, escaped in a shaky whimper.

Elena pressed her hand to my cheek and smiled. "I'll see you when you wake up, sweetheart."

When she was gone Aaryon, and I were left alone.

"Why are you helping me?"

He stepped around to the other side of the bed and folded his arms across his chest. Now that he was in full view and I could see him from my limited range of motion, I saw that he was dressed much like anyone else. The dark jeans he had on, hung perfectly on his hips and the T-shirt he wore showed off every muscle on his body. If you could get past the translucent skin and the myriad of geometric tattoos lining his upper body, he looked quite normal.

"There is a prophecy of which I'm sure you're aware?"

"Yes."

"It states that a Divine Sensitive will be born to battle the original if the balance is tipped." He paused looking at me before continuing. "We weren't sure you were the one, but we had to keep you safe until we were certain."

My breath caught as he stood beside me, his hand resting on the pillow.

"A young healer told us of you. She told us you were noble and on a quest to help those you love even when you foresaw your path leading you to Death's door."

"I don't understand."

His lips broke into a smile, and, in that moment, he was the most beautiful thing I had ever seen. His body seemed to glow from within, illuminating the marks across his translucent skin. The kindness radiated from deep inside and enveloped me like a big, warm hug. Tears poured out of me and I couldn't stop them even if I tried.

The emotions were running rampant thanks to whatever he did to unblock the dam.

"Faith told us that you helped her. Faith told us you are the one we've been waiting for."

Tears pricked my eyes. The little girl from St Augustine's.

"You must know, Divine Sensitive, this won't be easy for you. Mere Sensitives are not built to withstand such pain which will find you, but with the essence of the moon that runs though you, you should be able to."

Should be. That was comforting. I bit down on my lip and found his eyes, they shifted from dark to light to completely white. Without a word, he reached down for my arms and folded them across my chest.

I watched as one hand snaked behind my back and his other landed on the nape of my neck.

"Close your eyes."

I obeyed and braced myself.

As much as I tried to prepare, nothing would have readied me for what came next.

"Take a deep breath."

Before I could register what he'd just said he began to murmur, fast and low, too quick and too quiet to hear and then the pain exploded behind my eyes piercing my skull, reaching right into the parts of me I'd kept safe and close.

My breath was stolen from me as I screamed feeling the heat tear through me, ripping me apart from the inside as each nerve ending fired all at once.

I felt the tears before I knew they were falling and before I could scream again, I was silenced.

White light exploded behind my eyes and then the darkness came.

My name was called, but it was so far away.

The pain and horror mounted and grew until I couldn't feel anything but the chaos inside me.

As my body began to fall, drifting off into nothingness, I heard my name again. I felt the pain of loss, of fear. Then I felt nothing at all.

CHAPTER NINETEEN

ILLARION

Elena was with Ace for more than an hour, I kept glancing down at my watch impatiently and then back at Michael who, too, looked restless.

He was married to Elena for more than thirty years and knew Ace since she was born. It hurt me to think how hard it would have been for them to be excluded from her life.

Ace's parents had done the right thing to protect their child, but the fact remained, Elena and Michael had missed out on Ace.

They missed out on seeing her grow up and go to school. They never saw her learn to play sports or get in trouble in class. They missed out on seeing her rebellious years which made me smile, knowing that she had, in fact, had many rebellious years. Most importantly, they missed out on having her in their lives.

Michael moved to my left, drawing my attention. I followed his gaze to the room where Elena emerged. We both got up and strode over to her.

Her tired eyes were filled with tears but her mind was secure, I couldn't get a read on anything.

She smiled weakly and nodded. "They agreed to help her."

I allowed myself to finally smile.

Elena stepped closer to me and gently brought her hands to mine. In that small gesture, I felt the weight of the world shift.

"This will be hard on her. Aaryon spared me from the details. She's going to need you when she wakes up."

I nodded, pulling back. "I'm not going anywhere."

A lump formed in my throat when I thought about all that she'd been through. Bozhe, she had been through too much, much more than anyone deserved to see and experience.

"I'm sure Aurel would like to be updated." Michael wrapped an arm around my shoulder and smiled.

My heart sunk, Aurel. I let myself forget, or maybe I forced myself to forget. But Michael was right, it wasn't fair on him, it wasn't his fault, and it was something I had to talk to him about, in person.

Michael squeezed my shoulder. "Go and make things right between you and Aurel."

Before I could argue, I was led down the corridor and into Elena's car. She dropped the keys into my hand.

"Come back when you're done, not sooner."

I ground my teeth and nodded. In our world, where life and death were merely states of being, friends and family were more important than anything else.

I shifted the BMW into gear and took it out onto the main road, heading for home.

Only now, as I drove, and the adrenaline had died down did I feel the bruise along my jaw. Aurel had landed several good blows to my face, and I was afraid to think what damage I had done to him in my fit of rage.

I took the final turn onto the gravel path and slowed as I reached the gates. Keying in my code, I drove down toward my house.

As I slowed, coming to a stop, I spotted Aurel. He sat with his back against my front door with one knee drawn to his chest where his head rested. Elena must have told him I was on my way.

I turned the car off and stepped outside composing myself. Aurel got to his feet.

I didn't give him a chance to speak. Instead, I stuffed my hands into my pockets and looked at him.

"Elena asked the Celestial Beings to help her."

"What did they say?"

"They agreed to help," I added.

"Thank God."

The tension inside him snapped. Slowly, he backed up into the door and slid down to the ground.

"I don't blame you. I know whatever happened was an accident. I want you to know that," I said. "Elena will keep you updated."

***

ACE

A quiet, almost inaudible sigh woke me. My eyes fluttered open and darted around the room trying to gauge exactly where I was. As they landed on the small, open window a pang of pain shot through my head. God, that was bright. I drew my hands to my face. Then it hit me, *my hands moved.* I sucked in a deep breath and looked down at my legs, I tried wriggling my toes, and when the blanket at the end of the bed moved, I choked back a sob.

Fragments of the last few days came back to me in bits and pieces. *How much time had passed?*

I slowly, and very carefully, swung my legs over the side then stopped when I saw Illarion.

He was sleeping so peacefully that I considered not waking him. But I wanted him to see me, I wanted to feel him and hold him. I wanted to throw myself into his arms. I wanted things to be how they were before.

Carefully I tested my legs. First one and then the other. A fierce tingling spread through me as the pressure subsided and when I was sure I wouldn't fall flat on my face, I quietly padded over to him and knelt. Every movement was like a fresh slice of pain, but I pushed through.

Silent tears fell as I took him in. It was as though I hadn't seen him for months. God, whatever Aaryon did to me to unblock my feelings was as much a miracle as was the fact that I was standing and walking again.

I closed my eyes for a moment and searched the dark space inside where I'd previously felt Dalca and when I came up totally empty, I grinned to myself.

I was me again. Just Ace.

It was the truest form of fear, remembering how it felt not to have anything inside me, to not feel love or hate and have Dalca poking and prodding through my brain whenever he felt like it. There was nothing that terrified me more than touching Illarion and not feeling a damned thing.

I gently brushed my fingers along the violent bruise that spanned from his jaw down to his neck.

When he stirred, I moved my hand and waited.

After what felt like an eternity, his eyes opened and as soon as they found mine, a quick flicker of pure and unfiltered awe flashed through his eyes.

He didn't speak as he reached for me and found my cheeks. He finally smiled and brushed my tears with his thumbs as he helped me to my feet.

"I love you, Illarion." I reached up and cupped his cheek, feeling the stubble of his beard tickle my hand. "I love you, more than you could ever know. And I'm so sorry about Daniel, I'm so sorry about the things I said."

"Lyubov." He smiled, sweeping his hands over my arms. "I told you before, I'm not going anywhere Ace, as long as you want me here, I'm here."

CHAPTER TWENTY

ACE

It had been close to two weeks since my accident and Aaryon's magical healing spectacular. It wasn't an instantaneous fix to cure me of all my ailments, instead he kind of boosted my Divine Sensitive healing gene, giving me back what the Serum took.

Illarion walked by my side, gently helping me with each new step. I was practically learning to walk again. The pain was as fierce as I imagined it would be. The crutches dug into my underarms as I pressed my weight onto them.

A low, calculated breath escaped my lips as I gripped the crutch, taking each step one by one, up to his front door. Most of the evening was spent walking around the garden trying to get me stronger.

"Are you ready?"

Was I? I sucked in a breath and looked up at him, his eyes full of confidence in me.

"Can't wait out here forever, can I?" I whispered, hyperaware of the tingles spreading through my legs.

"Maybe having everyone over is too soon."

"No, dinner will be fine. I just need a minute."

"I'm not worried about dinner, Ace. This is the first time you're seeing everyone. I'm worried that you're putting too much pressure on yourself."

"I'm not. I just want to see my friends and have a quiet meal. It'll be fine."

"Okay then." He nodded, gesturing ahead.

Each moment my muscles and bones held me up was agony, each motion was torture.

I winced as a jarring pain consumed me. My toes had started going numb. I moved instinctively to the door for support.

Illarion held onto me. I let my hand hover over his arm afraid that if another wave of pain rocked me, I'd hurt him.

"I can take the pain from you, Ace."

"Absolutely not."

I heard him sigh and then his arms were around me. "Why?"

"Because it's horrible, no one should have to go through this."

"I would, for you, without a second thought."

"I know. And I love you for it, but I'm not letting you do that again, just help me get through this walk. Please."

"Of course." He sighed.

My eyes watered when I applied pressure on my left leg. I suppressed a hiss and grit my teeth. I felt the wetness in my eyes, clinging heavily to my lashes, before the anger began to bubble. Illarion tightened his hold on me.

"It's okay, Ace. You're doing really well; we knew this would be hard."

Once I was sure I could look at him without completely breaking into a fit of frustrated tears, I swallowed hard and looked up.

"Hard is a fucking understatement."

"Here," he said, gently taking the crutch from me. "Lean on me, I'll take your weight, you just focus on the motion."

"Got it."

Through the pain pulsing through my body and the tears in my eyes, I focused and pushed on. Illarion was by my side through every painful step.

Trying to convince him that I was fine was harder than convincing myself. Feeling his emotions clashing against mine was even harder.

We slowed as we reached the end of the hallway.

Chatter filled the room behind the closed door. Aurel and Anna were there chatting loudly, and Elena and Michael were laughing with Daniel about something he'd said earlier. A smile found my lips. It was all so *normal.*

Illarion stopped us a few doors away and turned me to face him.

"We don't have to do this," he said, looking down into my eyes.

"I can't put this off forever."

"You know they'd understand if you needed more time."

Tightening my hold on his arm, I looked up at him.

"I can do this."

He didn't say anymore. Instead, he handed the crutches back to me then stepped away, letting me move forward on my own. I gripped them tightly. My bones screamed in protest and beads of sweat broke out across my face.

I let out an even breath, focusing on each step rather than the pain.

As we neared, Illarion moved ahead and pulled the door open. The chatter died down and Daniel shot to his feet first, moving cautiously over to us but stopping a few feet away.

Elena's eyes swept across me, I forced a smile looking over at Michael. He nodded, smiling back.

As Aurel pushed past them, he stopped a tentative foot away, briefly locking eyes with Illarion. There was so much tension between them that it made my head feel like it was splitting in two. To ease him, I moved forward, trying my best to grin.

"I am so sorry." His voice broke.

227

If I could have slapped him on the head, I would have. "Don't, it was an accident and I'm good, I'm here. See?"

"But what I did…"

"It wasn't you."

"I don't understand." He looked up at Illarion before returning his attention to me.

Thinking of the best way I could explain it without delving into the details, I cleared my throat. "It was Dalca. He was getting into your head through me. That's what he does. Takes thoughts and twists them into what he wants."

Illarion shifted beside me.

"How is that possible?" Aurel asked.

"It's a long story, I'll explain later."

His eyes welled, but he nodded.

"Trust me, I know it wasn't you. It's okay," I added, knowing how much he was beating himself up over it.

"Fucking hell," he muttered.

When Aurel stepped back, I turned my attention to Daniel, Anna stood a few feet behind him. There was a different set of emotions I had to contend with now. I inhaled sharply, blocking them both out.

Daniel stepped away from her, keeping a foot between us giving my crutches a quick look. "When they told us how bad it was…well, shit. I can't believe you're here, *standing.*"

"Yeah, it'll take some getting used to, learning to walk and all of that."

Illarion shifted by my side again. He was doing well not to snap at everyone in this room. His nerves fired and sent jolts through me.

Daniel shook his head disbelievingly, stepping back as Illarion neared me placing a possessive hand on the small of my back. Daniel got the message.

"You should sit down. You need to take it slow," Illarion murmured to me.

I didn't argue, instead I followed him around the table and sat. I was quick to notice Anna's gaze sweep over me and land on Illarion, either he didn't notice, or he pretended not to see. His attention was solely focused on me.

Compassion ran through her veins, but laced within it was a pang of jealousy she tried to ignore. Unfortunately for her, she wasn't good at hiding her feelings at all.

As the evening progressed, Elena and Anna served us dinner along with Illarion's staff. I cautiously ate, taking my time to avoid a repeat of the usual after dinner show.

When I was sure I wouldn't be bringing up the amazing dishes Illarion's chef cooked up, I devoured the Honey cake they'd brought out.

Everyone laughed and talked. The mood was light and conversation flowed easily. I sat back and watched with love in my heart. Things were still awkward between Illarion and Aurel not to mention the tension between him and Daniel but, for the most part, everyone was civil.

Even though Illarion didn't say anything to Daniel I was pretty certain that he got the hint, Illarion was intimidating at the best of times.

There was little Agency talk, and no mention of anything related to Dalca which suited me just fine.

I didn't want to dive into that yet. I didn't think I could. Time to discuss what happened next would come soon enough and when it did we'd have to be on our A-game.

When Illarion's staff, led by Elsa came in and cleared the table, it was Michael who stood first.

"Thank you for a lovely evening, Illarion, Ace." He looked to us each before taking Elena's hand. "It's about time we head home and get some rest."

"You don't have to go yet," Illarion said, standing.

"I'm sure the two of you have a lot of catching up to do." Elena smiled warmly, turning her attention to Aurel. "It's late."

He too, stood, nudging Daniel in the shoulder.

God. They couldn't have made it any more awkward. Elena grinned to herself, keeping quiet on the other end of the table. I saw what she was doing.

"Come on, I'll drive you home," Aurel said to Anna.

She nodded, collecting her things.

Illarion argued with Michael to stay, and Elena quirked her brows at me knowing her husband was on her side. I felt my cheeks burn and a grin cross my lips.

"Thank you," I said to her, pulling her close.

"Make the most of your time together, Sweetheart."

"I will."

Before long, all our guests were gone. Daniel had made his way back to the guest house and Illarion and I were left alone at the front door.

I let out a long breath and tipped my head to the side watching him secure the perimeter through the internal keypad.

"You didn't have to kick them out," I said gently.

His fingers brushed my cheek before he pressed a soft kiss to my forehead. "Believe me, I didn't kick them out. That was all your aunt."

I smiled to myself. Of course it was.

Illarion took my hand leading me back to the kitchen.

"Where do you want these?" Elsa appeared behind us carrying a brown box which looked to be filled to the brim with papers. "And I'll have this cleaned up before dawn."

"No rush, and in my office please."

She gave me a curt nod before disappearing down the hall.

"What's with the box?"

"Research. Nothing important."

"You're being secretive."

"It's nothing, you're welcome to take a look," he said wrapping his arms around my waist. "But right now, I think there's something more urgent."

"What's that?" I asked.

We were surrounded empty bottles of wine and half-eaten desserts, specifically the honey cake. I secretly contemplated helping myself to some more.

Illarion chuckled, obviously catching me eyeing it.

"More cake?" he asked, pulling the glass dome off the display tray.

"I think I'll eat the entire thing."

"It came from the best traditional Russian baker in America," he said with a smile. "The only one that's close to the one my mother made."

"I'm impressed, Agent Lazarev. And also really sorry."

"About what?"

"I know you're upset with your mother."

His brows furrowed. "I'd rather not talk about her right now. If that's alright with you."

"Okay, of course, sorry."

He turned his attention to the cake, serving a slice for me in a clean plate. Before I took it from him, he reached over for a fork and cut a piece off, bringing it to my lips.

"When did you even organize this?" I asked. Everything in this city required decent notice, especially cakes that weren't your run of the mill request.

"I have this baker on retainer."

I laughed. "You're ridiculous."

"You know I spare no expense."

"I know, I can tell." I grinned.

He chewed his bottom lip, holding the fork to my mouth. I kept my eyes locked on his as I opened my mouth and took the piece of cake. *God that was good.*

The sound that came from his lips made my knees all but buckle.

It was the single sexiest moment of my life.

When I finished the slice, Illarion set the plate aside and gently pushed me backward until my back was pressed against the island bench. He stood in front of me, pressing his hands on the counter on either side of me, caging me in.

"You're so beautiful, Ace."

"After I've eaten half your kitchen."

He chuckled. "After seeing you at peace, enjoying things you used to."

I bowed my head, lowering my cheek against his chest. "It's been hard, won't lie."

"I know, Lyubov. I'm so proud of you."

"I'm proud of me too."

I tipped my head up and met his gaze. I grinned like an idiot feeling the warmth within him spread through me. He was at peace too.

"Now the only thing left, is to let me help you," he said, brushing my hair behind my ears.

"Ila, no."

"You're hurting. I can help you."

"I've told you before, it's too much."

"And I've told you before that I want to do this. I want to see you get better; I want you to start living again."

When I tried to pull back, Illarion held me tighter and cupped my cheek.

"I can handle it," I said, quickly.

"I can't."

My eyes snapped back to his.

He shook his head, brushing his thumb across my lower lip.

"I can't handle seeing you like this every day, it hurts. I want to help you."

My heart slowed. "Well shit, Illarion. When you say things like that."

"It's only the truth."

I released a long breath and leaned back into the counter searching his eyes. He wasn't lying. It didn't take too much digging to understand the heaviness weighing between us. He was staying strong but every day that I struggled meant he did too.

"So, will you let me help?" he asked.

"Fine."

He grinned, pressing a kiss to the top of my head. I let him lead me to our bedroom all while I couldn't help the grin on my face.

He knew he could undo me with a simple touch and some sound, heartfelt logic. *Asshole.*

***

The transfer was much easier on both of us this time. Illarion didn't look as bad as he did last time, and I felt almost instantly better. The lingering sensation of Aaryon's healing was still there in the form of tingles and some spasms of mild pain, but for the most part, I felt great.

Illarion came back from the bathroom having showered and changed after he let me steam away the evening.

I couldn't help the smile which found my face as he brushed his hand across my cheek, drawing me to him in an instant.

"You're all hands, Agent Lazarev," I chuckled.

"All I've wanted was to be able to touch you once more, Ace, to hear you laugh. I never thought I would."

"I know what you mean," I sighed, hugging him.

"I've missed you. Have I told you that?"

My hands instinctively looped around his neck, drawing his face toward me. "Maybe you should show me?"

"I think that's a great idea."

The dangerous look in his eyes told me he knew exactly how he was going to do what I asked. He lowered his lips to mine, and, in a heartbeat, his tongue slipped past my parted lips brushing against mine in the sweetest tease.

Smiling against his mouth, I knotted my fingers through his dark hair.

He pulled back and slowly brought my eyes to his.

I reached down for his jeans, but he was quicker, stopping my hands.

I pouted but all that got me was an amused smirk.

He trailed his finger across my cheek sending shivers down my spine. Slowly, he trailed that same finger along the curve of my jaw, down to my neck and slowly down my bare arms, cupping my elbow.

He walked around me and wrapped his arms around my waist drawing my back to his chest. I leaned my head back, closing my eyes as he kissed my neck letting his lips trail across the sensitive skin there. I let out a low breath as goosebumps erupted across my exposed skin.

"You're my everything, Lyubov," he whispered as he slipped the straps of my tank top off my shoulders.

I shivered under his touch. When he pushed the straps down further, I held my breath. Dear God, I was going to combust.

Just as he was about to pull my top down completely, he stopped and I felt his hand tense.

"What is it? What's wrong?" I asked.

He remained quiet for a few moments and when I tried to turn, he held me in place.

"It's beautiful."

"What is?" I tried to turn around again, but again he held me in place.

"The mark the Being left."

"There's a mark? He left a mark?" I pulled back from him and rushed into the bathroom.

I twisted so I could try to get a look. I gasped. It was beautiful.

The intricate pattern was just like the geometric tattoos on Aaryon's skin, only mine wasn't completely black like his were, which explained why I hadn't seen it before when I showered and changed. The color was darkening as the days went by, probably as the damage he repaired, solidified.

My back was getting stronger and what Illarion did by taking some of the pain must have helped even more.

Illarion stood behind me, his eyes fell to the mark, pure awe filling his eyes.

"It's incredible, Ace."

My heart slowed and then sparked back to life in a flurry of emotion. I looked at his reflection in the mirror and smiled. This was real, this was so much more than I ever hoped for.

"Come here," he whispered, catching the change of pace.

His hands wrapped around my wrists.

"You're so beautiful."

A smiled spread across my face but the heavy feeling inside me refused to leave.

I looked down, chewing my bottom lip. "Even now? After all of this?"

"Nothing could change how I see you, Ace."

He tilted my chin up and the smile on his face melted away the coldness inside me where the ugliness was.

"You're beautiful. You always will be, no matter what."

With him, I believed it. This time, when I reached for his jeans, he didn't stop me.

I was well aware of what I did to him, and I loved it.

He reached down and slowly slid my underwear over my thighs, letting his fingers graze the delicate skin as he did. I did the same, releasing him from his black Calvin Klein's.

Finally, he stepped toward me, closing the gap until both our bodies were touching, skin to skin.

He wrapped my hair around his fist, leaned in, and kissed me.

Passion exploded between us. It had been months, months since I felt anything but pain and fear, anything but terror and helplessness…he knew every secret inside me and he was acquainted with every demon that hid in the depths of my soul, every ugly mark that tainted me.

He led us to the bed slowly easing me down onto my back. His eyes found mine and within a breath of a second, his lips were back on mine and his knees gently parted my thighs.

Before either of us could think, he brought me up toward him as he fit our bodies together. Long overdue desire peaked between us. I wrapped my other leg around his hip pulling him closer and deeper.

I felt the breath he held against my mouth as my heart hammered in my chest.

His hands roamed my body, feeling and touching, absorbing every burst of electricity while I delved into his mind and his heart, feeling every fiber of his soul unraveling.

Since evolving, I had never felt more alive. Everything was heightened. Everything was better than before. Arching my back, I gripped onto him, pulling him closer, needing to feel everything, needing this moment to erase the horror of the past.

I dug my nails into his back as he moved faster bringing us both closer and closer to the edge we had been seeking for so long.

It was more than just love, more than just passion. It was a new start, a beginning after the end, a clean slate, a chance to make new memories and toss away the old.

His lips crashed into mine stifling a cry.

He collapsed against me burying his face between my breasts. As the aftershocks rolled through us, I let myself open up to him completely.

Our ragged breaths slowly evened out, but his hands never left mine not even when we both fell asleep and the night claimed us, closing another day bringing with it, hope for tomorrow.

CHAPTER TWENTY-ONE

ACE

The sun warmed my face chasing the last fragments of sleep from my eyes. As I turned, I was stopped by a heavy, warm arm which drew me against a hard, toned body. I caught myself smiling like an idiot.

"You're so beautiful when you sleep."

I smirked, choking back a snort.

He laughed that same, intoxicating laugh I came to love so much.

"So beautiful I bet, especially with the drool pasting my hair to my face and my morning breath."

"Well, we both have morning breath and probably garlic breath from last night."

I laughed, turning in his arms. "God the food was *so* good."

"I'm glad you enjoyed it."

"More than you know." I almost drooled recalling the amazing cake again. "Dessert was nice too."

"Oh?" he teased.

My cheeks burned.

He grinned, peeling a few strands of hair from my cheek which had, in fact, stuck to my face overnight. Once they were tucked neatly behind my ear, he pressed a kiss to my forehead ticking me with the stubble on his chin, I couldn't stop the giggle that came from me.

God, I could get used to this, waking up beside him, feeling *safe*.

"I like this." I grazed my fingers along the stubble on his cheek.

He caught my hand and brought it to his lips.

"There was too much going on, I didn't even think about this."

He kissed the inside of my wrist and shook his head, slowly.

"You kept me alive; you know that, right?"

He swallowed and a muscle in his jaw moved.

"Stop blaming yourself, Illarion."

As much as I kept saying it, he never would and the pain that was weighing him down was suffocating. His eyes drifted away from me and fell on the scars along my arms.

Slowly, I tipped his chin up with my finger, much like he had done for me, so many times. Such a simple gesture but it was laced with so much.

"I need you; I can't do this without you." I reached up and pressed a kiss to his lips. "And I'm so sorry I made you question that. Dalca was blocking my feelings somehow. It was horrific. That wasn't me."

"I understand, Lyubov." He drew in a breath and pulled me against him. "And I'm with you."

"Good. And don't get rid of this." I smiled, pulling back.

"I won't."

Something inside him shifted, drawing my attention. It was familiar. He must have sensed me looking into it because he slowly turned onto his back and pulled me up so I could rest my head on his chest.

"Something's on your mind," I said, softly, listening to the steady beat of his heart.

For a moment I thought he was going to try and hide whatever it was, but instead, he let out a deep breath. "There's been chatter, at the Agency, about Dalca and his movements."

When my breath caught in my lungs, he tightened his hold on me and pulled me closer.

"I didn't want to bring it up, believe me. I've been trying to do whatever I can without involving you."

"You had no right keeping information like that from me. Is that what's in the box?"

I pulled myself free from his arms and sat up.

"I kept it from you because I don't want you to go through this again." He sighed, sitting up. "I'm telling you now. And no. That has nothing to do with Dalca."

"I get it, I do. But it's not your decision to make, Ila." I moved to leave, but he caught my arm and pulled me back down onto the bed beside him.

"Don't do that," his voice was firm but there was a desperate edge to the coarseness. "Don't run from me when things get hard. Please."

I chewed my lip and laid back down and turned to look at him. He raked his fingers through my hair, smoothing it down my back.

"The reason I kept it from you is because you've been through so much and you'd only just begun to smile again." He sighed, drawing my hands to his lips. "It's selfish, but I wanted *you* back."

"I am back," I murmured, finding his eyes.

"But if I told you what I knew, I would have lost you," he said firmly. "You were in a dangerous place. I made a call."

I blew out a long breath. I could have argued but there was no point. He was right.

"Aaryon didn't just fix my back, he unblocked my senses, you know, when I became a robot."

"You weren't a robot." Illarion tightened his hold on me. "And yes, Aaryon proved me wrong."

My heart sank. Illarion hadn't trusted the Beings since they couldn't help his mother, he'd never openly said it, but it didn't take much to work it out.

When I kept my eyes down, he tipped my chin up.

240

"Hey." He smiled. "You weren't a robot."

"Are you kidding?" I smiled. "Were you not there when I had zero emotion, and I didn't even respond when you kissed me? Because I'm pretty sure under normal circumstances, I would have ripped your clothes off."

"And probably traumatized Daniel."

"Yep."

"You were under a lot of pressure." He began pressing feather-light kisses along my jaw, trailing down to my neck against my wildly thundering pulse.

It was hard to concentrate on anything when he was doing that. And then his hands fell to my hips, drawing a quiet gasp from me.

"I just don't understand what happened, why I went, well, basically catatonic."

"It was a defense mechanism—block all your pain receptors, block all the memories," he continued, speaking softly. "Usually, it takes a highly experienced Sensitive to do that and it usually takes a great deal of pressure to trigger it and in your case, it would appear that Dalca helped push you there."

When I was able to take a breath and concentrate on what he just said, I considered his words for a moment.

"Why would anyone voluntarily push themselves to a point where they don't feel anything?"

He thoughtfully placed a few more kisses on my forehead while his hand snaked behind my back and slowly caressed the sensitive skin on my hip.

"Some agents who are deep under cover do it, especially when they're exposed to situations that they may not be able to handle mentally."

As his words sunk in, I realized how hard it must be to immerse yourself that deep into an assignment that you no longer had the luxury of doing what you thought was right, you only did what the job required.

That had been my mantra, hadn't it? I kept telling myself to push through because it was just another job and I had to do it.

His fingers grazed the side of my hip, drawing a startled gasp.

"What are you thinking about?"

Moving closer to him, I hid my face in the nape of his neck.

"I wish I had known about it...before, when I was with him." I swallowed hard and took a deep breath before I continued. "Some nights I think I was almost there, you know? I was so deep in my head; I didn't realize when it was over. I just woke up and he was gone."

His expression hardened.

"Sorry, I shouldn't have said anything," I whispered. "It's not exactly pillow talk."

He brought his hand to my cheek, slowly coaxing my face toward his. "I don't want you to ever think for one second that you can't talk to me, about this or anything else."

"Even if it's horrible to hear?"

"Especially then."

I drew in a long breath and searched his eyes. The pain was still there, and I didn't think it would leave him any time soon, just like it wouldn't vanish from my thoughts.

"I won't stop until he's dead. I promise you that, Ace."

"I plan on putting a bullet between his eyes myself."

Something inside him cracked. Silence fell between us for a moment.

"We should get up," I said. I would have loved nothing more than to stay in bed with him all day long, feeling everything that made this world right and forgetting all that made it wrong.

Part of me enjoyed feeling normal again, but the other part, the part that wanted revenge, grew impatient.

He agreed, "Sadly, yes. We have work to do."

I smiled, pressing another featherlight kiss to his lips before I peeled myself away from his arms and made my way to the bathroom.

I turned on the water and waited for the steam to fill the shower before stepping into the stream. I leaned my forehead on the tiles and pressed my palms above my head stretching my shoulders out.

The water was such a welcome relief for my tired and achy bones. In quiet moments like this, I let myself feel how painful everything really was. Groaning, I tipped my head down as my hair slipped past my shoulders and fell forward in a heavy mass.

Behind me, a cool, subtle shift in temperature drew my attention, but I kept my eyes closed. When his hands found the curve of my hip, I smiled to myself. His chest pressed flat to my back encompassing me in a tight embrace.

There was nothing but love and care in the way he traced lines across my body. There were no expectations, nothing but being in his arms.

He brought his lips to my cheek and placed kisses along my jaw and trailed down my neck, sweeping kisses along every inch of skin where his fingers trailed.

My knees weakened as his hands came to stop just above my hip where he slowly, carefully, swept his hand to the front, pressing his palm flat across my stomach.

"We never spoke about this," he said gently.

I closed my hands over his and looked over my shoulder into his eyes. Water clung to his lashes.

"We would have made great parents."

"We would have, Lyubov."

"We can never have that."

"I'm so sorry." He pressed his cheek to mine.

"I'm sorry, Ila, you deserve that chance with someone."

"I don't want anyone else," he whispered into my ear. "This life is you and me; I'm not thinking about anything else. I swear to you."

I closed my eyes and hung my head.

"I know you're hurting; I can't begin to imagine how this feels but, Ace, don't ever think that this is something that will make me love you less or question my life with you."

"You know that it's, it's definitive. There's...I can't have that."

"I know, Lyubov. I will be by your side to help you however you need me."

"I love you, Ila."

He tightened his hold around my body and pressed more kisses to my neck, feeling my pulse quickening with every touch.

He lowered his mouth to my ear. "When all of this is done, I want you to stay with me."

I leaned into his touch and pressed my back against him. "Where else would I go? I've got tenants in my apartment."

He pressed a kiss to my other cheek.

"I meant that I want you to stay with me, officially."

I turned my head to the side and met his eyes. His wet hair fell over his face, and his lips parted as water cascaded over us.

The warmth in his eyes was filled with a nervousness I'd never really seen in him. What had the unshakeable Illarion Lazarev, shaken?

His lips quirked into a half smile.

"I know you don't really believe in that sort of thing...I know it's not really something you'd have thought about, and this line of work, well it doesn't really accommodate for that kind of life."

I couldn't help the grin that came across me. I turned in his arms and looped my arms around his neck.

"Illarion, are you asking me to marry you?"

He gave me a quick, nervous nod. "I know you need to think about it."

"No," I said, with a shake of my head, slightly pulling back.

He swept his hand over my cheek and before he could panic, I smiled, pressing a kiss to his lips.

"No, I don't need to think about it, and yes I'll stay with you, *officially.*"

When the words I just spoke registered in his head, my heart melted. I never thought I'd see that kind of happiness in anyone's eyes.

He pulled me into his arms and drew his fingers through my hair, pulling me against him.

"I do have one condition though," I said, pulling back from him.

He brushed his thumb along the curve of my lip. "Anything, moya zvezda."

"I want to do it properly," I said, softly, pressing my hand to his cheek.

His eyes warmed with joy.

"You're right. Our life doesn't really allow for these things... that's why I want us to do it right. I want us to have some semblance of a normal life."

"Then we'll do it properly."

I smiled reaching up to kiss him and when I pulled back, I bit down on my lip and locked eyes with him.

"Ask me when it's over. Ask me when that son of a bitch is in the ground."

Chapter Twenty–Two

Ace

Six months ago, my whole world was turned on its head, and everything following became a living, hellish nightmare I was sure I'd never be able to wake from.

But somehow, I did. Daniel played the biggest part in that and the whole escape. If he wasn't there to keep me sane during the nights when I was certain I'd find a sharp object and end it all, I don't know what I would have done. I felt dirty admitting it. But going through something like that, brought a whole new meaning to learning about oneself, and what one would do when faced with the things I was faced with.

There were times I didn't want to continue, and I'd even hoped and prayed that somehow, I would die in my sleep or that Daniel would accidentally overdose me with the Serum or heroin, but of course that never would have happened. He was careful and meticulously executed everything he was doing.

I'd lived for a reason and seeing Illarion sitting beside me, smiling and happy told me this was the why. Why I was spared. Why I fought so hard. Why I survived.

Illarion leaned in, across the table and brushed my wet hair from my cheek and smiled.

"Everything alright?"

"Yeah." I nodded, smiling. "It is."

He took my hand and kissed my fingertips softly before placing my hand back on the table.

"Can I ask you something?" I asked, leaning forward, pressing a soft kiss to his lips.

"Anything."

"When I first started at the Agency, you said you chose my code-name, Spectre," I said, quietly, to which he responded with a downcast smile. "You never told me why."

"I chose it because you disappeared from that desert and rose from the ashes. You fought against all odds, and you survived. Not unlike now."

"Thank you for seeing me in that light."

"I see you in many lights, Ace, each one more spectacular than the last."

I grinned. I would never tire of that. "You do know how to treat a girl."

He laughed, shielding the blush forming on his cheeks. "We should go through a few things today if you're feeling up to it."

As much as I didn't want to admit that I wasn't too thrilled about the idea, I agreed, "Whatever you need."

"You know I wouldn't ask if there was another way."

"I know. It's fine, what do you need to know?"

"I need to know how much information he has now. I need to know who else is in danger and what we need to prepare for."

"The fact that you're asking this late in the game tells me you have some information already?"

"I do. I was able to piece together a few things from the name of the agents Daniel gave me and the rest from the moves Dalca has already made."

"Because of what I gave him."

"Because he forced you to," he corrected, moving his chair closer to mine. "Tell me about the Sensitives he made you collect. Everything you remember."

My mind went back to Dalca's house. I thought back to each one of the men and women I was forced to kill. I watched each one as their eyes glazed over under my power until, eventually, there was nothing left and the light behind their eyes faded.

"If you can't—"

"I can." I nodded, trying to convince myself. I *had* to do this. I owed it to them.

"What information did he want you to get?"

I sucked in a deep breath. "The first one, was Michael Romvi. He worked in finance, and he wanted me to find the accounts for all the funds the agency used."

Illarion's eyes narrowed thoughtfully.

"I don't know what information I gave him," I admitted, completely aware that I could have single handedly been responsible for embezzling billions from the Agency and their accounts.

He nodded rubbing a soothing hand on my knee. "Do you know what he wanted with that information?"

"No, he only told me what I needed to know."

"I bet he did, he's not an idiot." He shook his head and gently squeezed my knee. "Who was next?"

"David Maximos." I took another breath. "He was from the weapons team, I think he was field trained too."

"What did he want with David?" Illarion's voice was gentle, but I heard the pain in it.

He had known David. God. *How many of the others did he know?*

"He wanted to know what our weapons team had been working on and what we geared up with in the field."

"Do you remember anything about what you'd told him?"

"The Legion."

"Legion? You're sure?" Illarion's expression was neutral, but I felt something akin to curiosity rush through him.

"Yeah, why?"

"Not sure. It's something I've been running an information gathering job on."

"I've read about it too. Sketchy info at best. What is it?"

"I thought it was a weapon and if David gave you data, I'd say I'm right."

"Christ. What kind of weapon is it?"

"I don't know, Lyubov. I haven't been able to find anything other than several dozen unnamed bank accounts funding it all the way from America through to Turkey."

"With no links to anyone. Right?"

He nodded. "It's what's in the box. I'm hoping to find more information."

"Source?"

"An old Russian informant of mine."

"Sanctioned?"

"No. This is between us."

I nodded, tracing my fingers across the rim of the coffee cup. "Only other info I managed to find through my source, Vanessa, was that it's a bunch of genetically jacked ex-marines or something."

"I've read the same."

"On the books or off?"

"Off."

"I don't like this, what would Dalca want with a group like that?" I asked.

"I don't know, but it's an angle I'm taking seriously now."

"As opposed to?"

"When Michael gave me the job, I thought it was to keep me occupied when you were gone," he cracked on the last word.

"But you think there's more to it?"

"I know there is now. I don't believe in coincidence. Do you?"

"No."

The gravity of what this meant pushed me into my chair. We could be sitting here on the brink of a war I was responsible for starting and we had no idea what it even was.

Illarion ran a hand through his hair. "What else can you tell me?"

"He asked about lockdown protocols."

Illarion frowned.

"I honestly don't know what I told him, Ila. I could have handed him everything."

"Not likely, only four people in the Agency know who has the lockdown protocols."

"Right, I remember Josh telling me this. We're sure I couldn't have burned everyone?"

"We're sure." He shook his head. "One person knows the identity of one other, and so on and so forth. No one would know all four."

"Okay, good."

"It's bad, but it's not the worst outcome. The lockdown is safe."

"You should've left me in the desert."

He pinched the bridge of his nose. "Don't say that."

"All those agents are dead, not to mention how many more are in danger now because of me."

"They're trained to deal with these possibilities, they're trained to expect the worst, Ace. Just like us."

"I killed them. I did that. How could anyone be trained for a possibility that your own agency would come for you?"

A soft, gentle hand on my cheek brought my attention back to him. "You had no choice, Lyubov. And sorry to break it to you, allegiances change all the time."

"That's not funny."

I knew what he was doing but I was still a murderer, and no matter how he tried to dress it up, I was the monster with their blood on my hands.

"You had no choice, Ace. In any of it," he said again, sterner this time. "Whatever you did in there is because you were held hostage, drugged and threatened. This is not your fault."

"You keep saying that, yet it never makes it better."

Turning away from him, I wet my lips but it wasn't just because of the Serum.

"Ace," he murmured, lifting my chin up again. "Don't do this to yourself."

"He knew who you were. What you mean to me."

Understanding stunned him into silence. His brows creased as his lashes lowered. He dropped his hand and leaned back in his chair, steepling his fingers beneath his chin.

"You warned me to keep my mind safe with Damon. Guess that fuck up was worse than we thought?"

"That's why you didn't fight back."

It wasn't a question.

In a dizzying rush he was up, a furious rage boiling inside him. "God Damn it Ace, why would you put yourself through that for me?"

"What kind of question is that, Illarion?"

"My life is not worth more than yours."

"It is to me."

"You shouldn't have done that."

"I had Vanessa check on you."

His shoulders tensed and he turned to me slightly.

"I asked Daniel to get me some information. I couldn't risk Vanessa telling you, I couldn't risk you knowing about me. Dalca has eyes and ears everywhere."

He sat back down taking my hands into his.

"I feel it in you, you're ashamed talking to me." He shook his head as though he couldn't believe why such thoughts were on my mind. "You have nothing to be ashamed about. Especially not with me."

A harsh, humorless laugh escaped before I could stop it and I folded my arms across my chest.

"There's a lot I'm ashamed of, believe me, Ila. If I could articulate even half of it in words, you'd think differently."

"Nothing can change the way I think of you," he said simply, his voice firm yet hardly above a whisper.

With that, I continued. I told him about each Sensitive. One after the other, about all the information I'd gotten for Dalca, and all the gifts I'd collected at least the things I'd remembered.

All while I spoke, I couldn't ignore how hurt he was. I never wanted him to know, especially not that. He would never forgive himself, not that he was feeling peachy to begin with. When his mind was quiet I still caught moments of turmoil where he loathed himself for drinking and finding comfort in Anna. He hated himself for ignoring his dreams and leaving me there.

All while I told him about my time at the house, he listened quietly, never interrupting me, only pressing a comforting hand to my mine when I stumbled on my words or wiping a stray tear with his thumb as all the memories solidified in my mind.

Talking about it made it real. It meant admitting what I had done, and openly acknowledging my involvement in all those deaths. I bowed my head pressing my fingertips to my temple.

He gently swept my hair off my shoulders letting his fingers graze my skin.

"You're strong, Ace. Stronger than you're letting yourself believe in this moment." His words were heavy and full of emotion, and they set my soul on fire.

He never let me feel like I was less than him, not even when he was nursing my sorry ass back to health. He was so good like that. He made me feel loved and cared for, but he always made me feel like his equal.

"What else do you need to know?" I swallowed and found his eyes again.

"We don't have to continue right now."

"We do. I'll be fine."

He hesitated for a moment. "Tell me about the people he brought over, who were they?"

Pain filled his voice as he asked the second question. He didn't know for certain, but it didn't take a Ph.D. to work out what Dalca's friends were there for when we both knew what kind of man he was.

"They were private investors, basically bankrolling whatever he's doing. Assuming Legion related. Others wanted to see what I could do."

A muscle worked in his jaw as he lowered his hand to mine. I felt the tremble in his fingertips as he tried to hold it together as much as possible. I had to hand it to him, he had an insane amount of self-control.

He saw that there were things I was hiding.

When I quietened for a moment, he swept his hand across my cheek, bringing my eyes up to his.

"Did they ask you to collect other Sensitives?"

I shook my head. "They wanted to watch."

"But there's more than that."

"Yes."

His fingers tensed around mine as he drew in a shaky breath. "What did they want, Ace?"

I looked up into his eyes and blinked back the oncoming tears. I couldn't say it. I didn't have to.

Illarion turned away, stifling a chain of expletives I knew were on the tip of his tongue. I'd seen that look before. He was livid. Almost at the point of bursting at the seams.

"I held out as long as I could, but I caved, Ila, I couldn't do it anymore."

He pushed back the chair and knelt in front of me, taking my face in his hands.

"You survived. You fought with everything inside you."

"I wasn't strong enough. I wanted to die. What does that say about me?"

"You survived because you're strong and wishing for death in circumstances you faced is natural."

His words brought forth tears I was working so hard on holding in.

There was a wrenching feeling deep inside me, a fear and pain that felt so real I had no way of distinguishing it from my memories. *What if I never got over this? What if I was never normal again?*

"I promise you won't feel like this forever."

My heart fell as my eyes drifted up to his.

"That's enough for today."

"No, you need this information." I shook my head straightening in my seat. I took the coffee cup from the table and cradled it in my hand like a lifeline.

"Lyubov."

"I'm the same as any other witness. You need the information, and I have it. Ask your questions."

"It can wait."

"I can handle it."

He scrubbed his face impatiently. "You shouldn't have to handle it. I'm making you dredge everything up, it's too soon."

"The sooner it's done, the sooner it's over."

Illarion said nothing but every part of him was vibrating with rage that was fueling the Darkness inside.

The violence I knew he was capable of and that he wouldn't hesitate to do what he needed to, chilled me.

"What else do you need to know, Illarion?"

He bowed his head, yet somehow, his eyes managed to convey so much more emotion than I ever imagined was possible in a mere look.

"Tell me about Dalca."

His third and final question.

Leaning back in the chair, I composed myself though all I wanted to do was run away.

"He likes power," I began, hating that my voice shook knowing that he had done this to me. "He's cruel, and he's smart. He's wealthy and well-connected. He's a Divine like me, so he's hard to kill. He knows how to use his power; he's completely evolved and much stronger than me."

Illarion went uncharacteristically still.

"Yeah," I nodded, looking down at the space between our hands. "He told me, the first night I was there. Kind of figured I was screwed right away."

When I looked back at Illarion and saw the steely resolve in the lines of his face, my heart sunk as my stomach coiled into tight knots.

"He's descended from the Sun being, so his power is all about taking, where mine comes from Aaryon and the moon, I'm meant to give life, give power. Fucking ironic, isn't it?"

Illarion hung his shoulders.

I wet my lips, letting out a harsh laugh. "I can never give life because he *took* that from me."

255

His amber eyes darkened as his lashes lowered brushing his cheeks.

"He enjoyed the power over me, not because it was easy to get, but because he knew that without the Serum, he'd have no chance. He enjoyed knowing that."

"He knew you'd evolve and when you did, you could end him."

"Maybe." I bit down, chewing on the inside of my lip. "Anyway, he wanted me to know that if I tried anything, if I tried to escape, he'd find…" I couldn't bring myself to say it. "He knew I wouldn't do anything."

"Jesus, Ace…"

He drew his hand back and balled his fists at his sides as he got up. I moved to follow, but he held his hand out, stopping me in my place. A tired breath left his lips before he turned back to me, rubbing his face.

"How did you fight off the Serum?" he asked changing the subject.

"Something to do with my DNA." I shrugged. "I don't really know; it was the same in Iraq when Alex and I were being held."

"With Grimes?"

"Yep. Daniel did the rest though, started lowering the doses, as you know."

"Christ." Illarion dropped his head, and I quickly felt where his mind went.

He was back to kicking himself over what happened to me. A dizzying kaleidoscope of hate and anger went around in his head on repeat.

"I shouldn't have said anything," I murmured, moving closer. "I never wanted to tell you. I'm sorry."

"I saw it in my dreams."

"Some of it, yes."

He shook his head slowly turning back to face me. A heartbeat passed between us before he stepped forward, tipping my chin up with his fingers.

Wanting nothing more than to take the guilt that he carried, away, I reached up and looped my arm around his neck.

"I failed in my duty," he said.

He was on the verge of losing his composure which was so unlike him. I brushed my thumb across the rough stubble on his cheeks and pressed a kiss to his lips. "What other information do you need?"

Shaking his head, he wrapped me in a strong, powerful embrace that felt so good.

"No more, not today."

"What about the other men?"

"What about them?"

"I need to know what happened to me. I need to know who they were. I need closure." I sat, looking up at him. "I know Dalca may never be held accountable but those men need to be."

For a moment, there was silence. Then he sat in front of me, pressing his hands over my knees stopping my tapping.

"Do you remember their faces at all?"

As his hands settled on my thighs and that same concerned expression I'd come to know so well, met me. I inhaled deeply and looked down at the space between our feet.

"No, nothing."

"Is there anything distinctive you can remember about them; tattoos, scars, or even jewelry like signet rings?"

"No," I groaned. "I'll never know, will I?"

His gaze dropped from mine for a moment before he brought his eyes back to me.

"There is another way."

"Really? What is it?"

"It's dangerous and it won't be easy."

"Tell me," I said.

"I can try to look through your repressed memories. Maybe I can catch a glimpse. I'll only be searching on a surface level, nothing too invasive."

Suddenly I was overwhelmed by the prospect. I found myself shaking my head before I could stop it. What would he see in there? There was a reason I'd repressed them, right? His soft hand over mine brought my eyes back up.

"Forget it. I shouldn't have mentioned it. It's a bad idea."

"No. Do it. They need to be held accountable," I said.

"I don't know, Ace."

"I need to know, Illarion. Please."

He blew out a long breath. "You're apprehensive."

"I'm terrified."

"Then you're not ready."

"How could I ever be ready for this?"

He didn't bother replying. Instead, he swept his hand across my cheek drawing my eyes to his.

"Do it, Ila. I need to know."

His eyes locked onto mine, and he gave me a quick smile. "I'll be in and out before you know it."

I drew a deep breath into my lungs and gave him my hands. He was good at this; I had no doubt he'd stay only as long as he needed and no longer.

"Close your eyes and listen to my voice."

I did as he said, preparing myself. I waited. Nothing. Silence on my end, silence on his. I couldn't feel him inside my mind.

A few minutes later, his hold loosened, and I opened my eyes, meeting his. "What's wrong?"

He stayed quiet for a moment before shaking his head. "I can't do it."

"What do you mean?"

"There's nothing there."

"There has to be."

"You've pushed it too far into your mind, I can't reach it."

My shoulders sagged in defeat. "We need the information, Ila. I need it. I have to know what they did."

My voice fell flat, like I was terrified of the notion, yet so desperate for it.

"I'll start running through a backlist of employees, known associates, anyone who ran in his circle."

"That'll take too long."

"I'll get Josh on it too."

"No."

"Ace."

"No. There's another way," I said firmly.

He saw through the words he didn't want to hear. He shook his head, taking my hand in his.

"You know I'm right."

"Going that far into those memories is beyond dangerous, Ace. It's a risk I'm not willing to take."

"I am."

"I'm afraid if I do, that I'll hurt you."

"You won't." I forced a tight smile. "I'm giving you permission, Ila. I trust you and I know you're skilled enough to do it. That's how you got through Bob's head right? Found me when I ran last year?"

"Your mind might not be able to take that much right now."

"I trust you."

"I don't trust me."

I let out a long breath, scrubbing the fatigue from my eyes. "I need closure, Ila. I don't know how else to do it."

He sat quietly, taking in my suggestion before finally nodding. "The only way this happens is with complete trust."

"I trust you."

"I know." He sighed. "But I need to trust you, too."

"I'm not following."

"You've heard of safe words?"

My lips quirked up into a smile. "Like in BDSM?"

A glint in his eyes told me his mind raced straight there too.

"We can definitely explore that if you like, but for tonight's purpose, I'm not referring to that."

"Oh?" I smirked.

"Like I said." He leaned across and brushed his lips over my ear. "We'll get into that one night if you like. But not now."

My cheeks flushed and the heat inside me grew.

When he looked at me like that, my skin instantly warmed and everything inside me became a jumbled mess.

"What I meant by a safe word, for this, is that when I'm in your memories, I need you to promise me you'll call it, when it gets too much."

"I'll be okay."

"Normally when I do this, it's to interrogate criminals and it's usually with the aid of the Serum."

"Can you do it without?"

"I can, if you're receptive. I'm not going to push."

"I'm giving you permission."

"It's not always enough. If your mind and consciousness aren't aligned, there'll be barricades and I'll have to break them down."

"But you can do it?"

"I can. But I won't."

I sighed, pinching the bridge of my nose.

Illarion squeezed my hand. His pulse was skyrocketing.

He was nervous too. The more real it got, the more my nerves told me that I did not want Illarion seeing what I knew was probably going to be in those memories. I had some notion of what they did, obviously, but not everything, not the whole picture.

"I need to know that you're going to stop me if it gets too much."

"Ila, I'll be fine."

"I want your word Ace, your safe word. Say it now."

"Arrow."

He nodded. "I won't be able to pull you out myself, you have to say it."

"Got it. I promise."

"I don't like this."

"Ila." A million things were on my mind, but instead, I just squeezed his hand. "I can do this."

He rubbed his eyes and turned back to face me, taking my hands.

"I need you take a deep breath and close your eyes. Focus on everything here. Focus on my voice, the way my hands feel on yours, the smells, the sounds around you. Keep yourself grounded."

"I know the drill." I'd done it dozens of times.

"Let your mind relax. If you start drifting, remember that it's me. You'll need to be completely open to let me in."

"Got it."

Without warning, my mind was jolted, it was happening. His thoughts were inside me, completely flooding every memory, every hidden thought I'd ever had. He was moving rapidly, tearing apart every wall I'd somehow built up, knocking down every barrier that had kept me safe.

His grip on me tightened and my chest constricted.

Suddenly, they weren't his hands holding me and I wasn't in his house. I was back in Dalca's office, back on the desk, pushed into the paperwork on his table, held down by three of his friends and that memory I'd repressed—well here it was.

"Ace?" Illarion's voice broke through the haze in my mind.

My body was shaking with fear, the pain was unbearable, and I couldn't move, I couldn't breathe, and they were *so* rough.

Everything around me was a blur. All I heard with certain clarity was Dalca. His voice was right in my ear, his hot breath was too close to my mouth. God, everything was too much.

There were hands everywhere, so many, so rough.

Another sharp, violent ripple of pain jolted through me as the second or third man took his place.

"Please God!" I screamed into the desk as he held me down.

"God isn't here, Acacia, but the Devil is."

Horror mounted as his lips curled into a cruel smirk.

"Ace, call it. Use your safe word."

Vomit rose, but I couldn't let it out because every time I got a chance to breathe, someone was back inside, and my eyes burned with humiliation and endless tears.

"Call it, Ace!" Illarion shouted, but he was too far away. He was always too far away.

"If Lazarev finds us, you know he'll kill us all," one of them stammered out between his breathless moans.

My mind flashed back to Illarion, I just wanted to go home. I wasn't here, this wasn't happening, none of this was real. Illarion would find me, he'd stop all of this, he'd help me.

"Please Ila…" I whimpered, my hand on the table was outstretched, reaching for him as though I could really see him somehow.

My brows furrowed. I remembered this.

"Lazarev will never find out. When we're done here, she's going to push all of this into a place so deep in her mind, no one will ever know. Not even her." Dalca laughed.

The youngest of the three stepped up to me as soon as Dalca stepped back and roughly squeezed my face in his. "Bite and I'll cut your tongue out."

"She won't bite." Dalca yanked my head up by my hair.

He snapped his fingers in front of my face and when I finally looked up, he held out a tablet. It was Illarion's house in aerial view. "There is currently a UAV, ready to send coordinates for an air strike as soon as I order it. Understand?"

My voice failed me.

"You're going to behave, aren't you?"

"Yes," I hissed.

"See," he said to the three men. "She's going to be a good girl."

"Ila…please. Please help me."

"Ace! Call it, now, you're going too far!"

"No one is coming for you, pet. And even if Lazarev found you, do you really think he'd want to touch you after we're done?"

Tears fell from my eyes, wetting the desk beneath my cheek and then I couldn't speak anymore.

"No," Dalca leaned over me and breathed in deeply, smelling my hair, my skin, trailing his fingers along my bare back where the dress had been ripped. "When we're done with you, no man will want you. And that agent your heart beats for, well, he's going to take one look at you and see what you've become. But me? I'll always want you, Acacia."

He dragged his hand down to the center of my back and pushed me down.

"All I want from you is one, simple answer," he said, in my head taking this conversation private.

"Screw you!" I cried, ignoring the way the other three looked at me.

Dalca pushed me up further onto the desk and my heart stopped.

"Lockdown protocols. Who has them?"

"I don't know!"

"I will break you. And when I do, you're going to give me what I want."

The other two pulled my arms down, holding them firm against the desk and then the panic tripled.

"I know you have them, Acacia. I know you have the identity of the final agent."

"I don't know!"

"We'll see."

A devastated scream erupted, a scream I couldn't control. It was filled with so much pain and so much helplessness, I thought it would break me in two.

He was insistent, despite the resistance and my skull felt like it was about to split at the pain, the intrusion, the humiliation—it was all too much. I gasped for air and tried to scream for him to stop, but my lungs choked up with the bile building from the gag reflex. I was going to die, this was it.

If I closed my eyes, if I just let myself go, it would all be over. He'd win, and I'd be free.

It was so easy now, all I had to do was pretend that it wasn't me here, that it wasn't me lying on this table, being used and abused by four monsters, that it wasn't blood sliding down my thighs, but I couldn't. I wasn't ready to give up, I was stronger than this, stronger than them.

"Keep your eyes open!" one of them shouted, and like a slap to the face, I remembered why I was here.

This wasn't real, this had already happened. But I could control this now. I looked up at the man, his face burned into my memories and as Dalca roughly gripped my hips, I pulled back and he wrapped his free hand around my throat and squeezed, choking me, but it was worth it. A quick glance at both men beside me was all I needed. I saw their faces knowing Illarion would get them too.

Forcing my eyes closed, I sucked in a deep breath. "Arrow!"

It was over.

I was out.

I wasn't in the office anymore. I was on my knees, on the floor, gripping onto Illarion's arms.

It was too real. Too painful. My heart, oh God, my mind. I couldn't keep up. Without warning, my stomach brought everything up, and I doubled over.

That's when the tears came hard and fast. I couldn't look up. I couldn't breathe. I couldn't see. Everything flashed through my mind like a damn sped up video that I had no control over.

Illarion moved to me, reaching for my hair but I held my arm out, pushing him away.

"Ace. Bozhe, look at me, Ace. Open your eyes, look at me. Please."

"Don't touch me!" I scrambled away from him.

"Ace," his voice shook.

"Get away from me!" I screamed, when he reached for my hand again.

And when I tried to push him back, he caught me and held me tight against him until I stopped struggling and finally quietened, folding into myself.

"It's okay, it's over Ace. You're safe," he kept repeating, over and over.

And somewhere in the silence following my hysterical tears, all I could hear through the rushing in my head, were Illarion's short breaths.

Was he crying?

"Ace...Lyubov," Illarion's voice was rough.

"You're here."

It was a realization. A very personal, and painful one. He was here. After all of that, after all the things they did to me, after all the times I'd reached out to him and called for him when I was there...he was really here.

Had I...had I somehow seen this moment? Seen him come to me from another time through my own mind? Is that why I always kept calling for him?

Was that even possible?

"You're here," I whispered again, letting a broken sob free.

"I'm here. You never have to doubt that."

"The things he said..."

"None of what he said is true."

When I finally managed to look up through body shaking tremors, Illarion's eyes found mine. Tears clung heavily to his lashes but the pain in them is what cut me.

He was in shock. Just like me.

His face had paled several shades, and I didn't know if he was about to pass out or throw up.

We'd both just lived through the worst moment of my life.

"I couldn't remember any of those things..."

"You buried it so deep I don't blame you. It was your way of surviving." When he reached to brush my cheek, I flinched, jerking back.

Hurt flashed through his eyes, but he didn't attempt to touch me again. Instead, his lips tightened into a straight line and the dark, penetrating stare of his eyes burned right through me.

266

Folding my arms over my chest, I focused on taking long and deep breaths. In then out. That's all I had to do, that's how I was going to survive this, *again*.

"Say something, Lyubov."

What could I say? I trembled, hating how I was breaking.

"Did you get a look at their faces?" I asked quietly.

"Yes."

"Good. I need some air." I got up and looked around, at anything but him.

"Ace—"

"I need you to give me some space."

"Alright."

Cracks in the dam I'd built myself were finally showing. The pain was back, and it was real, just when I thought I'd managed to make some progress.

But this was a part of it, right? Getting justice, getting those pigs into prison for the rest of their lives where they'd feel a fraction of what they made me feel.

Somehow, it still didn't make me feel any better.

Illarion was on his feet, but he didn't come to me.

I made my way upstairs.

When I finally crashed, all I could do was let out a long, shattered breath, but no more tears. I was done.

***

ILLARION

Her body was wired tightly and I was so afraid that if the Darkness took her, I'd never find her again.

When she disappeared up the stairs, I let out a long breath and slammed my fist into the table.

Whatever it took, those animals would be held accountable, they would pay.

My hands shook as I sat down dragging my laptop over. When the anger settled enough for me to type, I started searching the database. I remembered their faces, all three of those assholes who raped her.

She was right, Dalca was untouchable by legal, Agency and internation treaty means. These three men were not. It was a start.

Benefits of my clearance were that I had access to every database linked to our servers. A few hours, maybe less, would be sufficient to find them.

As I clicked through hundreds of faces, of men and women affiliated with Simon Dalca, I stopped, straightening in my seat.

"Got you, you son of a bitch."

I followed the links, followed his patterns, everything he did, everywhere he went, where he worked, where he drank, and, within the hour, I had all three names.

I picked up my desk phone and rang a number that had been saved to every phone in my possession. I only had to wait a few rings until the line connected.

"Hale."

"It's me," I spoke calmly.

"Illarion?"

"I need to call in that favor."

"What do you need?"

"I have three names for you. I need you to get your I.T. guys on it."

Ethan Hale was an FBI contact I'd met years ago. I helped him with some cases that overlapped some of mine, earning him a promotion.

"What am I looking for?"

Rubbing my jaw, I exhaled, "Videos, photographs. Anything on their personal and office computers, phones. Tablets. Everything."

"What are we looking for?"

"These men gloated about an assault on an Agent of ours. I have reason to believe they'd have it documented."

"What's the goal?"

"Complete destruction. I want them finished."

"Got it. I'll call you when it's done."

***

ACE

The next day, I was surprisingly less miserable, if that's what you could call it. I was breathing properly; I even managed to shower and get changed without feeling the need to throw up. But the moment I got downstairs, and my eyes fell on Illarion, all that confidence, was suddenly gone.

"Hey," I said quietly, sitting down, taking the coffee, he placed in front of me.

Aurel joined us a few minutes later, followed by Daniel.

"I made you breakfast." Illarion turned his attention to the plate of food he'd slid over.

"Can we go somewhere today?"

He looked back up at me. "Where would you like to go?"

"Anywhere." I forced a tight smile. "I just want to get out of the house."

"Okay. After breakfast?"

"Is that safe?" Aurel asked.

Illarion shot him a look across the table. "It's fine."

I frowned at the exchange.

Illarion didn't say anymore as he served the others and then himself.

My gaze shot up when I felt Aurel's mood drop.

I didn't miss the slight faltering in his aura which told me he was deeply concerned by the way mine was probably pulsating erratically, matched only by Illarion's tightly wound posture. But he didn't say anything and for that, I was grateful even if I couldn't tell him so.

Illarion sat down beside me, but he didn't make mention of the rollercoaster from hell we'd both been on, and I didn't dare look him in the eyes. I felt the anger bubbling inside him. I saw it every time I chanced a look across at him, his jaw seemed to be permanently grinding and the heat emanating from him, was suffocating. Aurel saw it too but he had enough tact not to ask.

I moved a mushroom around my plate ignoring Illarion. He was two steps away from losing it completely, and whatever was holding him together, must have been some seriously strong shit—maybe I could ask him what it was, God knew I needed something.

"If you can't eat it, I'll make you something else," he said, startling me.

"This is fine."

"Don't force yourself," he warned.

Taking every mouthful slowly, I chewed, swallowed and waited a moment to see how my stomach would handle it. Once I was sure it would be safe to proceed, I took another bite.

As I ate, the tension in the room grew. Illarion was keeping his eyes firmly glued to the table. Neither Aurel nor Daniel said a word, but it wasn't hard to miss the way their eyes skipped from me to Illarion.

Simply put, it was the breakfast from hell, a nice compliment to the ride we'd had.

When everyone was done, Illarion took their plates to the sink and sat back down beside me.

Daniel excused himself and left to use the gym while Aurel stayed behind reading through the files I'd brought back with me. I remembered asking for them, and I vaguely remember Daniel bringing them to me.

But my head was all over the place and I didn't even realize that I had forgotten them. After everything that happened with Dalca then the whole being paralyzed thing, my mind was not on the same page.

And as his father's name came to the forefront of my mind a choked gasp caught in my lungs as every single vivid image from that night flashed through my eyes.

Illarion reached over, finding my hand. I winced as another bout of nausea rushed through me. I didn't risk vomiting all over the floor. I got up and ran, making it to the powder room, throwing myself at the toilet bowl, bringing everything up.

Like always, Illarion was by my side, pulling my hair back. "You're still not keeping your food down."

His voice was laced with concern, and he tried not to let the fear show, but it did. How could he be here, acting like he didn't see what happened to me?

"You must be starving."

Another change of topic. Was he going to pretend that nothing happened?

"Why didn't you say anything?"

When I pulled back, flushing the toilet, I closed the lid and sat on it. "I didn't want to worry you."

"You didn't think I'd worry seeing you get weaker as the weeks went on?"

He had a point.

"Ace, you have to tell me these things," Illarion said, cupping my cheek and forcing my eyes to his. "You're being too hard on yourself. You need time to deal with what happened."

My breath shuddered and came out in a quiet gasp. "I'm broken."

"You're not broken."

"You saw what happened to me last night. If that's not broken. Christ, Illarion, tell me what is."

His eyes flared, flicking away from mine. I was right. He didn't want to talk about it. Maybe it was too much for him, maybe that whole event was just what he needed to really see what a fucked-up mess I was—

"Stop," he whispered, capturing my hands looking at me again.

"I don't want your pity."

"And you're not getting it."

Dropping my hands to my lap, I looked down at the twisted mess of toilet paper I'd shredded. Tears burned my eyes again. I was sick of crying.

Illarion tipped my chin up meeting my eyes. Nothing but love coursed through him. Not pity. Not judgement.

"Nothing that happened in that house can make me stop loving you, Ace. Nothing. And you'll never get pity from me. I think you know that don't you?"

"You've been...distant from me."

"I have." He hung his head. "But it's not because of you and certainly not because of what happened there."

"But it is because of what you saw."

"Because I failed. I should have protected you, and when you were calling for me..." He shook his head slowly, like he was confused by it all. "We will get through this together, I give you my word."

"I should have said something. I'm sorry."

A questioning look met me.

"About being sick," I clarified. "I should have said something."

"Come on." He stood up holding out his hand. "I'm taking you out. You said you wanted to get out of the house."

"Is that safe?" I echoed Aurel's logical questioning. "I wasn't even thinking…"

He drew me against him and rested his chin on top of my head, "I've got it covered. It's safe, I promise."

"I don't want to make things harder for you, I'll stay put if that's what we have to do."

"What we have to do is make sure you're feeling better, living. I've got it covered. Okay?"

I pulled back and looked up at him. His voice was firm, sincere. I nodded. "Okay."

CHAPTER TWENTY-THREE

ACE

A dress, something nice. That's what I needed. I rummaged through my wardrobe. I wanted something that would make me look like less of a walking corpse and more of a presentable woman who would be seen with a man like Illarion.

I stopped when my hands trailed across a silky, floral dress with thick straps. A smile spread across my face as I pulled it out and pressed it against my body. It was perfect, it was everything I would have worn in my past life.

I changed into it and pulled my hair back into a ponytail wearing it just like I knew he liked it. I picked out a lovely pair of nude sandals Elsa had obviously ordered for me. The heel was just over two inches, and it did wonders for my calves. I even managed to slather on some makeup and really complete the look with some simple jewelry. How this woman got all the right styles, was beyond me. I smiled at my reflection. The bruises were gone for the moment and the scars were faint under the foundation.

My hand grazed the spot where Troy's chain used to hang. I swallowed back the sadness. I didn't even know how he was; I hadn't even thought to ask about him.

What did that say about me? God, I was getting too used to asking that. I missed him and the small token I'd carried of his, was lost.

Subconsciously, I smoothed my hands along the fabric. A deep, niggling feeling of sickness welled inside me making hot flushes kick my heartrate up. An anxiety attack. That's all this was. It wasn't Dalca. Aaryon had made sure he was gone and I was triggered by the dress, that's all.

I sucked in a sharp breath, composing myself. This was nothing like the dresses *he* made me wear. This was all Ace and Illarion. I had to reaffirm that to myself. It had a deep, yet conservative plunge in the front and had I not been so sickly thin, I would have filled it out nicely, but nonetheless, it was still pretty. It was a lot like what I would have bought myself before...before everything.

Swallowing hard, I smoothed the straps down and readjusted them for the tenth time. Why did I feel so off wearing this?

It wasn't revealing, it didn't make me uncomfortable. The hem came to a stop just above my knees, firmly tightening around my thighs elongating my legs. The pink and purple flowers splashed sporadically against the white backdrop was a stunning combination for my tanned skin tone.

But my arms were ugly. The skin there was scarred and pinkish with violent, blue bruises lining the inside of my elbows. Nothing could fix that, not even the Being with all his power and supernatural healing. I bowed my head at my reflection and folded my arms across my chest.

I couldn't go out like this. Deep in my core where all my demons used to hide alone, now lay a pit of endless self-loathing and misery. At least they weren't lonely anymore.

I pulled out a cardigan and slipped it on. I looked like I was trying to pull off a super, preppy outfit so no one would look twice at it.

Without thinking about it too much, I stepped out into the hall before I could psych myself out. I made my way downstairs and stopped just short of the door drawing in a deep breath. *I could do this.*

He wouldn't think any less of me and the way I looked. He wasn't like that. He never was.

My eyes fell on him. I had to hold my breath as it caught. Whatever he said I did to him, it could never compare to what he did to me.

He was dressed in light-colored chinos with a blue and white checked button-down shirt which was rolled up to his elbows and, instead of his usual combat boots, he had on a pair of brown, lace up shoes. His hair was tied back in a bun but those same, few, stray hairs always fell over his eyes, framing his face.

My god.

Cautiously taking the steps down one by one, I let out the breath I was holding. He turned catching my eye and a wide smile spread across his face.

"You are so beautiful." He stepped up meeting me on the last step.

He brought his hands to mine and slid them up, over the cardigan coming to rest over my elbows.

"You don't look so bad yourself, Agent Lazarev."

He laughed and pressed a gentle kiss to my lips. When he pulled back, he led us to the car, as was his customary way, he opened the door for me and closed it once I was inside.

As soon as we were both seated, he shifted the new Hummer into gear, and we were on our way.

"I've been meaning to ask you a serious question."

"Sure," he said seriously.

"Do you have car dealerships on speed dial?"

He laughed. "Something like that."

"In order of importance, where are they in relation to the bakery?"

He laughed, the sound warming my heart. "On par."

I grinned, glancing around, as we drove past all the main turnoffs I recognized around this part of Long Island. "Where are we going anyway?"

"It's a surprise, but you'll love it."

"Come on. You know I don't like surprises."

"I know, but you'll like this one."

"If you say so."

He laughed softly before turning his attention back to the road.

After about twenty minutes on the road, he finally pulled up to a large mansion overlooking the beach nestled amongst three long piers filled with massive yachts.

My eyes scanned the horizon. Dozens and dozens of small white boats dotted the shoreline and there were hundreds of people.

"You got us a boat for the day?" I glanced at him.

"Not quite. Come on."

He got out of the car, and I followed him down to the shore until we reached a small, paved path which led down past the trees to the marina.

A middle-aged man walked up toward us from a large, white yacht by the end of the dock with a smile. He waved Illarion down. I glanced back at the yacht. Damn. It was probably the biggest one there, too.

Illarion greeted him with a smile.

"Mr. Lazarev."

"Salvador, this is Miss Hart," Illarion said with a smile.

"It's an absolute pleasure, Miss Hart." He shook my hand before he turned his attention back to Illarion. "Mr. Lazarev, everything is ready, as you asked."

"And my order?"

"Due to arrive by the time you dock."

"Great, thank you." He smiled. "Please make sure Roza calls me if she needs anything."

He nodded, gracefully shaking Illarion's hand.

"We'll be back in a few hours," Illarion said taking hold of my hand bringing my attention back to him.

"You okay?"

My mouth dried up.

"Ace?"

"There are a lot of people here."

"Just focus on me."

Easier said than done. I looked up at him and then back at the other people on the pier. Couples and families all around us were getting into their boats, some were already alive with the sound of people partying. No one was paying us any attention, and that relaxed me slightly.

Then, I caught unmistakable flashes of scope reflections in the afternoon sun glistening from several vantage points. Before I could bug out, Illarion's hold tightened on me and he drew his hand over his ear and tapped it. "Delta Unit, confirm positions."

My eyes snapped up to his.

Illarion remained quiet for a moment listening to what I assumed was an earpiece before nodding.

A quick succession of flashes off to my right caught my eyes. Morse code flashes reading *five by five*.

"You have a whole security team out here," I said.

"I've had a team on us the second we reached home soil."

"Do they know what they're protecting?"

"They know what they need to."

"Agency?"

"Private detail."

"Illarion—"

"It has to be done. You know as well as I do how far Dalca's reach extends."

"Don't need to remind me."

"Come on," he said, gently drawing me against him.

I sighed, hating that I needed round the clock security detail, but I wasn't ignorant. I knew how powerful Dalca was and I knew that the only reason we were able to come down here today was because Illarion had people watching us. It was probably the only reason I were afforded so much freedom without being ushered into witness protection in the first place.

Knowing how much that kind of security went for, made my eyes water. Illarion spared no expense. I knew that already but knowing it was spent on me, made me sick. Dalca screwed everything.

Together we walked down along the wooden slats and when we stopped, my breath caught as we came up to the one Salvador had come from. Briefly taken aback by the mammoth sight before me, I looked up, stunned. It towered over every other boat here and it sure as hell looked better than the rest.

"After you," Illarion said, softly in my ear as he came to stand beside me and nodded to the gangway.

I climbed up, absorbing every single inch of the yacht's beauty. It was incredible, every step was like walking into a dream. As I reached the second deck, I noticed two security guards take flank position and step out of view. Discreet to most but obvious to anyone trained to see them.

Once we'd reached the main deck, I stepped up and over the last steps and waited for Illarion to join me. My eyes swept the vastness of the boat. It must have been at least two-hundred feet. Who on Earth owned this thing?

"Do you like it?" he asked, stopping beside me.

I turned on my heel, pulling my gaze from the horizon of crystal blue skies and endless expanse of sea ahead. "It's amazing."

He smiled taking my hand. "I know you hate the need for security."

"You're right." I looped my arms around his neck. "But I understand it and I appreciate it. I appreciate you. Thank you, Ila."

"I appreciate you, more than you know," he said, easing me back. He reached for my cardigan and when I pulled back, he pressed his hands to my shoulders.

"Ila, I don't think—"

"You don't need it." He shook his head slowly. "You don't need that around me; you know that."

I looked away.

He caught my chin and tilted my face back to his. I hadn't even realized that I had wrapped my arms around myself.

He brought his hands to my elbows, slowly sweeping down and unfolding my arms. He waited patiently until every muscle slowly unlocked and I placed my hands on his arms.

"You can relax, enjoy the sun. I see the yearning in your eyes." He cupped my cheek and smiled. "It's just us here, my staff won't bother us."

"This is yours?" My eyes shot up to his.

He chuckled. "Why would I bring you to someone else's boat?"

"This is what you meant when you said we'd sail the world together."

He tipped his head to the side with a small, confused smile.

"At the warehouse showdown, before I, you know, died in your arms and all that. You said we'd sail the world together and eat a lot. It sounded perfect."

His jaw squared. "I meant everything, and that'll never change. We've got a lifetime of things to do together."

"I like the sound of that."

"So do I, so come on, take this off and enjoy the sun with me. It's a perfect day."

I nodded, taking a deep breath, pulling the cardigan off my shoulders. Illarion took it and handed it to a man dressed in white whom I hadn't even noticed had just appeared. He gave us each a quick nod before disappearing down the narrow walkway.

Illarion kissed my forehead and led us away from the bow and curious crowds. I didn't need to have any super-heightened senses to hear the people below talking about the boat and how incredible it was, questioning who owned it, what kind of job the person had. All the usual questions people asked when they saw something like this in public. Usually, only celebrities and billionaires were privy to this sort of thing, and, well, Illarion.

The four decks were a sight in themselves, it was impossible to fathom such a grand piece of architecture.

The sleek design of the yacht was out of this world. Tinted, glass windows surrounded each deck, and the rest were some incredibly designed panels that glistened in the sun.

Another well-dressed man approached us.

"Mr. Lazarev, we're ready to sail. Weather is clear, with an expected high of eighty-two degrees on the ocean."

"Perfect."

He bowed courteously and took his leave.

A few moments later, the yacht began to move. I could only imagine how extravagant a boat like this looked to people on the shore, and I wasn't at all surprised by the small crowd of people forming to watch it leave.

Illarion kept us moving up until we were on the sundeck.

There was an entire tan leather lounging area with a sleek, square glass table in the middle which was set out with everything one would expect in a high-end restaurant.

"Sit?" he gestured.

I followed wordlessly and took a seat, Illarion sat opposite me.

For a moment he looked at me thoughtfully before leaning back in his seat. "You know I'd do anything for you, Ace."

"I know." My heart grew heavy.

He'd done a lot for me, gone through a lot for me. This gesture out on the ocean, the surveillance, it was beyond anything I could have anticipated. Guilt had consumed him for months.

"And you know I'm not doing any of this, out of guilt or obligation."

I tipped my head to the side, watching him. What he said rang true, there was only love and a deep desire within him to protect me. It was the same feeling that coursed through me when I knew I could never let him get hurt when I was with Dalca when I knew I would do whatever it took to keep his secret safe.

But a part of me now wondered whether I knew this man before me as well as I thought. He was haunted. Nightmares chased sleep from him every night. I knew it whether he admitted it to me or not. And the kind of surveillance he had and was capable of paying for, meant he was serious business and not the kind that just inherited money from his folks. There was more to Illarion Lazarev than I'd thought.

"What's going through your head?" he asked gently.

"Are you a double agent, Illarion?"

He laughed at first but then, when he must have realized I wasn't joking, he leaned forward, meeting my gaze.

"No, Ace. I am not."

"You'd tell me if you were."

"I'd tell you."

"Because you trust me, right?"

"Yes. What is this about?"

"Ila." I shook my head, looking around at the boat, the guards I wasn't meant to know were there, the set-up, his house. "You're not just inheritance rich."

"You're right."

"So, there is something more."

"Something off the Agency's radar. But it's not for another agency."

"Black ops?"

"Not quite. Personal work."

"Personal work you've never told me about."

He covered his mouth with his hand, his eyes leaving mine for a moment.

"Illarion?" I leaned forward.

He looked back at me just as two staff came back around and set down some assorted chocolates and a bottle of champagne that cost more than a month's rent in New York.

He ignored the staff and the bottle, holding my gaze. "I never told you because it never came up."

"What kind of ops do you run?"

"Some information gathering, a lot of direct requests. Relocations and security."

"Human trafficking?"

"Yes, sometimes. Most requests come from a friend in the UN. He knows I can find homes for them without people asking too many questions."

"How?"

"I have a lot of connections, relationships I've built over my years in various positions of employment."

"In Russia?"

"Yes, some contacts are Russian."

"Okay."

"Okay?"

I nodded, chewing my bottom lip. I saw the pain in his eyes.

"Ace. I'm not a double agent."

"I believe you. I just wanted to know where it all comes from. I trust you, Ila. I know you're a good person and now I know how good."

His brows furrowed but when I reached for the champagne, he took it from me, gently closing his hand over mine.

"I'd never be involved in anything that puts you at risk, do you understand?"

"I do."

"And you trust me?"

"I trust you." I held his gaze.

"Do you?"

"Always."

Still holding my gaze, Illarion tipped his head to the side searching my eyes. I closed my hand over his cheek.

"I'm sorry I brought it up. I didn't mean to insinuate anything," I said.

"I'm glad you did. I don't want there to be secrets between us."

"Agreed. Now, enough work talk, let's drink."

He relented, giving me a little smile. He took the bottle from me and poured two glasses of champagne. He handed me a glass and held out his.

"You know your vintages," he said when I grinned.

"This was on my dad's bucket list."

"Then we toast your family."

He raised his glass again, making me chuckle.

"A toast to my family."

I took a sip of the champagne and closed my eyes. The sun was warm on my face and Illarion stayed quiet, letting me enjoy my moment.

Not long after we'd left the marina the engines came to a stop alerting me. Illarion got to his feet drawing me up to mine. He took my glass from me and replaced it on the table before leading me down another set of stairs which led down to the lower deck and around to the bow.

Once we stopped, he moved to me, closing the gap between us.

He turned my body around, so I was facing the large white, hull. A giant version of the Lazarev crest that adorned his home, was printed on it.

How did I miss that?

He wrapped his arms around my stomach pulling me back to lean against his body.

"My father thought it was appropriate." He chuckled. "The Lazarev men were quite fond of this sort of display. I don't really care for it, but it was important to them and so here it is, I kept it as he wished."

"It's amazing."

"I wanted to show you because this is where my dad proposed to my mom." He paused to sweep my ponytail over one shoulder where he placed a soft, tender kiss on the curve of my neck. "This is where he came to ask her, where he told her that he wanted her to share his name. Well not this boat, but you get the idea."

I was transfixed by the gravity of the words he'd spoken. He wasn't only being sentimental when he offhandedly mentioned that he wanted me to stick around. He'd let me into his heart and his home, he opened up about his family.

"I know you want to wait. But I wanted you to know that I meant it, every word. I'll wait as long as you need me to wait."

Illarion tightened his hold on me, and exhaled deeply, drawing my attention to him.

My insides tightened; he was on edge. "What's wrong?"

"I already told you have contacts."

I nodded.

"I need to show you something," he said softly, scratching the back of his neck.

When I turned around, he handed me his phone.

The phone had a video loaded on it. I pressed play. When the video started, I was confused, until I saw one of their faces and then I felt sick. My hands instantly turned to ice as I gripped the phone in my hand. The screen split into three simultaneous feeds—police bodycams from three separate units.

The voice on the first screen belonged to a man.

"Jarrod Sharpe. You're under arrest for the rape of Agent Acacia Hart..."

His voice trailed off and everything else became a blur.

Illarion wrapped his arms around me, tightening his hold and before I could swat away the tears, his thumb coasted across my cheeks and wiped them away.

"How?" my voice was barely a whisper.

"I told you, Ace, I'd do anything for you. Whatever it takes. I'll never stop until you're safe, until you know you don't have to look over your shoulder anymore."

He tucked his phone back in his pocket and swept his thumb across the curve of my lip, bringing his face down to mine.

My body reacted moving up against him, pulling his body closer.

"It's not the justice you want, it never could be, but it's a start."

"Oh, Ila."

His lips found mine, and he kissed me like he hadn't kissed me for months. And this, this huge thing he'd done for me, it was beyond what I needed. My heart was healing, slowly, and I knew, without a doubt. He was here, with me. Completely.

I reached up, looping my arm around his neck, deepening the kiss until I felt it drown out every other thought.

"Thank you."

He smiled against my mouth. "You don't need to thank me for this."

His fingers brushed through my hair, gently sweeping it down my back.

Slowly, we pulled apart still leaving no space between us and I was completely open to that idea. All I wanted was to be close to him, to show him how much I loved him and appreciated what he'd done for me.

"Lunch should be ready by now."

When I replied with another kiss, he laughed softly tickling my neck with his breath.

"If you actually want me to eat any food, we should leave now." I managed, pushing him back.

He was loving every minute. Jerk.

When he reluctantly agreed. I grinned letting him draw me against his body.

He led us back up the stairs onto the main deck and around to a table which hadn't been there earlier.

We sat, and I downed the rest of the champagne the staff had brought over.

The food came out and Illarion watched with careful precision as I took each mouthful. Once the steak and salad were gone from both our plates, we moved on to the small serving of dessert.

"How do you feel?"

I sensually licked my lower lip forcing my eyes to his. "Like something sweet."

He grinned, eyes narrowing. "That *is* sweet."

I shrugged, seductively picking up another strawberry with my fork. When I saw his lips part with longing, I placed it in my mouth and he let out a low growl.

Again, I casually tossed my hair back over my shoulder, tilting my head back in an exaggerated maneuver as I took a cherry and toyed with it.

He grew restless, watching my lips, but he stayed exactly where he was. He patiently watched until I had both lemon tarts, every single strawberry and cherry.

And as soon as I was done, he got up, startling me. He pulled me up and before I registered what was happening, he moved us backwards to the tinted windows. Before we crashed into them, they slid open silently revealing an overwhelmingly, huge bedroom.

My eyes took everything in.

As soon as the doors slid shut again, we were surrounded by three hundred and sixty-degree views of the ocean and sky above us.

The room was basically floor-to-ceiling-windows, and the rest was lined with sleek, black and white, leather lounges and a massive, king size bed centered right in the middle. The roof was lined with the same tinted windows, the sun and the blue horizon washed over us.

"Oh my god."

"Is this sweet enough?" he whispered, coming up behind me, letting his lips linger by my ear.

"Well, Agent. Lazarev, when you speak like that, a girl might just melt."

He chuckled, his chest rumbling against my back.

My legs weakened and pulse quickened all at once.

He moved us toward the bed and gently lowered me onto it. He followed pressing his knee between my legs and gently pushing them apart. A shaky gasp left my lips.

His lashes lowered, leaving only a sliver of his dangerously dark eyes visible. He pressed his lips to mine and quietly stifled another gasp as he trailed his palm across my thigh and under the hem of my dress.

"Is this okay, lyubov?"

"Perfect, Ila."

The way my body responded to his touch made me realize that no matter what uncontrollable things went wrong, he would always be right.

He swept his hands under me and in one, fluid motion he flipped me up and on top of him, so our positions were reversed, and he brought my face down to his.

A deep, hungry kiss spread between us as his hands worked their way up my thighs pulling with them, my dress. Up and over it went. He threw it to the floor haphazardly. Bringing his hands back to my skin, he trailed his fingertips up along the curve of my hip coming to rest just below my breasts.

Through hooded eyes he watched me, every breath I drew was laced with a desire so deep it transcended mere physical touch. He was more than just someone I loved, someone I wanted to be with. He was *everything.*

He brought his hand to my cheek, leaving a blazing trail behind wherever he touched.

"I love you, Ace."

Those words burned a hole in my chest. "I love you, Illarion."

He reached up again only this time he pulled me down, so our bodies were touching, length to length and no more room was available between us.

Less than a heartbeat later he had unclasped my bra, expertly, before he tossed it aside with my dress.

A quick moment later he lowered me back onto the sheets. He pressed an elbow into the pillow beside my head. A line in his jaw feathered as he drank my body in. He moved carefully, lowering his lips to mine, crushing me against him as though there would never be another day like today. And in our world, maybe there wouldn't be.

His dark eyes found mine, seeking permission.

He snaked his hand under me pulling me up and, arching my back I let him in. His soul swam through me, infecting every corner of my essence.

His calloused hands coasted across my breast, drawing another breathless whisper of his name.

Suddenly, he was everywhere, he was everything, inside me and around me. He filled every crack in my bones, every chip in my soul. He knew how to fix me completely.

His hand slipped to the nape of my neck, and he brushed his fingers through my hair, deepening the kiss, letting no space escape between us.

A broken cry was lost as he pressed his hot cheek to mine and gripped my body like a silent plea.

Nothing else mattered but the way he held onto me, the way he smoothed his hands over my trembling body.

The heat burned, scolding inside me. By the way his breaths quickened and the muscles in his arms tensed as he held me, I knew we were both close. He closed his mouth over mine, stifling both our broken gasps as it finally broke inside us, exploding.

My nails dug into his sweat slicked skin, and I threw my head back, arching my body.

He buried his face in my hair and breathed out deeply, fast, shallow breaths consuming him.

Letting the aftershocks slowly quieten and disappear, I turned in his arms and held him, letting my hands trail over the planes of his taut abdomen.

In his arms, I lost track of time, but I couldn't care less. I knew who I was, and I belonged right here, with him. He drew me closer, removing all the space between us as our breathing returned to normal and my dizziness settled.

Eventually, when the engines roared back to life, we got up and got dressed. I didn't want today to end, but I knew that he would do everything in his power to make sure we had a thousand days like it.

CHAPTER TWENTY-FOUR

ACE

As we disembarked and walked down, I tried my hardest to ignore the massive crowd which had formed. Despite the breathtaking afternoon we'd just shared, I hated how quickly the anxiety returned.

Salvador was waiting down on the pier with a smile and a small white bag that he gave to Illarion. With a quick smile, Illarion passed it to me. When I shot him a questioning look, he simply smiled and thanked Salvador.

Glad that I pulled my cardigan back on before we got here, I cringed as dozens of eyes were on us, most wide with awe. Others narrowed with envy, mostly from women who kept staring me down. I rolled my eyes walking beside him.

Illarion tightened his hold on me, throwing a possessive arm around my shoulder. "Still with me?"

"There are a lot of people."

"I'm sorry," he said, quietly. "I should have warned you about that, maybe this wasn't a good idea."

"No. It was perfect, I'm just…I'll be alright. I need to get out more, it's fine."

He grazed a finger along my cheek with a smile.

"Just focus on me."

Ignoring the looks and chatters and the women giving me death stares, I did just that. I looked up into his eyes.

"People here are usually more...*tasteful*. They're just tourists."

"You always know what to say."

He chuckled. "I only know what to say because it's the truth."

Once we'd reached the Hummer, and we were safely inside, he nodded at the bag in my lap.

"Open it," he encouraged.

I smirked and reached into the bag. My fingers tightened around a medium sized, rectangular box. I slowly pulled it out of the bag and held it in my hand.

"I had it made, when you came back but then...the accident happened." A line in his jaw worked and then his hand was on mine. "I wanted you to have something. From me."

"I have a lot from you, Ila."

"Something you can keep with you, until you get a ring from me that is."

A flutter rushed through my heart at the sentiment.

I returned my attention to the box and opened it. The black box held a white gold chain and, at the end, hung a delicate Celtic knot clasping a stunning diamond.

"Traditionally, it represents what a many people believe to be the holy trinity, but others see it as the unity between mind, body and spirit," he said, softly. "You've gone through so much, yet your mind is strong, your body endured, and your spirit remains pure."

Tears stung the back of my eyes as the box grew heavy in my hand. I was speechless. I set it down in my lap and drew my hands over my eyes.

"It's too much," he said.

"No, Ila," I replied quickly, turning to face him, "it's perfect."

"Really?"

"Yes, I love it. I'm just, I feel unworthy of this."

"You're worthy, Ace."

I wet my lips looking down at the stunning necklace.

"You're worthy," he repeated, gently taking the box from my clutch. "Let me."

It took a moment for my brain to communicate with my body. I turned in the seat and he swept my hair off my shoulders and gently placed the chain around my neck letting it fall just above the curve of my collarbone.

"I know you lost the one Troy gave you and I remember you liked wearing white gold."

My heart sunk, oh God, how could I have gone all this time and not once asked how he was? Jesus, I was a selfish jerk and a shit friend.

"You've been hyper focused on surviving, Ace. Don't be so hard on yourself."

Of course he'd caught all of that. "How is he?"

He tucked a strand of hair behind my ear, caressing my cheek with his hand. "He took it hard, like we all did. I went to see him twice, to check in on him."

"Oh, Ila." I bowed my head.

"When you're up to it, we'll go and see him."

"Thank you, for everything." I nodded, leaning across the console pulling him against me.

Once I released him, he shifted the Hummer into drive, and we left the beautiful coastal town and made our way back home.

"How are you feeling?" he asked, as we pulled up and around the driveway to his house.

"So far so good." I shrugged, getting out with my little bag.

"Later, if you're up to it, I want to run through some ideas with you. Get a team ready."

"Whenever you need me, I'm good."

He nodded and we parted ways at the foot of the stairs. He went left toward the main living area where we'd set up our makeshift Agency workstation and I went up, toward my room. As much as I enjoyed playing house and looking pretty I desperately wanted to change and hit the gym.

Once I changed, I made my way to the bathroom, scrubbed off the makeup and braided my hair. My eyes fell to the knot around my neck, and I felt myself smile.

But as my attention went to my less than toned arms and thighs, I scoffed at myself. A gym session was in order. I was eager to get back into shape and get some mass back on my spangly arms.

Before I made a move to leave, I felt it, in the pit of my stomach, rapidly creeping up on me. Not again. First, my mouth watered and then my vision dimmed, I rushed back to the bathroom and dropped to my knees above the toilet.

Tears rapidly formed, and I swatted them away with an angry force. At least Illarion wouldn't have to know about the epic waste of a ten-thousand-dollar bottle of champagne, and a nice array of fruits that just went down the toilet. Literally.

I peeled myself away from the bowl and flung my braid back over my shoulder. Just as I was about to get up, a violent convulsion surprised me forcing me back to the ground. I threw my hands out in front of me, narrowly missing the basin. That could have been really, really bad.

Although I didn't crack my head open, I did smash shoulder first into the wall before landing with a thud cradling my bruised shoulder.

Before I could assess how bad it was, Illarion came rushing through the door. Great.

"Ace?" he yelled, before he reached me.

When he finally spotted me, a moment of panic rushed through him and then it was replaced by amusement.

"Yeah, yeah," I muttered, still sprawled out on the floor like a drunk college girl. "Help me up."

He smirked and held his hand out.

"What happened?" he asked, smoothing my clothes down as I stood.

"Ah you know, the usual, fell over my own feet."

"Were you sick again?" he asked, leading me to my bed, throwing a quick glance around the bathroom.

I nodded, still nursing my shoulder.

"How did you fall?"

The concern was back. Guess he didn't believe the whole, *I'm clumsy, and I fell*, spiel.

I looked across at him as he sat down beside me, he pulled my hand away and moved the strap from my top drawing in a sharp breath.

"Ace. What happened?"

"I was sick," I said, simply.

"And?"

"And then there was a sharp pain and a convulsion—"

"A seizure?" his voice rose, two full octaves. "How long has that been happening?"

"I don't know…" I peeled my eyes away from his. "A while."

"A while?" He shook his head, incredulously. "Why wouldn't you say anything?"

Being chastised by him was the world's worst torture. I dragged my gaze away from his and sunk into myself. The disappointment in his eyes was bad enough, but the tone in his voice? That shattered me.

"I'm sorry."

"Are you trying to get yourself killed?"

"What?" I stammered. "No, why would you think that?"

"You tell me. You don't seem to care about your health, you're keeping things like this from me, what else haven't you told me about?"

"Nothing!"

"I don't believe this." He shook his head again, standing. "I'm calling a doctor."

"No, don't, I don't want to see anyone." My eyes flicked up and, in a moment of panic, I realized that I sounded like a child.

"Having episodes like that can be due to a more serious condition. You're seeing someone."

"I'm sure it's nothing."

"If you weren't living off Serum and heroin for the last six months, I might have believed you."

I closed my mouth pulling my ego down a few notches.

Several moments of silence passed before I felt the tension inside him shift and slowly dissipate. He let out a breath and knelt, pressing his hand over mine, squeezing it gently until I turned my head toward him, giving him all my attention.

"Please, Ace. For me."

"It's a waste of time. They won't find anything we don't already know."

"Humor me."

"Fine." I conceded turning my head from him.

He smiled at my pouting and pressed a soft kiss to my lips.

"Will you call the doctor here?" I whined.

"I'll call Donna. We can trust her."

He had a hard time letting anyone in, especially when it came to me. He was always guarded and overly cautious. Some called him paranoid. But he wouldn't have entrusted my health to just anyone, Donna meant a lot to him. And the little time I did get to speak with her, made me feel at ease. She was kind, and sweet and I could see why Illarion cared about her.

He pulled out his phone and sent off a quick message. A moment later a chime sounded alerting him to a new message, "We're set."

"Can you stay with me?"

"I'll stay as long as I can, but she'll want to see you in private too."

Suddenly anxious, I wrapped my arms around my chest.

He cupped my cheek, turning my face toward him. "I wouldn't let her near you if I didn't trust her." His eyes grew warmer. "You'll like her."

"When will she get here?"

"In a few minutes. She was seeing another patient down the road. She helps the those who can't afford to come to the hospital."

"She sounds like a good person."

"She is. This will all be okay."

Maybe it was a good idea.

Illarion got up before a knock at the door drew my attention. When he got up, I quickly grabbed my hoodie and pulled it on.

Illarion pressed a quick kiss to the top of my head and went to the door. Elsa must have walked her up here, she was probably well acquainted with Illarion's old *friend*.

"She's here," he said, softly, brushing my cheek with his thumb. "It'll be alright, I promise."

I swallowed back the nerves and stood, waiting, as Illarion went to the door, letting her in.

Her eyes found mine. She didn't miss a thing as her gaze landed on my heavily clothed body in a room which was at least seventy-five degrees.

"Ace, you remember, Donna," he said.

"I do, it's good to see you again."

She smiled and gave Illarion a curt nod for the introduction.

Illarion waited by the door as Donna stepped closer to me with a wide smile, hand outstretched.

Her sapphire eyes were framed by dark blonde lashes and a thick framed, designer pair of glasses. Her blonde hair was tied back in a sleek ponytail secured with a gorgeous black ribbon. Her light purple blouse sat just above her hips, tucked neatly into a pair of black, high-waist, suit pants which cropped just at her ankles revealing a stunning pair of sky-high, nude pumps. Everything about her was alluring.

Inside her there was nothing but good. She was a pure and decent person, and if he trusted her, she must have been an incredible woman.

He caught my eye from by the door. *"Do you want me to stay?"*

"No, you were right, it's fine."

He smiled in response before leaving and closing the door.

I brought my attention back to Donna. She was already unpacking her equipment, setting up at the table. She neatly placed her Prada handbag by the foot of my bed and turned to me.

"Have a seat," she said, softly.

Sitting down, I looked up at her.

"You can take your hoodie off."

Feeling a lot less comfortable now, I did as she asked and instinctively wrapped my arms over my skin as much as I could.

She pulled the chair over to me and sat. "Let's take a look."

She gently took one of my hands and drew my arm to her, she turned it in her hand running her fingers along the marks, examining the depth of the cuts and the bruises along the injection sites.

"They're healing on their own, which is typical for Sensitives. But I'll give you some cream to keep the skin soft, it'll minimize scarring where your genetics haven't been able to boost the healing."

I nodded.

"I know the doctors took care of some of the other superficial injuries when you were admitted a few weeks ago and then even more with the aid of your Celestial Being."

"Yep."

She smiled looking up at me through her wide-rimmed glasses. "Tell me about how you've been feeling."

"Sick, nauseated." I rubbed my head and turned to her. "I start to think I'm getting better, but it always comes back."

"Any times you remember it being at its worst?"

"It's always there, but mostly after I eat, I can't hold much down, and the convulsions have started coming more frequently."

She looked at me thoughtfully. "Those are common effects when coming off such potent drugs."

"Even the Serum?"

"Yes. I've been well accustomed to the effects that drug has on Sensitives. I'm sure you know what the chemical composition is."

"Yeah, I do."

"Then you know how serious an addiction to heroin is. It's not a simple thing to detox from, even harder when you add in the rest of the ingredients within the Serum."

"Right, so what does all that mean for me?"

"It's not uncommon to see some lasting and concerning aftereffects."

"You're talking about the seizures."

She looked at me pointedly and nodded. "They are concerning."

"Is it permanent?"

"Fortunately, I don't think so. But I'll run some tests to make sure." She pursed her lips and looked down for a moment. "I'm sorry for what you went through."

"You know?"

"Not all of it, no. Illarion respects your privacy, but he did divulge enough so I know what I'm working with."

"Right."

"The rest is up to you to tell. If you wish. It will make this easier for me, to know what I'm treating you for."

"Sadly, I don't think you could help me, no offence."

She smiled. "None taken. Will you speak with someone if I recommend a therapist?"

"Not sure I have the luxury for that."

"Mental health is not a luxury, Ace. You have a right to feel safe and well."

"I'll feel safe and well when I finish this job."

She ground her jaw and handed me a pack of tablets. "They're stronger than what Daniel gave you. They'll help with the nausea."

She pulled out a small flashlight, bringing my attention back to her. She turned it on and instructed me to follow the light with my eyes.

"Now the seizures, depending on the cause, should ease on their own."

"If they don't?"

"There are medications."

I nodded, blinking back the tears that formed from the light.

"I'll take some blood, run a quick test here. If that comes up clear, we'll stick to waiting them out. I don't want to load you up with more medication. I don't think your liver can take it if I'm completely honest and we need you well and healthy."

Again, I nodded. She drew a couple of vials of blood.

"What are they for?"

"To run more in-depth tests back at the lab."

I was sick at the thought that I didn't even flinch anymore when it came to needles, my heart rate even spiked a little, in some sort of sick anticipation. I swallowed that thought back and looked up at her when she was done.

"It was you…" I said, looking up at her.

A questioning gaze found me.

"You did it, you were the one who had to tell Illarion."

"Yes. It was one of the hardest things I've ever had to do." She pressed her hand to my arm. "Lie down, I'll check your abdomen."

I obliged, and she lifted the hem of my tank top up.

"Everything looks good here."

I sat up and pulled my hoodie back on as soon as she was done.

"Now, this part will be uncomfortable but it's important, Ace."

"You want to do a pelvic exam."

"Considering what you were subjected to, I think it's important."

I drew in a long breath and nodded.

"Did the men use condoms?"

My eyes snapped up to hers immediately sending my guard up. "I never said there were other men."

"Illarion mentioned it to me when he called," she said tipping her head to the side. "I'm sorry, I shouldn't have said anything."

She watched me intently. Her aura was steady, her face placid albeit a bit uncomfortable since I was probably staring at her. God I was losing it.

"No, sorry. You just caught me by surprise. I'm finding it hard to talk about all of this."

"Completely understandable, I'm sorry. I'll be more considered in my approach."

When I gave her a curt nod, she forced a tight smile and pressed her hand to her hip. "Can you tell me if you remember them using protection?"

"Not all the time." I swallowed back the bile building in my throat.

"That's okay, I'll run some tests for STDs."

"You think I caught something?" I asked, immediately hating my-self for not thinking about that when I slept with Daniel or Illarion. Jesus.

"It's okay, Ace."

"No, it isn't okay. Fuck, I'm so stupid."

"If they used condoms, chances are low you caught anything. But I'm going to test for everything to be sure. I'm mostly just checking your health. Okay?"

Tears burned my eyes, but I nodded.

Donna turned, giving me some privacy to undress. I pulled my underwear off and screwed it into a tight ball gripping it like a lifeline.

Donna got to work all while I held my breath, squeezing my eyes shut at the intrusion.

"Nearly done, Ace," she said gently.

Once it was over, Donna packed up her equipment and dropped her gloves into a disposable trash bag, then sat in the chair opposite me.

"There might be some spotting for a few hours, a light pad should be enough. If there's more, call me."

"Thanks." I nodded, folding my hands uselessly in my lap.

She finished writing up the labels on my samples and turned to me.

"Did you know about me before we met?" I asked.

"I did. Illarion was always quiet, he never really smiled much and then, eventually, I noticed a change. He would laugh more, he'd smile. Whenever I asked him about it, he refused to tell me. He always said he'd have to kill me if he told me.

"Eventually, on one of our coffee dates, he told me about you, that he was assigned to watch a young soldier in Iraq."

Hearing about him like this from someone else was so different, I felt like I was learning about him, things he'd never tell me.

"I was so jealous." She chuckled. "I was right here in New York, and he was hung up on a girl on the other side of the planet, he'd never even met. I hated you for it. And then, when he went to find you in Iraq when you went missing, I don't know, I think I kind of got the point."

"The point?"

"The more time I spent with him and the more I saw how happy he was just *knowing* about you, I realized that I was being an idiot. How could I hate someone who made the man I loved so happy? Eventually I got over it, took a while of me brooding and sulking, but ultimately, we became close. He's one of my best friends. And you know in your line of work, how rare that is."

"I do."

"Same goes on my end. The shifts are long, you don't get much normalcy. So, his friendship meant a lot."

"I'm glad you're in his life."

She smiled and a moment later that smile was gone. "When I had to do what I did, it wasn't easy, Ace. I had a choice and I made it. God knows he hated me for it, but I had to try and save you."

"You did what you had to; I know that. Illarion does too."

"Your injuries were so bad. The baby was already gone by the time you were brough to me."

My eyes watered. "I know."

She looked up at me.

"I felt it, in the warehouse. The exact moment she died."

"She?"

"I see her, in another life. In my dreams."

Donna's gaze flicked down from mine and she shook her head, taking her glasses off for a moment.

"It'll never cease to amaze me, hearing about you and what you can do."

"It's ironic though, I'm meant to do all these great things, but I couldn't stop that."

"You couldn't fight them, not all of them. They made sure of that."

"I know."

She balled her fists in her lap, shaking her head. "You died on my operating table and I…"

"You had a chance to save my life, you took it."

"When I had to tell him. The way he looked at me." She shook her head again. "I'll never forget that look."

I looked away. I read his letters and felt the pain in the words and in the residual energy left behind by his touch.

Everything inside him held on to a tiny thread of hope. A hope that I was still out there somewhere.

"I'm glad you're here." She smiled, finally. "He's happy again, happier than I've ever seen him."

"Yeah, he's happy you're here too." I chuckled. "He would have dragged me to the hospital if you didn't come."

"He said you had a bad fall earlier?"

"This seizure was worse than the ones before. I lost my footing and smashed my shoulder into the wall."

She reached for it, taking a quick look. She gently squeezed it and maneuvered it back and forth.

The little device she brought to check my blood, beeped, alerting her to its completion.

She checked it and smiled at me. "Everything looks good here, you should be fine to just let them pass on their own, but you'll need to be careful, no driving, no working. And your shoulder is fine as long as you don't apply too much pressure."

I opened my mouth to protest, but she held her hand out when she got up and started scribbling out a prescription.

"As long as it's desk-based, you're clear. No field duties."

I sighed and took it from her. The signature at the bottom caught my eye. It was signed *D. Martin.*

"Everything okay?" she asked without looking at me.

"Martin?"

"Mm-hmm," she murmured. "Is there a problem?"

I frowned. "No, there's no problem."

"Great, Illarion will get my report, don't bother trying to keep it from him."

"Thanks, Donna," I nodded, getting to my feet.

"No problem. Keep taking those pills and keep checking in with me. I'm happy with how everything else has been going." She handed me a note with instructions on when to keep applying the cream and when to keep taking the pills.

For a moment I looked at her and then when I finally pushed the nerves down, I looked up at her.

"Can I ask you something?"

"Of course." She sat back down.

"Obviously I was cut up inside and well he didn't waste time getting on with the program. Is that bad? Could that have done permanent damage?"

"Normally we would keep you in for a few days to check on the healing. We would advise against sexual activity for at least six weeks to avoid any infections and for all the incisions to heal."

Sexual activity. I cringed, wrapping my arms around my middle. I released a shaky breath and when she walked over to me and pressed a gentle hand to my forearm, I swatted the tears away.

"He didn't wait six weeks. I can tell you that for certain."

"Are you feeling abdominal pain?"

"No."

"What about during intercourse?"

"No."

306

"Then I'd confidently say you're fine. If infection was a concern, I'd see other symptoms and signs."

"Would your blood tests confirm that?"

"Yes, and considering they're all clear, I'd say you're fine, Ace."

"And STDs?"

"All clear."

I let out a relieved breath and nodded. "Thank you."

She smiled, squeezing my arm. "Are you comfortable with me talking to Illarion about today's appointment?"

I looked up, finding her eyes. Was I? For a moment I didn't know what to say, I didn't know if I wanted her sharing everything with him but then, knowing that Illarion and I were going to someday be married, I didn't see the use in hiding anything.

"Yes, that's fine."

"Great. Call me if anything changes. And if you're up to speaking to someone I'll send over the number of the therapist I know."

"Got it," I forced a tight smile.

She packed her things and left; I heard her just outside the door talking with Illarion. I knew what she was telling him, and I didn't need to be there to hear it.

He took the steps down with her and the door opened and closed, and I heard her car take off down the driveway and away from the house.

Once I was sure she was gone, I sprinted outside, starting with a few laps around the house to clear my head.

Chapter Twenty-Five

Ace

I focused on clearing my head as much as possible and running always worked. Today though, it didn't. I finished my lap and jogged back to the house with a frown on my face.

"Hey." Illarion got to his feet when I walked in. "Everything okay?"

"Fine." I nodded, holding my small pile of clothes against my chest.

"You left quickly."

"I just needed to take a breath." I smiled. "I'm going to change, then we can go through this."

"Okay."

I took my time taking the stairs to my room, letting my mind wander back to Donna and the things she'd said.

Swallowing back the niggling feeling in the pit of my stomach, I put it down to irrational jealousy. She said she'd performed the surgery but the name I saw on the hospital records didn't state that unless she went by a different name. Or unless she wasn't who she said she was.

No. That was ridiculous. I'd seen her aura and felt all the way through her soul. She was clean. She was a good person. I, on the other hand, was bordering paranoia. I was making something out of nothing, and the point was moot, what was done was definitive regardless of whose hand was holding the scalpel.

I showered and changed then took another couple of those tablets she gave me and jogged back down the stairs.

Illarion hadn't moved and was still looking over the files Daniel had brought back with us.

"Are you sure everything is okay?"

"Everything's fine, I'm good."

He searched my face, digging just beneath the surface. I pushed my shield up, forcing a tight smile. I didn't need him to know I was letting my paranoia creep up on me and that Donna, one of his closest friends was at the forefront.

Illarion was still suspicious. I cleared my throat pulling my gaze away.

"What's the plan?" I asked, taking a seat beside him.

"Back to Alabama."

"What do you need from there?"

"He was tracking Sensitives with specific skillsets and knowledge. He'd have all that saved somewhere. I doubt he would have memorized everything."

"Agreed, not that much information."

"I want to head a team and go back."

"I can guide you." I nodded.

"No, Ace." He shook his head turning his body to me. "No field work."

"Fine, no field work, I'll sit in the van with Josh, but you need me there."

"You stay in the van, I mean it."

"I will not leave the van." I nodded, smiling. "You have my word. Now what information do you need exactly? He has several offices where he kept different information."

Illarion pulled up a decrypted file which Elena had given him. "I had I.T. run through the information you gave me. These are the agents that we now know were burned."

"Agency I.T. or yours?"

"Both." He frowned.

My heart sunk. They were burned because of me.

"We need to know where he kept the other list. Those agents had information about the offsite servers."

"The lockdown?"

His face hardened. "It's been forced into safe-mode."

"Safe-mode?"

"When the first code is entered without prior confirmation, it forces the agency into a systematic safe-mode, to ensure unauthorized access even with all four codes."

"So, he accessed at least one?"

He nodded.

My eyes widened.

"I was careful," I whispered.

"This isn't your fault."

"I thought I kept that information hidden."

Suddenly, I had no idea what I'd let him have. Maybe, maybe I didn't save anyone. Maybe I wanted to, and my guilt made me think that I'd selected what information I allowed through.

I'd just been brutalized by those assholes that night. Maybe I blocked everything out including who I'd handed over to Dalca.

Illarion's hand tightened around mine, bringing me back to him.

"None of this is on you, Ace."

I pulled my hand free pressing my fingers to my temples. *Had I really sold everyone out?*

No. There was at least one who I knew for certain was still safe.

"Ace," he said firmly, drawing my eyes back to his. "You need to stop torturing yourself. You saved many lives with the information you held back."

As a moment of silence fell between us, I felt the shift inside him, his mind went back to *that* night and so did mine.

"All those agents…"

Illarion shook his head vigorously, "The agents who died knew there was a risk, especially holding that kind of information."

"It's not good enough."

"Ace…"

"Don't," I snapped. "How many?"

He didn't say anything and for a moment, I thought he would argue.

"Two."

"Two?"

Two out of four Sensitives who knew the lockdown protocol. Two Sensitives who were now dead.

"The two who're alive…they'll be at risk now."

"Michael has eyes on those agents. They're safe."

I was going to be sick. I rose to my feet and pressed my hands to the top of my head.

Illarion drew in a long breath. "When we infiltrated the house a few weeks back he'd already cleared out."

That didn't come as a surprise. It was a few days after Daniel broke me out, of course he'd have cleared everything out. When we'd gone on the run, Daniel drove for days, not stopping until we were across state lines.

Mulling over my failure wouldn't help the agents who were in danger now and more importantly the last two with the codes.

I sat back down and pulled the files toward me.

"If he left anything behind, it'll be in the south office," I said.

"Okay, I'll brief Aurel when he gets in. Give me a minute, I'll call Michael and organize a team."

He quietly got to his feet but pressed a kiss to my lips before he dialed a number on his phone and pressed it to his ear. "I need a few agents; we're running a team to the Alabama house again."

He nodded to himself, keeping his eyes downcast.

"Yes, we have a new lead. Information pertaining to the compromised codes."

I flinched when he nodded a few more times, keeping his face neutral.

"Yes, thank you Director. I will."

"What was that about?"

"He wants to make sure I keep an eye on you."

My brow furrowed. Was he really trying to lie to me?

"We're set. We have four agents who will meet us there and the rest is up to us."

"You know you don't have to babysit me."

"I'm not babysitting you. It's as much for you as it is for me," he said lightly.

Illarion's heart was heavy, his eyes looked tired and body worn like the first time I'd seen him since coming back.

"Seeing you makes me feel better. Like I won't wake up and realize it's all been a cruel dream, that you never came back."

"I'm sorry."

"Don't be, I understand. I'm suffocating you. I give you my word I'll try to take a backseat. I'll give you space."

"I don't want space, Ila." I closed my hand over his. "Just trust that I'll be okay, that I can make it through this."

"I know you can make it through this. I never doubted that."

"But you're still worried."

"I'm always going to worry."

I sighed before he pulled my hand into his.

"I know it's not easy, dealing with…everything." I let out a soft laugh trying to hide the sadness in my voice.

He immediately caught on. "No. This isn't hard, I know what you're feeling. You think you're a burden."

"Aren't I?"

He didn't respond, but his silence said infinitely more than words ever could.

"You don't have to lie, I'm not naïve. I know this is taking a toll on you."

He was tired, he couldn't hide that as much as I couldn't hide how messed up I was. He tightened his hold on my hand. "We will finish this, I swear to you—when this is all over, we're both going to be okay."

***

Illarion drove in silence, each of us quietly contemplating what the mission would bring.

Aurel was uneasy in the back seat. His emotions flipped all over the place giving me a migraine, and Illarion was quiet beside me, his face set with steely determination I'd seen only once before. It shook me to the core.

And throughout it all, I was oscillating between insatiable desire to run and hide with my tail between my legs or find Dalca and take him on headfirst, show him that he didn't destroy me. Only I didn't believe that at all as my palms grew sweaty and my breaths became shallow.

Illarion reached over and squeezed my hand in his.

Jesus, my feelings must have been flashing all over the car like a neon sign.

"It's going to be okay," he said, softly. "You'll be safe with Josh."

"I want you with me."

He glanced over at me, a pained expression on his face. "You know you can't be in the field."

"I feel fine."

"You'll be a liability."

Opening my mouth to bite back, I stopped when Aurel nodded, siding with Illarion.

"Damn it," I ground out.

"I can't have you in there, knowing you might have a seizure at any moment," Illarion said. "It will compromise the safety of everyone in the field."

"I know."

"We'll both be nearby," Aurel added.

Rubbing a knot from my shoulder, I nodded.

We drove for the remainder of the journey in silence.

As the airstrip came into view, Illarion pulled around the back and parked where we met Josh and one other field Agent.

"Agents," she acknowledged us.

"Ace, this is Agent Simms."

I shook her hand, glad to see another woman in the field. She had long, blonde hair pulled back into a braid and standard Agency gear like what we had on. Black pants with a black t-shirt and jacket. Though her insignia was different.

"They're a specialized division of the Agency, they're sometimes called in for black ops missions," Illarion explained catching me eyeing the emblem.

"We're called in when the Agency want to keep things off the books, you know, shake shit up a bit," she said with a grin.

"Or in other words, when they want expendable fighters." Aurel added.

"That too," Illarion said, a hint of anger lacing his words. "In any case, they're invaluable to us."

"Glad to be of service." She winked at him.

She was flirting. She was definitely flirting. I tore my gaze from her just in time to spot Josh running toward us.

He pulled me into the biggest bear hug I'd ever had the pleasure of receiving. Illarion darted out of the way, narrowly avoiding getting bowled over, and let out a soft laugh leaving the two of us with some privacy.

"The last time I saw you…"

"I know."

"How are you?" he asked, looking me over.

"I'm good, much better now." I couldn't help the smile that came so naturally around him.

As we neared the jet, he nudged me in the ribs. "So, you and Lazarev?"

I blushed turning from him, spotting Illarion up ahead, who always seemed to have a watchful eye on me. He smiled and turned back to the small group of agents who had gathered, no doubt giving them a brief of what we were doing tonight.

"Yeah," I turned back to Josh.

"It's good, I'm glad. He's a total babe and so are you, plus I saw how he looked at you when he brought you around to see me last year."

"Was everyone aware of this except me?" My eyes widened.

"That's usually how it goes."

"I guess you're right," I shrugged as we reached the jet. "How's that cute I.T. guy down the hall?"

"He's fine," Josh flushed.

"I'll bet he is."

"You are a fiend." He laughed, shaking his head. "Besides, I have to occupy my eyes now that Lazarev isn't around to look at anymore."

"Yeah, I'll bet he misses his biggest fan."

Josh gave me an exaggerated eye roll. "That man has fans all over the world, by no means am I the biggest, believe me." He nodded his head in the direction of the blonde agent who seemed to be glued to Illarion's side.

"Ha. Ha." I punched him in the shoulder. "So, when are you and I.T. man going to give it a go?"

"When my heart recovers from the heartache that is the loss of Illarion Lazarev."

"So, do I get a name or is he forever shrouded in secrecy?"

"His name is, James."

"James," I mused with a grin. "Cute."

He laughed again and pressed a kiss to my cheek as we neared Simms and Illarion. "Ah how I've missed you, Hart."

Illarion nodded for us to board and when we did, I chose a seat beside Josh. Illarion and Aurel left us to catch up and I couldn't help but notice how Simms found a convenient seat right next to him.

***

The three-hour flight was filled with laughter and stories shared by friends, the mood was light and the nerves were settled. It was a perfect prelude to a war.

We landed just before midnight and everyone filed out silently.

I took my bag from Illarion and followed him down to the transport.

When we were all seated, the driver took off.

"We're going to park at the north entrance. A surveillance van has been left there for us. You two will run ops from there. Aurel and I

316

will head the first team in through the back, and the other agents will take the side."

Josh and I both nodded and when the van pulled up to the familiar driveway, I felt my heart speed up and my palms became sweaty again. The driver pulled over beside a dark, blacked out van.

I drew in a long breath and composed myself. Inside, the van was fully decked out with all the tech we'd need. Josh and I connected all the short-range comms and handed them out to each agent.

When they all left, I waited for Illarion to come to me.

"Have I told you today, Lyubov?"

"What?"

He leaned in and cupped my cheek. "That I love you."

"You have, Illarion. And I love you too." A frown tugged at my lips. "Be careful in there."

"I've got you watching my back. I'm as safe as possible." He smiled, giving Aurel a quick nod.

When they were gone, I closed the door, turning my attention to the screens set up along the side of the van and took a seat beside Josh.

"You good to go?" Josh asked, putting on his own headset.

"Ready."

We watched for a few minutes as the first team made their way to their designated targets, closely followed by the second team who flanked them.

At this point, it was an information recovery mission only. Although we were pretty sure there was no one here, there was always a chance that someone had stayed behind watching the property.

I leaned back in my chair chewing on a Twizzler as Josh monitored the other agents. When Illarion came into view, I wheeled my chair closer to the console.

"Alright, Nighthawk, I've got you. If you take the corridor down to the end and follow it around, you'll see the first office we're hitting."

He nodded and continued walking.

I glanced across at Josh, he was keeping the rest of property covered and our signal off the radar.

Josh didn't know what went on here and he didn't need to.

As Illarion continued down the corridor, I brought my head back to the game. When he reached the door he stopped, pausing briefly. I couldn't see his face, but I imagined that he closed his eyes, trying to calm himself down. I would be doing the same thing. Thoughts and feelings were powerful and undeniably overwhelming to a Sensitive like Illarion, especially when the emotions were negative, and especially when they were related to someone they loved.

"What you need will be in the desk, there should be three locked drawers," I explained.

Illarion was aware of exactly what he needed to do, we'd only gone through the details fifty times, but his straying from the mission had Josh's attention.

Illarion glanced up at the camera before he made his way inside, pushing the loosely hanging door. Since Daniel had smashed the lock when he broke in there to come after me, it made no sound unlike the heavy footfalls of Illarion's steps. I bit down on my lip as memories of the room flooded me. The last time I was in there, I was getting flung around like a rag doll after the son of a bitch double dosed me.

I gripped the edge of the table forcing myself to remain calm. Shattered glass still lay strewn across the floor, broken artwork too. Illarion's boots crunched across the shards echoing loudly through the silent comms channel. Slowly, I swiveled my chair further away from Josh. I took another Twizzler and popped it in my mouth as I worked my hands across the keyboard, bringing up several other surveillance points leading up to and away from Illarion's location.

We were probably alone here but the sound of the teams moving through the damaged rooms, including the one Illarion was in could have drawn unwanted visitors.

Confirming that we were clear, I returned my attention to Illarion.

He walked around the dark, untouched room, tracing his fingers across the surface of the chairs, the table, the shelves. His sense gave him a definite advantage. He felt, and saw, whatever took place somewhere and, if he tried hard enough, he could probably feel exactly who was in here and when providing there were no wards set. That was a learned aspect of his gift. It took someone truly exceptional to be able to home in on that level of control and from experience, I knew how hard it was.

I knew he was doing a good job keeping composed because I saw how angry he really was. The tell-tale sign of his slightly trembling hand hovering across the shattered frame on the hardwood floor was enough to put me on edge.

He walked around touching the furniture until he stopped at an upturned chair. My heart sunk as he knelt and lowered his hand to the wood.

His face was turned from the camera but I saw him grip the edges of the chair, knuckles blanching, before he pulled himself back up to his feet.

A dangerous anger simmered inside him.

"Keep moving, Nighthawk, the desk is where you need to be."

Josh looked curiously at the scene unfolding until he brought his attention back to Aurel's team moving silently through the house.

Illarion moved over slowly.

I blinked and looked away as more and more images and memories running through the room found their way into his head.

Everything that had happened to me here, all the things I'd done to the other Sensitives were right there for him to see like an open book.

Finally, he reached the desk and pulled the drawers free from their locks. He promptly located all the files and tucked them safely in his backpack.

"Titan is about to finish up too, make your way back the same way you came. You're clear."

The more time he spent in this house, the more my nerves began to twist on themselves.

Fear crept up inside me, so, I kept him moving and distracted from what I imagined was a severely strong pull toward the other side of the house where my *bedroom* had been.

Illarion slung the backpack over his shoulder and made his way out, leaving the office as he found it.

I watched as he hurried through the hallways trailing his hand across everything he could touch and get a read from.

Then, like a breath was sucked from him, he stopped. He looked up at the cameras looking directly at me and my stomach dropped.

He felt my residual energy intensify toward the lower end of the corridor and abruptly he changed his course. That's when I began to lose it. Terror seized my insides, fear of what he would see, fear of what he would *feel* took over.

"Don't," I warned.

He ignored me and continued down the hallway, making all those familiar turns and corners I had done for months and months.

"Do not do this."

"What's going on?" Josh moved his chair over to me.

I fought back the tears and kept my attention focused on Illarion.

Suddenly, he stopped, and I thought my heart would too. He was at my room. At *the* room where too much had happened.

320

"Ila, *please.*" To hell with caution, I didn't care who was listening to our transmission.

His hand hovered over the door handle. Slowly, he brushed his fingertips across it and drew his hand back like he'd burned himself. I felt it through him, the pain I had suffered, as if I was suffering it all over again.

It was too late. I couldn't block him out, I couldn't block out my own feelings.

He was so emotionally charged right now it was flooding into my brain, suffocating me. It was like a beacon of light and energy bouncing off the walls and, if anyone was monitoring the building, we'd definitely be made now. That much power was hard to ignore, and it was impossible for me to control.

"Ila, don't do this, *please.*"

Josh looked at the screen and then back at me. "What's going on, Ace?"

"Keep your eyes on Aurel," I snapped. "We might have company now."

"Ace—"

"Do it."

He threw his hands up defensively and moved back to the monitor. I heard him advise the other agents to watch their six.

Illarion was still standing, transfixed, at the door. Damn him.

"I'm begging you, Illarion. Do not do this."

He ignored me and pushed the door open, just as he did, his hand went to his heart as the other reached for the wall.

All my emotions and feelings that were etched into the essence of those four walls, exploded around him. The wards were well and truly faded now.

Illarion wasn't prepared for the emotional tsunami that was just released. He struggled, he dropped to one knee holding onto the door for support.

"What the hell is going on?" Josh hissed beside me.

I couldn't answer him.

"Please…" I whispered to Illarion.

My tongue grew heavy in my mouth and the sickness inside me rose.

He struggled to his feet and on unsure legs, he walked around, touching and feeling me in everything, until finally, he stood a tentative foot away from the bed.

And in that moment, every thought I'd ever had, every plea I'd made to die, was right there, open like a book. He would see it all and there would be no coming back from this.

Illarion knew what those men had done to me. He knew titbits of information about Dalca's abuse but I never wanted him to know the extent of it all.

I ground my molars. "Don't."

Illarion dropped to his knees and with trembling hands, he grazed the sheets. I grit my teeth as I watched Illarion's head drop. Seconds later, he ripped the sheets from the bed and threw the bedside table against the wall smashing it into hundreds of pieces.

Josh did his best to keep his eyes on his own screen, but I saw the shocked expression from the corner of my eye.

"Shit, Ace we have company. Get him out of there," Josh muttered beside me.

I glanced at all the other screens confirming what he'd said. Damn it.

"You need to leave now, Illarion. We have company," I shot, swiping the tears from my eyes.

322

He pushed the rest of the furniture around violently until the whole room was ripped apart. From the rug to the wardrobe filled with beautiful gowns to the bed and the writing desk where I'd read all his letters.

Movement off to the right of one of the monitors, drew my attention. Josh caught on and warned the other agents.

"You're clear on the south side," I said, checking back to make sure there weren't any more bogies.

When Illarion cleared the building, he was intercepted by one of Dalca's men that I hadn't seen.

I held my breath as he blocked the right hook coming at his face. Aurel was hit from his side as well. Two men ambushed him from behind the building, throwing him to the ground.

"Sparrow," Josh called out to Simms, "Titan is down, get to him now."

Confident that Josh had his team handled, I returned my attention to Illarion.

He was on the ground, fighting off a knife aimed right at his heart. My heart sped up as the man on top of him got the upper hand and pressed his forearm to Illarion's throat. A sense of panic ran through me. Illarion was struggling, badly. He was a better fighter than most people I'd ever met, what was happening?

When he finally threw the man off, he turned his face, and I got a good look. His eyes were completely black, just like the guy I fought in Bob's pantry last year. Where the hell were they getting these supercharged freaks?

Illarion jumped to his feet and threw a kick, launching his foot right into his attacker's chest. He dropped and Illarion moved. He spun on the spot, scissor kicking him, knocking him out.

Illarion picked up the bag he'd dropped and ran.

Glancing over at Josh's monitor, I let out a shaky breath. Aurel and Simms were safe and heading back to rendezvous with us.

Illarion pulled the door open and rushed through the dark pathways making it back to the designated meeting point.

Aurel was heading toward him and was about two minutes out. The other two agents took down three bogies with Aurel narrowly avoiding being made by another. Christ, we were lucky this didn't go worse.

"Keep moving, Illarion," I spoke while I focused on keeping an eye out on the other monitors. Illarion moved stealthily through the dark grounds. Once I saw he that he'd cleared the garden, I pulled the headset off and threw it on the table.

"Keep your eyes on them," I barked at Josh.

"What? Ace, wait!"

Ignoring him, I shoved the back doors open and jumped out. I stormed down the path knowing that Josh would go back to the job. I needed to find Illarion.

The familiar garden path leading past the fountain came into view and it took every effort to keep my eyes averted and keep walking.

I swallowed back the anger building inside me and pulled myself together.

Illarion came into view. Before I could stop myself, I walked up to him and slapped him.

"Damn you!"

He didn't even flinch, I slapped him again, this time harder. And when I reached to slap him for the third time, he caught my hand and pulled me against him.

"You're a fucking jerk!" I screamed, trying in vain to pull back.

He remained silent, but his arms were tight around me.

"Why did you do that?" I cried against him.

The anger I had moments ago, was replaced by a relentless pain followed a violent torrent of tears that consumed me wholly.

He felt everything.

"You shouldn't have gone in there!"

"I should have listened to the dreams."

He let out a deep breath as his eyes found mine and his dark lashes lowered.

"I should have known. I *knew* that you weren't gone, I knew you couldn't be…But there were so many wards…they must have finally faded now."

His mind was scattered, all over the place, just like mine. We didn't have time for this.

"We need to leave, now."

"Ace, I—"

"Get in the damn van, Illarion."

I turned from him and made my way back down the same way I came. As we rounded the last of the garden, he followed me into the van.

My eyes landed on Aurel and the dark bruise forming rapidly across his jaw. Jesus. This was an utter disaster.

He looked like he had a lot to say, but the expression on Illarion's face must have told him to back off. Aurel pulled the van out onto the road then we were moving.

When we reached the jet, I stormed back up without a word. The tears continued to fall, and the silence was suffocating.

I was completely bare, and I'd never expected to have felt like that, because of Illarion.

Chapter Twenty-Six

Ace

The cobblestone mansion came into view and before the car had even stopped rolling, I was already out the door.

"Ace wait!" Illarion called.

"Get the hell away from me."

"Please stop," he said firmly, gripping my wrist.

When I pulled back, I spun on my spot and shoved him so hard that he barely managed to keep his footing.

And when he moved again, I stepped forward closing the gap between us, making sure that we were eye to eye and there would be no mistaking the next words to come out of my mouth.

"What you did is unforgivable, Illarion. I will never forget it. Do you understand me?"

He stepped back, pain flaring in his eyes.

Daniel appeared beside us. "What's going on?"

"Feel free to explain to him how you just fucked that job," I said, without turning from Illarion. "And how you almost got half our team killed."

When neither of them said anything further, I made a beeline for my room and left them.

ILLARION

Ace was gone, leaving me and Daniel in the hallway, reliving the aftermath.

"Can I talk to you?" I said without giving him the chance to follow her.

He turned around looking like he was lost for words.

"Ah, yeah sure."

I led him down to my office and when we were both inside, I shut the door with a loud thud.

He was intimidated by me, but he was standing tall and standing his ground. I pressed my hands flat to my desk and looked up at him.

"I know what happened between you two."

His eyes flared for a moment before he stepped back, defensively folding his arms across his chest.

I'd taken a backseat, letting this play out. But enough was enough. "I know what she went through put you both in a difficult position. You were there when she needed someone."

"She was in a really bad place, Illarion, she wasn't thinking straight."

"Damn it." I hit my fist against the table. "That's exactly why you should have been."

He flinched and opened his mouth to argue but then promptly closed it.

"She needed you to be better than that."

"You're right. You are." He shook his head, dropping his gaze. "I'm so sorry."

"I don't want apologies, Daniel. I don't want your reasoning. I want you to take a step back now. Do we understand each other?"

"Yes, we understand each other."

"Good. Don't mistake my tolerance of you living here for anything other than what it is."

He looked like he had a lot more he wanted to say but it wasn't the first time I'd exerted my will to silence someone.

"I know she cares about you, and you're a good friend to her. But don't overstep your bounds again."

He nodded and his emotions ran wild. I felt the anger simmering inside him. He was frustrated with me, furious with himself but he remained calm on the surface.

"I've got some work I have to do. Aurel's going to start deciphering the intel we gathered. You can help with that. It should be familiar information."

"Yeah, no problem."

"Good. See yourself out."

I sat and turned my attention away from him. He stayed frozen in place for a while, before finally turning from me and leaving.

***

ACE

As soon as I slammed the door shut, I pulled my tactical vest off, dropped it at the door and stripped. A quick, military style shower had me clean and dried in less than sixty seconds. I shoved my feet into my pajamas and pulled on my sweatshirt.

Glad now that Elsa was the one who picked my clothes out, I relaxed into the soft cotton. They weren't pretty or sexy, they were warm and comfortable. And comfortable is exactly what I needed tonight. I wanted to crawl under the covers, watch a bad movie and eat chocolate until I threw up which, going by my recent track record, wouldn't have been too long after.

A quiet, quick succession of taps at the door drew my attention to it. I sighed, rolling my eyes.

I'd worked so hard on keeping my shield up, I hadn't even realized that it was Illarion at the door. My heart sped up.

"Can I please come in?" His voice was muffled by the door.

"No."

A new sensation which somehow didn't surprise me, originated deep inside. First it was static, buzzing around me, and then came the hum making the small bulb beside my bed, flicker. When the air in my lungs caught, I had to remind myself to breathe. As soon as I took a calculated breath, the flickering stopped, and I exhaled.

"Can we talk?"

"There's nothing to talk about right now."

He pushed the door open anyway. My mouth gaped. *Was he kidding?*

"I can't talk to you through the door."

"That's the point, Illarion, why are you here?"

He crossed the distance between us and stood just a foot away from my bed. I didn't bother getting up, he wouldn't be staying long.

"Please talk to me," he begged.

"You ignored me."

Illarion bowed his head and ran a hand through his loose hair. "I want to apologize—"

"You could have listened to me, why didn't you? I was calling to you, telling you to stop."

My voice was growing louder and less stable.

He didn't have a response, nothing at all. He stayed silent, but the bulb began to flicker again catching his attention.

"You hurt me so much. I *begged* you to stop, and you know what, Illarion?" I shook my head looking away from him. "All I could think was that no matter how many times I pleaded, no matter how many times I said *no*, you didn't listen, you didn't care about my wishes or what I was asking of you."

Illarion's body stiffened, his eyes widened as his aura pulsed erratically digesting the words I just said.

"I don't know how to get past this, Ila."

"Don't say that…"

"You directly chose to ignore me when I was pleading with you to stop. You *chose* to do what you did. I gave you permission when I let you search my memories, I gave you permission to feel the things I let you feel, I let you in. But this? No, I did not give you permission to do this."

"I needed to know, Ace."

"Why?" The bulb flared. "What good came of it?"

He remained quiet but his eyes moved to the light beside me.

"You were the only safe place I had left."

He remained rooted to the floor, but I didn't miss the way he flinched as he watched the light pulse erratically. I was losing my composure, and the light grew brighter and brighter but at this point, I didn't care about controlling it.

His eyes filled with tears, he tried to step closer, but I focused everything I had inside me and stopped him. "Get out, Illarion."

"Ace…"

"Go!"

When he refused. I felt the rage inside me grow. His eyes flicked from the flaring light, back to me and then I felt it snap inside me.

"Get out!" I screamed just as the bulb exploded, shattering into a thousand pieces and Illarion…I'll never forget the look of terror on his face as he jerked back, shielding his face from the glass.

He was afraid of me and honestly, it was probably for the best. I passed out the moment my head hit the pillow.

By the time I'd woken up the next morning, they had already begun working on analyzing the files that we had managed to gather last night. I ignored the pang of pain that shot through me when I saw Illarion, sitting at the table. That same terrified look haunted him. He didn't even look up at me.

I turned away and poured myself a coffee, taking a seat beside Aurel.

He leaned over, handing me a pile of papers to go through. "As far as I can tell from all of this, he's meant to be in New York tomorrow."

I read over the names on the list, three of the five agents on it were stationed here, somewhere. So, it only made sense that he'd try to locate them first.

"So, we go to each of them and wait?" I asked.

Illarion cleared his throat. "He'd be expecting that, we need to lay low."

"We can start by setting up a perimeter around Starbucks, stakeout for a few hours, take a few surveillance shots," I suggested.

Aurel looked at me and then Illarion. "She's got a point. Surveillance can be done by us, no point bringing in everyone."

"Correct." I nodded, glad that he was catching what I was throwing. "If he's expecting it, he'll have contingencies in place, most likely signal jammers, EMPs." I looked at Illarion. "We remember how bad that went for us, we don't want any more of our vehicles taken out like that."

"Agreed. Josh has all the specifics about that particular weapon used, if they're still relying on the same tech we should be able to arm ourselves with counter weapons," Illarion said, handing me another pile, his eyes lingered on the small yet painfully large gap between our hands.

I pulled back, regaining my composure.

He cleared his throat. "You take this Agent; I'll take Riggs and Aurel will watch Mason."

"Why haven't they been warned yet?" I looked at Aurel.

He shook his head pointing at another column beside their names. "They're too far undercover, there's no way to get information to them without burning them."

Awesome. This was going to be easy, nothing to it. I pinched the bridge of my nose and sighed.

"We'll leave tonight." Illarion nodded to me and then Aurel, we both gave him a quick nod back.

Trying to be civil and professional was a lot harder than I thought and every time he looked at me, I wanted to burst into tears.

"Who else is in?" I asked, focusing my question at Aurel even though Illarion was heading this operation, as he always did.

He didn't say anything, instead he remained quiet letting Aurel answer.

"The three of us, Josh in the van and the four agents from last night. That is, if we get what we need from the stakeout."

"Full house." I nodded.

"Yeah, we'll need it for the amount of people we're watching." Aurel leaned back in his chair sighing. He scrubbed his chin looking across at Illarion before casting a sideways glance at me. "So..." he said, quietly, "anything I should know?"

"No," both Illarion and I said in unison.

"Right," Aurel responded, sarcastically. "Look, I don't care what you're having a disagreement about, but I need to know that your heads are in the game. Because if we have a repeat of that shit storm we sailed through last night, we're going to have issues."

"I'm fine." I cringed. Aurel's face was bruised up from last night's run in and I felt worse seeing that they were both tightly strung. "Good to roll."

Illarion nodded too.

"Alright, get your shit together, we're leaving in six hours," Aurel added.

Six hours until we headed out to stop that asshole once and for all.

I got up and nodded to both men, determined to get out of there as soon as humanly possible. There was nothing I had to say to him right now. I walked back upstairs with the intention to hit the gym again.

As I rounded the corner, Josh stood at the landing.

"Got a minute?"

"Really don't." I forced a smile.

"I'll be quick."

"I'm heading to the gym. You can walk over with me."

As we walked outside into the warm air, he cleared his throat. "We need to talk about last night."

"It won't affect the team. We're both professionals."

"Last night was horrific."

"Last night was a mistake."

"Last night was a disaster," he corrected.

I flinched. "I know."

"What happened?"

"There were bogies we didn't anticipate."

"You know that's not what I'm talking about."

Letting out an exasperated sigh, I rubbed the back of my neck, stopping. "Illarion broke formation."

"Yeah," he said. "I was there, I saw."

"It won't happen again."

"I didn't think it would, but I'm worried about you."

"There's nothing to worry about."

"That's not what I saw last night."

"He shouldn't have strayed from the mission."

"That goes without saying." He ground his teeth. "What was that about?"

I composed myself by taking a calculated breath but when I didn't answer, Josh sighed.

"What happened in that house, Ace?"

"A lot happened, Josh," I said, pressing my hands to my hips. "Honestly, I don't want to talk about it."

"I can understand that, but I need to know that every person in this team is safe. I'm responsible for all of us when I'm in the van."

The jab hurt. I glanced up and released a long breath before looking back at him. His brows were up, waiting for my answer.

"I was held hostage in that house for six months," I said, "that's where I was taken after I died. He tortured me. Kept me on the Serum. Came to me in the night."

Josh's eyes widened with understanding.

"Illarion obviously knew...when he came for me, I was a mess. I didn't know who I was half the time. Nightmares were one thing; the injuries were another. He understood there was a lot that happened to me, but I didn't want him to *feel* it all."

"And he ignored you."

I nodded.

Josh draped his arm over my shoulder.

Swallowing the building emotions, I got up, not letting him say another word. "There won't be a repeat of last night, we're good."

He gave me a sympathetic nod as I turned to leave. I broke into a steady jog pretending there weren't tears burning my eyes again.

Whatever it took, tomorrow the Taker would die.

CHAPTER TWENTY-SEVEN

ACE

Four laps in, I could barely keep my breathing steady. I came to a panting stop pressing my hands to my thighs, forcing deep breaths into my lungs.

I looked around, realizing that I'd run all the way to the property border. I'd never been down here before. I let my eyes wander over the horizon, sweeping the scenery, absorbing everything.

From my bedroom window, I could just make out the clearing where I was now. It was some sort of field and curiosity got the better of me. I began a slow jog toward it and carefully made my way down and over the embankment. As I neared, I recognized it as a training pitch, much like the one Aurel and I used when he kicked my ass back at his house.

A large, wooden training dummy caught my eye, and I dropped my water bottle by the side while scanning the rest of the area.

Eager to let some of my seriously pent-up anger out, I started by warming up and when my muscles were loosened up, I began with punches. I let out all my anger on the dummy, striking it with an open palm, followed by elbow jabs and blocks. Ignoring the splitting pain from my raw skin hitting the wood, I moved on to kicks. I spun on the spot kicking the dummy where its head would have been. When I landed back in position, I launched a front on assault of strikes with my hands and elbows and finished off with a kick, shouting out in anger as the impact broke the skin along my knuckles.

"Wanna fight something that fights back?"

I rolled my shoulders turning on my heel. Aurel stood at the end of the training pitch with his arms folded across his chest.

No one here seemed to get the damn hint.

"Wing Chun dummy is great, but he ain't gonna fight back."

"What do you want?" I shot back.

"Came to talk to you."

I rolled my eyes and he moved to the centre, holding his arms out.

"Come on," he said, tossing aside his sweater. "It'll be good for you."

"You don't want to do this with me right now."

"Kinda do. Come on."

He squared off with me assuming my silence was my agreement.

I steadied my breaths looking down at the blood dropping at my feet. His eyes followed my gaze and then narrowed when I grinned, squeezing my fists. We bowed at each other, locking eyes.

"Form?" he asked.

"Keep it interesting. No rules."

"You sure you want to do that, Ace?"

"You're the one who wanted to fight. Let's fight."

A dangerous glint in his eyes told me he wasn't going to be holding back this time. Good, I inhaled through my nose and drew my hands up, ready. I wouldn't be either.

The fight was on. He lunged right at me with a closed fist strike to my face. I stopped it with an x-block, throwing both forearms up in front of my face. I took my chance to grab onto his hand, pulling him close enough so I could grab him in a side mount choke hold.

He countered that by kicking out behind him, striking me in the shin. When I stumbled, he took the moment to distract me with a jab and as I moved to block another hit, he got me in the face with a right hook.

As I jerked back, I swung out, hitting him square in the chest with an open palm strike.

The fight drastically changed. We were no longer training and that glint in his eyes darkened. The ferocity with which he came at me was on par with my own rage. Pent up anger and months and months of fury bubbled underneath and sped to the surface. There was something deeper driving us both.

Before I had another chance to defend myself, he surprised me with an elbow strike to the right side of my face, followed by a roundhouse and hook kick combination, which forced me to the ground like a completely untrained civilian.

"You're distracted," he muttered.

I spat the bloody saliva out and balled my fists, getting back to my feet.

"That distraction could cost you your life."

"Here to lecture me or fight?" I shot back.

He smirked, "That depends."

"On what?"

"On whether you're planning on getting your head in the game or fighting like a rookie."

I ground my jaw, taking my stance again before rushing forward.

I reached up and grabbed his right elbow with my left hand and pulled him down toward me. Before he had a second to react and retaliate, I planted my left leg to balance myself and launched my right knee up into his stomach. As he grunted, jerking back, I swept my leg in one fluid motion, catching his knee sending him crashing to the ground.

He grunted loudly as the wind was knocked from him. He tried to get up but I moved quicker. I launched myself over him, crouching over his torso.

I pressed my forearm across his throat, pushing down. I lowered my face to his until our lips were a mere inch apart.

"Do not fucking test me, Aurel. I'm not in the mood."

His nostrils flared and a moment later he tapped my arm, surrendering. I released him and got up as he remained sprawled on the ground.

"Remind me not to piss you off," he stated, getting up.

"Don't piss me off."

He hopped to his feet. I ignored him and turned away.

"Ace, wait!" he called out, coming after me. "Can you just wait for a minute?" He took a hold of my arm, and I just lost it.

Hell. No. I briskly turned on my heel and swatted his arm away.

"Back the hell off," I hissed, stepping right into his space.

"You need to calm down."

"You need to stay in your lane."

He folded his arms across his chest.

Deep inside me, I felt the Darkness surging. It began to rear its head, threatening to erupt at any moment. It was like Larry's apartment only this time, there was no barrier of inexperience holding it back. No, this time when I moved, *it* moved with me. It spurred me on, and I knew just how much damage I could do and how far to go.

Closing the gap between us, my eyes narrowed, and I was ready to do whatever I had to.

He started backing away.

The space around us grew dense, electricity pulsed through the air as I took purpose driven steps toward him.

Through his wide eyes, I caught a glimpse of myself. My eyes were black. Small, dark veins webbed around the corners of my eyes. There were no green irises, no warmth.

My hair rose off my shoulders as though a gust of wind had blown it behind me, only it didn't fall, it floated, billowing gently. The static charge hummed all around us, growing in intensity as the electricity in the air became supercharged.

His mouth gaped and he drew his hands up in surrender.

He feared me.

I'd seen that look before. I'd seen it back in Iraq when I single-handedly took down the heavily armed soldiers who were torturing me. I'd seen it when I killed Mike. I'd seen it last night when I blew the bulb and nearly hurt Illarion.

"Ace, I'm sorry."

"Everyone's fucking *sorry*. Everyone fucking *understands*. Yet they keep doing the same shit over and over."

He kept backing away from me.

"You know what that is, Aurel?" I hissed. "Fucking lunacy, that's what. Stay out of my way."

I pushed the Darkness down and I turned on my heel, picked up my bottle and left.

I was naïve to ever think that this could have worked. There was no way that me coming back after six months of hell would ever just be fine.

Who had I been kidding? I stepped heavily, crunching the gravel and leaves beneath my feet, letting my anger simmer inside me.

A fresh gust of wind picked up around me making the branches of the cherry blossom overhead shake and tremble sending its tiny petals tumbling to the earth below.

As I neared the house, I sucked in a deep breath and went in search of Illarion. He wanted to talk, so I was going to give him exactly what he wanted.

As I neared the library, I felt him. He was still, concentrated and focused. I made my way in quietly. He was sitting in an armchair with a massive pile of papers and files around him.

His hair fell over his eyes and when I neared him, they shot up. He rose to his feet and took a few tentative steps around the desk but he didn't come closer.

"This isn't going to work," I said.

For a moment, he didn't say a word and for a moment I thought I'd cave, and then he folded his arms across his chest and looked at me with a tight jaw.

"I shouldn't have done what I did."

"That goes without saying," I agreed, shifting my balance onto my other foot. "But that's not what this is about."

"What do you need me to do, Ace? I'll do whatever you need."

Taking a deep breath, I shook my head. "I need your help to finish this."

"You know I will."

"And then I'm leaving."

His eyes snapped back to mine. "I don't understand."

"I don't know how either of us thought this would work, you know?" I shook my head again, this time wrapping my arms around my chest as though that would stop the crushing weight in my heart. "We were both so blinded by whatever this is, to see the truth."

"What truth?" his voice shook, he was on the verge of losing his shit.

"That I am too far gone, too broken to be fixed or to belong with you, to be here."

He stepped forward, and I stepped back.

"You don't need to be fixed. And Christ, Ace, you belong with me, you belong right here."

I let out a sarcastic laugh and looked around, pulling my gaze away from his.

"Your optimism isn't going to make this better, Ila. You know as well as I do, there is *nothing* inside me worth fighting for. You felt it. You saw what he did to me. He ruined me, Ila. There's no coming back from that."

Again, he stepped closer, but this time I didn't move. His eyes narrowed, burning me.

"Everything about you is worth fighting for, Ace, *everything* and what he did to you is inexcusable, but it doesn't change how I feel about you. You're not ruined, you're not broken."

"I had sex with that asshole's son." Saying it out loud made me realize just how absurd the whole thing was.

His jaw tightened, and he stepped toward me again.

"You weren't in a good place."

"No," I agreed, "but I knew what I was doing. I *wanted* it. How can you be okay with that? What's wrong with you?"

"I'm not okay with it!" he shouted, and I stepped back, completely stunned. "I'm not okay, not even close."

Words failed me.

"But I'm dealing with it. I'm trying to get past how much it hurts, and having him here, in my house, is another level of torture. How do you think I feel?"

I'd been so caught up in my own misery that I hadn't even stopped to think about how this had affected him. He was always so level-headed and calculated in everything he did but the man before me was not.

"I can't pretend that it doesn't hurt me Lyubov, it does, but I don't want to lose you."

"You're blinded by it—"

"By what?" The anger was finally catching up with him.

His feet were firmly planted on the dark hardwood floors, and his arms shook at his side, fists clenching and unclenching.

I stood my ground.

"By your love for me. You're blinded, you're desperate to have me here because you feel guilty about what happened to me."

His fists balled.

When he remained silent, I continued. "You feel responsible, and it consumes you."

"Because I am responsible!" his voice faltered. "I should have been there for you; I was meant to protect you and I failed!" He pressed his hand across his chest. "I wasn't strong enough. And then I failed you again when I slept with Anna and continued to fail you when I let her stay here!"

He stopped abruptly as the words left his mouth. I sucked in a sharp breath and looked down at my feet. Hearing that kind of bluntness from him was like a vicious slap to the face.

"And then, this is where it gets even better," he snapped with a harsh laugh. "I failed you when I drank myself to sleep every god damned night trying to block you out instead of looking for you!"

"You didn't fail me," I said, when I regained my thoughts.

He scoffed shaking his head in disbelief.

"That asshole raped you for months because I was too weak to do anything!" He raised his hand and pointed to nothing in particular and when I shook my head, he threw his arms up in defeat. "Tell me how I didn't fail you. Tell me how I am not responsible."

"It wasn't your fault, there was nothing you could have done, but who I am now...I'll never be that girl again, Ila, and I..." I paused wetting my lips. "I can't pretend that I can be. You deserve more. You deserve someone who can give you life, to let you be a dad, to—"

"Don't do this." He shook his head. His fight was gone, and his voice shook with each word. "Don't turn this into that, you know where I stand. You know how I feel."

"One day you're going to wake up and realize what this has cost you and by then it'll be too late. I won't let that happen."

"And you're making this decision for me."

"I loved you, with everything that I had left, but it's different now, I'm different. I feel differently."

Like I'd slapped him in the face, he remained still, pleading, his eyes brimming with a sheath of tears that would be falling because of me, again.

"Differently, how?"

"I don't love you like that anymore."

"Is that the truth?" he challenged.

"Who I am now can't love or live, or even think the same way anymore, Illarion. So yes, it's the truth. It is my truth."

"Please, Ace."

*Maybe one day…*I shook my head, stopping that thought. I had to be strong. This was the only way he'd let me go. I reached up and unclasped the necklace he'd given me. In that moment, I saw the pulsating of his aura turn erratic. He must have known for certain that this was as definitive as it would get.

He walked over to me, closing the final distance between us and when I didn't move, he reached up and cupped my cheek. My own body betrayed me and instinctively reacted to him. I leaned into his touch feeling my tears wet his calloused palm. I gripped the pendant in my palm and felt my own fingers shake with tension.

"Please, Ace…don't do this to us," he whispered, his lips so close to mine, his breath dancing across my skin.

"I'm sorry." I pulled back, taking his hand and placing the necklace in his open palm. "I've made up my mind. Please respect that. Please do what I'm asking this time."

I heard him inhale sharply before he dropped his hand from me.

My heart screamed in agony, there would never be another touch or another kiss. Nothing would ever bring peace to my heart like he could. But this was the right thing to do.

***

Before I even realized that I'd been up the whole night, Josh and Daniel came down the stairs, chatting about movies as was their customary choice of discussion, and when Daniel spotted me, he abruptly stopped talking and rapidly moved down the stairs, away from me.

What the hell?

Aurel followed behind them. When his eyes landed on me, the atmosphere changed. I didn't miss a beat, all three of them looked at me like I was some kind of unhinged psycho.

I forced my attention back to my work, everyone seemed to have had a rough night.

Before long, Aurel brought me a coffee and placed it beside me.

"You doing okay, punk?" he asked without looking at me.

"Fine. Thanks for the coffee."

"No problem."

He sat across from me keeping his eyes down. I didn't blame him. I'd single-handedly destroyed the team dynamic, nearly killed him on the training pitch and broken his best friend. All in a day's work.

I downed the hot liquid and got up.

Illarion still hadn't made an appearance, and my insides began to do back flips. *What if he didn't want to do this anymore? What if he decided that it wasn't worth the trouble?* That *I* wasn't worth it.

As soon as I rounded the corner, heading up the stairs, I ran right into him.

Illarion stumbled back a few inches, grabbing my shoulders, stopping me from tripping down the stairs.

"Sorry," I murmured, pulling back from him.

He held onto me until I was stable before he reached up, brushing a strand of hair from my face. At this point we were inches apart on the entirely crowded staircase.

"You haven't slept," he said calmly as though nothing happened between us mere hours ago.

"Neither have you."

A smile that didn't reach his eyes, met mine. "I had a lot on my mind."

I was having trouble focusing on his words when all I could think about was the way my heart and body felt so right when he was close. Tears stung the back of my eyes, but I pushed him away.

"I need to get ready," I whispered, breaking both the proverbial and literal hold.

He nodded, and I noticed now, in the light, how dark the shadows that had formed under his eyes truly were. My heart sunk.

"I'll see you downstairs," I said as gently as I could.

"You will."

Before he could do anything else that could make me second guess what I knew was right, for both of us, I took the stairs two at a time, slamming my door shut.

It took me less than ten minutes to shower and dress and a quick check of the time told me it was already six in the morning, which meant that we'd be heading out in less than fifteen minutes.

Suddenly, my steely nerves were anything but. My legs were buckling with fear as I took each step down the stairs. Dalca would be there.

I had no doubt, I could feel the dread building with each passing minute.

As I neared the front door, I slowed. There was equipment everywhere, bags stacked two or three high. It looked like we would probably never be coming back here. Not *we*, I stopped myself. Illarion.

I released a long breath, composing myself. Daniel and Josh stood a few feet away, looking somber with downcast expressions.

When I reached the table, Daniel came over, stopping beside me. I kept my eyes down, doing a quick double check of the plans on my laptop.

"Be careful."

"You've been avoiding me," I said without looking at him.

He didn't deny it.

"Did Illarion say something to you?"

"No."

"Why bother lying to me?"

He sighed. "Yeah."

I let out a disbelieving breath, turning my face slightly. "He shouldn't have said anything."

"But he was right to. I was out of line."

I bit back the anger, "I probably won't see you again, after today."

"Why?"

"I'm leaving," I said, simply, turning my attention back to my laptop.

"You're quitting the Agency?" he asked, lowering his head, keeping his voice low.

"Yeah."

"Illarion's going with you?"

"No, just me."

"I don't understand."

"I need time to sort myself out. I think, after everything, I need time to heal," I said. "If I don't see you again, I wanted to say thank you. For everything you've done for me."

"Don't say it like it's goodbye."

"I need you to know how much you've helped me. You saved my life."

"What is this really about?"

"It's about me needing to find out who the hell I am now." I squeezed his hand with a tentative smile. "Thank you, Daniel. I'll never forget what you've done for me. I promise, one day, I will make it up to you."

"You don't have anything to make up for."

"I do," I disagreed, "I owe you a lot, and I will repay you."

"Please be careful."

"Always am." I winked, gently squeezing his arm again.

We said our goodbyes and soon we were back in the Hummer, the four of us.

No one spoke, no one breathed a word about what was waiting for us. The heavy realization that not everyone would make it home today, settled over me in the silence.

There were four other agents who would be meeting us, the same four who came to Dalca's house and helped us. Men and women who had dedicated their lives to the cause, who answered and took orders regardless of what it could cost them.

Illarion pulled up to a factory a few streets over from the part of town we needed to be in. It looked like it backed into the loading bay of a grocery store.

"There's minimal staff and almost no security aside from the rent-a-cop doing the rounds every few hours," Aurel explained.

"Right."

347

"It's also good cover. No one would anticipate a team coming out of here," Illarion added.

"Makes sense to me, boss."

His eyes met mine for a moment as we both exited the Hummer at the same time before he turned away. Josh shifted beside me; I caught the sympathetic smile he offered as he opened the trunk.

Great. I turned my attention to weapons and started gearing up.

"We'll be clear to make our approach from here," Illarion explained. "Simms and Wright will take the approach from the adjacent street."

"Got it." Aurel nodded.

"You and Aurel need to take that exit there." He pointed to the large roller door just behind us. "This will take you to the storefronts. Ace, you're in civilian gear so you can take surveillance from the street once you're clear."

"Okay," I agreed.

Soon after, a van pulled up and parked beside us, the four agents from yesterday got out dressed in all black, weapons holstered and ready to go.

Josh jumped into the back of their van and left with the driver.

"Everyone on comms?" Illarion asked.

We all nodded.

Once he was done helping Simms set up her earpiece, we were set.

As Aurel and I began to move, followed by the other agents, Illarion stopped me gently catching my wrist in his hand. I also didn't miss the look Simms threw my way.

"Be careful out there, Ace," he said, ignoring everyone else. "Stay close to Aurel and if anything changes you let me know."

His eyes lingered on mine as did the heavy air between us.

I smiled tipping my head forward in a nod. "I will."

I pulled free and broke into a jog to catch up with Aurel.

He led us through the factory and down to the back. He was right when he said there'd be minimal staff. I counted maybe six people including the security guy who was seated in his small Hyundai devouring a coffee that was bigger than my head.

"We'll hang back here for a few," Aurel explained.

We stopped, staying close to the walls and out of sight of the cameras panning the ancient fit out.

I glanced around trying to make out what kind of factory this was. A quick look at the items stacked neatly in the pallets confirmed it was a canned food manufacturer.

"We're clear," Aurel said quietly.

We followed him out into an underground car park beneath the factory which came to an end just as we reached the far side of the building.

We split into three groups from here. Simms and another agent went through the front entrance, two others took the elevator shafts into the building and we walked through the roller door. When we reached the storefront, Aurel stopped, gesturing left instead of right.

"What? This isn't the plan."

"No, but neither was the almost empty street. We can't blend in when there are hardly any people."

I looked up, confirming that it was indeed lacking in the usual foot traffic one would expect at this time of morning. There were hardly any people lining up for their morning coffees or having pre work meetings.

"Down here." He nodded to the sewer grate that we'd stopped beside. "We'll approach the street from below. Trust me, it's safer this way."

"Fantastic," I shot.

"After you."

He lifted the grate, and once the gap was big enough to get through, we dropped down into the darkness.

Aurel tossed over a flashlight which I quickly flicked on as soon as we started trekking through the wet, smelly slush.

When we reached the end of the tunnel the bright, morning sun shone through the cracks in the street above illuminating a path for us.

"Our target is up there." He pointed, glancing at the coordinates on his watch.

"How long until we move?"

He glanced down at his watch again. "Half an hour. Got some time to kill."

I crouched down, Aurel did the same and leaned against the wall.

"Do you think they know we're here?" I asked quietly, keeping my eyes averted.

"I doubt it. But Dalca might."

Yeah, that was a real possibility. One that would be bad news for all of us. Silence fell in the sewer until Aurel shifted slightly beside me.

"I can't begin to understand what you went through."

Sweet baby Jesus. "I don't think this is the best time to talk about that."

"I beg to differ," he said, softly, turning his body in my direction. "You've not spoken to me at all."

"And I'm not going to while we're down in the sewer, quite literally up to our knees in shit."

He cracked a smile. "Best time to talk about a shitty situation, don't you think?"

"I appreciate it, but we're not talking about it."

"You've been through more than anyone could imagine. It's normal to be scared, Ace."

"You're wrong, I'm not scared." I shook my head, finding his eyes. "I'm terrified, Aurel. Terrified out of my fucking mind."

He shifted, looking at me.

I sighed. "I don't want to talk about it because talking about it makes it real. It makes what he did to me real."

"You don't need me to tell you how to process all of this, but acceptance is part of starting to heal and let go."

"I know that. I do. But I'm not ready for it to be real. Not yet. I don't know when I will be."

He bowed his head. "You're not staying, are you?"

"No. Not after last night, I can't."

"Illarion loves you. He fucked up, we know that, he knows that but he will protect you with is dying breath. You know he will."

"I know, but I can't."

I expected him to argue, but he didn't. "When we move, stay close," he said, quietly, changing the topic, "don't try to be a hero."

"I'll try not to."

"I'll head out first, this will take us to the alleyway," he explained. "We'll have our vantage point there."

As soon as our time came, he reached for the grate and moved it. He climbed up first and pulled me up.

"Come on," he whispered, running along the wall, staying in the shadows.

He dragged us both behind a dumpster where we had a good view of the apartment building our agent was in. Surprisingly we didn't dredge up half the sewer with us. With a few strategic kicks along the brickwork, the remaining slush came off leaving us with wet, but relatively acceptable attire, which was just as well, we were still going to have to fit in among the people on the street.

"We're in position," he said, through the comms.

"Copy that," Illarion replied. "Has everyone else got their target in sight?"

The other agents all responded as had we, once we were positioned, we waited.

From the corner of my eye, I caught movement, but it was more than that, it was a feeling, sort of like mine and Illarion's connection. I turned my head in that general direction and my breath caught. *God no.*

"He's here," I heard myself whisper.

Aurel rushed over, placing his body in front of mine, "Stay low."

My breath was stuck in my throat. Nothing could shelter me from Dalca. No shield, no barrier, no Sensitive. He knew I was here long before I felt him.

"What's happening?" Illarion's voice came through the earpiece.

"Dalca's here," Aurel responded when I failed to.

"Damn it! Keep her out of sight! Keep her safe, do you hear me?"

Aurel nodded, turning to me, but my eyes were glued up ahead. Those eyes, I could see those eyes, those same eyes that tormented me for months.

"Ace." He shook my shoulder, cupping my cheeks. "Look at me."

I peeled my eyes away and locked onto Aurel's.

"We need to stay quiet. Can you do that?"

"It won't make a damn bit of difference. He can sense me," I choked, feeling my blood chill.

"Okay, that's alright, we'll figure something out."

I could feel Dalca enjoying my fear, that sick smirk of his was in my head, he was under my skin.

"He knows she's here," Aurel said, into the comms.

"Where is he?" Illarion shot.

"South side."

"I'm coming," Illarion responded.

352

"No," I whispered, as soon as I found my voice. "He knows you'll come out, that's what he wants."

Aurel glanced across at me. "What do you suggest we do?"

"Give me a minute. I need to think."

"We don't have a minute," Aurel clipped, looking down at his watch. "Our target is heading out soon, he knows that."

"Stick to the plan," I said, finally. "We're here for a reason."

"No," Illarion replied, swiftly. "If he knows you're here, he's waiting for you. You're now the target."

"I'm not important, they are."

"Ace—"

"Don't argue with me, you know the job comes first. We came here to finish this!"

Aurel pressed his hand to my shoulder which I shrugged away.

"Acacia." Dalca's voice was in my head.

I jumped, looking around, he was still on the street, but he was looking right at us, *at me.* No. This wasn't possible. Aaryon had pushed him out of my head. He couldn't be here.

"I know you're there; you think I wouldn't be able to sense you? After all the time we'd spent together?"

My heart hammered against my ribs. I was frozen.

"We both know why we're here."

I couldn't move.

"We're here because you came to protect those you let down." His melodic voice drew me out, making me forget how terrified I was of him, *"I'm here to offer you a solution."*

My eyes burned with tears, and I was vaguely aware of Aurel shouting for me and then he was talking to Illarion through the comms. He was telling him that something was wrong that I was in trouble. I couldn't snap out of it; I couldn't tell him I was fine.

No. He'd draw Illarion out then all of this would be over. He'd use him to get to me and if I refused, he'd kill him.

But I couldn't move, not a single coherent thought formed, not a single word came out of my mouth. Nothing I wanted to say, came out. I was frozen, like a deer struck by headlights.

"I will let these agents live, I'll even let your friends walk away from here…" he lowered his voice to a whisper in my head. *"I only want you."*

Silence enveloped us. Aurel's shouting stopped, Illarion's panicked calls for me stopped. Dalca's voice stopped.

The street was plunged into an eerie, silent blackness.

Then, as though a switch was flipped, the world was plunged into a whiteout. I was no longer behind the dumpster; I was no longer in my black jeans. I was out in the open, in the New York streets only they were empty, not a soul was around, and I was dressed in a beautiful yellow summer dress. I was on a date, Illarion's kind eyes found mine as he handed me a bouquet of roses.

I smiled as his hand reached for my cheek, grazing his thumb along the curve of my parted lips. That smile, the way it reached his eyes, full of warmth and love, made my breath catch.

"You're so beautiful," he whispered, lowering his lips to mine.

My free hand pulled him closer, deepening the kiss, passion and forgotten lust exploded between us, my name was a whisper on his lips as the street disappeared and we were in his bed, in his house, his hands roaming my body, tangled beneath the sheets, feeling every curve, drawing ragged breaths from my lips. I looked up into his eyes as he smiled down at me.

When I blinked, we were in another room, sunlight bathing us as we sat by the bay window in his house. He whispered words to me, caressing my cheek, letting his fingers run through my hair.

"I love you both so much," he said, softly. "My two beautiful girls."

I turned my gaze to the yard outside. I watched a young girl, *our daughter* playing in the sun with another little girl. Aurel and Josh were with them, chasing a puppy around the yard laughing with the widest smiles on their faces. She was beautiful. She had my dark, wavy hair and Illarion's beautiful smile. Anna was standing by the large oak, laughing as our children ran around the garden.

Happiness swelled inside my heart making me choke on tears. She was perfect, she was our daughter, and she was here. She was real, she was alive, but I knew immediately it was an alternate reality.

I brought my eyes back to Illarion, when he cupped my cheek, with that same warm smile.

"We can still have this; you just have to go to him."

My heart stopped. *What?*

"Just go with him, Lyubov. Then you and I can have this, forever. Our own little family just like you've wanted."

"No, Ila, this isn't real."

"It's real in another time."

"Not our time, it couldn't be."

"You're not even willing to try?" he said, he was upset.

"Get out of my head, this isn't real!" I shoved him back.

Before my mind could keep up, Illarion was gone, and I was outside, in the dark, wind whipping my hair around my face as torrential rain lashed my cheeks. I was screaming, crying hysterically on my knees.

Illarion's wide, unseeing eyes were glued to the sky above, blood poured out of his body, spilling endlessly as his Kevlar vest grew red. Beside him, Aurel laid sprawled on the ground, a hole was right between his eyes.

As my heart raced inside my chest, a guttural, all-consuming scream erupted from me, from the darkest, most shattered parts of my soul, and then it was all gone.

I was back in the alley, back in New York, Aurel's wide eyes found mine. He was desperately shaking my shoulders, trying to bring my attention back to him. All I could do was let out a broken whimper.

"That is your future, Acacia. That is what you do to the people you love."

No. No I could never hurt them...

"You know as well as I do how volatile your power is. You've seen what it can do."

Bile rose in the back of my throat. Beside me I heard Aurel yelling for me, in my earpiece I heard Illarion say that he was coming.

"I can end him before he even makes it past that street. Do you really want to risk him like that? Do you really want that to be his end?" Dalca cooed.

No one else was dying because of me. I was done being a coward.

I ground my jaw and got up. I pushed past Aurel.

Before he could stop me, I forced my hold over him. Aurel went silent, and his eyes flared then the aura surrounding him grew brighter as he struggled to break my hold.

Throwing him a quick glance, I moved with a heavy heart. I broke into a slow jog trying to control my breathing. But no matter how much I thought I'd prepared myself, my breath caught in my throat as I spotted him up ahead.

With each step, my breaths grew shorter and sharper, panic was hastily rising, but I was close, so close now, I could end this. But I needed a plan, something that didn't involve me becoming a slave again and killing innocent people.

His grin widened, and when I was about ten feet out, he was knocked down by Illarion.

"Ila!" I screamed, closing the distance between us.

The two of them grappled on the ground and my hold on Aurel broke. Before I knew what was happening there was a shootout across the street. I didn't know who fired first, but the war had begun.

Dalca's agents were shooting at our men and Aurel was now fighting another one of Dalca's recruits who'd been hiding in the shadows. I raised my gun and shot two who came running at me, I dodged a third and threw myself behind a clutter of trash cans.

Illarion and The Taker were out in the open now. He had Illarion pinned to the ground in a choke hold, but Illarion was quick to move and pulled Dalca's arm down leaving his jaw free for an open palmed strike.

He stumbled backward and Illarion got to his feet. He lunged forward, kicking him in the chest. He was fueled by rage as he kept landing blow after blow on him. He was a skilled fighter and in hand-to-hand combat, I'd never met anyone better than him, but Dalca had other skills, skills that Illarion couldn't match.

He found a moment in Illarion's defense that was blinded by his rage and lunged at him again.

I deflected another attacker and screamed for Dalca as he came at Illarion.

Whatever strength he had was nothing compared to the brute force Dalca was throwing behind every hit. Illarion kept fighting, he kept getting back up after every violent hit tore him down.

Dalca looked amused; he was toying with him. He could end his life with a single thought, but he was relishing in the game.

As I ran toward them an explosion rocked the street about a block away and my attention was pulled to it as a group of panicked people spilled out from the nearby stores and cafes.

"Agent down!" someone yelled in the comms channel.

My eyes darted around the chaotic scene and landed on an agent lying unconscious on the road. Her leg was bent at an unnatural angle, and she was too still. I knelt beside her and gently turned her over. It was Simms.

A strong arm pulled me back, behind a car.

"We have to help her," I hissed to Aurel.

"She's gone, Ace."

"Fuck."

"I know, stay down," Aurel shouted, firing off a few rounds over the roof of the car before dropping back down beside me. "Are you hurt?"

I shook my head.

My eyes darted across the urban battlefield landing on Illarion. He was on the ground. Although he was fighting back Dalca had the upper hand. Illarion was exhausted and badly injured.

"He's killing him!" I screamed, trying to pull free from Aurel.

"I'll help Illarion, you stay here!"

When I shook my head, Aurel pulled me back down, and forced my eyes to him.

"Stay here," he ordered. "Do not move!"

I glanced over, across the hood. Aurel reloaded his weapon and fired off another round, this time at a female shooter.

She went down and my eyes followed to where she had just been standing.

Right behind her, another shooter raised his gun and aimed at Illarion. The shooter pulled the trigger, a heart stopping scream erupted from within me as Illarion went down.

Chapter Twenty-Eight

ACE

I watched as time slowed around us. My breath came out in a staggered, broken scream and the sounds around us quietened.

I shoved Aurel out of my way, ignoring his warning, and ran across the street. Nothing mattered but reaching Illarion. My eyes watered, hindering my sight as I ran away from the safety of the car.

Dodging men with guns raised, I ducked, evading the bullets that sped past me, narrowly missing my body.

Behind me I heard Aurel shooting, taking out whoever was still on my tail. Fear should have been on the forefront of my mind, but it wasn't even close. The only thing that kept repeating was that I'd told Illarion that I didn't love him.

I jumped up onto the hood of a grey sedan that was discarded on the side of the street, slid across it landing heavily on the sidewalk.

Dropping to my knees, I grabbed his arms and pulled him back, taking cover behind the car.

The second we were safe, everything erupted back to life. The sounds, the firing...had I slowed time somehow?

It didn't matter. I gripped Illarion's face in my hands. His eyelids fluttered, fighting to stay open. His dark lashes fanned across his cheeks and closed momentarily. A fine sheen of sweat broke out across his face, dissolving in the trickle of blood spilling from his mouth.

Dalca was nowhere to be seen.

"He's rabbited," Aurel muttered, dropping to his knees beside me.

"Christ, help me, give me something." I pressed my hand over the wound in Illarion's chest.

He coughed, choking on his blood. The bullet had pierced his lung, it was collapsed and rapidly filling with fluid.

"Here." Aurel pulled his hoodie off, and I bunched it as tightly as I could, pressing it down over the hole.

"Keep your eyes open, Illarion!" I shouted, cradling his head in my lap.

His eyes slowly found mine, and I saw the desperation in them to hold on. I knew he was memorizing my face, trying to commit it to memory.

"Don't you dare leave me!" I shook his shoulders.

The pull of the connection between us pulsated, weakening with every breath. Tears spilled from my eyes as I felt the wetness spread under my hand.

There was too much blood. Aurel's hoodie was almost soaked through. He ripped the bottom off the tank top he had on and shoved it into my hand. I tossed the soaked hoodie and pressed the fresh makeshift gauze to the wound.

"Come on, brother, keep your eyes open," Aurel said beside me.

I let out a stifled sob as his body tensed in my arms. A low, painful sound escaped his lips as I pushed down harder.

"Why weren't you wearing your vest?" I choked out through sobs. I wiped my tears with my shoulder, pressing down harder on his wound. "I'm sorry, just hold on, please, Ila. Please fight."

He smiled weakly as he looked up at me. Tears fell from the corners of his eyes as he tried to reach up, but he'd lost so much blood, his strength was depleting. I pressed my cheek to his, breathing in his scent.

"So beautiful," he whispered, closing his eyes.

"Please don't leave me like this. Oh God, Ila, I'm so sorry. Please hold on."

A warm, fierce feeling began to spread inside me. First, I felt it start from the mark on my back then it made its way up through my heart and into my arms, finally reaching my fingers where they touched his skin.

Desperation consumed me. If I lost him…No. I wouldn't let my mind go there. I needed him. God, I *needed* him to survive this.

I had no idea what I was doing, but it felt so right. My hands moved on their own, one resting on the wound while the other reached for the nape of his neck. I desperately ignored the seeping blood that spilled through my fingers, wetting my gloves.

He understood what I was doing before I did.

"No…" he stammered. "Don't, Ace."

Ignoring his pleas, I closed my eyes and focused. As soon as I did, the heat inside me intensified. It grew hot as my fingers burned on his skin.

"What are you doing, Ace?" Aurel whispered.

"Stay back."

A violent shudder rocked Illarion's body, and his rasping screams lacerated the air around us.

Or were they mine? I couldn't tell where time ended and where it began, I couldn't see anything, but I saw everything at once.

The static around us began to crack and all the surrounding colors intensified, everything flowed into me like I was seeing and hearing everything in high definition.

Cold air twisted inside my lungs, coiling and bucking, burning for an escape as searing pain sliced through all my nerve endings then fused them back together.

My grip on him tightened. I pressed my palm down on his chest with urgency, pushing harder against the gushing blood and as the heat spread through me, the bullet came free.

As it fell from the wound, the damaged muscle began to repair itself and the hole in his chest closed, stopping the flow.

I let out a shaky breath.

He moved.

He was alive. It was the last thing I saw before I blacked out.

***

Silence.

Unforgiving silence deafened me as I stood in the streets of New Jersey alone.

I was still behind the grey sedan, but the crumpled bodies and the attacking shooters were gone. Illarion was gone. Great. I was dead.

"You weren't really alive to begin with."

I turned on my heel, recognizing the voice immediately. Aaryon stood in the middle of the street with his hands stuffed neatly in his pockets.

Today's outfit consisted of a dark, well-fitting three-piece suit.

"What do you mean? And where is everyone?"

He smirked. "Well, you don't just survive an accident like the one you had, do you?"

"I know I died." I paced the street impatiently, remembering Donna's confession.

Shaking his head, he stepped forward, "That's not the accident I'm referring to."

"You're going to have to stop being cryptic for a moment."

"You died on the operating table. Your aunt has a brilliant ability to compel even the most powerful Sensitives. So, you see, it wasn't hard to keep your condition hidden."

"I—I thought my spine was…"

"There were complications, things the non-Sensitives didn't foresee." He paused for a moment and came to stand beside me. "When they gave you adrenaline to shock you back to consciousness, your already weakened body shut down."

"I had a heart attack?"

"Yes. Your heart stopped beating."

That was like a slap to the face.

"You didn't just heal my body? You brought me back to life?"

His silver eyes narrowed. "I gave you a new life, a better, stronger one. You're what you were always meant to be now."

My heart raced in my chest—I immediately felt the change in me when I woke up, only I didn't know to what extent.

"What is this?" I looked around at the empty streets. "My own personal hell? A concrete jungle?"

He laughed a cold, unnatural laugh.

"You're now able to move between planes, like us, and control them to an extent," he said, simply. "Normally this wouldn't be possible. But you're powerful. We haven't seen that before. At least, not for a few centuries."

"What am I?"

"You're nothing and you're everything," he stated, stepping forward.

Normally, I would have instinctively pulled back, but I didn't feel the need to with him. He took hold of my hand and turned it over, looking at my palm.

"You needed the final piece to complete your evolution, and now you have."

"Death," I stated, a morbid curiosity rose inside me.

He nodded, trailing his translucent index finger along the middle of my palm.

"And life."

"The Giver and the Taker."

He nodded as the pieces clicked into place.

"What does it mean?" I followed his finger as it lingered, hot to the touch.

"It means that you're one of us, Acacia. You're exactly where you were meant to be, since you were born." He looked at me, narrowing his silver eyes. "You were meant to go through everything you did because it led you to this moment, right here."

A breath left my lips as his eyes, which were now completely white, found mine.

I didn't understand. *Was I meant to stay here forever? Was I going to stay with them? Could I never go back to my life, to Illarion?*

"Only when your mortal body dies, will you come to us."

My heart hammered in my chest. That was somewhat of a relief. At least I could still spend whatever was left of my mortal life on Earth.

"How did this happen? How am I...how was I made?"

"Your mother was offered a gift. After what happened with the man who made her conceive Damon Cale."

His name burned like acid inside me.

"Once we saw how she handled such evil, our council knew she would be the perfect Sensitive to raise you, the purity in her soul was unmatched."

"Why?" I was frozen. "Why me?"

"We needed a mortal who was strong enough to survive these gifts you've been given. We thought that the prophecies were referring to you and once we heard from Faith, we had our answer."

"But you must have known before that."

"We saw your future, your path."

"You saw my future?"

"Do not dwell on that, Divine. It will do you no good."

How the hell was I meant to ignore the fact that someone saw how my life would unfold and refused to tell me?

When I remained silent, he stepped around me, the same static charge that I felt when I was calling on the Darkness, sparked around him.

"You were born of fear and evil to hope and goodness," he said, quietly. "The power of Darkness rules you, the essence of the Celestial Beings is strong inside you—you're neither good nor evil. You're a perfect balance. The perfect Divine Sensitive destined to restore order."

I took a deep breath and folded my arms across my chest.

"What do you need from me?"

"We need you to defeat the Taker."

There it was. The kicker.

"You knew that jerk would be born and that he would eventually give you all hell, why didn't you just kill him in the womb or something?" I shook my head. "You could have gone all *Terminator* and just killed his mom or something."

Again, he laughed. "Like I said, you needed to go through everything in order to complete your evolution. That is how this works."

"That sounds convoluted."

"To a mortal mind, yes. But we don't live and abide by linear rules."

"Right." I sighed. This conversation could go on for days and I didn't have days. "How do I do it?"

"We don't know." His white eyes glistened with amusement.

"You transcend literal space and time, but you don't know how I'm meant to kill him?"

"We don't know everything."

How convenient. I rolled my eyes.

"You are Hart of Darkness, and he is Dalca of Light. You give life, he, by the same token, takes it."

When I shook my head in utter confusion, he smiled, and the smile creeped me out much more than I cared to admit.

"Just as you're a descendent of the Moon, of me—and have an affinity for the Darkness. He is a descendent of the Sun, Solaris—he has an affinity for the Light. Because of this you cannot kill him, you complete each other. But there can only be one."

"So, on the one hand, I can't kill him because we're one in the same but on the other, I have to because he's out of control?"

"Something like that."

"That doesn't make any sense."

"Like I said—"

"Yeah, I know, you don't obey linear rules."

He smiled, nodding.

"Is there anything I should know?"

"Keep your mind strong. He can show you things, he can take your soul to places where only we would normally be able to."

"The things he made me see…they're real?" My heart sunk as the words grew heavy on my tongue. A newly formed ache settled in my heart, crushing it into oblivion.

"Real in another plane, another dimension. Not yours and not this time."

"Can't it still be real?"

"I think you know the answer to that question."

"Why couldn't you fix that?"

He looked away for a moment, before looking back at me.

"Fixing what happened to you is as impossible as replacing a limb that is gone, or a mind that is lost."

"But you brought me back from the dead."

"Death is easy, it's simply a displacement of essence. Missing parts that cease to exist no longer exist anywhere. We can't make them reappear."

When I remained silent, he stepped closer.

"There are limitations to what we can do, I'm truly sorry, Acacia."

My brain couldn't keep up. Dimensions and timelines, planes and transcendence. I felt my heart rate pick up. This was too much. I was just a girl, no one special. I couldn't go up against him. Hell, I froze when he spoke to me.

"We wouldn't have chosen you if we didn't believe that you could do this."

"What if I can't?"

"We've never been wrong in our appointments of Divines. You can do this." The cool, white light from within grew warmer until a slight smile adorned his lips. "But you must face the fear which holds you back. When you do. You'll be unstoppable."

"Will you be with me?"

"Until the end."

***

My eyelids were heavy, too heavy, everything was dark again. I couldn't move or focus. Everything rolled into one like crashing waves of confusion. Voices, echoes, screams. There was gunfire exploding around me then I heard my name being called.

"Open your eyes!" I heard his voice clearly now. Illarion was right beside me. He had me in his arms, he was running.

"What's wrong with her?" I recognized Aurel's voice frantically shouting over the noise as he shot off a few rounds.

"I don't know," Illarion responded, and I felt him pull open a door and then climb into a car. "She's in there. I can feel her trying to wake up."

As my head lolled to the side against his chest, I felt the car begin to move.

"Hold onto her," Aurel shouted, "this will be rough."

God, it *was* rough. I felt my body moving as the car skidded around corners, careering up gutters and back down onto the street.

Illarion pulled me against him, holding me steady.

"I know you're in there, Ace, just open your eyes."

I wanted to, God, I was trying. I really was.

"Why would you do that?" His voice lowered, his angst cut through me. "Why would you put yourself at risk like that?"

The car was maneuvering and swerving every which way.

"Is she okay?"

Illarion tensed against me. "She's not waking up."

"Fuck." The car swerved again, hitting something. Aurel corrected the course we were on and accelerated. "What happened? She was fine healing you."

"I don't know, maybe she exhausted herself."

"Christ." Aurel's voice was sharp and on edge just like the mood in the car. "Brother, what if…"

"No." Illarion tightened his hold on me.

"You have to think of the possibility."

"Don't," he said, firmly, his hand trembled against my face. "She'll wake up."

I opened my mind up to Illarion's. He was *so* angry at me. He was furious that I had risked my life for his. I would always, always risk everything for him. But mostly he was scared. One painful thought kept circling around in his head. His mother's sacrifice.

That wasn't something that even crossed my mind when I healed him. All that was going through my head was how I couldn't live in this chaotic world without him. I couldn't do all these crazy things or continue this crazy mission alone. I *needed* him. I needed him by my side even if it was just as my friend.

He cupped my cheek. "Please, Ace, fight."

The mark on my back warmed and tingled every time he touched me fading in and out of focus.

"Come on, Ace. Open those eyes."

The car finally came to a stop.

"We'll be safe here for a few hours at least," Aurel spoke.

Illarion pulled me up into his arms and stepped outside. I heard a door open and then we were inside a warm, quiet place.

"I'm going to check the perimeter," Aurel said. I heard footsteps then a door open and close again.

Then I felt Illarion lower me into what felt like a soft couch. The cushion beside me dipped with his weight as he sat.

"Ace…" He sighed, pressing a hand to my cheek. "I'll never forgive you for this, if you don't wake up…"

My heart ached, he carried so much guilt and so much pain. It all rushed through him at breakneck speed.

As he fell silent, my mind drifted to Dalca.

He was there, he was *so* close. I could have finished it had I just known how and, unfortunately, my translucent friend wasn't so helpful in that department.

My mind wandered over a million scenarios, there was nothing that came to mind. Nothing at all.

Uh. This wasn't going to be a cake walk. I had to actually think this through. There wouldn't be a regular "Ace Special," where I ran in, guns blazing, hoping for the best. This required a plan.

How could I defeat him when I couldn't kill him?

There can only be one…an insidious voice inside me whispered. Two sides of the same coin…

My mortal form would die, then I'd join them. The same would be true for him.

He was strong here but when he found me in the other plane when he was in my head, I was stronger. I pushed him out and he wasn't expecting that. If I could learn how to get there, if I could somehow bring him to me…

Then, like a glorious, sunshine with a rainbow kind of day, it came to me. I knew how to kill him. I knew how to end this.

ACKNOWLEDGEMENTS

This is the third edition. The third time I've poured my heart and soul into the black and white pages of this story. The third time I've sat here and wondered how I could put into simple words what a journey, what a rollercoaster this book has been and capture even a fraction of the gratitude I have...

What started as a humble fanfiction project for my own book, became so much more over the years. The story grew, so too did Ace's world and thus, the King was born.

King of Hart gave rise to a rich world filled with love and pain, heroes and villains and most importantly, lifelong lessons and self-discovery. Perseverance, dedication and sacrifice were the things I took away—if I believed I could, then surely I would and here we are!

Once again, this wouldn't have been possible without a plethora of people who formed my support team. Balancing life, running my business, parenting and writing while still having some semblance of a social life is tough but we did it!

This is a shout out to the wonderful humans who supported me, cheered me on and believed in my project. To my family who was patient and encouraging. To my friends who listened to my concerns and eased them.

To my wonderful team at Vulpine Press; Lisa and Sarah, all the folks in the back end and the design team, you've outdone yourselves. Ace and I thank you eternally.

And most importantly, to the fans, the loyal readers; without you guys, there'd be no world for Ace and Ila.

We will be back!

Based in Melbourne, Violeta M Bagia is an accomplished author with a passion for delving into challenging and thought-provoking topics. With a Master of Arts degree under her belt, Bagia brings a depth of understanding to her writing that enriches every narrative.

Whether crafting tales of futuristic worlds or weaving intricate narratives of love and human connection, Bagia is a storyteller with a passion for exploring human emotion.

If you're ready to explore narratives that push and challenge you, pick up a copy of Bagia's latest books, which are available now.

Instagram: @violeta.m.bagia_writer
Facebook: Write Point Coaching
Website: www.writepointcoaching.com

www.ingramcontent.com/pod-product-compliance
Lightning Source LLC
Chambersburg PA
CBHW020513260626
47156CB00006B/1991